Loaded
for
Revenge

Dark Sheriff • Book 2

ROMEN GRAPHICS - San Antonio, Texas

Check out other books
by Roger Mendoza

Non-Fiction:
My Little Cowboy: My Reincarnation Story
Migrants: Exploring the Colors of my Family History
Jesus Mendoza: His Life through Letters

Fiction:
Purging Purgatory
Loaded for Justice (Book 1 of the Dark Sheriff Series)

Loaded for Revenge

Dark Sheriff • Book 2

ROGER MENDOZA

Published by
Romen Graphics · www.RomenGraphics.com
Author Website: www.Roger-Mendoza.com

This is a work of fiction.
Names, characters, places, and incidents are either the product of
the author's imagination, used in a historical or genealogical
context, or are used fictitiously. Any resemblance to actual
persons, living or dead, events, or locales is purely coincidental
unless otherwise stated.

Disclaimer
The author and publisher have made every effort to ensure the
accuracy of this work. However, they make no representations or
warranties regarding its content and disclaim any implied
warranties of merchantability or fitness for a particular purpose.

Cover Design and Photography
Roger Mendoza
Crows and gun rendered with AI-assisted artwork

ISBNs
Hardback: 978-1-938962-38-7
Paperback: 978-1-938962-28-8

Library of Congress Control Number: 2025924166

To my mother – Carmen.
She called me to this life and nurtured and cared for me.

To my brother – Richard.
He was the first to edit this book back in 2019 and encouraged me to keep going.

* * *

TABLE OF CONTENTS

PROLOGUE

Joseph Pruitt

They say justice has a price. I've paid it in silence.

My brother, Randall, and John Walker brought their gang to my land—my land. I let them stay. Not because I wanted to... but because I had to. For my wife, Elizabeth. Her life was on the line. And I wasn't about to gamble with that.

I kept the secret. Buried it deep. Let the town think I was still the law, even as outlaws slept on my land.

The darkest secret I ever kept was to keep the town... the whole town... safe from Silas Gentry. That man and his henchmen, worse than Randall. Tried taking the town. Gunned down the sheriff. Came for my goldmine. That was before I married Elizabeth, before I wore the Sheriff's badge. Sheriff Buchanan and I drove Gentry out, but he came back. He chased Buchanan out of town. Almost killed him. That's when I got the badge. I got rid of him for good. Cost me plenty. He knows better than to set foot in my town. Not while I've still got breath in me.

I wasn't the only one with secrets. Randall had a son, Alexander. A truth he kept hidden, even from himself. And Alexander was a threat, working with the Law to expose the very men who'd promised to kill Elizabeth. They'd come after her if Alexander succeeded.

Then Thomas came back. Fifteen years gone, and suddenly my son was standing in front of me, carrying more pain than I could name. He found love in Rebecca. He found purpose. And when the time came, he did what I couldn't... he crippled his own uncle, Randall, with one shot—a bullet through his hand. Ended Randall's stagecoach-robbing days. There's no telling what's coming for Thomas for doing that.

Randall and Walker's gang scattered. I paid them to leave... and most of them did. But Walker didn't leave empty-handed. He left me two lockboxes filled with stolen gold. He left those damn boxes like a warning—loaded for revenge. Said if I ever turned on them, they'd come for Elizabeth.

1

So I kept quiet. I kept watch. And I kept those lockboxes hidden.

Thomas and I—we're trying. Mending what broke. But the past doesn't stay buried. Not in this town. Not in this family.

And revenge… revenge has a way of finding its way home.

CHAPTER ONE

Crimson Brooch

It was a bright morning in Sacramento, California, in 1842. Sheriff James Buchanan sat on the hotel bench beside his wife, holding their infant, Rebecca. Twelve-year-old Charlie fidgeted next to his mother.

Sheriff Buchanan handed his son a six-shooter and said, "Go practice like I taught you."

"Yes, sir," said Charlie as he took the weapon. His eyes flicked to his father for approval before he turned toward the practice stump.

Mrs. Buchanan's eyes narrowed. "You gave him a loaded gun?"

Sheriff Buchanan snickered, holding up the six bullets. "It's empty. He's gotta get used to handling it."

She rolled her eyes and went back to fussing with her baby.

Charlie jumped down from the porch and pointed the gun at the bushes where the rabbit had taken cover. The rabbit twitched in the underbrush.

Charlie squinted at the rabbit's hiding spot, picturing an outlaw ducking behind cover. He leveled the barrel like Pa taught him, heart thudding with pretend danger.

He crept closer, eyes locked on the trembling leaves. With a sudden leap forward, he pulled the trigger. "Bang! You're dead!"

A frightened animal let out a piercing, raw scream that echoed the cry of an abandoned infant. Then it bolted, a blur of fur and panic.

Charlie turned to his parents.

Mrs. Buchanan huffed. "Poor thing."

His Pa chuckled. "Charlie, go fetch your sister. The coach'll be here soon."

Charlie's pulse still buzzed with excitement. He liked seeing the rabbit bolt—liked the way it screamed when it thought it was about to die.

He turned to his mother, not out of defiance but out of habit. Her word carried more weight than his father's.

The corner of Mrs. Buchanan's lips curled. It wasn't quite a smile, but something close. "She's probably out back. Go get her."

"Yes, Ma."

Charlie rushed to the rear of the hotel and ducked behind a dilapidated wagon. He'd spotted Charlotte, two years older than him, just ahead. He crouched low in the overgrown weeds, heart thudding.

Charlotte stood across from her boyfriend, John Walker. He and two other boys sat on the fence.

Charlie knelt, raised his gun, aimed it at John, and pulled the trigger. "Bam, you're dead," he whispered. As he pushed himself upright, his hand struck something hard. He reached for it. "A bullet!"

Grinning, he brushed away the dirt and fiddled with the gun. He'd seen his pa load it countless times, though he'd never been allowed to try. Slowly, carefully, he replayed each step in his mind and slid the bullet into one of the chambers. He beamed at his handiwork. His gaze locked on John. He aimed and fired. Nothing.

John's cackle snapped Charlie's attention toward him.

Charlie's pupils grew pinpoint sharp.

John hopped down from the fence and planted a kiss on Charlotte's cheek.

"John! I oughta slap you," Charlotte yelled. "My ma's just right around the corner. How could you?"

Charlie's breath caught. His eyes narrowed. His grip tightened against the gun, his finger planted on the trigger. He charged, gun raised, shouting, "You stay away from my sister!"

Charlotte snickered. "Put that thing down!"

John's two friends burst into laughter and tore across the yard toward the boy.

One of them shoved him, knocking him to the ground as his pants caught on a jagged stone and tore. He lay stunned on the ground, his fingers wrapped tight around the gun handle. He didn't cry. But the ache in his chest wasn't from the punch—it was from Charlotte's laugh.

Boots crunched on the gravel next to him. It was his father, the real sheriff of this town. The edge of his lips curled up slightly. His father was there to avenge him.

His father turned to the two boys. They ran. He turned to Charlotte and waved her to come.

She walked up and helped Charlie to his feet.

Then Sheriff Buchanan said in a stern voice, "Go get in the coach! We're leaving. Your mother and the baby are inside waiting for you two."

Moments later, Sheriff Buchanan settled into the stagecoach, ready to depart. His wife sat beside him on the front bench, Rebecca asleep on her lap. Charlotte and Charlie faced him from the rear.

His face was filled with frustration as he gazed at his children. Charlie shifted restlessly in his seat, fingers tapping the barrel of his gun. Charlotte held a smirk on her face as she slid the curtain aside. She smiled and gave a quick wave.

Sheriff Buchanan looked out his window and saw John standing near the entrance, waving. He barked to the driver, "Let's get a move on!"

He pulled back inside, his eyes narrowing on Charlotte. Her gaze flicked to his, then dropped to her lap. She let the curtain fall, jaw tight, and sank into her seat.

Sheriff Buchanan exhaled sharply, his gaze settling on his son. He'd once imagined the boy growing into the badge one day. But fate, it seemed, had other plans for Charlie.

Mrs. Buchanan nudged him. "He's told me so many times he wants to be just like you when he grows up."

He grimaced. "At least he's learned how to hold a gun properly."

Charlie lifted the gun again, carefully lining up the sights with Charlotte's face. He pulled the trigger.

Mrs. Buchanan muttered, "I wish you hadn't given him that. It's made him loud and rowdy. I liked it better when he was quiet and reserved."

The sheriff half-smiled. "It's about time he's excited about something. I should have put a six-shooter in his hands long ago.

5

Maybe he would have been shooting by now. Charlotte knew how to handle hers by her tenth birthday!"

Outside, six majestic horses led the stagecoach away from Sacramento, headed to Auburn. The driver, perched high above, whistled a tune as he always did on this route. But a half hour later, his tune disappeared. He tightened his grip on the reins as the road narrowed with a canyon wall on the right and a dangerous drop on the left.

The coach lurched as it rounded a bend, a shower of rocks falling from the stony wall ahead. The driver leaned into the reins, guiding the coach through the debris with practiced ease, dodging the larger boulders. The wheels crushed the smaller stones, their crackle lost in the dust.

Another twenty minutes passed. He pulled back on the reins as he approached a thicket of trees off to his right. The horses snapped out of their rhythm, ears twitching, pace faltering as something unsettled them.

The driver reached for his rifle, eyes fixed on the road and its many hiding places. This was the site of a robbery that had occurred the previous week. His gaze lingered on the brush ahead just long enough to spot a stray dog scurry away. Yet he remained vigilant. A deep unease settled in his gut. The coach crept on, its pace cautious.

Further down the road, three men crouched in silence, poised to strike as the stagecoach approached. Each had a finger curled around the trigger of his rifle, eyes fixed on the bend. Their breath came slow, measured—seasoned hands at a familiar job.

A fourth man, Silas Gentry, stood near the roadside, shotgun leveled toward the curve. His coat flapped in the breeze, dust gathering at his boots.

"Wait for my signal," he rasped, voice low and gravel-thick.

They weren't after blood. Word was, the Sacramento coach carried a lockbox loaded with gold dust. Easy pickings. Only a driver up top—no guards, no trouble.

The leader's eyes narrowed. He'd timed it to the minute. The driver would be slowing now, horses twitching at the canyon's edge. Any second...

* * *

Inside the stagecoach, Charlotte wore loose-fitting pants instead of the pretty dress her mother had insisted on. Her father had promised her an afternoon of target practice in Auburn, and she meant to be dressed for it the moment they arrived.

She looked at Charlie and shook her head. Earlier, she'd carefully pressed his pants and his shirt, polished his shoes, and made sure he was ready for their trip to town. She'd even helped him pin that shiny sheriff's badge onto his shirt. It was a toy, sure, but his eyes lit up bright when she gave it to him.

Now, his shoes were scuffed, his trousers torn just below the knee, and a black eye gave him the look of a one-eyed raccoon. At least he hadn't lost that little badge of his.

"Bang! Bang!" yelled Charlie as he pointed his gun at her.

She glared at him. "Put that thing away!"

She turned to her mother.

Mrs. Buchanan's lips were tight as she covered her sleeping baby's ears. Charlotte watched as her mother shifted in her seat. Pinned above her heart, an ornate red brooch gleamed against the deep blue fabric. The large stone at its center caught the light, fracturing it into a tapestry of crimson hues that shimmered across the cloth.

Charlie had helped fasten it.

Charlotte glanced at his black eye and sighed.

He leveled the barrel at her, his finger hovering on the trigger.

"Stop putting that in my face," she squawked. She spun around to her mother and pointed at Charlie. "Mother!"

Mrs. Buchanan blew out a tight breath. "Charlie, you know how I hate violence. Don't point that at your sister!"

Sheriff Buchanan grinned at his wife. "At least he's holding that thing like he knows how to shoot." The sheriff shook his head. "He's too soft. I should have let that other boy beat the tarnation out of him. Maybe it would've toughened him up."

Charlie glared at his father.

Charlotte chuckled. "He sure is soft."

Charlie slapped her arm hard. "No, I ain't!"

Mrs. Buchanan gasped, her eyes wide. "You're not supposed to hit girls. Not even your sister. She's liable to give you another black eye." She glanced at Charlotte.

Charlotte narrowed her eyes at her brother, her patience waning. "He needs another black eye to have a matched pair."

Sheriff Buchanan cleared his throat. "You should have protected your little brother!"

Charlotte's eyes shot to her father and then swung back to Charlie, narrowed.

He sneered at her. "When I learn to shoot, I'll be better than you."

He pointed his weapon at his mother. "See, Ma. I know how to hold a six-shooter."

Charlie pulled the trigger. A loud explosion followed.

Charlotte's gaze snapped to her mother.

Mrs. Buchanan gasped and brought her hand to her chest. Blood stained her hands and darkened her dress as it dribbled down the face of her brooch. Her eyes were white, her mouth hanging open as she slumped over. Young Rebecca fell onto the seat next to her and began to cry.

Charlotte's eyes flicked to her father. His face was frozen as he reached for her. He didn't seem to be breathing.

She grabbed the infant and brought her to her chest, shielding her from the chaos.

Charlotte choked back her shock as she turned to Charlie. "Charlie! No!"

He sat frozen, his eyes brimming with tears, his weapon still fixed on his mother. Smoke oozed from its chamber, his hand twitching. "I didn't mean to…"

She snatched the six-shooter away from him and tossed it to the floor. An explosion of gunfire erupted outside. A bullet flew into the cabin, splintering the ornate wood trim above the window, and Rebecca cried louder.

As the stagecoach lurched forward and jostled them about, Charlotte tucked her baby sister on the floor behind her feet.

Time seemed to stop as she watched her father. His mouth was open, his face pale. He gently laid his wife across the bench. He avoided looking at her face. An instant later, he withdrew his rifle from the compartment below. He yanked the curtain aside and fired out the window.

Time continued, fast and furious, as he snapped at Charlotte, his voice rasped with urgency. "Stagecoach robbers! Get your brother down before the boy gets shot, and grab your weapon!" He turned back to the window, bracing the rifle against its frame as another shot cracked through the chaos outside.

Charlotte pushed her brother down beside Rebecca and yelled, "Take care of the baby!"

She grabbed her rifle from under the bench and leveled it out the window. Her aim was steady. She squeezed the trigger. Her pupils narrowed, sharp and dry, as tears threatened and bullets ripped from the chamber.

Charlie crouched on the floor, clutching Rebecca. He looked across at his mother, whose eyes bore into his. A single tear traced her cheek as she reached for the baby. Then came a long, weary sigh as her final breath left her.

He recoiled in horror as his mother's lifeless, accusing eyes remained fixed on him. He'd forgotten about the bullet. Now, with tears clouding his vision and guilt pressing on his chest, he whispered, "I killed her!"

The gunfire still roared, but for Charlie, it had faded into silence. Only the ringing remained in his ears. The brooch caught the sunlight coming through the window. The crimson light, sliced by the gem, scattered across Charlie's stricken face.

CHAPTER TWO

Elizabeth Roberts

On January 25, 1850, the Auburn, California, sun beat on Elizabeth Roberts's sunbonnet as sweat trickled down her forehead. Three months had passed since she'd pulled into this boomtown with her husband James and Aunt Helen, each with dreams of gold nuggets dancing in their eyes.

Joseph Pruitt arrived with them from New York on the same wagon train. The two men had been close throughout the trip from New York to California, and Joseph partnered with James in a gold mine shortly after arriving.

She stepped down from the porch and looked down the road. Nothing.

James was gone, perhaps buried under tons of unforgiving mud and rock. Joseph promised to keep up the search."

Elizabeth wiped her eyes with a calloused hand and straightened her shoulders. Grief could wait. Today, survival was all that mattered. She started for the porch and then stopped suddenly.

A galloping horse was headed her way, a whirl of dust in its wake. She reached for her rifle, a familiar comfort in this unfamiliar world.

The rickety cabin door creaked open. Elizabeth turned to see Aunt Helen walking out of their shack that was barely large enough for the three of them. The older woman moved quickly to Elizabeth, who stood at the foot of the stairs. She squinted in the direction of the approaching rider. "Elizabeth?" Aunt Helen asked, her voice soft and raspy. "Is that James?"

Elizabeth's gaze hardened. "No."

Silence settled between them, heavy and suffocating. Helen came west with them, and both Elizabeth and James persuaded her to invest most of her life savings in the mine alongside Joseph. Now, they struggled to survive on what little remained in their bank account.

Elizabeth rested her rifle against the wall. "It's Joseph. It doesn't look like good news."

Joseph galloped up, the horse's hooves hammering the ground in frantic rhythm. Dust billowed around them, clinging to his sweat-soaked shirt as he dismounted in a rush. His boots skidded on the dry earth, and he stumbled toward Elizabeth, breath ragged, eyes wide with something that smelled like panic. His face was already grieving what his lips hadn't yet spoken.

Elizabeth saw it before he spoke. Joseph's face was a map of mourning—swollen eyes, red-rimmed and puffy, a crease dug deep into his brow, and his mouth held tight as if damning a flood. The news was already there, etched into his features like a wound that wouldn't heal.

Elizabeth covered her mouth as tears filled her eyes. "No... it can't be." Her shoulders slumped.

"There were no survivors. Sheriff Buchanan is at the mine site right now. He officially called off the search."

A short, loud breath caught in her throat. "He called it off?" She turned to Helen.

Helen's hands trembled as she reached for her mouth, her face pale and unreadable.

Elizabeth brought her close.

Joseph's voice rasped. "I'm sorry. They searched for three days. Buchanan said it was too dangerous to continue."

Helen yelled at Joseph, "It's your fault."

Elizabeth's cheeks tightened. "Aunt Helen! Please!"

Joseph stepped close to Elizabeth and touched her hand. "You know that I care for you and James deeply. I would never hurt you."

Elizabeth withdrew her hand. "I know."

Joseph took a deep breath and let it out all at once. "I've always considered you family. James was like a brother to me and a great partner. And...well, there's the matter of the mine." He hesitated, his gaze shifting uncomfortably.

Elizabeth's heart hammered against her ribs. "The mine, Mr. Pruitt?" she asked, her voice tight. "You want to talk business already?"

"No, of course not." Joseph cleared his throat.

Elizabeth stepped back.

Helen stood beside her. "Go inside and rest, dear. I'll talk with Joseph."

Her eyes, still red from tears, locked with Helen's as she raised her head. "I'm okay." She shook her head and straightened up. Her chin went forward as she turned to Joseph. "What is it that you wanted to discuss?"

Joseph blinked, surprised. "The mine's business can't wait. The miners need to return to work. Some have found jobs at other mines. I can't afford to lose any more workers. I need to reopen the mines and get those workers back."

Dread curdled in Elizabeth's stomach. "I..." She paused. "We have an interest in that mine, too."

Joseph's eyes fell to the ground and then back to her. "Not any more. We agreed. If one of us dies, the other holds the claim."

Elizabeth's brows narrowed, her mouth agape. "We're left with nothing?"

Joseph froze, his eyes locked on hers.

She took a deep breath and met Joseph's gaze. "I may not know the first thing about running a mine." Her voice was steady. "James wouldn't have been happy for his share to disappear and leave us penniless. Half of the money for this mine came from Aunt Helen. She's your real partner. Shouldn't she be your equal partner now, Mr. Pruitt?"

A surprised smile played on Joseph's lips. He cast a sideways glance at Helen and then turned back to Elizabeth. He shook his head. "James was the co-owner. But with the purchase of that house in Sacramento, his remaining share in the mine is quite small."

A new fire burned within Elizabeth, a determination to survive and fight for what was rightfully hers. "What house?"

"James mentioned that you and Helen haven't been happy living in this little shack."

Elizabeth turned briefly to Helen and then locked eyes with Joseph. "That's true. But what does that have to do with anything?"

"He bought a place where you and Helen would be proud to live. It has plenty of room for the two of you. You could keep chickens, a cow, and horses, and have space to plant vegetables. I thought he told you."

Elizabeth gasped. James had promised that someday he would give her the home she deserved.

Aunt Helen stepped toward Joseph. "Where is it?"

"It's in Sacramento, about thirty miles southwest of here. I'm sure you both would love it."

Aunt Helen muttered, her voice suddenly lighter, "I see."

Elizabeth blinked as curiosity stirred within her. "How? When?"

Joseph's face softened, and he said, "I was with him when he bought it."

Elizabeth's breath caught.

Aunt Helen turned to Elizabeth. "He's trying to get rid of us."

Elizabeth shook her head.

Helen said to Elizabeth, "I poured my life savings into that mine, and what has it gotten us? Pain, loss, and a life of want." She turned to Joseph. "What about the rest of our investment?"

"It's all in a bank account in Sacramento. Our mutual friend, Douglas Holt, the bank owner, personally handled all the paperwork. You can move in as soon as you're ready." Joseph's gaze settled on Elizabeth. "Does that sound fair to you?"

Elizabeth's frown transformed into a slight smile as she thought of James's surprise. She glanced at Helen, then nodded to Joseph. "When can we see it?"

Joseph's eyes twitched. "How about tomorrow?" He extended his hand to Elizabeth.

She shook his hand.

The following day, Joseph accompanied Elizabeth and her aunt, Helen, to visit the beautiful house on two acres on the outskirts of Sacramento. When Elizabeth first walked up to the porch, she expected James to greet her at the door.

True to Joseph's word, there were chickens, a cow, and a large garden beside the barn. It was everything that James had promised her and so much more.

After James's funeral, Joseph helped Elizabeth and Helen move to their spacious home.

Over the next four weeks, Joseph often visited Elizabeth and her aunt, helping them settle into their new place.

But at the start of the fifth week, he lingered.

Elizabeth paused, a slight curl of her lips forming. "I've seen you more in the past month than I ever did back in Auburn."

Joseph's eyes glanced away, then back—his gaze steadier this time. "I want to make sure that you're okay. You know I've always cared about you."

Elizabeth tilted her head slightly, watching him.

Joseph straightened up. "We're digging a new mine shaft, so I won't be able to come by for several weeks. I've asked Sheriff August to check up on you occasionally."

"I was wondering why he came by earlier. Thank you. You've been very generous. I appreciate everything you've done for us."

Joseph hesitated as his eyes caught hers. "Well, I'd better head home. If there's anything I can do for you, please send me a letter."

Elizabeth's face flushed. "Thank you."

He winked.

She stood on the porch waving goodbye as Joseph rode away. She smiled as warmth embraced her heart. Aunt Helen walked out.

"Sheriff August seems like a good man. He reminds me of James. He's a good fit for you."

Elizabeth chuckled. "Aunt Helen!"

Over the next few weeks, Sheriff August visited Elizabeth often. Soon, the casual visits turned warm and friendly as they grew close. They frequently sat side by side on the bench right outside the front door, laughing. Elizabeth's chuckles would elicit boisterous laughter from Sheriff August.

One particularly grueling morning, Elizabeth visited the sheriff at his office, frustration clinging to her like dust. August, uncharacteristically quiet, was at his desk with a six-shooter pushed aside. He looked up as she entered, a flicker of concern in his eyes.

"What a pleasant surprise!" he said, his voice gruff. "Is everything okay?"

Elizabeth sank into the chair next to his desk and sighed, defeated. "I brought my horse into the blacksmith's and..." She shook her head. "People in this town treat me like I shouldn't be here."

August poured her a glass of water and patted her hand. "I'm sorry, Elizabeth," he said in a comforting tone. "They aren't used to a strong, independent woman." He smiled. "I appreciate you."

She nodded as a smile crept onto her face, and she blushed. "You always know what to say to cheer me up."

Silence settled over the room, thick and expectant, broken only by the soft hiss of the oil lamp. The air smelled faintly of gunpowder and pine soap—August's scent, familiar and steady.

Taking a deep breath, she looked up, meeting August's gaze.

He rested his hand on hers. "Elizabeth, you mean a lot to me."

"August," she began, her voice barely a whisper. "I can't."

He leaned closer. "Please. I know you feel something for me, too."

The door slammed against the wall with a splintering crack. Joseph stumbled in, reeking of whiskey and sweat, his boots dragging like dead weight across the floorboards. His breath came in wet gasps, and the sour stench of alcohol filled the room.

August straightened.

Joseph blinked, eyes glassy, and steadied himself. His face lit up at the sight of Elizabeth at Sheriff August's desk. He lurched forward, arms half-raised. "Elizabeth! I missed you. I love you."

August stiffened, breath caught in his throat. He turned to Elizabeth.

Elizabeth's jaw tightened. Her eyes shot to August and then back to Joseph, her voice cracking. "That's the whiskey talking."

CHAPTER THREE

Sheriff Joseph Pruitt

On October 11, 1864, Sheriff Joseph Pruitt gripped the window frame, his knuckles white. He hated that he even knew the trail leading to the remote corner of his land—the corner where his brother, Randall, and his outlaws were hiding. Joseph inhaled deeply, a gravelly voice echoing in his memory: "Would be a shame if something happened to your wife if you told anybody about us."

Joseph gasped, cold fear seizing him at the thought of Randall or his men harming Elizabeth.

Elizabeth tapped his arm. "Are you expecting someone? You've been staring out that window for a while now."

"No. Just thinking."

Elizabeth followed his gaze and then sighed. "I'd like to think you'd tell me if there was something I should know about. We're in this together. Right?"

"Being a sheriff is always about keeping people safe." He half-smiled. "I'm headed to town to take care of some business. Be sure to keep your gun close. Alright?"

Her shoulders dropped as she exhaled loudly. "I always have it handy."

Joseph kissed her cheek, grabbed his rifle, and rushed to the door.

"Wait! Did you forget? Aunt Helen and my friends are arriving today from Sacramento. I telegrammed them I'd be waiting."

He blinked several times, and his jaw slackened.

"Now I know something's weighing heavily on you." Elizabeth's lips tightened as she locked eyes with him.

Joseph shrugged.

"I suppose I couldn't convince you to stay home instead."

She kissed his cheek and rushed to the door. She showed him the leather pouch where she kept her weapon. "See. I'm taking my gun."

Barely fifteen minutes later, Joseph's wagon stopped at the hotel, and he helped Elizabeth down. "I'll be at the Sheriff's office. I'll send the deputy to wait with you for your guests."

Elizabeth rolled her eyes. "That won't be necessary. I'll be inside the hotel. There are plenty of people there to keep me company. Now off you go."

Joseph glanced toward the sheriff's office. "Okay. But be careful." He was back in his seat, reins in his hands.

Soon after, he parked the wagon in front of his office and walked inside. The two deputies were dozing, with their legs propped up on their desks. Joseph grinned and slammed the door shut behind him.

Both deputies nearly fell from their chairs. "Sheriff!" they said together.

"When is the morning stagecoach from Sacramento due in?"

The deputy whose desk was closest to his stood abruptly. "The telegram we received this morning said they left an hour early. It should be here any minute now."

"Good." He glanced at the door and then stopped next to his desk.

"There's a matter to discuss that requires discretion," Joseph said, his voice low. "I need you both to watch out for a man named John Walker. He's a well-known outlaw, but I have my reasons for needing him to move on quietly." He paused. "I want to handle him myself. Just leave him be. Keep your distance and don't engage."

The standing deputy hesitated briefly and then smiled. "Oh, I get it. He's another one who needs some 'Sheriff Pruitt' style encouragement to move on. I wish everyone knew how hard you work to keep this town safe."

The sitting deputy nodded.

Joseph shrugged. "The sooner he moves on, the better."

He picked up the newspaper and sat at his desk.

Barely thirty minutes later, the door flung open. Elizabeth rushed in.

"Elizabeth!" Joseph put the paper down and stood.

Her face was etched with worry. Elizabeth's voice trembled, her hand clenched into fists at her sides. "The stagecoach is late.

Something's wrong."

Joseph checked the time. "It's an hour overdue." He grimaced at his deputies. "Let's ride out there to see what happened." He turned to Elizabeth. "I'm sure they're fine."

Joseph motioned to his deputies. "Let's go!"

He and his two deputies left and soon after found the delayed stagecoach. It was snuggled up against the brush about thirty feet from the main road. It was missing a horse. Further down the road, men were lying motionless, face down.

Joseph shook his head. "Looks like half a dozen or more fools met their maker. We're gonna need a cart." He pointed to one of the deputies.

"Yes, sir. I'll be back in twenty minutes," he said and raced away.

As he walked past the stagecoach, a woman peeked out. "Who are you?" yelled Rebecca. The horses whinnied.

Joseph said, "Is everyone okay? I'm Sheriff Pruitt."

"Joseph Pruitt?" another woman from inside shouted.

His brows tightened with confusion. He was uncomfortable that a stranger knew his name. "Who are you?"

"My name is Gertrude," she said as she peeked out the window. Her head disappeared behind the curtain.

"I'm Sheriff Joseph Pruitt. We're here to help." He waited for one of the women to walk out or open the door, at the very least.

Rebecca called out, "We've been stranded here! We have an injured man and need a horse to get moving again. Please hurry, Sheriff."

Joseph pointed to the nearest deputy. "You get that stagecoach back on the road to town. I'll go check those men up ahead and make sure they ain't a threat."

Two women, one young and one older, approached them. Joseph nodded and then rode past them to the dead men. He kept his gun at the ready in case any of them lying on the ground moved. He collected their pistols and kicked away any rifles he found.

Joseph smiled proudly at the resourcefulness of his deputy. His deputy's horse had been harnessed in place of the missing lead, filling out the team of four. Also, the injured Sacramento deputy was up top with the driver, eager to go.

Joseph signaled for them to leave. The driver returned a wave, whistled at the horses, and yanked the reins. The stagecoach lurched forward and disappeared down the road headed to Auburn.

The deputy approached the sheriff. "The cart should be here soon." He smiled and pointed at the men in the road. "Those women told me they shot these men. Imagine that?"

"Is everyone okay?" Joseph asked.

"Yeah. They're all okay except for a wounded deputy. He'll be fine. Rebecca and your Aunt Helen were with them."

"She's Elizabeth's aunt, not mine!"

A plume of dust rose from the road coming from Auburn. The other deputy, driving a large cart, was heading toward them.

Joseph watched as the two deputies loaded each of the dead men onto the cart. His breath caught when he saw the bloodied face of one of them. His skin prickled. He recognized the man from the day he'd visited John Walker's outlaw camp.

He shook his head as worry crept toward him. He stared at the cart filled with the dead men who had belonged to John's gang of outlaws. Soon, the outlaws would be traced back to him. He'd be accused of aiding them.

He rubbed his forehead hard, the headache already staking its claim. "What if John Walker blames me for the death of these men?" he muttered.

The deputy tapped Joseph's arm. "Sheriff?"

Joseph jumped and glared at him. "What about the other woman? Why did she go to Sacramento?"

The deputy nodded. "The older woman, Gertrude, said her niece, Martha, commandeered a passing carriage and left for Sacramento. The driver of that carriage took the stagecoach's spare horse to chase after her."

Joseph shook his head. "Shoot! This is bad!"

The deputy glanced down the road leading to Sacramento. "Should we head that way? Help them?"

Joseph cocked his head back and wrinkled his nose. "No! Let Sheriff August deal with their troubles. We've got enough on our hands."

CHAPTER FOUR

Rock Bottom

Hooves thundered across the clay trail into the outlaw camp on Joseph's land. The ground trembled beneath them. The riders yelled, while others grunted as they stopped in the middle of the camp.

Frank rushed out of his tent to investigate the commotion.

He spotted Randall and Charlie at the front.

Charlie jumped from his horse and helped Randall get down.

Frank ran up.

Charlie said, "Where's John's men? They were over in Auburn. They should have been back before us."

Frank said, "They're all dead." He gasped when he saw Randall. "Your leg is bleeding!"

Randall grinned. "Someone shot me. The bullet tore into my leg, and it hurts like hell." He paused, pointing at his leg. "Charlie wrapped it."

Frank's eyes widened. One of Randall's eyes was swollen, and his face was scraped and bright red. "What happened to your eye?"

"I tripped and went face-first into the dirt when I got shot."

Frank's nose twitched at the sight of Randall's eye.

Randall spat to the ground. "They were shooting down on us —picking us off, one by one."

Charlie rubbed his face. "Could it have been Alexander? I saw him peek out from behind the stagecoach, aiming his gun at us."

Randall shook his head rapidly. "Did he see you?"

"No."

Randall nodded.

Frank narrowed his eyes. "We've gotta get rid of that man. He's a menace."

Randall winced when he put weight on his bloody leg. "It wasn't him. The bullet came from up the hillside."

Frank gasped, his eyes widened, and his face drained of color.

"What's wrong?" Randall barked. "Was that you shooting down at us? Did you follow us?"

Frank cocked his head back like he'd seen something revolting. "No! I was here. Ask anyone." Frank looked away abruptly, and then his gaze rose back to Randall.

Randall was staring at him. "Son! You know something. Don't you?"

Frank stood frozen. "I told Thomas. But he wouldn't have shot at you. He wouldn't have."

Charlie gasped.

John rode up and jumped down from his horse. He sprinted to Randall and shoved him to the ground. "We're done. Your stupid, supposedly brilliant plan didn't work. Thanks to you and Charlie, all eight of the men I sent there are dead. You both botched that robbery. I've had it with you."

Frank stepped back, his jaw slackened.

Charlie's voice cracked. "What? I was supposed to go with them."

John glared at him.

Randall moaned in pain as he struggled to stand. "It ain't my fault. You agreed to this. Some of mine got killed, too."

Frank started to pull his gun on John, but Charlie tugged his arm and whispered, "Let them be. You and I can help Randall after they're done fighting."

Frank returned his gun to its holster and watched.

John closed in on Randall. "I don't think you care about your men. You keep getting them killed." John kicked at the dirt. "To be clear, I'm in charge now, not you, not Charlie."

Randall shoved John, "Get out of my face."

John lunged at him.

Randall fell to the ground and struggled to right himself. "I—"

Frank winced and narrowed his eyes at John.

John's eyes were bright with fire. "Shut the hell up!" His gaze swept past Charlie and then landed on the group. "Everybody, get ready. We'll stay here as long as we can. We might have to run if the law comes looking for us. In the meantime, we'll be lying low. I don't know if it will be days or weeks—no way to tell." He turned to Randall. "If you and your men come with us, you'll do as you're told. Got it?"

Frank gasped at Randall's vacant look.

John gestured for his men to follow him and stormed away.

Frank stood frozen in shock as several men, including some of Randall's, followed John.

He'd never seen Randall treated that way.

"John is a dead man," Randall muttered. "He's soft. He's weak."

Frank's eyes shot to Randall, and his breath caught at the threat. He rushed to Randall. "Everything will be okay, Uncle Randall." Frank wanted to call Randall his pa, but 'uncle' sounded safer.

The edge of Randall's lips cracked up slightly.

Frank gestured to Charlie. "Let's get him to the doctor."

Charlie said, "Let me take a look at his wounds. They don't look too bad."

Frank hesitated. "And his eye, too."

Frank and Charlie led Randall to his tent. Frank whispered to Randall, "Charlie and I are both on your side."

Fixing Frank with a piercing stare, Randall didn't blink. "We visit Thomas tomorrow."

Frank gasped. "But—"

Randall rasped, "Do you know where he lives?"

Frank's voice cracked as he said, "Yeah. He told me."

"Make sure you have a wagon ready to go. I won't be able to ride my horse anytime soon."

The next day, Randall sat beside Frank, silent, while Frank held the reins. Frank pulled into the road leading to Agnes's house and stopped just outside the gate to her property. The modest house sat back away from the road on a lot bordered by large bushes and shrubs. An unassuming small barn stood to the left of the house. He'd expected to find Thomas sitting on the porch drinking whiskey or working in the yard, but it was quiet there.

He grunted when he tried to move his injured leg. He stepped down from the wagon and almost fell. He grimaced and limped to the house.

Thomas ran out of the house and stood at the top of the stairs, aiming his six-shooter at Randall.

Randall kept walking and winced when he heard an old woman yell out from the house.

"Thomas, what's going on out there?"

Thomas glanced back, his gun fixed ahead of him. "Agnes, don't come outside. I'll take care of this."

Randall stopped a few feet away from the bottom of the stairs. "I'm alone. I came to talk."

Thomas, his eyes narrowed, shouted, "I've got nothing to say to you. You turn around and get going. I'll shoot you if I have to."

Randall cocked his head. "You're the one who shot me yesterday. Aren't you? I know Frank told you about our plans."

Thomas's voice cracked. "I could have killed you if I wanted. I got you in the leg instead. The same as you did to me back in New York when I tried to escape you."

Randall chuckled. "I suppose I should be grateful that you spared my life, like I spared yours?"

Randall glanced over his shoulder. "Frank, come on out."

Frank emerged from behind the shrubbery, his six-shooter fixed on Thomas, and stopped next to Randall.

Randall turned back to Thomas. "You look a little pale."

Frank, his voice hoarse, yelled, "You'd better put your weapon down."

Thomas shook his head and kept his gun on Randall. "You're not my family anymore. I don't care what happens to you. You'd best go back to New York."

"It's your fault I'm losing half my sight," said Randall.

The edge of Randall's lips curled up slightly as Thomas's gun wavered.

At lightning speed, Randall pulled his gun and pointed it squarely at Thomas's middle.

"I'd holster those guns," came a voice from the side of the house. "I'd do as he says," came another voice. Randall caught sight of a man standing on the side of the house. And another on the side nearest the barn.

Randall gasped when he saw the barrel of a shotgun poke out from the porch window.

"You two had better turn around and get off my property," yelled the woman from inside.

Randall grinned as he held his gun sideways. "I guess I ain't got family here."

Thomas straightened, his voice hardening. "You too, Frank. Holster your gun, and let me see your hands. Looks like you've made your choice — me or Randall."

Randall nodded to Frank.

Frank stowed his gun.

Thomas stepped forward. "Randall, stow that gun and leave before I put another bullet in you."

Randall's eyes flared with rage. He lowered the gun toward his holster—then snapped it upward, aiming at Thomas.

Thomas fired.

Randall's gun, slick with blood, crashed to the ground.

He screamed, "My hand! You put a bullet through my hand." His eyes darted to Thomas, disbelieving at what he had done. He saw the smoke oozing from Thomas's gun as he looked down the barrel and then up at Thomas.

Thomas yelled, "I'm not that little kid who used to look up to you. I don't feel anything for you." He paused. "Frank, you'd best take care of his hand. He won't be able to use it for much anymore."

Randall's heart was pounding, his hand was trembling, and the pain was growing.

Thomas chuckled. "I know you're lousy at shooting with your left hand."

Randall bristled. He leaned over and reached for his gun with his uninjured hand.

Thomas fired. The bullet landed an inch from the fallen weapon. "Leave it. No sense in messing up your other hand, too."

Randall growled. He spat at Thomas and motioned for Frank to help him.

Thomas yelled, "One more thing. I saw Alexander's son."

Randall, his eyes wide, spun back and locked eyes with Thomas.

Thomas's gun was still trained on him as he said, "Funny how Alexander's boy looks just like you, his grandpa." Thomas paused.

"That boy will learn who his true family is."

Randall's jaw fell open, and his eyes shot to Frank.

Then he choked on his breath. His head shook, and his body trembled. He looked up at Thomas slowly, eyes dulled and fractured, as if every lie he ever leaned on had crumbled. His mouth moved, but no words escaped his shock.

Thomas said, his voice steady, "You're responsible for killing my ma, Martha's ma, and — Alexander's ma."

Randall dropped to his knees, clutching his hand. His face was etched with creases as his deepest, darkest secret was laid out for all to hear. His jaw hung loosely as his eyes darted from Thomas to Frank, to Agnes's boys, and back to Thomas. For the first time in his life, Randall's eyes filled with shame.

His gaze fell to the ground. Their deaths were indeed his fault. He never expected his family, his nephew Thomas, to take everything that mattered to him away—his shooting hand and the secrets that had held him prisoner long before Thomas was born. The only two people living who knew that secret were Joseph (Thomas's father) and Frank. Randall gasped and narrowed his eyes at Frank. "You told him?"

Frank's mouth fell open.

Randall shook his head, disbelief carved into every line of his face. He looked down at his bloody hand, then up at Thomas. "You've taken everything from me, nephew. I thought family took care of family."

Thomas's voice thundered. "So the secret's out. Alexander's your son — and just as vile. No wonder you bent over backward to protect him."

Frank yelled at Thomas. "Traitor!" He spat the word, helping Randall to his feet. "Let's go."

Thomas said, his voice booming, "Next time I see you, Uncle, I might just put a bullet in that cold heart of yours." He stepped closer. "Your stagecoach-robbing days are done."

Randall, breathing hard, turned away from Thomas.

"And stay away from my pa!" Thomas yelled.

Randall hesitated, his chest hollow.

Frank tugged Randall's arm, and they started walking away. Randall's mouth hung open, eyes vacant. He stumbled toward the cart, limping and half-aware. Climbing aboard was a battle.

Thomas's face flushed with satisfaction. For the first time, he felt powerfully in control of his destiny. He felt nothing for Randall—no love, no sympathy, not even hatred.

The boy who once idolized Randall was gone. In his place stood a man who'd buried his illusions.

But when he saw Frank's eyes swimming in tears, his heart sank. His heart ached as he watched his best friend glance back at him, his eyes filled with hatred.

Frank spat on the ground. He climbed onto the wagon, flung the reins, and vanished in a cloud of dust.

The friend he'd loved like a brother was gone, and in his place stood something cold, calculating, cruel.

Agnes stepped out onto the porch, and one of the boys went to retrieve Randall's six-shooter.

Thomas turned to Agnes.

Her face held a soft, supportive smile. "I'm proud of you, Thomas."

"Thank you!"

CHAPTER FIVE
The Reckoning Within

Frank flung the reins harder, and the horses flew into a gallop. Frank glanced at Randall.

Randall wrapped his hand tightly with a filthy rag he'd found on the bench. Blood turned the once-white cloth into a soggy, red mess.

Frank's heart pounded as he jerked the reins. "We're almost at the doctor's place. How could Thomas shoot you like that?"

Randall's breathing was hard. "I can't stop the bleeding. Blood's gushing from my wrist."

Frank's eyes widened with shock at all the blood. "Press harder!" His eyes darted back and forth from the road to Randall.

Randall's face grew pale as the blood pooled up in the foot well. He closed his eyes.

"There's the office!" yelled Frank, pointing ahead.

Dr. Martin sat on the porch, reading the newspaper.

Frank pulled hard on the reins and almost crashed into the hitching post.

Dr. Martin jumped to his feet, his eyes darting to Frank. "I remember you. New York?"

Frank yelled, "His hand is bleeding all over the place. It's not stopping. You've gotta help him. He's all I got!"

The doctor's eyes shot to Randall's blood-soaked hand and rushed to him. "What happened?"

Randall's eyes snapped open and locked menacingly on Dr. Martin.

The doctor flinched. "Let's get you inside before you pass out. That isn't good—bleeding from the wrist. That's a lousy place to bleed from."

After Randall was on the bed, the doctor administered ether.

Frank, his eyes crazed with worry, rasped, "Can you help him?"

Dr. Martin nodded. "I'm not even going to ask what happened."

He worked quickly and put a tourniquet on his upper arm. Then, he removed the makeshift bandage. Soon after, he cleaned the wound and sutured it shut. He locked eyes with Frank for a few seconds.

"The last time I saw you… New York, maybe… You brought your best friend in for a leg wound, if I remember right."

"He ain't a friend no more!"

The doctor shrugged and turned to Randall. "Did he try to kill himself? That's one of the ways people try it."

Frank cocked his head back like he'd been insulted. "No!"

Randall was unconscious, his breath rasped as he inhaled and whistled when he exhaled.

"Why was he limping?"

"He got shot in the leg."

The doctor pulled Randall's pant leg back and recoiled at the blood-encrusted wound. "That wouldn't have ever healed. It would have killed him eventually."

Frank shook his head. "My friend, Charlie, took care of his leg. He said it was a flesh wound."

The doctor rolled his eyes. "That isn't a flesh wound." He thoroughly cleaned the wound and pulled a bullet. "He's damn lucky. The bone isn't broken all the way through, but it needs healing. He'll need to stay off it for a while." He bandaged the leg.

"His right eye is messed up, too."

Dr. Martin shook his head and then examined Randall's left eye. The doctor wrinkled his nose. He drew a glass of water from the basin next to the bed and gently rinsed the swollen eye, washing away the grit and gore that didn't belong. Once satisfied, he took a clean cloth, folded it into a small square, and placed it over his eye. The doctor used a piece of twine to secure it in place.

He turned to Frank. "Is there anything else wrong with him?"

Frank hesitated and shook his head. "Is he going to be okay?"

"His leg and eye will heal. I think the bones in his hand and wrist are broken. I found bits and pieces of bone. Hard to say how he'll ever use that hand again, with bones in splinters. But who knows? I've seen worse."

"Smart thinking, bringing a wagon with you this time. You can take him home in an hour or two." He pointed to the wall. "There's a crutch for him."

The doctor handed Frank a small envelope of pills. "Make sure he only takes one if the pain is unbearable."

Soon after, the doctor and Frank laid a sleeping Randall in the back of the wagon, and Frank set off with him.

Randall stirred as the camp came into view.

"What's going on? What am I doing back here?"

Frank glanced over his shoulder. "You were hurt something awful. You're on the mend now. The doctor took care of your wounds."

"I feel fine."

"That's because of a shot the doctor gave you." Frank rounded the corner and pulled into the camp.

Frank helped Randall to his makeshift tent, a hundred feet from the rest of the group, where he was isolated from the others.

"All this damn fuss!" he rasped as he lay down and fell asleep.

That evening, Randall awoke to the loud chatter of men outside his tent. He inhaled uneasily and looked down at his right hand. It was the hand he used for shooting, writing, eating, and even pulling himself up to the saddle. He gasped as he tried to twist it. The pain was excruciating. He shut his eyes, bracing against the torture. No luck.

How could this now useless hand become his weakness? His downfall?

With his left hand, he reached into his pocket and withdrew a little envelope with the pills from the doctor. Seven pills.

He took one, swallowed it, and tucked the envelope away. Randall closed his eyes, a shiver of fear, cold and unfamiliar, running through him. How easily a man could fall.

His thoughts drifted back to a time long past. An old memory surfaced—one he had tried to forget. He remembered Alexandria, the woman he'd loved deeply, whose love he'd pushed away until she found solace with his best friend, CJ, and married him.

Randall harbored resentment toward the union. In a moment

of vulnerability, Alexandria betrayed CJ and succumbed to Randall's charm. Despite her indiscretion, she confided in him that she was expecting his child. Randall dismissed her, declaring he wanted nothing to do with the child. He promised never to reveal their secret to CJ. But as time passed, Randall and the child became very close, showering him with gifts.

Alexander was eleven when Randall told Alexandria that he wanted to tell their boy the truth. When CJ overheard, Alexandria fled in shame and took her own life. The following year, CJ disappeared. Randall was shocked. He committed to ensuring that Alexander had everything he needed. Randall had many opportunities to tell Alexander the truth, but never did.

Years later, when he was twenty-seven, Alexander Johnson and his family moved from New York on the same wagon train that Thomas arrived on. Randall and his outlaw gang chased after Thomas and ended up at Joseph's ranch.

Frank peeked into Randall's tent. "Are you okay, Randall?"

Randall jumped and wiped his face. "Yeah."

"You need anything?"

Randall shook his head.

Frank said, "Thomas needs to pay for what he did to you."

Randall cocked his head back. "He's never stood up to me like that before. He's changed."

"I'd say he's changed. He won't stop until all of us are in jail."

"No. He wants to settle down. He was angry. He's been angry with me for a long time because of what I did to him and his pa."

"What? He just shot you! That man is crazy. Thomas betrayed you. He betrayed me. He needs a bullet in his heart!"

Randall narrowed his eyes. "We don't kill family. I consider you family." Randall glanced at his bandaged hand. "You shouldn't have told him about Alexander."

Frank blinked as his head bounced back, and his jaw dropped. "But—"

"You're not going to shoot Thomas. Got that?"

Frank's eyes grew wide, and his breath choked in his throat.

Outside, amidst the cacophony of voices, several men engaged in animated conversations punctuated by the occasional shouts.

Randall glanced at the tent entrance. "What's going on out there?"

Frank hesitated, taking a deep breath before responding. "John is gathering everyone." He kept his voice steady despite the worry gnawing at him. "He's been yelling at anyone who crosses his path."

"Help me up."

Randall and Frank went to where the men were gathered.

Charlie smiled as he walked over to Randall. "I'm glad to see you out. How's your hand?"

"It's useless. I'm done for without this hand." Randall let out a sharp exhale. "What's John doing?"

Charlie's eyes darted to John and then back to Randall. "John's getting everyone ready to leave."

"What?!" Randall yelled.

John stopped talking, glared at Randall, then turned back to the rest of the men. "Make sure you got everything. We're heading out in two days."

"Everyone?" asked Charlie.

John snarled at Randall and then looked at Charlie. "Yup. Everyone."

Randall, his jaw clenched tightly, narrowed his eyes at John.

Meanwhile, on the other side of his land, Joseph stood by the window, lost in thought, as thoughts of his brother, Randall, came. Randall had warned that if Joseph spoke a word about the outlaw group staying on his land, his wife, Elizabeth, would suffer the consequences.

Joseph's situation became increasingly tangled: his honesty to his wife tugging at one side, his brother's looming threat at the other, and the weight of his duty as town sheriff pressing down on him. But above all, he had to protect the secret that outlaws were camping on his land. What choice did he have? Especially with old deals still whispering at the edges.

The last time he visited John and Randall at their camp, he'd noticed tensions simmering beneath the surface. Maybe that was something he could use. If he played it right, he might be able to peel a few outlaws away from the group.

Would they blame him for John and Randall's botched stagecoach robbery? Think he'd sold them out? They shouldn't. If anyone deserved the blame, it was Alexander Johnson and Douglas Holt. This mess was theirs.

He needed to restore peace to his family and his town. But a darker storm was coming, its first signs tied to Thomas Pruitt's upcoming wedding to Rebecca Buchanan.

The celebration that should have been a moment of joy for him was instead overshadowed by Randall's threat and the outlaws hiding on his land.

As the wedding day approached, Joseph couldn't shake the feeling that something terrible was coming for him. Something that would alter their lives forever.

CHAPTER SIX

A Perfect Morning

On January 7, 1865, in Auburn, California, an ornate brooch, its blazing crimson sun at the center, glimmered in the light as an elegant woman delicately held it. Rebecca Buchanan sat at the dressing table, dressed in a beautiful wedding gown, her fingers fumbling to fasten the heirloom. She examined the clasp, tried again, and sighed—determined to make it sit just right.

A soft knock came from the door, and then a familiar voice. "It's me."

"Come in," said Rebecca.

Thomas stepped in, smiling, dressed in a dark frock coat and vest, with a tie slung carelessly over one shoulder.

His breath caught. She was beautiful beyond words. A huge smile spread across his face, mirroring hers. His eyes brimmed with joy, and his jaw slackened.

She smiled at him and showed him the brooch. The light from it caught his eye. "Thank God you're here. I can't get this on."

"You decided to wear it?"

"Yes. It still unsettles me that my mother died wearing it, but when Charlotte gave it to me yesterday, she said it would be like Mother was here with me, keeping me safe."

"Let me help you with that." Thomas took the brooch, carefully opened the clasp, and then fastened it to her dress, just above her heart.

"My mother was wearing this when she died." Rebecca touched the brooch lightly. "Life can be so fragile."

Thomas kissed her.

A smile grew on her face. "That tie giving you trouble?"

Thomas walked to the full-length mirror and fussed with his tie, trying to get it right. "Doesn't it bother you that my father is paying for all this? He's been out of my life for over fifteen years. It's like he's trying too hard to be close to me."

Rebecca said, "It was Elizabeth's idea to give us this beautiful wedding. Besides, Joseph is the richest man around these parts, thanks to that gold mine, and wants to share that with you."

"I don't think he's the kind of man who does something without expecting something in return."

"Your father is trying to make up for lost time. How old were you when he left New York?"

"I was about ten when Uncle Randall threatened my Pa." Thomas sighed. "I guess my Pa didn't have much of a choice."

He once again untied his tie and turned to her. "Can you help me get this blasted tie on?"

She hurried to him, her fingers finding the knot and easing it into place with practiced care. "Your father is trying to make it up to you. That's why he wants to do this for you. And you know as well as I do that he loves you and Elizabeth. I have no doubt he'll do anything for both of you."

Thomas raised an eyebrow. "And I'll do anything for you."

"You already have. You made me the happiest woman when you accepted my marriage proposal." She walked back to the chair and sat.

Thomas chuckled. "I hope you didn't tell anyone it happened that way. I fully intended to propose to you."

"Don't worry. I didn't tell Elizabeth." Rebecca chuckled. "I think Helen did."

"I was all set to ask you to marry me that day."

"I know. I guess I was a little quicker to the draw than you."

Thomas leaned in and kissed Rebecca, his hand brushing the brooch. "I promise you, I will give you the life you've always dreamed of."

A loud sigh escaped her lips.

Thomas's heart clenched. "Is something wrong?"

Rebecca ran her finger across the brooch, her voice low. "Do you think I made the right decision telling my sister to stay away? She took care of my brother and me after my mother died."

He leaned in, steady. "Charlotte shows up out of nowhere, wanting back into your life now that you're getting married. Whatever the reasons, I trust you did the right thing."

"She's still tangled up with that outlaw crowd and married to that snake, John Walker."

"John Walker? Was he with her?" he asked, brows furrowed.

"No. Thank goodness. He's a real troublemaker. When I was young, Charlotte was always trailing after him. A bunch of good-for-nothing boys surrounded them. I don't want those criminals anywhere near us."

"I understand." Thomas wrinkled his nose like he'd smelled something sour. "Sounds like my uncle, Randall. He's about as bad a criminal as they get. I wonder sometimes if I'm taking after him."

She gasped. "From what you've told me, you're nothing like your uncle."

"Thanks. I wonder how your sister found out about our wedding. Do you think Elizabeth told her?"

"No. Elizabeth never met her. My sister was long gone by the time I met dear Elizabeth. I'd be embarrassed if she knew that I have an outlaw for a sister. Please don't tell her."

"I won't. Until you told me about her yesterday, I knew only of your brother Charlie."

"There are three of us. Charlotte is the oldest, Charlie's the middle child, and I'm the youngest."

"Maybe Charlie told her?"

Rebecca shook her head slowly. "I doubt it. He's annoyed by her. Although Charlie told me yesterday that he's known her whereabouts for years."

Thomas shook his head. "Is he going to walk you down the aisle?"

"No! When I asked him, he laughed. Since Pa left, he seems to have gotten crazier. He's sticking around, though. Elizabeth told me she asked Charlie to help her here and there with the reception."

"If your father were here, he would be right by your side in that church."

"I hope he comes back someday. He was the sheriff here before your pa. Sheriff Buchanan."

"Really?"

She nodded. "I do miss him. Charlie told me that our father wasn't the same after our mother died. Charlie thinks he went back East."

The edge of his lip tightened as his gaze fell away. A glint from her brooch caught his eye. "Your mother is always with you in your heart."

"She is!" Rebecca sat up taller, a grin filling her face. "You know what? I don't need anyone to accompany me up that aisle. I'll march into that church and head straight up to you."

"I love that you never hesitate to go after what you want."

She chuckled. "That makes you my prize."

There was a soft but urgent knock at the door. They jumped, startled.

The knocks grew louder with more determination.

"Thomas! You better not be in there!" A woman shouted from behind the door.

Rebecca winked at him and whispered, "It's Elizabeth. Go let her in."

Thomas made a beeline for the door and swung it open. Elizabeth stood tall in the hallway, draped in a dress fit for royalty.

Elizabeth exhaled sharply. "Thomas! I'm trying to make sure everything is perfect for you two."

Thomas nodded. "Everything IS perfect."

She narrowed her eyes, suppressing a grin. "Your father is waiting for you at the church."

Thomas chuckled, backing out of the room with the grin of a man gently scolded but thoroughly enchanted—like a schoolboy caught sneaking one too many cookies.

Elizabeth closed the door behind Thomas and then turned to Rebecca, a broad grin on her face. "He's just like his father."

She stepped toward Rebecca, eyes wide. "Oh my goodness! You are radiant."

"Thank you! I'm so happy."

The crimson brooch caught Elizabeth's eye.

Elizabeth brushed it gently, letting the light catch its gleam. She looked up at Rebecca.

Rebecca smiled, her eyes shimmering with tears. "It belonged to my mother."

"It's beautiful! I'm sure your mother would be proud of you. It suits you well."

CHAPTER SEVEN
Wedding Day

Thomas marched out of the hotel and onto the bright, sunlit road. He squinted against the glare until his eyes adjusted.

The town park ahead shimmered with lavish decorations. Tables and chairs lined the lawn, white linens fluttering in the breeze. He grimaced at the extravagance.

Two men were hoisting a banner that read, "Congratulations, Mr. & Mrs. Thomas Pruitt."

A wedding band had assembled in the far corner near the water's edge. Their tuning drifted across the lawn—light, cheerful, and painfully out of step with the weight in his chest.

Thomas crossed to the church. As he reached for the doorknob, a burst of angry voices echoed from within.

He hesitated, then crept down the side steps to a narrow window near the foundation. Crouching low, he peered inside.

Joseph, his father, stood impeccably dressed, speaking to a shorter man. Their conversation rang out with startling clarity, as if Thomas were standing right beside them.

The short man said, "My wife told me she gave you a list of my men's names. What the hell? Why'd you want that damn list? Risky writin' their names down like that."

"John, how else could I pay your men! I can't do that if I don't know their names?"

John narrowed his eyes at Joseph. "I reckon."

"Tell Charlotte I appreciate her doing that for me."

When Thomas heard Charlotte's name spoken alongside John's, it struck him. That was the man Rebecca had named—John Walker. And his Pa was talking to him. His stomach churned. What business could his Pa possibly want with a man like that?

John said, "I'm still wonderin' why you'd need the names of my men."

Joseph looked dead-on at John. John cocked his head back. Joseph stepped closer. "I hear the banks aren't moving gold on

37

this morning's coach."

John winced. "Guess there's no point in robbing any stagecoaches today."

"Nope."

Thomas gasped at the mention of robbing stagecoaches. He shifted on his feet as he continued to eavesdrop.

John shook his head and blew out a sharp breath. "This spells nothing but trouble for business."

"Maybe it's time for you to get into a new line of business. A respectable one."

John leaned forward. "You ain't thinking of turning us in, are you?"

Joseph's brow furrowed. "No! You asked me that before. You're lucky I have a reason to be generous today, being that my son's getting married. Accusing me of that after I let your men hide out on my property while I looked the other way."

John grinned. "It's not like you had a choice, but I do thank you for that." John shook his head. "It's a shame we ain't friends. Could've made a hell of a team."

Joseph grimaced. "You got anyone left there? I have someone moving in there in a few days."

"We're heading South, just outside of Sacramento. We'll be gone soon." John hesitated and then smiled. "No hard feelings?"

Joseph sucked in a long breath and blew it out all at once. He patted John on his shoulder. "No. I'm good."

"Your brother says you were a great stagecoach robber back in the day. Too bad you ain't with us instead of Randall."

Thomas gasped, eyes wide. Randall's in with John, and Pa knows. He's known all along.

Joseph stepped back, "That damn brother of mine is leaving with you, ain't he?"

"Yeah, I think so. He's still recovering from getting shot in the hand."

Thomas shook his head.

Joseph's brows narrowed. "Is he okay?"

"He's changed. He's not as nasty as he used to be. I almost feel sorry for him. His shooting hand is messed up. I doubt he'll ever be able to fire a gun with that hand. Randall doesn't believe that."

"He was a lousy aim using his left hand." Joseph grinned. "Maybe it's time for him to find a respectable line of work."

"He's gonna have to. He ain't much use for robbing anymore." John leaned in. "He stays to himself these days."

Thomas muttered, "I'm glad I shot him. He's done being an outlaw!"

A sudden cacophony of crows erupted in the tree above, their black wings slicing the morning light.

Both Joseph and John turned toward the window where he stood.

Thomas ducked and bolted behind the building, peeking out the side.

Joseph and John burst through the door and stopped near the tree.

The crows went wild—frantic, shrieking, their caws shattering the silence as they flailed from branch to branch.

"It's just a bunch of crows," John muttered, pulling his six-shooter. He fired once.

The birds scattered like smoke.

Joseph yelled, "Stop shooting! There's a wedding about to start."

John shrugged. "Alrighty then. I'll see you later." He holstered his gun and strolled to his horse.

Across the road, Charlie stepped out of the saloon in his best Sunday clothes. He froze as the gunshot cracked through the morning air. A flurry of crows burst into the sky, their wings sliced past him. He watched curiously as John holstered his gun and walked away from Joseph, who then disappeared into the church.

Charlie squinted. "What's John doing talking with Joseph?" he muttered, suspicion tightening his brow.

As John rode away, Charlie stepped toward the church, then froze when Thomas peered out from behind the building. Charlie's brow lifted in surprise. He was tempted to rush over and congratulate his soon-to-be brother-in-law. But before he could move, Thomas sprang from the bushes, dusted off his coat, and rushed to the church door. He jiggled the knob until it gave, then slipped inside.

Charlie smiled wryly, waited a minute or two, and then walked across the road to the church. He climbed the stairs and sat on the bench by the door. He was impatient as he watched the hotel entrance, tapping his foot on the wooden porch. The loose planks rattled from his constant thumping. Soon, Rebecca and Elizabeth would arrive. He huffed as he remembered his conversation with his sister the day before.

"Come on, Charlie, Pa isn't here. I want you to walk me down the aisle," Rebecca said.

"No! I can't handle all those people judging me, watching me. Besides, I can't sit through the long, boring ceremony."

"Fine! Just don't even bother. I never could count on you for much." She stormed away.

He snapped out of his recollection as he rubbed his forehead. Her words lodged in his chest like splinters.

He'd been up most of the night, struggling to find the courage to accompany her down that aisle. That morning, he discovered it at the bottom of a shot of whiskey.

The guests arrived over the next half hour. As each walked up, Charlie jumped up, opened the door for them, and returned to the bench. He jumped to his feet when Elizabeth and Rebecca exited the hotel.

Now, he thought, we can get this wedding started. He took a deep breath and almost forgot to exhale. Charlie had never been prouder of his sister. He went to the edge of the porch as Elizabeth and Rebecca rushed hand-in-hand toward him.

Charlie held the door open—and froze. Pinned to Rebecca's dress was his mother's brooch. The same one she'd worn the day she died. The last time it had caught his eye was as a boy, when his mother was wearing it, just after he shot her.

His gaze rose to Rebecca's face. Her face held no smile, no frown. It was just still like those porcelain dolls she played with as a child. Her dress was adorned with those frilly ruffles that high-society women wore. His breath choked in his throat as he said, "I changed my mind—"

Rebecca walked past him and entered the church.

Elizabeth smiled at Charlie. "Charlie, would you mind handling things at the park? I'd feel better knowing someone I trust is there in case anything comes up."

His smile disappeared when he peeked inside. Rebecca was marching alone toward Thomas. Charlie locked eyes with Elizabeth. "Sure thing," he said with a painted smile.

"Thank you." Elizabeth patted Charlie's arm and then rushed into the church.

The music grew louder through the still-open door. Charlie glanced inside again. All of the pews were filled with guests. Elizabeth caught up with Rebecca and accompanied her to the first row. Rebecca continued to Thomas, and Elizabeth sat with Joseph. Charlie grimaced. He took a deep breath and exhaled as he walked across the road to the park.

He liked Elizabeth. Even though she was four years his senior, she reminded him of his mother. She always looked out for him, unlike Joseph, who was always cruel and condescending toward him.

Inside the church, Rebecca focused on the perfect wedding, though adrenaline surged through her. Her heart fluttered with excitement. After a deep breath, she managed to calm herself.

The minister stood before her and Thomas at the front of the church, adjusting his glasses and flipping through the worn pages of his book.

Thomas leaned in toward her. "The whole damn town is here."

"If we'd gotten married back home in Sacramento, we wouldn't have nearly as many people."

"That's true. Although Agnes would have come."

Rebecca smiled. "She's very proud of you, of the man you've become."

"I owe her plenty."

Rebecca let out a soft sigh. "I was hoping that Martha would be here."

"Need I remind you that her husband threatened to kill me if I came anywhere near her?"

Rebecca rolled her eyes and then grinned. "You and Alexander must get over your little feud."

Thomas took a deep breath and said nothing.

Rebecca sniffled. "I'm disappointed Elizabeth's Aunt Helen didn't come. She's like a mother to me."

In a poor rendition of Helen's voice, Thomas said, "These old bones are too brittle to sit in a stagecoach for hours."

Rebecca let out a small laugh. "She said she didn't feel well. I don't blame her. After that last trip, when those stagecoach robbers attacked us…. She's given up traveling. That frightened her terribly."

The edge of Thomas's lips curled up. "If your coach hadn't come upon those outlaws, I might never have met you."

The minister cleared his throat. "Shall we get started?"

Rebecca took Thomas's hand, and they turned to the minister.

The world around Rebecca faded as she focused on Thomas and the minister's words. He was the love of her life, a love she never expected to find. When the minister said, "Do you take Thomas…" She responded, "Yes." Before the minister completed the ask.

When he said, "You may kiss the bride," she let out a long breath as a new calm washed over her. In that instant, after the kiss, the world around her opened up. The guests were clapping and cheering. Her tears were streaming down her cheeks.

After the wedding ceremony, they walked hand in hand out of the hotel and strolled across the road to the park to the reception.

Rebecca's eyes swept across the park, drinking in the colors, the flowers, and the laughter. "Isn't this beautiful?"

Thomas said, "It's hard to believe a sheriff in a town like this can afford all this."

"You are incorrigible! You know he has that goldmine. Besides, Elizabeth told me these folks pitched in for the decorations. They sure do love their sheriff."

"I guess so."

"Thomas, would you mind getting me something to drink? My mouth is parched."

"Of course, my dear." He kissed Rebecca and rushed away.

CHAPTER EIGHT

Reception

At the other end of the park, Joseph held Elizabeth's hand as they greeted the guests. Elizabeth leaned over and kissed Joseph's cheek. "Thank you for giving them this beautiful wedding. It means the world to them, and me."

"Darling, you know I'd do anything for you and Thomas. I have to make up for lost time with him."

Joseph glanced at the road toward the sheriff's office. Two deputies stood there waving at him.

"Elizabeth, I'll go see what they want. It'll just be a second. You know this town can't run itself."

"Okay, dear. Please don't be long."

Joseph kissed Elizabeth's hand and rushed away to the waiting deputies. He chatted briefly with the two men and then sprinted off to the sheriff's office.

When Joseph walked in, Howard, a peculiar soul with a fondness for whiskey and a heart too soft for outlaw life, was asleep in an unlocked jail cell.

At one time, Howard had been one of John's trusted men. Joseph felt a closeness to Howard, partly because he was respectful and courteous toward him. But mainly because Howard had left John's group of outlaws and vowed to walk a more righteous path. Joseph had given Howard a small house on the edge of his property — a shack, really, but Howard cherished it. That house was the same one where Elizabeth and her late husband had lived when they first arrived.

Joseph hesitated at the sight of Howard balled up on the bunk, snoring like a bull. How could whiskey have done so much damage to that man's life?

Joseph reached for the jail door, as the memories of the night before tugged at his heart:

Howard was curled in the alley behind the saloon,
drunk and delirious, his body wound tight like a

child hiding from a storm.

Crows had gathered in the trees above, watching with eerie stillness. One by one, they swooped down, pecking at his clothes, testing his stillness, drawn by the scent of spilled whiskey and weakness.

Howard whimpered, crying out for help.

Joseph stepped forward, his voice low and steady. "Come on now. Let him be."

The birds paused, confused. They remembered Howard's bullets. But they also remembered the scraps Joseph had left for them—on fence posts at home, beneath windowsills in town.

A pair of dark brown eyes watched silently from the branches as Joseph waved for his deputy. The man approached slowly, careful not to meet the birds' gaze.

Together, they lifted Howard and carried him to the jail, where he could sleep off the drink.

Joseph brushed the memory away and tapped Howard's arm.

"Wake up!"

Howard grunted and squinted at Joseph. "I was just resting my eyes." He rubbed his eyes and sat up. "Sheriff!" His eyes darted about in confusion, and then he yawned.

"I need your help. Come over to my desk. I gotta show you something."

Howard followed Joseph and sat in the guest chair.

Joseph lowered himself into his chair and pointed at the list that Charlotte had made for him. "Howard, take a look at this."

Howard wiped the sleep from his eyes and examined it. "I recognize those names." He pointed to the paper. "There's my name," he said, half amused, half ashamed.

"Charlotte wrote down the names of everyone in John and Randall's camp.

"She did?" Howard asked. He rubbed his temple to soothe his throbbing headache. "I like Charlotte."

Joseph nodded as he unlocked his bottom drawer and withdrew a stack of money and several envelopes.

Howard's eyes flew open. The adrenaline pulsed through his

body, softening his headache.

"Howard, I'd like you to take this money to John's men before they leave."

"What for?"

"I want them to know there's a way out. John's not giving them enough to live on. Some have wives."

"Yup. There are a few of 'em that even have little ones."

Joseph shook his head with concern. He brought the paper closer to Howard. "Also, I'd like the men to know they could count on me to help them get out and find a way to make an honest living."

"You're a decent man, Joseph. Always looking out for others."

"Thanks." Joseph withdrew a stack of envelopes from the top drawer.

Howard said, "Wait. Please don't give it to all the men. Some of them are married to that life. Especially Randall's lot. They'd slit your throat for a silver coin."

Howard took the list, circled some names, and returned it to Joseph. "These men don't deserve anything!" He hesitated and then grabbed it back and circled his own name.

Joseph raised an eyebrow. "Why yours?"

Howard looked down. "So you don't give me any more. You've done enough."

Joseph smiled. "I'm proud of you." He copied each uncircled name onto a separate envelope, tucked a banknote into each, and stuffed them into a pouch. "Could you go to John's camp and discreetly deliver these? They're leaving soon, so you'd have to hurry."

"Sure thing," said Howard.

Joseph gave Howard the pouch along with a gold coin. "You know I'll always take care of you."

Howard's eyes lit up brightly.

Back at the park, Elizabeth sat patiently on the bench, watching the park fill with smiling guests and laughter. She thought about how loyal those deputies were to Joseph.

A waving hand caught her eye—Rebecca, rushing toward her, radiant.

Elizabeth jumped to her feet, grinning. "There you are!"

Before Rebecca caught up with her, Joseph snuck up behind her and planted a quick kiss on her cheek.

"You're such a romantic!" Elizabeth beamed. "Look who's coming."

Rebecca arrived, eyes glistening, joy dancing across her face. "You've done a wonderful job here. Thank you."

Elizabeth kissed her cheek. "I'm thrilled for you on this glorious day."

"You and Thomas deserve it," Joseph added warmly.

Rebecca hugged him. "I don't know how this day could get any better."

Thomas walked up with a glass of lemonade and handed it to Rebecca. She kissed him before taking a sip. "Even the lemonade is heavenly."

Elizabeth teased, "You were a bit chatty at the start of the service."

Rebecca's smile turned sheepish. "We were just talking silly nonsense while the preacher got ready." She nudged Thomas. "Weren't we?"

Thomas chuckled. "Just nervous, silly nonsense."

Joseph clapped Thomas's shoulder. "Are you enjoying this fabulous celebration that Elizabeth orchestrated?"

Elizabeth smiled.

"Of course," Thomas said. "Seems like the whole town's here. Must've cost a stagecoach full of gold."

Elizabeth noticed Rebecca nudge Thomas's arm.

Joseph straightened. "These folks came with open hearts. I've always considered them family. Kind, generous—I'm proud to be their sheriff." He smiled at Thomas. "It was worth it."

A well-dressed man in polished boots walked up. Douglas Holt.

Elizabeth's eyes lit up bright, "Douglas! We're so glad you could attend. I thought you'd be too busy with bank business."

"I am busy, but I couldn't miss this," Douglas said, his eyes narrowing briefly at Joseph before softening toward Thomas and Rebecca. "Rebecca, you've caught a true gentleman."

Rebecca giggled. "I'm very fortunate."

"Great to see you again, Thomas. Congratulations."

Thomas shook his hand. "Thank you."

Joseph's glare didn't go unnoticed.

Elizabeth, ever the peacemaker, stepped in. "Joseph is thrilled for them, too."

Douglas nodded at Joseph with a tight smile.

Thomas cleared his throat. "What brings you to town?"

Douglas's posture stiffened. "Looking into the stagecoach robberies."

Elizabeth's gaze shot from Douglas to Joseph.

Joseph's head cocked back. "Elizabeth, shouldn't we greet the guests?"

Elizabeth turned to Douglas, a soft smile gracing her lips.

The edge of Douglas's lips curled upward. "I should get to the bank." He nodded at Thomas. "Congratulations again."

Douglas's eyes lingered on Elizabeth for a moment before he turned and walked away.

"Stagecoach robberies?" Thomas muttered. "Sounds suspicious."

Elizabeth's breath caught when Joseph said, "Everybody's gotta make a living. Right?"

She turned to Rebecca and Thomas. "Will you come to the house for lunch tomorrow?"

She took Joseph's hand.

Joseph winked at Thomas. "Afterward, we can ride out to my secret hideout."

Thomas laughed. "That would be exciting!"

Elizabeth shook her head. "Rebecca and I have our own secret place."

Rebecca said, "We'll be there."

"Excellent." Elizabeth smiled and then gazed at the crowd. "Joseph, let's visit with these wonderful people."

Elizabeth hugged Rebecca and patted Thomas's arm. Joseph winked at Thomas and walked off hand in hand with Elizabeth.

Thomas watched them go, wondering about the wink. Had Joseph seen him earlier at the church?

Rebecca tugged his hand. "What's wrong?"

He hesitated. "Before the wedding, I overheard Pa talking with a man named John—John Walker, I think—about robbing stagecoaches."

Rebecca's face darkened. "That's ridiculous! Joseph wouldn't involve himself with someone so tawdry."

"He called the man's wife Charlotte."

Rebecca scanned the park. "Then Charlotte must be nearby. She promised me she would stay away."

"He said they were leaving town soon. It sounded like Joseph was helping them."

Thomas hugged her, eyes following Joseph and Elizabeth.

"When Charlotte stopped by the other day, she seemed apologetic. For a moment, I thought she might walk away from that group—leave John and come back to me. But then she said she hoped to grow old with him on a farm. That's when I knew she hadn't changed."

Thomas paled. "I shouldn't have told you. I'm sorry."

His breath caught when he saw Rebecca's eyes flare.

She said, "Don't even think of keeping secrets from me. That would not bode well for our marriage. Promise me."

"I give you my word." His grin returned, warm and sincere. "Let's forget about John, Charlotte, the robbers—everything unpleasant. Today is ours. Agnes always said to focus on the bright moments."

Rebecca smiled. "Agnes is a wise old woman."

"And you, my dear, will always be the brightest part of every day."

"I'll never forget this day." Her gaze swept the park. "This town is beautiful. Everyone's so friendly. I wonder what it would be like to live here."

She glanced at Thomas. "Especially now that those tawdry folks are leaving."

Thomas nodded. "It would be peaceful."

He leaned in and kissed her.

CHAPTER NINE
The Offer

On the day after the wedding, John Walker stepped onto the saloon porch. A well-dressed man walking out of the hotel caught his eye. With his polished boots, the man strode like he owned the place. John's face soured as the bank owner disappeared into the bank. John marched into the saloon with a mission. Joseph's unmistakable laughter spilled from the far corner. Joseph's brother, Randall, had the same laugh. That laugh, when Randall wore it, needled its way under his skin.

The bartender eyed John suspiciously.

"Whiskey, please," said John

The bartender nodded and, a few seconds later, slid the drink over without a word, eyes narrowed.

"Thank you kindly," said John. He grabbed the glass and glanced Joseph's way.

John chuckled and headed to the chair across from Joseph.

The chair creaked as John plopped down.

Joseph's head jerked back, his brows furrowed. "John! What are you doing here?"

John slid the glass with the amber drink in front of Joseph. "Howard was in my camp yesterday."

Joseph's eyes flicked to the whiskey, then to John. "Did you get my little gift?"

John nodded slowly. "I did. Are you trying to bribe us?"

"Of course not! I want to make it easier for your men to move closer to the right side of the law. That's all. The envelope for you had a little extra in it."

John's smile disappeared as he fixated on Joseph. "You got all the money you could ever want, and you give it away — hoping you'll change someone's life to your liking."

"You got plenty too, mostly other people's money. There's hope for you. You and Charlotte could settle down and raise a family."

John's gaze fell away, and he shifted in his seat. He suddenly straightened up. "I saw that bank owner just now, the highfalutin-looking one. He was going into the bank."

John's eyes flicked to Joseph's whiskey glass as Joseph pushed it away.

Joseph said, "That was Douglas Holt. He owns several banks, including the one here in town. He's here because of the stagecoach robberies."

"I know who he is." The edge of John's lip curled up slightly. "We haven't robbed a stagecoach in weeks. He couldn't be looking for us."

"He's here to stir up trouble. If he finds out I've helped you…"

John rolled his eyes. "Relax. We've been lying low. We'll be gone long before he knows we were here."

Joseph narrowed his eyes. "Is my wife safe now that you're leaving?"

John grinned. "You're lucky that Charlie has a soft spot for her. Says she reminds him of his mother."

"Is she safe?"

"You worry too much. We wouldn't have touched Elizabeth. But I'd think twice about sending the Law our way. I don't want a reason to hurt someone in your family. Especially now that there are more to choose from."

Joseph immediately thought of Rebecca, Thomas's bride, another family member to protect from John.

"Did Randall tell you to threaten me with that?" asked Joseph.

John's head jerked back, and he scoffed. "He wanted to come here with me, but I told him no. He said he's got something important he wants to tell you."

"And what's that?"

"How should I know? He keeps babbling about you, Thomas, and Alexander. He's not acting like himself. He said he was sorry about a bunch of stupid stuff he did."

Joseph stared at the whiskey. His eyes darted to John. "That doesn't sound like him."

The edge of John's lips curled up. He wondered why Joseph didn't even take a little sip of the whiskey. His gaze drifted to

Joseph. "That nephew of his and Charlie are worried about him."

Joseph's brows furrowed. "Thomas?"

"No. The other one—Frank."

Joseph guffawed. "Frank isn't his nephew. Where'd you get that idea?"

"Frank's been calling him uncle."

Joseph's laugh caught, twisted. "Frank's been calling him uncle?" He rolled his eyes. "That's rich. That boy, Frank, ain't right in the head. He ain't no relation to us!"

John shrugged. "I don't trust him like I do Charlie."

Joseph's eyes narrowed. "He's leaving town with you. Ain't he?"

The edge of John's lips curled up slightly.

Joseph stared expressionless at John. "Is he?"

"No. Charlie's staying." He paused. "I'll stop by your house tomorrow afternoon at half past three to drop off something I need you to keep safe for me."

Joseph's eyes narrowed. "I don't want anything from you."

John's slivering tongue wet his lips. "I insist."

His smile spread as he met Joseph's stare.

Joseph grabbed his hat and stood. "Steer clear of the house. I'll be by the river, waiting. Don't let Elizabeth see you. She doesn't know anything about you, and I'd like to keep it that way."

"Okay," said John.

"If you don't mind, I've got somewhere to be right now." Joseph winked and then left.

John held a grin until Joseph walked out the door. He reached for the whiskey he'd brought for Joseph and drank it down.

Within the hour, Joseph and Thomas rode from town to the cabin at the edge of Joseph's property. They hitched their horses next to the porch.

"This was my house when I first moved here. These hands built this," said Joseph, holding his hands up. "My best friend, Juan Cortez, and others helped me build it."

"Incredible," he whispered. "Looks like someone's been keeping up this place."

"We put a lot of work into this place to clean it up. You

should have seen it before."

Thomas peered inside through the window. "Who lives here?"

"No one yet."

Joseph opened the door and walked in. Thomas followed behind.

Thomas's eyes darted about, his face filled with a smile. "Elizabeth told me you gave up drinking after moving here."

Joseph hesitated. "Still get tempted now and then. I came close to taking a sip recently."

"I rarely drink," said Thomas.

Joseph withdrew two glasses from the kitchen cabinet and set them on the table next to a pitcher of lemonade. He poured the sweet drink into each of them. He opened the icebox and used a pick to chip away two pieces of ice from the block sitting at the bottom.

Thomas rubbed his fingers lightly along the smooth surface of the table. His gaze wandered through the warm and inviting room. A broad smile filled his face as his eyes danced with excitement.

Joseph stepped up with the drinks, condensation tracing down the glass.

"You like what Elizabeth has done with the house?"

Joseph offered a glass to Thomas.

"It must have cost a small fortune to furnish this place," said Thomas.

"What can I say? Elizabeth knows quality. She did a great job. Didn't she?"

"Yes. It's incredible." Thomas's head was slowly bobbing up and down.

"Now that you're a married man, do you have any plans for the future?"

"Rebecca and I are moving in with Elizabeth's Aunt Helen back home—at least long enough to get work to save for a house."

Joseph's smile grew. "Really?"

"Yeah. Rebecca deserves everything that I can give her and so much more. We want to start a family, too."

"That could take a while."

Thomas's gaze fell away. He took a deep breath and then let it out all at once. "We've talked about it. She's okay to wait."

Joseph took another drink.

"Elizabeth and I have wanted a baby for years."

"You're a great father," said Thomas.

Joseph's breath faltered in his throat. "Thank you, Son. That means a lot to me, considering."

Joseph patted Thomas's shoulder. "You need a faster way to get Rebecca that home she deserves."

"What? No! I promised her that I would find a respectable job. I'm not about to rob a stagecoach or some nefarious way of making money."

A furrow creased Joseph's brow, and his head cocked back. "Hold on there. You got the wrong idea. I have more than enough money to share if you ever need any. There's never a reason for you takin' what ain't yours."

Thomas blinked, surprised. He looked at his father with questioning eyes.

"Son, I'm telling you that you and Rebecca should move here instead of waiting!"

"Nah! I have a little money saved, but nowhere near enough to live in this town. I would need to get work, buy land, and build a house."

Joseph shook his head and let out a huff. "You're not understanding me, son. I'm trying to tell you that Elizabeth and I are giving you this cabin."

Thomas's eyes opened wide, and his head jerked back as the offer sank in. "But…"

"We want you both to have this place as a wedding gift."

Thomas's breath choked in his throat. He shifted in his seat. "That's generous of you. But I couldn't possibly accept it. I mean, I have to talk to Rebecca."

Joseph leaned in. "Son, I want you close. I spent years wishing you were here with me. Hell, my damn brother wrote me that you were dead."

"Randall told me the same thing about you. I didn't believe him."

"He came looking for you a couple of months ago," said Joseph. "I never expected he'd leave New York."

Thomas cocked his head back. "He arrived here in California at the same time I did. That's when he and his men attacked Alexander's place. I thought he was going to kill me that day."

Joseph winced. "Randall won't hurt you. He has a soft spot for you." He grimaced. "And one for Alexander, too."

Thomas flinched and took a sip. "Randall's not too happy with me right now since I put a bullet through his shooting hand."

"He'll bounce back. He always does."

"Not this time. He's done for." Thomas blinked, his eyes drifting away before returning to Joseph. "I know Randall's secret."

"What secret?" Joseph's eyes tightened slightly. Randall had many secrets.

"I know that Alexander is Randall's son."

Joseph's jaw slackened. "He told you?"

"No. Frank did. Randall's eyes went wild with shame when I told him I knew about it."

Thomas hesitated when his pa's eyes flicked down for an instant, the way Randall's had.

Joseph took a long sip.

"I was surprised you weren't with Frank the day Randall showed up on my porch. You two were always together."

Thomas took a sip. "I never could convince Frank to leave his outlaw life. I tried. He looks up to Randall." Thomas sighed. "Frank was there when I shot Randall's hand. I'd swear he wanted to kill me for hurting Randall."

Joseph paused, "I'm proud of you, son. Convincing men to leave their criminal life behind ain't easy. I doubt those two are worth saving."

"The day before, his band of outlaws had Alexander's stagecoach pinned down a few miles this side of Sacramento. His wife, Martha, and I picked them off one at a time." His mouth twitched at the memory.

A wide grin broke across Joseph's face, eyes lit with pride. "Thanks to you, that stagecoach was safe that day."

Thomas sat up taller, his warm smile turned into a grin. "That's when I met Rebecca."

"She reminds me a bit of your Ma."

"She does? Do you ever think about Ma?" Thomas inhaled deeply. "I miss her."

Joseph shifted in his seat. He took a sip of his lemonade. "I think of her all the time. I'll always love her. I love Elizabeth, too."

Thomas's gaze lifted slightly as he remembered Elizabeth knocking at Rebecca's hotel door. "I like Elizabeth." He paused. "Does she know about Randall?"

"I've told her everything about our family. She's written most of it down, but I didn't tell her that Randall was here in California."

"Why not?"

"I want Randall as far away from Elizabeth as possible."

"Do you think he'll hurt her?"

Joseph locked eyes with Thomas. "Yes. I do."

Thomas blinked at Joseph's worry-filled eyes. "I won't tell her. But, I just swore to Rebecca that I would never keep anything from her."

"Just give me a little time to tell Elizabeth myself."

"Okay. But if Randall comes near my Rebecca, I swear, I'll make him regret it."

Joseph leaned in. "You're a natural at safeguarding people's lives. You should work as my deputy."

Thomas's brow bounced up. "Sheriff August, over in Sacramento, hired me as one of his deputies. He had me doing menial chores. I couldn't stand it after a few days. I quit."

Joseph winced at the mention of the man who had threatened to woo Elizabeth away from him before he had a chance to prove he was a worthy husband. He'd promised to give up the drink. He despised Sheriff August. "Here, you would be my trusted deputy. You would run things now and then. This would be your chance to make your Ma proud. She always wished the best for you, and so do I."

"I don't know what to say."

"Son, I'm happy you came back to me. I don't ever want to lose you again."

The edges of Thomas's mouth curled up. "This seems like a peaceful town."

"It's peaceful because I maintain law and order here. It's safe here because I keep the criminal elements away." Joseph glanced away as he remembered Silas Gentry. "You'd like being a lawman. Maybe someday you'd become the sheriff."

Thomas's face brightened. "Rebecca would love it here."

Joseph pulled a fancy gold watch from his pocket. It was a gift from Elizabeth after they married. It had belonged to her first husband, who was his best friend. He treasured it. He checked the time, his thumb tracing its worn edge.

"You could move in today if you wanted. It's got everything you need."

Thomas swallowed hard.

CHAPTER TEN

A Caress by the River

That afternoon, Elizabeth sat next to Rebecca on a sun-warmed boulder by the river's edge. The gurgling water tumbled over the moss-covered rocks and snagged at the branches with a low, melodic hum. Towering over them like giants, the trees cast shadows that danced across the women's faces as a gentle breeze flew by. Wildflowers dotted the grassy bank that sloped gently down into the water. Rebecca leaned back, letting out a contented sigh as the cool spray tickled her face. The smaller birds warbled a sweet melody as they hopped between branches, while the larger ones sat watching Rebecca with wary, unblinking eyes.

Elizabeth said, "Whenever I feel tired, I'll come down here, sit on this boulder, and let the breeze caress my face."

Rebecca inhaled deeply and let it out through a smile. "It's beautiful here."

Elizabeth rested her hand on Rebecca's arm. "I sometimes bring snacks for the birds. They're amazing creatures."

Dozens of pairs of chestnut-brown eyes stared at her.

"There are so many of them," said Rebecca, her voice cracking.

Elizabeth stood, narrowed her eyes at the crows, and pointed to Rebecca. "This is my friend Rebecca!" She stepped down from the boulder, walked a few feet away, and put some apple pieces on the wooden table. "I love these crows. They expect me to feed them each time I come here. They're smart. And I think they like me."

She went back and stood next to Rebecca. "I can tell they like you."

Elizabeth smiled as she kept her gaze on the apple pieces, waiting for the beautiful, black crows to notice the treats.

The crows wasted no time and flew to the feast Elizabeth had left for them. One by one, they flew down and took some fruit. They would caw as if saying "Thank you" and then fly back to the safety of their tree.

Rebecca's eyes danced in amazement as she watched the crows enjoying their meal.

Elizabeth was eager to share the details about the wedding gift of the cabin that she and Joseph had decided to give them. She was sure that Rebecca would relish the idea of moving closer to her and Joseph. Elizabeth fought back the temptation to tell Rebecca the great news. It would be better for Thomas to surprise her, she thought.

Elizabeth cast a momentary glance at the house over her shoulder and then settled back on Rebecca. "Let's go have some Queen Cakes."

"Would you mind if I just sit here for a minute longer? It's so peaceful."

"Don't be long; the men will be back soon." Elizabeth jumped to the river's bank. She glanced at the water and then back at Rebecca. "Just be careful. That moss is beautiful, but it makes those rocks slippery."

Rebecca nodded, closed her eyes, and smiled, her face bright from the sun.

Elizabeth walked up the trail to the house. As she reached the top of the hill, she heard Rebecca humming a beautiful tune. She turned to see Rebecca swaying back and forth, waving her arms in a dance. Elizabeth smiled and then continued to the house.

Thomas sat on the porch swing as she stepped onto the porch.

He jumped to his feet. "Where's Rebecca?"

Elizabeth stopped at the door. "She'll be here shortly. She wanted to enjoy the river for a little while longer. I'm going to go freshen up. I'll be back."

Thomas nodded as Elizabeth disappeared into the house.

Thomas yawned and sat back onto the porch swing, about to close his eyes, when he heard steps coming from the trail behind him. He smiled, expecting to see Rebecca. It was Frank pointing a gun ahead of him. Thomas glanced at the front door and then rushed down the stairs.

Frank kept his gun pointed at Thomas. "Ain't you afraid I'm going to shoot you?"

"I thought you were my friend," said Thomas as he walked closer to Frank. "I ain't got my gun."

"I oughta shoot you for what you did to Randall."

"He deserved what he got. He's caused trouble for as long as I've known him."

"You shot his damn shooting hand. You must have known what that would do to him. He's turned into something different. He's not the man he was before. You took that from him."

"He can't rob stagecoaches anymore. What's wrong with that?"

"You took everything from him. He's—"

"Weak?" Thomas narrowed his eyes at Frank.

Fire danced chaotically in Frank's eyes. "You'll pay for what you did."

Thomas closed in on Frank. "I've been paying all my life." Thomas let out a huff. "It's about time you snap out of your blind allegiance to Randall. I tried to help you. Lots of times!"

Thomas's eyes flicked to Frank's trembling weapon.

Frank rasped, "I watched out for you, Thomas!"

"Frank, stop!" yelled Charlie. "Put your damn gun away."

As Frank turned, Thomas kicked the gun out of his hand.

Frank lunged at Thomas and punched him in the gut.

Thomas crumpled, eyes locked on Frank.

Frank picked up his gun and walked away. He turned back as he holstered his weapon. "We'll finish this conversation another time."

Thomas sat on the ground as Frank disappeared down the trail.

Charlie walked up. "You okay?"

Thomas stood and brushed the dirt from his clothes. "Yup. I'm fine."

"You two seemed like you used to be close."

Thomas looked down the trail Frank had gone, then back to Charlie. "He was my best friend. But that was a long time ago."

Charlie nodded. "I'd better make sure he's gone."

"Thanks."

Back at the river, Rebecca's eyes shot open as heavy footsteps traipsed behind her. A large man closed in on her. She jumped up and slipped. Randall grabbed her wrist with his left hand and righted her before she could fall into the water.

"I didn't mean to frighten you," said Randall as he let go. "I thought Joseph was here."

"He's probably back at the house."

Randall touched her face and said, "You look familiar."

Rebecca shoved his arm away and slapped him, her eyes wide with annoyance. She smelled the acrid scent of whiskey and sweat. She stood taller. "How dare you touch my face!"

"I meant nothing."

Rebecca's eyes grew into tight slits. "Who are you?" She noticed his bloodshot right eye.

"I'm Randall, your husband's uncle." He grinned. "I'm disappointed Thomas didn't invite me to the wedding."

Rebecca gasped, and her eyes widened. "Thomas told me all about you. You killed his mother."

"That ain't true. Joseph did that. He shot her dead just a few feet in front of me."

Rebecca wrinkled her nose as if she'd smelled something awful. "Why are you here, disturbing my peace?" She'd met people like him before and knew how to handle them. She used to sing in the Sacramento saloons when she lived there, and too often the rougher crowd would try getting familiar in ways she'd rather forget. She found that directly confronting them was the most effective way to disarm them.

Randall cracked a smile. "Joseph and I haven't been too civil to each other for far too long. I was hoping to chat with him and see if we could work something out somehow. I thought he'd be here."

"I told you already. He's at the house."

Randall glanced over his shoulder at the house and then rubbed his bloodshot eye.

Rebecca, feeling a bit of sympathy, studied his face. She had a talent for sizing up a person. "What's wrong with your eye?"

"I can't see out of it too well." He seemed like a child whimpering about an injury. He glanced down as if embarrassed.

"What about your hand?"

Randall's eyes narrowed. "Your husband shot my hand. It ain't good for nothing now. He stole the one thing that made me who I was."

Rebecca huffed. "I guess that means you can't rob stagecoaches anymore, either. Now, you'll need your family's help. Huh? You're scared, too. Aren't you?"

Randall stepped back. "I ain't scared! I don't need anybody. Things have changed—that's all."

Heavy footsteps crashed through the brush behind them, fast and furious, tearing through the quiet like a storm.

Rebecca's head jerked back as Joseph lunged and struck Randall with a sharp punch. Randall crashed into the water, sending a spray that soaked Rebecca's dress.

She gasped and stumbled back, the chill clinging to her fabric.

Randall surged upright. "What the hell, Joseph? Is that any way to treat your brother?"

Rebecca stood trembling as Joseph turned to her. The violence left fear etched across her face.

"I'm sorry," he rasped.

Her breath stuck in her throat, her eyes wide. She cast a sideways glance at Randall.

His face held a grin. He winked at her and said, "Joseph thinks I'm going to kill Elizabeth."

He turned to Joseph. "I don't kill family. That's what you do."

Rebecca's gaze snapped to Joseph, and her jaw slackened.

"Rebecca, please don't tell Elizabeth anything about this."

Randall grinned. "I've been here all this time, and you kept me a secret from her? I'm almost offended." Randall huffed. "I came here to chat, but you ain't ready for that!" He marched away.

Rebecca bolted back to the house.

CHAPTER ELEVEN

The Lockbox Trap

At the water's edge, Joseph stood frozen, watching Rebecca running away with his secret.

"Shoot," Joseph muttered. He yelled after her, "Rebecca, please!"

Joseph rubbed his knuckles as his gaze swung to where Randall had gone. Joseph's eyes widened when John and Charlie stepped from behind a large rock outcrop directly beneath the dark birds and walked up to him.

John chuckled. "She's a firecracker, ain't she? Just like her sister."

Joseph glared at him. "Where'd Randall go?"

John wrinkled his face. "Why were you surprised to see Randall? I told you he wanted to see you before we left. Something about making peace with you."

Charlie shook his head. "Randall shouldn't have touched Rebecca's face like that. Women don't like men touching them that way."

Joseph winced. "How would you know what women like?"

Charlie closed in on Joseph. "I didn't know you were keeping Randall a secret from Elizabeth. When you came to our camp, you said you kept nothing from her. Maybe Elizabeth and I need to have a little chat."

Joseph's eyes grew large with rage. "Mind your own business! I'll run you out of my town faster than—"

Charlie bared his teeth like a rabid dog. "I ain't going nowhere."

Joseph stood firm and narrowed his eyes at him. "You don't have much respect for the law."

John stepped between the two. "Charlie, let's get something to drink before I head out."

Charlie glared at Joseph, his mouth widening into a grin. "Finally got something worthwhile on you." He turned and walked to his horse.

John shook his head. "Joseph, I appreciate you letting us stay on your property."

Joseph's nostrils flared, and his breathing was hard. "What choice did I have?"

John's eyes darted to the barn and then back to Joseph. "I left something by the barn to show you my appreciation and to make sure you don't tell anyone about us."

Joseph gasped and glanced over his shoulder at the barn. An old, dilapidated cart stood there.

John started for his horse and waved at Joseph. "Pleasure doing business with you."

Charlie was on his horse, staring daggers at Joseph.

John climbed up on his and snickered at Charlie. "Come on. Let's get that drink."

Charlie's brows bobbed up at Joseph. "Sure. You're buying."

Joseph stood simmering in rage by the river as John and Charlie rode away.

Back at the house, Rebecca, her clothes wet, rushed inside through the back door. No one was there. She ran through the kitchen and saw a stack of little cakes on the table. Those were Elizabeth's famous Queen Cakes. She went past them and burst out the front door.

Thomas was alone on the porch bench, swinging back and forth. Rebecca rushed up and sat down next to him.

Rebecca caught her breath and said. "Where's Elizabeth?"

"I thought she was inside. You okay? Why is your dress wet?"

"I almost fell in the water. I feel a little tired. Can we go?"

Thomas cocked his head back. "What about dessert? I love Elizabeth's Queen Cakes."

"I don't want any. Can we go?" Her eyes darted to the trail and then back to Thomas.

She stood when she heard footsteps coming from inside.

Elizabeth peeked out the front door. "I thought I heard you. I dozed off."

"We have to go," said Thomas, his face etched with worry.

Elizabeth frowned. Her shoulders sagged. "Oh no!"

Rebecca shrugged and whispered, "I'm sorry."

Elizabeth nodded and glanced at the door. "Wait! I'll be back." She disappeared into the house.

Thomas hugged Rebecca as he glanced toward the river. "Did something happen?"

"I'm fine. I'm just tired."

Elizabeth walked out carrying a small package. "Here are some cakes to take with you."

As Rebecca reached for the cakes, she gasped. Her wrists had begun to darken where Randall had grabbed her. Her eyes darted to Elizabeth.

Elizabeth's face was serious, and her eyes were focused on the bruises. "What happened to your arm? Are you okay?"

Rebecca's breath caught. Her hand trembled as she quickly took the cakes. "It's nothing."

Elizabeth blinked and then hugged Rebecca. "We'll stop by tomorrow. We can have lunch and talk."

Rebecca's breath caught. She nodded, offering Elizabeth a small smile.

"Where's Joseph?" asked Thomas

Elizabeth shrugged as she glanced toward the road. "I don't know. I'll tell him goodbye for you."

Rebecca glanced back at Elizabeth as she and Thomas walked to the coach.

Elizabeth watched as Thomas and Rebecca's carriage left. Something caught her eye. Charlie and a man she didn't recognize were riding toward the road.

"Charlie!" Elizabeth yelled.

Charlie rode to her. The other man continued, then stopped at the road.

Elizabeth squinted to get a better look at the man as Charlie stopped beside her. "Yes, Ma'am?"

Elizabeth's breath hitched in her throat. "Have you seen Joseph?"

"He's by the water." Charlie glanced at the trail of dust still hanging over the road that led to town. "John and I saw Rebecca running away from Joseph a few minutes ago. He was pleading with her to hide something from you. You should ask him about it."

Elizabeth's eyes grew wide with concern, but she maintained her composure. She pointed to the man. "Who's that man?"

Charlie said without hesitation, "John Walker."

She took another look at the man and then said, "Thank you, Charlie."

Charlie nodded at her, hiding a devilish grin, and quickly caught up with John.

Elizabeth watched as Charlie and John Walker rode away. She marched down the trail to the river, shaking her head. She shuddered as she approached the water, and the air grew damp, making breathing uncomfortable.

Joseph was at the water's edge, staring into the distance. She inhaled deeply and exhaled into the wind. She stopped next to him.

He turned to her with a troubled expression and a hint of guilt in his eyes.

"What did Thomas say about the cabin?"

"He seemed hesitant. Says he's going to talk it over with Rebecca."

Elizabeth glanced at the rock where she and Rebecca were sitting. It was wet. "What happened with Rebecca? She was upset about something when she left."

He glanced at the house and then took a deep breath.

She stepped closer to Joseph.

"What are you keeping from me? Did you hurt Rebecca? She's a respectable, precious woman," Elizabeth said, her eyes moistening with tears. "I thought we didn't keep secrets from each other."

Joseph's eyes grew bright with fire. He glanced at the trail and muttered, "Charlie!"

He turned back to Elizabeth. "He's trying to cause trouble between us. You know he hates me."

"Forget about him. Just tell me." She blinked several times as her eyes bore into Joseph's crimson face.

His breath stuck in his throat as his eyes locked with hers. "There's nothing to tell."

Elizabeth's eyes narrowed. "So, you're not going to tell me?" Her patience exhausted, she turned quickly and stumbled.

Joseph's eyes widened in alarm as he reached for her, but missed.

Elizabeth fell hard face down, hitting her head on a rock. She wailed as a sharp pain throbbed in her middle. She struggled to right herself, not unlike a turtle trying to get back on its feet.

Joseph helped her up.

She was wobbly as she brushed the dirt from her clothes.

"You okay?" He asked, his voice cracking.

Elizabeth glared at him. She took a step and yelped loudly, grabbing again at her middle. "Help me get back to the house. I need to lie down."

Joseph supported Elizabeth's arm as they slowly walked back to the house. Her other hand pressed firmly across her abdomen.

Joseph reached around to carry her.

"Don't carry me."

Once safely in bed, Elizabeth turned away from him and closed her eyes.

Filled with guilt, Joseph went to the kitchen. A lone tear spilled from his eyes as he wiped his face and gazed out the window. A cart stood next to the barn. He'd forgotten that John had left something for him. He glanced at the bedroom on his way out the door.

A rickety cart sat next to the barn by an old wooden table. Inside were two boxes. Joseph shook his head in disbelief. He recognized them as the type of lockboxes the stagecoaches used to store valuables. He looked back at the house to ensure Elizabeth wasn't watching him. He opened one and discovered it was brimming with riches, undoubtedly from a stagecoach robbery.

"Damnit!"

He couldn't turn it over to the bank without admitting he'd helped the stagecoach robbers. He cursed at John Walker, who had left those crates, to ensure that he wouldn't be able to extricate himself from the outlaws.

CHAPTER TWELVE

Doubled Over in Pain

The next day, the sun, a blazing inferno in the sky, cast a harsh glare over the dusty road in front of the hotel. The air hung heavy as Thomas and Rebecca sat beneath the porch awning.

Rebecca fidgeted in her seat as she fanned herself with her hat. She glanced down the road. "Do you think Elizabeth is coming alone?"

Thomas glanced at her. "Joseph will be with her."

"Of course."

Thomas moved closer. "Are you sure you're okay? You've hardly said a word since yesterday."

She half-smiled. "I'm fine. I needed the rest." She sniffled and rubbed her wrist. "The last few days have been a whirlwind of excitement."

"I know something unpleasant happened to you yesterday. Please tell me what it was. I don't like seeing you in this state."

She let out a sharp breath and eased her shoulders, as though releasing something she'd been holding onto for too long. Her eyes lingered on him with quiet sadness, the corners of her mouth drawn but gentle. She turned to him. "When was the last time you saw your uncle?"

He looked at her, steady but soft, and shifted in his seat. "It was the day I shot his hand, at Agnes's house."

Her eyes flickered with a trace of understanding, but the tightness around her mouth didn't ease. She seemed to search for words, weighing what she ought to say against what might hurt. "You mentioned that time already. Have you seen him since?"

"No. He's long gone. I told you not to worry about him."

Rebecca took a deep breath, the kind that gathered steadiness before stepping into uncertain ground. Her voice stayed soft, but something beneath it braced. "He was at the creek yesterday."

Thomas lurched to his feet, breath snagged mid-thought. "Did he hurt you?"

"No. When he walked up, he startled me, and I almost fell. He caught me before I did." She rubbed at her wrist, as if remembering the moment more than feeling it. "I was alarmed when he touched my face. That was inappropriate. He smelled of whiskey. I don't think he meant anything bad by it. He was different than the way you've described him. Soft-spoken. Apologetic. Like a broken man."

"That doesn't sound like Randall. Are you sure it was him?"

"Yes. He said he wanted to make peace with Joseph."

"Really?"

"Then, Joseph ran up and shoved Randall into the water. He made a huge splash that left my dress soaked."

"Did they talk?"

"As I ran off, I heard them arguing. When I reached the top of the hill, I glanced back. Randall was stomping away."

"I wonder what he's up to."

Rebecca shrugged. "Wouldn't it be wonderful if he turned his life around. That's what you did?"

"I think he's beyond saving. A man who is that far gone doesn't wake up one morning and turn noble. And without someone like Agnes to steer him back, there's not a chance." Thomas's right cheek twitched. "I spent years trying to get an old friend to straighten out, but it didn't work." He exhaled, sharp and short. "I owe Agnes plenty for steering my life in a more positive direction."

Rebecca watched him closely. The way he looked past her, the way his voice thinned. This wasn't just about Randall. Not entirely.

"Maybe you could be that person for him—to help him change."

"Not me." He smiled. "You've got a gift for seeing the best in people, even when it's buried deep."

Rebecca chuckled and took his hand. "I like the challenge— digging into someone's heart for the hidden good and helping it surface. But Agnes... she's miles better at that than I am."

"I wonder how she's doing?" Thomas grinned.

"We'll see her in a few days, when we go home." Rebecca glanced away, then back. "Joseph said Elizabeth doesn't know

Randall is here in Auburn. Do you know if she knows?"

Thomas rubbed the side of his face, jaw tense. "No. I didn't tell her. I didn't see a need. I figured tearing up Randall's hand would keep him away. I told him I'd shoot him dead if he ever showed his face again."

"I hope you don't do that."

Thomas shrugged.

Rebecca half-smiled and looked down the road, hoping to catch sight of Elizabeth and Joseph coming. "I wonder why your father didn't tell her."

"Maybe he's in league with the stagecoach robbers."

"Being involved with Randall doesn't mean he's tied to the robbers."

"I suppose you're right."

Rebecca took Thomas's hand. "Promise me you won't keep anything from me, even if you think it might hurt me. Okay?"

"You already have my word. Though... I've kept something from you."

Rebecca's jaw slackened. "Thomas!"

He grinned. "My pa offered us a cabin as a wedding present."

Her breath caught in her throat. "Really?"

"He said it was Elizabeth's idea."

"I should have known. Yesterday, she seemed like she was itching to tell me something."

"I visited the place. It's everything we've ever dreamed of. And, it's ready for us to move into."

"It's not every day someone offers you your dream," Rebecca said, her voice rising with delight. "It's everything you've always wanted. Isn't it?"

Thomas paused. "I don't know. Something doesn't feel right."

Her expression softened. "Elizabeth is watching out for both of us. She told me your father cares about you. She trusts Joseph."

"He offered me a job as his deputy."

Rebecca's smile grew wide. "What did you tell him?"

"That I wanted to talk to you first."

"I'd be happy with whatever you decide. I've loved these last few days with Elizabeth. Living near her again would be wonderful. We could start our family right away. We wouldn't have to wait."

Rebecca's eyes lit up. "Imagine living here—the cabin, the town, all of it!"

Thomas chuckled. "We could go see the place later today if you'd like."

"That would be wonderful!" Rebecca beamed, but her attention flicked to the road. She sprang to her feet, pointing. "They're coming!"

Thomas followed.

The wagon rolled to a gentle stop in front of the hotel. Joseph held the reins steady while Elizabeth stepped down.

Rebecca rushed toward her, joy brightening every step.

Joseph said to Thomas. "How about you come with me to my office? I want to introduce you to my deputies."

Rebecca kissed Thomas. "Have a great time!"

Thomas smiled at Elizabeth and climbed up next to Joseph.

Elizabeth patted Thomas's arm.

Rebecca watched the exchange between Joseph and Elizabeth.

When Joseph nodded at Elizabeth, her smile faded, and her eyes cooled.

She sighed.

Joseph glanced at Rebecca and quickly looked away.

He said, "We'll be back in a few hours."

He snapped the reins hard, and the horses surged forward, pulling the wagon into a rising plume of dust.

Elizabeth exhaled. "Let's go inside. It's too dusty out here. I've got to get off my feet."

Together they stepped into the hotel.

Douglas was at the counter, ahead of them, chatting with the clerk. He crossed the room quickly. He nodded at Rebecca and then turned to Elizabeth.

"Elizabeth, may I speak to you for a moment?"

Elizabeth tapped Rebecca's arm. "Please go ahead. I'll join you in a minute."

Rebecca glanced at Douglas and then nodded. "Okay. Let me know if you need me. I'll wait for you by the stairs."

"Thank you, dear."

Rebecca moved to the chair beside the staircase and sat.

* * *

Elizabeth stood next to Douglas in the far corner of the lobby, where they had their privacy.

Douglas leaned in, voice low. "I have reason to believe your husband may be connected to the stagecoach robberies. The bank plans to take action if it proves true."

Elizabeth's voice burst out. "That's preposterous. Joseph is the sheriff, for God's sake! He's the wealthiest man in town. He wouldn't be involved in that."

Douglas grimaced. "I hope you're right."

Elizabeth took a breath, her tone clipped, "Those accusations are serious. Perhaps we should speak with Joseph at the sheriff's office and see what he has to say."

Douglas's eyes widened. "No. We're still investigating. I came to you as a friend. We've known each other a long time, and I thought you should hear it from me."

Elizabeth's jaw set, her gaze steady. "Then, as a friend, know this—my husband is *not* guilty of whatever you suspect."

Douglas lowered his voice. "I'm sorry, Elizabeth. I didn't mean to upset you."

Down the road at the sheriff's office, Joseph and Thomas climbed down from the wagon.

As Thomas stepped up on the porch, he turned to Joseph. "My wife wasn't quite herself yesterday on the way home. What happened by the river?"

Joseph's breath caught. "She almost slipped into the water. The rocks there can be treacherous."

Thomas studied him, suspicion flickering. He wondered why his Pa hadn't mentioned their encounter with Randall.

Joseph asked, his eyes bright with excitement, "What did she say about the cabin?"

Thomas hesitated at the sudden shift in tone. "She said she'd be happy with whatever I decide. But, I want to make sure she really liked the place."

"How could she not?" asked Joseph.

Thomas smiled, remembering Rebecca's joy. "I'd like to take her there this afternoon."

Joseph's shoulders relaxed, a smile forming. "That's a great idea!"

He opened the office door and held it for Thomas.

Thomas stepped inside. Joseph followed, his face beaming with a smile.

Meanwhile, in the hotel room where Rebecca and Thomas were staying, the two women sat sipping coffee and each enjoying a Queen Cake.

Elizabeth rubbed her side and shifted in her chair. "These chairs are so uncomfortable."

Rebecca glanced at Elizabeth's side. She paused and then said, her voice cracking, "I have to tell you something. I'm afraid it might upset you."

"Dear, you can tell me anything. You know that."

"Yesterday, after lunch—"

Elizabeth took Rebecca's hand. "You and Thomas left a little early."

Rebecca blurted out, "Joseph asked me not to tell you his brother, Randall, was there."

Elizabeth blinked in surprise. "Randall is here—in Auburn?"

"Yes."

"So *that's* what he's been keeping from me."

"Randall said he wanted to make peace with Joseph. He seemed sincere."

Elizabeth inhaled sharply and let out a slow breath. "Why was your dress wet? Did that brother of his have something to do with that?"

"Before Joseph walked up, I almost fell. Randall grabbed my arm and kept me from hitting the water. After he helped me up, he touched…" Rebecca rubbed her cheek. "He acted as if he recognized me. It was odd. I've never seen him before. That's why my wrist was darkened."

Elizabeth leaned in. "Oh dear!"

"He was subdued. Nothing like what Thomas had described him. His right hand was bandaged, and one of his eyes looked terrible." Rebecca's face pinched as she watched Elizabeth's mouth fall open, and her eyes dimmed. "I should've minded my own business. I hope you're not angry with me."

"Heavens, no! I knew something was off. Right after you left, I asked Joseph about it. He didn't mention his brother."

"He didn't?"

"I love my husband, warts and all. I knew he was hiding something. It's the only thing we've ever fought about. Being a sheriff means dealing with unsavory people. I've told him never to keep threats from me. How else can I be prepared? Now that I know, I'll talk to Joseph."

Rebecca said, "I didn't know what to do."

"Don't worry anymore. It'll work itself out." Elizabeth rolled her eyes. "Who knows why Joseph kept this from me. Maybe he's worried Randall might harm me. Randall was somehow involved in his first wife's death."

A teary-eyed Rebecca hugged Elizabeth. "I don't know what I'd do if anything bad happened to you. Please be careful."

"I'll be fine. Let's talk about something else." Elizabeth smiled. "Has Thomas mentioned anything about our big gift yet?"

Rebecca wiped away her tears and nodded. "He told me as you were coming up the road."

Elizabeth's face lit up. "What did you decide?"

Rebecca's eyes sparkled. "I told him it was up to him, and I would be happy with whatever he chose."

"It would be wonderful if you lived close by. You've always dreamed of a home like this one. It's ready to move into—perfect for both of you."

"Thomas was excited about the cabin and about working as the deputy."

"He'd make an excellent deputy. That was Joseph's idea."

Rebecca's cheeks reddened with joy. "I'll talk it over with Thomas."

"Oh dear…" Elizabeth's smile vanished. Her jaw slackened, and her eyes drooped. She gasped, clutching her stomach. "I feel light-headed."

Rebecca's brow furrowed. She jumped up, her face taut with worry.

"I took a hard fall yesterday," Elizabeth murmured. "It's a little warm in here."

As Elizabeth stood, her legs wobbled, threatening to buckle.

Rebecca rushed to steady her. "Are you okay?"

Elizabeth gripped the table. "My leg's gone to sleep." She shook her right leg. "I need some air. Would you mind opening the window?"

Rebecca hurried to the window and opened it. When she turned, Elizabeth was about to sit when her mouth fell open, and her eyes squeezed shut. She doubled over and crumpled onto the floor.

"Elizabeth!" Rebecca cried, her voice cracking.

But Elizabeth didn't answer.

CHAPTER THIRTEEN

Recovery

Having fallen minutes before, Elizabeth lay curled on the hotel room floor, clutching her stomach. Her face was pale, twisted in pain.

Rebecca dropped to her knees, panic rising in her throat. "Elizabeth!"

"Doctor," Elizabeth gasped, barely audible between moans. "Go…"

Rebecca bolted to the front desk.

The clerk looked up slowly, irritated at the interruption. "What can I do for you?"

"Elizabeth Pruitt needs a doctor!"

The clerk's eyes darted toward the room and then back. His face seemed distant.

"Now!"

The clerk jolted from his shock. "Yes, Ma'am! He's in the room next door." He rushed around the counter and pointed to the corner room near the front door. "He sees patients there three times a week."

Rebecca turned and sprinted back, the door crashing against the wall as she entered.

"Help me," Elizabeth rasped, reaching out.

As Rebecca eased her up onto the bed, Elizabeth let out a sharp cry that echoed through the room.

Fast approaching, heavy footsteps startled Rebecca. "Thank God!"

The doctor raced in through the open door and pushed past Rebecca.

Elizabeth was in tears and winced as the doctor poked at her.

"Relax," said the doctor.

Elizabeth shrieked as the spasms in her middle intensified.

"Elizabeth, try to calm yourself," said the doctor. "It will ease the pain."

The doctor's breath caught as he examined her. "Your side is black and blue. And the bump on your head…"

"I fell yesterday."

He lightly touched her rib section, and Elizabeth yelped. A large bump protruded from her head, just above her ear. He shook his head.

"Did you hit your head?" he said as he pressed the syringe to her skin and delivered the dose. "This will ease the pain. Your body is in shock and is trying to right itself. You should have seen me immediately. With that much trauma to your body, I wouldn't be surprised if you cracked some ribs." He took a sharp breath. "…or worse."

Elizabeth gritted her teeth and squeezed her eyes shut. The medicine pulsed through her, leaving a tingling warmth in its wake. After a long, uncomfortable two minutes, she cracked open her eyes, inhaled a deep, shuddering breath, and released it.

"You need to keep off your feet for a while. I can't guarantee that everything is okay yet," said the doctor. "I'll check in on you later today. That shot will help in the meantime." He dug a vial out of his bag and pressed it into her hand. "There are seven pills. Please don't take them unless the pain's unbearable. They're dangerously addictive if used casually."

Elizabeth nodded.

He cleared his throat. "Feeling better?"

"Much better," she whispered.

Rebecca took Elizabeth's hand. "You can stay here in this room. Thomas and I will be in the room across the hall."

Elizabeth squeezed Rebecca's hand. "Joseph. He should have been back by now."

Rebecca nodded and started for the door.

"I'll wait until you return," said the doctor.

She raced away. When she reached the desk, the clerk jumped up from his chair and said, "Is Mrs. Pruitt all right?"

"She's doing better. Where's the sheriff?"

His shoulders eased. "The deputy told me that he hasn't seen him since this morning."

Rebecca ran outside to the porch and paced, unsure how to

find Joseph. She walked into the street to get a better view of the road leading into town, but there was still no sign of the two. When she went back to the porch, the sound of galloping horses fast approaching echoed behind her. It was Thomas and Joseph racing down the road toward the hotel. They laughed riotously as they came to a stop beside her.

Rebecca, her eyes brimming with tears, said, "Joseph! Elizabeth needs you upstairs! The doctor is with her."

Joseph, his voice laced with panic, asked, "What's wrong?"

He tossed the reins aside and darted inside, not waiting for an answer. He rushed past the clerk and up the stairs, taking two at a time. He was breathless when he entered the room. His heart missed a beat when his gaze fell on Elizabeth.

The doctor was in the chair by the bed. "Sheriff, your wife will need plenty of rest for the next few days. I'll come by later and check up on her. If she needs anything, come get me downstairs."

The doctor smiled at Elizabeth and left.

Joseph, his eyes heavy, took Elizabeth's hand. "My love, I can't lose you."

"I'm going to be fine, Joseph." She winked at him. "All this fuss about a few bruises. That shot the doctor gave me has made me feel wonderful. The pain is gone."

"About yesterday…"

She took Joseph's hand and squeezed it. "I know about your brother being here."

Joseph's eyes, moist with guilt, started to ramble. "This is all my fault. I'm supposed to protect you. I should have told you about Randall. I'm…"

He choked on his words and kissed her hand.

Elizabeth's face filled with a warm smile, "It was a devastating shock, but we'll worry about your brother later, if we need to."

Thomas cleared his throat as he and Rebecca walked in.

Full of tears and raw emotions, Joseph turned away.

Rebecca noticed Joseph's reaction and tugged at Thomas's hand. She half-smiled at Elizabeth. "Call out if you need anything."

Elizabeth nodded. "Thank you, dear."

They left the room, closing the door behind them.

Rebecca led the way to the room across the hall.

Once inside, they sat at the table near the window.

Rebecca covered her mouth. "This is terrible."

Thomas said, "My father was crushed. He cried just like this when my mother died. Powerful men aren't supposed to cry."

Rebecca took a small breath. "Everybody cries. He loves Elizabeth. He must have thought he was losing her. That kind of thing rocks a person to their core."

Thomas nodded. "You're right. I don't know what I'd do if I lost you."

"You'll never lose me." She kissed his cheek. "We can't leave Elizabeth alone. We have to stay until she recovers."

"We can stay as long as you want. I'll take care of the hotel arrangements later."

"After Elizabeth goes home, can we move into the cabin? I want to be close to her in case she needs me."

Thomas glanced at the door and then at Rebecca. "You want to move here?"

"Yes, with all of my heart."

"I'll let Joseph know in the morning that we'll accept their gift. He and Elizabeth will be happy to have family around them."

Thomas hugged her.

After three days in the hotel, the doctor suggested that Elizabeth return home to complete her recovery. Rebecca and Thomas helped Joseph get Elizabeth home safely and comfortably. Joseph rented a stagecoach for Elizabeth. And the four of them traveled to the Pruitt place.

"Don't leave yet," said Joseph to the driver when they arrived.

Joseph opened the door and assisted his wife. He grunted as he picked up Elizabeth, a strain evident in his voice.

Elizabeth gasped. "Oh dear!"

"Hold on. I'll take you to your bed."

Rebecca and Thomas waited on the porch.

A few minutes later, Joseph stepped out. "Rebecca, Elizabeth is asking for you."

Rebecca tilted her head at Thomas.

He quickly nodded and turned to Joseph. "Rebecca wants to be near Elizabeth if she needs something. Can we move into the cabin now?"

Joseph's face lit up bright. "Of course." A wide smile filled his face. "It's ready and waiting."

Rebecca jumped up, a huge smile on her lips. "I'll be right back. I must tell Elizabeth the good news."

She ran inside and found Elizabeth sound asleep. She smiled, closed the door softly, and went back outside.

Joseph and Thomas were waiting next to the coach.

"How is she?" asked Joseph.

Rebecca smiled. "She's sleeping. She looks so much happier now in her bed."

Joseph's shoulders relaxed. "That's great to hear." He gestured to the coach driver. "These two need a ride to the cabin."

"But the horses?" asked Thomas.

"I'll take care of them."

Moments later, Thomas and Rebecca arrived at their new home. Thomas stepped out of the stagecoach and extended his hand to Rebecca.

She stepped down and paused when she laid eyes on the house. "It's magnificent."

She followed the path to the front door and pushed it open.

She walked over to the table. A beautiful bowl of fruit sat next to a lavish vase of flowers. "Elizabeth must have added this welcoming touch." She turned to Thomas. "This place is perfect."

"Joseph said it was ready to move in, but I expected we would still need to do something to make it our own."

Rebecca picked up a small note sitting by the flowers. She read it aloud. "Family takes care of family." She smiled. "And it's signed Joseph and Elizabeth."

She noticed the writing wasn't smooth and flowery like Elizabeth's. "What a kind sentiment that Joseph must have written. I can't think of a lovelier housewarming present." Her eyes brimmed with tears. She turned to Thomas and hugged him. "I love this house. It has plenty of room."

Thomas nodded.

They sat at the table and ate the fruit.

Rebecca's brows went up. "I have an idea. Let's send for our things?"

"Elizabeth's aunt Helen won't appreciate strangers showing up at her house to collect your things. We'll head to Sacramento in two days and pack up our belongings," said Thomas. "And say a proper goodbye to Helen and Agnes."

Rebecca said, "I hope Helen won't be disappointed that we won't stay there with her after all."

"I think she loved having you there before we were married, but I don't think she was too keen on me living there, too."

Rebecca chuckled. "She loves her privacy."

"Yup," said Thomas. "She'll enjoy the extra space once we move your things out of her house."

"I don't have that much. I think Agnes will be sad to see you go, too."

"That's true. She was like a mother to me — maybe a grandmother. I liked living with her and her family." Thomas glanced away and then smiled at Rebecca. "Within the week, we'll have all our things here, and we can finally call this place home."

Eight days later, Thomas arrived with Rebecca in a large, covered wagon, laden with all their worldly possessions. Rebecca jumped down and ran to the front door. Thomas followed her and opened the door, then carried his wife across the threshold.

Within minutes, Thomas was trekking back and forth, carrying Rebecca's belongings from the wagon to the house. He didn't have much himself. Everything he owned fit into one trunk. When he was done, Thomas sat exhausted at the kitchen table. There in the center lay a shiny deputy's badge. He picked it up and smiled.

Rebecca walked up. "I'm so proud of you."

Thomas stood and hugged her. "Both of our dreams have come true."

She leaned into the hug, her eyes glistening with possibility. "I can't wait to see what's in store for us in our new life here."

Rebecca rode to Elizabeth's house every day to help with her recovery. They often sat on Elizabeth's porch, enjoying tea and cake and bubbling with laughter. Joseph and Thomas would disappear to the sheriff's office, the gold mine, or out riding. Most evenings, Rebecca, Thomas, Elizabeth, and Joseph laughed together at the dinner table. Fifteen days after Elizabeth's collapse in the hotel, the doctor told her that she could go back to her usual routines.

CHAPTER FOURTEEN

Housewarming Party

Elizabeth tended to her chickens early the next morning, on January 25th. She chose one of the larger hens and carried it behind the barn, well away from the others. With a firm grip and a swift flick of her wrist, she silenced it.

Feathers flew. She plucked and gutted the bird with practiced ease, and moments later, it was simmering in a pot of bubbling water.

She scrambled eggs for breakfast with the same quiet efficiency. Beneath it all, she was brimming with excitement.

Joseph walked in just as Elizabeth set the food on the table.

"Smells delicious!" he said, kissing her cheek. "How are you feeling?"

"I feel great—just a little tenderness around my middle. I've been cooped up in this house long enough. I'm anxious to see what Rebecca's done with the cabin."

Joseph smiled. "Shouldn't you rest a little longer?"

He sat and began eating.

"No, the doctor said I'm healing wonderfully and that I should get plenty of exercise."

"In moderation," he said, a grin spreading across his face. "You're a strong woman. That's what I love about you."

Elizabeth smiled. "Have you gone over there?"

Joseph's gaze drifted toward the window, thoughtful. "Not since I left that deputy badge for him with Rebecca."

Elizabeth chuckled. "Rebecca said that Thomas's face lit up when he saw it."

Joseph gazed at her—silent.

Elizabeth shifted in her seat, her brow furrowing. "What's wrong?"

"It's been two weeks, and you haven't said a word about my brother."

"You should have told me about him. I get why you don't share every detail about the criminals you deal with. But, he's family—no matter what."

Joseph's voice hardened. "You don't know him like I do. He's dangerous. He could hurt you. I have to rid this town of him and keep you safe."

"He doesn't seem like much of a threat anymore. Do you know where he is?"

"I'm hoping he's long gone by now."

Elizabeth looked at him, unconvinced. "From everything you've told me over the years, I doubt he's far."

Joseph's jaw tightened. "He'll regret it if he comes around here again."

She glanced sideways at him. "Do you think there might come a time when you and he could work out your differences?"

Joseph choked on his breath. "He threatened to kill you!"

She gasped. "Did he even try?"

Joseph stared incredulously at her. "I can't bear the thought of anything happening to you. You're my life."

Elizabeth softened. "I'm just trying to understand. He's led a life of crime. He tore your family apart. He's been cruel to you, to Thomas, and countless others."

Joseph shifted, set his fork down, and locked eyes with her. He paused.

She held his gaze. "What?"

His voice dropped. "It's his fault my first wife is dead."

Elizabeth's jaw slackened. "I thought her death was an accident."

Joseph looked down and shook his head. The gleam in his eyes caught the light as he tried to smile at her. "He shoved her into my gun."

Elizabeth gasped. "Oh my!"

Joseph's gaze drifted. "When Randall and I were younger, we were inseparable—hunting, fishing, carousing around town. He even stood up to my father on my behalf. He looked out for me. But when I met Rose, everything changed. I wanted to spend time with her, not him. He didn't take that well."

"So he did care about you."

"When Thomas was born, Randall was the proud uncle, always bragging about his nephew. Thomas adored him. Clung to him."

Elizabeth frowned. "That doesn't sound like the Thomas I know."

"Thomas broke away from Randall and his criminality." Joseph turned to her, eyes shadowed with regret. "I'm sorry."

Elizabeth smiled gently. "Thank you for telling me. I understand why you didn't want to mention Randall being here in California. I'm hoping we can move on now and focus on the future and be happy."

Joseph's voice softened. "I've always been in awe of your passion. It keeps me trudging forward, no matter the difficulty. And you carry it with love and compassion."

Elizabeth rushed over to Joseph and wrapped her arms around his shoulders. "I can face adversity as long as you're by my side."

Joseph's face warmed with a smile. "When do we head over to Thomas's house?"

"In about an hour. I need to finish up in the kitchen."

"Perfect. I've got a few tools I want Thomas to have. I'll load them and bring the wagon around front."

"I'm sure he'll appreciate that. After lunch, maybe you and he can make yourselves scarce so Rebecca and I can chat."

Joseph nodded. "I'll take Thomas for a ride while you two women gossip."

Elizabeth chuckled, placing her hand over her chest as her eyes glistened. "Joseph! We don't gossip."

"If you say so," he said, grinning.

"I just enjoy talking with my friends. It's not my fault they tell me intimate details, and I feel compelled to share them."

Joseph raised a brow. "Is that why you write everything down? You've got boxes of journals. What are you going to do with all of that?"

Elizabeth shrugged. "I've dreamed of writing books since I was young." She rolled her eyes. "Ma and Pa thought it was a silly dream. God rest their souls."

"I don't like reading much, except the newspaper, but I'd read your book."

"Really?" Elizabeth blinked as if a candle had illuminated the dark corner of her mind where her dreams lay hidden.

Joseph smiled. "I can tell you plenty of stories about my family."

Elizabeth's eyes lit up. "That would be lovely!"

On the far side of Joseph's property, at Thomas and Rebecca's place, Rebecca was busy with housework while Thomas and Charlie dashed from the barn to the chicken coop, to the well, and back again. Thomas was eager to finish his chores so he could enjoy a relaxing afternoon with Elizabeth and Joseph.

Thomas went to the barn where Charlie was about to start chopping wood. "Would you mind finishing that up later?"

"No problem. I understand. I'll finish it after your company leaves."

Thomas handed Charlie a few coins.

"Thanks, Thomas," said Charlie. "You're mighty generous."

"You're a hard worker, and you deserve it."

"I enjoy this kind of work. It gets my mind off my problems."

"I know what you mean." Thomas smiled. "I really appreciate your help. I couldn't have got this done without you."

"Thanks. I'll be back later."

Charlie mounted his horse with ease, gave a backward wave, and rode off.

With a bounce in his step and a sense of restored order, Thomas stepped onto the porch. Clumps of mud broke loose from his boots, trailing behind him as he entered the cabin.

Rebecca gasped. "Oh dear! You're tracking mud inside!"

Thomas froze. "Sorry."

Rebecca chuckled. "I've got the tub ready. Hurry before it gets cold."

"You're the best!"

"Wait! Leave the boots!"

Thomas stepped back outside, returned barefoot, and tiptoed to the back room. Rebecca smiled as she cleaned up the mud from the entryway.

"Don't take too long. Elizabeth and Joseph will be here soon," she called.

"I'm hurrying," came his voice, mingled with splashing water.

Back at Joseph's house, Elizabeth climbed up onto the wagon as Joseph loaded two baskets of food.

Joseph settled into the driver's seat and took up the reins. "That's a lot of food."

"Rebecca will appreciate the leftovers."

Joseph chuckled, clicked at the horses, and snapped the reins. "Let's go."

The carriage pulled away, rolling toward Thomas and Rebecca's cabin.

They were both silent for a while. Elizabeth leaned forward, her hands resting on the bench beside her.

Joseph glanced over. "You've had a grin on your face ever since we left."

Elizabeth laughed. "I can hardly wait to get there."

His face lit up. "Well, you don't have to wait long. We're coming up on the cabin."

"How exciting!"

Joseph guided the horses onto a narrow trail. The cabin came into view.

Thomas sat on the porch bench, brushing mud from his boots. He jumped to his feet, slipped on his shoes, and ran to the coach as it came to a stop.

"Welcome. How are you doing?" he asked, helping Elizabeth down.

"I'm great," she said, as she followed him along a narrow walkway. "You've done a lot of work out here. The porch looks wonderful—new floorboards, fresh paint. You must've worked day and night."

Joseph followed with the baskets and set them by the door. "Thomas, I brought you some tools. Help me get them to the barn."

Elizabeth said, "You two enjoy yourselves. Rebecca and I will handle the food."

Joseph kissed Elizabeth's cheek and patted Thomas's arm. "Let's go."

Thomas grinned, and the two trotted off like schoolboys,

ready for recess.

Just as Elizabeth raised her hand to knock, the door swung open.

Rebecca's face lit up, eyes moist with joy. "Elizabeth, come in!" she said, pulling her into a hug.

Elizabeth gasped softly. "My ribs are a little tender."

Rebecca eased back. "Oh—sorry. Please, come inside."

Elizabeth stepped in, swinging the basket in front of her. "I've been waiting for this day since we talked about you moving here."

Rebecca picked up the other basket and rushed in, letting the door swing shut.

Elizabeth winced as she lifted the basket, her ribs still tender. She managed to place it on the dining table with care. "Joseph and Thomas left."

Rebecca placed her basket beside the other. "We won't be seeing those two for a while."

Elizabeth nodded. "I hope you're hungry."

"Oh heavens! That's a lot of food!"

Elizabeth pulled out a tin. "I brought Queen Cakes, too."

"My favorites!"

Out came the chicken, along with the rest of the meal.

Rebecca's eyes widened. "You must've spent hours on this. It smells delicious."

They chatted as they set the table, arranging serving dishes brimming with food.

Elizabeth stepped back, admiring the spread. "I think it's perfect. Don't you?"

Rebecca beamed. "It's a banquet fit for royalty!" She glanced at the door. "Let's go get Joseph and Thomas before it gets cold."

They giggled like young girls as they slipped out the back door and headed toward the barn.

Joseph's voice wafted toward them. "Let's go riding after we eat. You could get familiar with the land."

"I'd love that!" Thomas replied.

Rebecca called out, "Lunch is ready."

Thomas turned, surprised. Rebecca ran up and took his arm.

Elizabeth chuckled and snuggled up to Joseph. "Let's race, I sure could use the exercise."

Joseph took her hand and kissed it. "Darling, let's stroll back. No need to over-exert yourself."

Rebecca nodded. "Joseph is right. You've got to take it easy."

Elizabeth's brows bounced. "The doctor told me to exercise. I think a brisk walk counts."

Joseph, Thomas, and Rebecca stared at her, incredulous.

Elizabeth rolled her eyes. "Okay. I'm outnumbered." She winked at Joseph, then sprinted back to the house.

The trio gave chase.

Elizabeth reached the front door, breathless. "I win!"

The others caught up and followed her inside.

The four sat around the table, savoring the food and each other's company.

"This is the best chicken I've ever had," said Rebecca. "You'll have to teach me how you make it."

Thomas turned to her. "Yours is delicious, too."

Elizabeth smiled. "Thomas is right. Yours is better than mine."

Time slipped by, and the conversation was filled with joy and anticipation.

Soon after, Rebecca and Elizabeth stood on the porch, watching Joseph and Thomas ride off to explore the property.

Elizabeth smiled. "I'm so thankful they found each other."

Rebecca nodded. "I am too. It's made Thomas so happy." Then she walked to the front door and held it open.

"Let's go inside. I've been dying for one of those Queen cakes. They've been calling to me ever since you arrived."

CHAPTER FIFTEEN

Exploring

While Joseph and Thomas explored the outer edges of Joseph's land, Elizabeth sat across from Rebecca in the quiet of their parlor, sipping coffee and savoring the Queen Cakes—small, sweet, and speckled with currants.

From the barn came the steady rhythm of an axe striking wood. Charlie had returned not long after Joseph and Thomas rode out, saying little, and gone straight to work in the barn.

Rebecca glanced toward the window. "Charlie always did prefer the barn when he needed space. Especially when Joseph's around."

Elizabeth nodded, watching the steam rise from her cup. "Joseph doesn't make it easy."

"No," Rebecca said softly. "Charlie's lucky that Thomas likes him."

"I like him too. He used to do a lot of work at our place until Joseph ran him off."

Rebecca shrugged. "How about you and Joseph? Are you still upset with him?"

"No. Joseph and I talked about his brother." Elizabeth's tone turned somber. "I just wish he'd told me himself that Randall was in town. We've never kept secrets from each other."

"I hope neither Thomas nor I is responsible for causing you and Joseph trouble. That would be dreadful."

Elizabeth grimaced. "No, of course not."

Rebecca glanced away at the memory of seeing Joseph punch Randall by the creek. "I suppose he wants to keep you safe."

"That's Joseph." A smile played on Elizabeth's lips. "I love him with all my heart."

"I think he draws his strength from you."

Elizabeth looked down at her cup, the warmth fading against her palms. At times, she wasn't sure she deserved Joseph's devotion, but she cherished it all the same.

She reached for Rebecca's hand and patted it gently. "No matter how troubled I am, you always draw me toward hope," Elizabeth said, smiling.

Rebecca smiled. "I'm glad we live near each other. You and I can chat as often as we like, like we did in the old days, when you lived in Sacramento with your aunt."

"I'm thrilled. Joseph is, too, now that Thomas is back in his life. He's talked about him for as long as I've known him. He regrets leaving his son behind in New York. He was a young boy at the time."

"Thomas is still adjusting to their renewed relationship. He's overwhelmed with the money and gifts that Joseph gives him."

"Joseph has a big heart and a generous nature. He likes sharing his wealth with those he cares about."

"Thomas is like that, too. I suppose," said Rebecca. "He doesn't talk about it much, but I think he broods over those lost years. It's as if he's trying to make up for time he never got to spend with his Pa."

Elizabeth nodded. "After my first husband died, Joseph told me when life knocks you down, it's okay to flounder for a time, but eventually, you get up and move forward."

"That's so true." Rebecca took a bite of her cake and a sip of coffee.

Elizabeth glanced at the door and then back at Rebecca. "How does Thomas like the cabin?"

"He loves it. We both do."

"Joseph is thrilled Thomas agreed to be his deputy."

"You should have seen his face when he found that badge. He hesitated when he reached for it, and then a huge grin filled his face. He was so happy. He wears it proudly," said Rebecca.

"That's wonderful."

Rebecca took another bite. "Your cakes are heavenly."

"It's Aunt Helen's recipe."

Rebecca leaned in with a mischievous smile. "I've always liked yours better."

A smile played at Elizabeth's lips as her brows arched. "Did you know she and I used to practice shooting?"

Rebecca's face tilted slightly. "Really? I've never seen her touch a gun."

"It was a long while back," Elizabeth said, her gaze drifting.

"Thomas said Joseph told him you're a better shot than he is."

Elizabeth smiled broadly and nodded. "Perhaps when I was younger, but not so much anymore."

"We should practice together. I don't have much need for shooting these days, but no sense in letting my talent go to waste."

"Sure. I line up cans out back now and then and use them as targets." Elizabeth nodded and then glanced away. "A few days ago, Joseph insisted I carry my six-shooter when I leave the house."

"Sounds like he's worried for you."

On the far edge of Joseph's land, the two men rode toward the mine entrance, where the hills sloped into shadow, and the air grew still. Crows squawked in the distance.

Joseph said, "Now and then, my men turn up something of value there."

"Is this how you got rich?"

Joseph chuckled. "That gold made me wealthier than I ever dreamed."

"I've never been in a gold mine before. Rebecca would love exploring here."

Joseph half-smiled at Thomas. "For now, let's keep this between us. Our secret, okay?"

"Secret?"

Joseph inhaled deeply and then exhaled all at once. "Don't go in there alone. It's dangerous! You could get lost."

Thomas cringed. "I won't."

A growing cacophony of crows squawked louder.

Thomas's gaze rose to the trees. "What is that racket?"

Joseph looked up, "The crows saw us coming."

"I've never seen so many in one place." Thomas pulled his gun, about to shoot.

"No! Don't!" Joseph shook his head. "It's best to leave them be. All this racket has to do with you. Those damn birds tell each other when there's a new face." Joseph chuckled and continued, "Soon, every crow in the area will know your face!"

An instant later, the squawking ceased. The silence was so sudden it felt unnatural. Thomas's gaze shot up to the trees. Dozens of beady eyes stared down, unblinking.

Joseph grinned. "Someday, you'll meet my friend Howard. Those crows hate him with a passion."

"Howard Jackson?" asked Thomas.

"Yeah."

"I met him in Sacramento. He's an interesting fellow."

Joseph smiled and then nodded. "They attack him whenever he's alone."

"Really?"

"Yup! Crows are smart, crafty, and conniving. They never forget a face. Those beady eyes of theirs are as sharp as a hawk's eyes. They're always watching. A crow will tell other crows, even the young ones, about those faces who mean them harm. They'll remember your face until the day they die. Crows protect their family, especially their young. They will threaten you, attack you, and try to kill you to keep their families safe. Don't mess with them."

"He must have done something to incur their wrath."

"Howard messed with them when he first moved here. He'd shoot at them, thinking he could drive them off. He was wrong. They went after him. And then he climbed trees, shot into nests, and killed their young. But he didn't realize that they remember faces. They hate him. And he drinks to deal with it all."

Thomas glanced up at the trees. "I promise. I won't bother them!"

Back at the cabin, the scent of coffee and cakes lingered as Rebecca and Elizabeth sat together, their laughter fading into quiet comfort. Rebecca stood, then staggered slightly, her hand shooting out to steady herself against the table.

Elizabeth's eyes widened with concern. "Are you okay?"

"I got dizzy all of a sudden. That's all," said Rebecca, and then settled back into her seat.

Elizabeth glanced at the door. "The men should have returned by now."

"I'm sure time got away from them."

Elizabeth went to the door. "I'll send for the doctor, just in case. You look a bit pale." She stopped at the door. "I'll be right back. Will you be okay?"

Rebecca shrugged. "You're making too much of a fuss." She rolled her eyes in surrender. "I'll be fine."

Elizabeth smiled to hide her worry. She stepped out onto the porch.

Charlie was working on a hitching post. Elizabeth yelled out to him, "Charlie!"

He glanced over.

She stepped to the edge of the porch, her face creased with worry. "Get to Doctor Hammond's and ask him to come by. Tell him it's an emergency. And see if you can find Thomas and tell him to come home immediately."

"Yes, Ma'am."

"Thanks, Charlie."

Elizabeth watched as Charlie raced to the barn and then rode away. She smiled uneasily and walked back into the cabin.

An hour went by before Dr. Hammond arrived.

"I'm glad you're here," said Elizabeth. "Rebecca is in the bedroom right over there. I told her to lie down."

Dr. Hammond stepped in briskly, his bag swinging at his side, without saying a word.

Elizabeth sat in the front room, tapping her foot. At the sound of approaching hooves, she gasped and sprang to her feet. She rushed to the door and burst onto the porch.

Thomas was walking up the porch stairs.

"Thomas, come quickly."

His breath stuck in his throat. "What's wrong?"

"It's Rebecca. The doctor is in there with her."

Thomas rushed inside.

The doctor stood beside her and said, "You're fine. I'm guessing you're with child. We'll have to wait and see if your courses return."

Rebecca smiled at Thomas. "I had a feeling this morning when I woke up."

Thomas froze, his mouth slightly open, eyes wide with wonder. Then, slowly, a smile broke across his face.

Elizabeth smiled. "I should have noticed that glow in your face."

"That's wonderful news," said Thomas, grinning ear to ear.

Thomas rushed to Rebecca and kissed her hand.

She pulled him closer and kissed him. "I'm so happy."

Rebecca turned to the doctor.

The doctor's eyes darted from Rebecca to Thomas. "I'd suggest rest."

A smiling Elizabeth said, "I'll care for you until you're better."

The doctor gave Rebecca a spoonful of his tonic.

She wrinkled her face as she swallowed the dark liquid. "That tastes awful."

He put the bottle on the table beside the chair and turned to Elizabeth. "Please make sure she takes a teaspoonful daily."

"I will." Elizabeth winked playfully at Rebecca.

Rebecca scrunched her face. "I feel perfectly fine!"

Elizabeth chuckled. "Must be the doctor's special tonic."

Rebecca nodded and then giggled.

"You need to take it easy," said Thomas.

Rebecca took a deep breath and let it out all at once. "We've got to have a party!"

Thomas laughed in disbelief. "A party?"

"Yes! To celebrate our new home and the fabulous news that we're having a baby!"

Elizabeth's face was creased with concern. "Won't that be a bit much for you?"

"I'm fine. And you know how much I love parties." Rebecca turned to the doctor. "Would that be okay?"

The doctor blinked, taken aback by Rebecca. "I suppose it would be okay, as long as you don't over-exert yourself."

Rebecca raised her brows, a slow smile forming as she turned to Thomas.

Thomas acquiesced. "It should be a small party."

Rebecca nodded excitedly. "That's perfect. Let's have it the day after tomorrow."

Elizabeth shook her head and smiled broadly. "I'll stop by in the morning. If you're up to it, we can go into town and invite a few friends."

Rebecca hugged Elizabeth. "It's going to be wonderful!"

Elizabeth's gaze drifted from Rebecca to Thomas and back. "The doctor and I will show ourselves out."

The door closed, leaving Thomas and Rebecca alone.

"Do you remember when you said you dreamed of a home filled with laughter?"

Rebecca nodded, eyes glistening. "It's coming true."

Later that day, Charlie was feeding the horses. He glanced toward the house. Rebecca was alone on the porch, her eyes closed, enjoying the cool breeze.

Charlie walked up and roared, "Congratulations."

Rebecca's eyes shot open, and she jumped in surprise. "Charlie! You startled me!" She caught her breath and said, "Thank you."

He stood at the bottom of the stairs. "I've been meaning to tell you I saw what Randall did to you at the river that day after the wedding. He shouldn't have done that."

Rebecca jumped to her feet. Her eyes darted toward the front door, and she rushed to the edge of the porch. "You were there?"

Charlie stepped up closer to her.

She raised her hand to her nose, catching the scent of sweat, tobacco, and whiskey.

His eyes darted to her covered nose, and he stepped back. "I walked up after you ran away."

Rebecca grimaced. "It was nothing." Her concern deepened.

Charlie's head cocked back. "Yes. But—"

The door opened suddenly, and Thomas stepped out. He glanced at Charlie and then turned to Rebecca. "Is everything okay?"

Charlie grinned. "Thomas! I was telling my sister congratulations."

"Thanks, Charlie." Thomas hugged Rebecca. "We're excited about it too."

"You two are going to make wonderful parents. That means I'm going to be an uncle. I like that."

Thomas smiled. Rebecca's gaze dropped to the ground, and then she forced a smile.

Charlie said, "Well. I'd better get back to the horses." He nodded and sauntered back to the barn.

When Charlie was out of earshot, Thomas said, "Who did he say touched you?"

Rebecca wrinkled her face and rolled her eyes. "No one. Charlie doesn't know what he's talking about."

Thomas's gaze shot to Charlie and then back to Rebecca. "What did Charlie say to upset you?"

"Nothing. I'm still angry with him because he didn't want to walk me down the aisle. He knew how much it meant to me since our Pa couldn't be here." She kissed Thomas's cheek and continued, "You probably think I'm being silly. But I don't think I can ever forgive him for that."

"Do you want me to speak with him?"

"No, of course not. He's not worth the trouble," said Rebecca.

"Have you talked with your sister since the wedding?"

"No," Rebecca said, her voice short. She started for the door. "Let's have some of those cakes."

Thomas glanced at Charlie and then followed Rebecca inside.

CHAPTER SIXTEEN

Meeting Alexander

Early the next morning, Elizabeth and Rebecca sat on a sun-dappled bench near a glassy pond, scattering bits of dried bread to a resting family of ducks.

"Elizabeth!" came a familiar voice from behind them.

Douglas and Alexander strode toward them.

Rebecca rose, her smile blooming at the sight of Alexander.

Elizabeth's gaze narrowed at Douglas as he approached.

Her voice cooled. "Douglas." Her tone softened as she turned to Alexander. "Hello, Alexander."

Rebecca nodded, her gaze lingering on Alexander.

Douglas smiled at Rebecca and then his gaze shot to Elizabeth. "I apologize for interrupting your picnic. I believe you've met my bank manager, Alexander Johnson."

Elizabeth extended her hand to Alexander. "It's nice to see you again, Mr. Johnson. Last time we met was after that awful stagecoach robbery where Martha, Gertrude, and Rebecca held their own against those outlaws."

"Of course," he said as he shook her hand. "I'm—"

Rebecca stepped closer, her voice light but edged with mischief. "I didn't mean to embarrass you last time. Sometimes I speak before I think."

Alexander smiled awkwardly. "Think nothing of it. Martha was very impressed with your marksmanship."

Rebecca blushed, extending her hand, palm down. "It was quite the thrill."

He kissed it gently, then released it as she tugged back.

"I'm a married woman now," she said, with a playful tilt of her head. "Mrs. Rebecca Pruitt."

Alexander nodded politely, stifling an urge to say something rude about her husband, Thomas. He cleared his throat. "I'll be working with Douglas to address the uptick in stagecoach robberies."

Rebecca said, "That's encouraging. Those robberies have shaken the passengers. Elizabeth's Aunt Helen hasn't slept well since. That ordeal left her rattled."

Alexander blinked. "That's a shame."

Douglas leaned in toward Elizabeth. "Elizabeth, could I have a word with you? It's important."

"Certainly." Elizabeth turned to Rebecca. "I won't be long."

Rebecca watched as Elizabeth and Douglas walked to the water's edge. She leaned over and tried to hear what they said, but their voices were too soft.

Alexander's mind buzzed with thoughts of Thomas: resentments, suspicions, and half-formed judgments that swarmed like gnats in the corners of his mind. He couldn't quite name them, let alone silence them. He dismissed them, closed the distance, and said, "Shall we sit?"

"Of course," said Rebecca.

At the water's edge, Elizabeth's gaze lingered on Rebecca and Alexander sitting together.

She turned to Douglas. Her mind wandered back to the last time they spoke. His voice had been sharp with accusation, casting a long shadow over Joseph's name.

Douglas's voice dropped. "We caught one of the men behind last week's robbery. He claims there's a gang, organized and efficient, moving up and down the stage routes."

Elizabeth's breath hitched. "What does that have to do with Joseph?"

"The man said a Lawman gave them shelter. Somewhere nearby."

She stiffened. "There's no one hiding on our land. That's absurd."

Douglas leaned in. "I'm coming to you first, Elizabeth. Not Joseph. You know this town. Maybe it's one of his deputies."

Her voice sharpened. "Steer clear of Joseph. His deputies are beyond reproach."

Douglas grimaced. "I'm hiring men to protect the stage lines. I'll eliminate that threat one way or another. If there's a Lawman giving shelter to criminals, I'll see to it he's removed—quietly, if I'm lucky."

Elizabeth let out a huff and rolled her eyes. "I understand."

Her eyes flicked toward the sheriff's office. Her breath caught. Joseph was walking toward them, his stride calm, deliberate. Her heart thudded against her ribs, a warning drumbeat beneath her calm. She glanced at Rebecca and Alexander. She turned back to Douglas, bracing herself.

Alexander leaned back, his breathing measured, as he tried to wrangle the unease in the pit of his stomach.

Rebecca sat on the edge, her eyes darting to Alexander. Thomas crossed her mind. He would disapprove of her chatting with Alexander. She hesitated, Thomas's stern voice echoing in her mind. But the joy was too much to contain. "Thomas and I... we're having a baby!" Her voice trembled with excitement.

"Congratulations. Martha will, no doubt, be thrilled for you."

"Last I saw her, she couldn't wait for the baby to arrive."

Alexander's lips curled up. "He arrived! His name is Marcus."

Her eyes lit up with glee. She leaned back and clasped her hands in excitement. "How wonderful! Please tell Martha how happy I am for you both."

"I will," Alexander said with a soft smile. "His older brother, Alex, is almost five now. I'm proud of both my sons."

"I met little Alex and look forward to meeting baby Marcus."

Douglas and Elizabeth walked up.

"Alexander, are you ready to go?" asked Douglas, his voice tinged with urgency.

Alexander sprang to his feet, as if caught in a moment he wasn't meant to enjoy.

Rebecca stood. "It was lovely chatting with you about your family," said Rebecca as she offered her hand to Alexander.

"Yes, of course. The pleasure was all mine," he said as he shook her hand and almost bowed to her.

Rebecca pulled her hand back and gasped when Joseph walked up and stopped next to Elizabeth.

Joseph's voice sliced through the air, sharp and sudden. "Have I interrupted something?"

Elizabeth tugged at Joseph's arm. "I thought you were with Thomas."

Joseph grimaced. "I came back to get some supplies."

Douglas leaned in. "I want you to meet Mr. Alexander Johnson, my new bank manager."

Alexander hesitated and then extended his hand to Joseph. "It's…"

Joseph shook Alexander's hand with an almost painful grip. "I've known Alexander since the day he was born."

Elizabeth noticed the way Joseph's jaw tightened as he spoke.

Alexander's head cocked back as he pulled away from Joseph's tight grip.

Douglas continued, "Alexander will be working here on my behalf now and again. He won't be here often unless we have some trouble."

Joseph put his hand around Elizabeth. "We'll have no trouble in this town."

Douglas glanced at Elizabeth and smiled. "That's what I like to hear."

Joseph smirked. "How long will you be here?"

"Just a day or two; Alexander needs to get back home to his family," said Douglas.

Joseph grinned at Alexander. "Congratulations on extending the family line." His eyes narrowed. "I guess you and Thomas have that in common." He cast a sideways glance at Rebecca.

Alexander grimaced.

Joseph's stare bore deep into Alexander. "What kind of trouble exactly are you looking for?"

Alexander's breath almost choked in his throat. "I'll be working to curtail the stagecoach robberies." He leaned forward, voice low. "You wouldn't know anything about that… would you?"

Joseph's eyes shot daggers at Alexander. "No!" He pointed to Alexander and then to Douglas. "And you two skulking around here are likely to bring those criminals to my town."

Elizabeth gasped.

Douglas flipped open his pocket watch. "We've got to go."

Joseph started back to his office and then doubled back and

said to the two bank men, "Don't overstay your welcome. Around here, surprises aren't always pleasant."

Alexander glared at Joseph.

Joseph huffed and marched away.

Douglas nudged Alexander's arm and then turned to the women. "We need to get back to work. Good day, ladies."

Rebecca leaned toward Alexander. "His bark is much worse than his bite. Isn't that right, Elizabeth?"

Elizabeth stood stone-faced, fixated on Joseph as he disappeared down the road.

Rebecca smiled. "In any case, I enjoyed chatting with you, Alexander. We're having a party in a couple of days. Perhaps you could bring your family. You too, Douglas."

"I'll ask Martha."

Douglas tugged Alexander's arm. "Let's go."

The two men were halfway to the bank when Rebecca followed Elizabeth's gaze. Elizabeth watched as Joseph reached his horse outside the Sheriff's office.

Rebecca cleared her throat. "There's a quiet strength in Alexander. I can tell he's a man of principle."

"He is," said Elizabeth as Joseph rode away.

Rebecca smiled. "I hope that Martha comes to the party."

"That would be wonderful. I think I last saw her at that lovely get-together at Aunt Helen's back in Sacramento."

"That was the day I fell in love with Thomas."

Elizabeth shook her head. "I'll say. I almost choked when I walked out onto that porch, and you and Thomas were in a passionate embrace. I mean, you just met him."

"The moment I first laid eyes on him, when he rescued us from those stagecoach robbers, I knew he would be my husband."

"Joseph told me that you 'hitching up' with Thomas was the best thing that ever happened to him."

Rebecca smiled. "Why was Joseph so upset?"

Elizabeth sighed. "He's not too fond of Douglas. They had a falling out after arriving from New York."

"Douglas and Joseph came together from New York?"

"Yes. About fourteen years ago. But they've always been civil to each other."

Rebecca glanced at the Sheriff's office. "Joseph doesn't appear to like Alexander either. I had no idea that Joseph knew Alexander."

Elizabeth stared across the pond, her breath catching as she exhaled. "Another mystery," she murmured. "Another secret."

Joseph tore back to the mine in fury. He was sure Douglas and Alexander's antics would drag the stagecoach robbers back to his town. Worse yet, John might wrongly assume Joseph had informed them about the outlaws.

When he arrived, he saw Thomas standing outside the entrance, waving him over.

"Pa, I'm glad that you're back. We've been having a great time."

Joseph jumped down and tied his horse next to the watering trough. The horse slurped up water, trying to quench its thirst from the hard ride.

Thomas's smile disappeared. "Is something wrong?"

"I'm afraid so. Let's sit in the shade. We have to talk."

They walked to the nearby trees and sat on a fallen tree trunk. Thomas's face was filled with concern.

"I was headed here when I spotted Douglas Holt chatting with Elizabeth in the park."

"What were they talking about?"

Joseph glared at Thomas. "Don't know, but Rebecca was alone with Alexander, chatting up a storm. Real cozy, from what I saw."

Thomas's jaw clenched. He looked away, blinking hard. "Alexander has no business speaking to her."

"Did you know he's the Bank Manager back in Sacramento?"

"Yeah."

Joseph exhaled sharply. "Anyhow, I saw quite the spectacle. Rebecca and Alexander were laughing and having a grand old time. I'd swear he was flirting with her."

"What?" The color drained from Thomas's face. "You must have misunderstood."

"Rebecca seemed infatuated with him. When you get home, ask her. I thought you'd want to know."

Thomas's eyes narrowed with suspicion. "Yes. I do." His voice was riddled with doubt.

"If I'd thought this was something that you'd rather not hear, then I—"

"No. Thanks for telling me."

Joseph hadn't expected Thomas to crumble so quickly. A flicker of guilt passed through him. He'd wanted Thomas to see Alexander clearly, not to hurt him. He patted Thomas's back.

"What did you want to show me?" asked Joseph.

Charlie sauntered out of the mine and glared at Joseph.

Joseph's eyes widened. A tremor of hate shuddered within him. His hand jumped to his holstered gun. "What's he doing here?"

"He was helping me. You told me not to come here alone." Thomas turned to Charlie. "We'll talk later."

Charlie nodded, cast a sideways glance at Joseph, and muttered something under his breath—too low to catch, but sharp enough to sting.

Joseph's eyes narrowed as he watched Charlie go. "That scoundrel is always hanging around. Sweet as pie to everyone else, but he gets under my skin. There's something off about that man, always has been."

Thomas shrugged. "He's been a huge help at my place ever since we moved in."

"Just watch him. I don't trust him. He isn't even respectful to his sister."

Thomas furrowed his brow. "Rebecca can take care of herself. She doesn't need him."

Joseph's mouth curled with unease. He had meant Charlie's other sister, Charlotte. "Why don't you head home and be with your wife?"

Thomas softened. "Rebecca means the world to me. It's hard being away from her."

Joseph's voice quieted. "I know what you mean, son. I feel the same about Elizabeth."

"Thanks, Pa," Thomas said, "I'll put that stuff away first."

"I'll take care of it," Joseph replied. "Go on, be with her."

A grin lit up Thomas's face. "I'll see you tomorrow," he called, already springing toward his horse. He mounted and galloped away.

The wind rushed past him as he rode, Rebecca's smile already forming in his mind. The trail blurred beneath his horse's hooves, and for a moment, everything felt right.

But as the trees thinned and the outline of his home came into view, something shifted. His eyes filled with shock.

Frank stood beside his horse next to the trail.

Thomas jumped down and ran to Frank. "Frank! What are you doing here?"

Frank shoved Thomas hard. "We didn't get to finish our talk."

Thomas scoffed and wrinkled his face in disgust. "Our talk?"

"You betrayed me. You told the Law about Randall's plan."

Thomas's breath stuck in his throat. "It was the right thing to do."

"Randall blamed me. But it was your fault."

"I couldn't sit back and do nothing. Rebecca was almost killed. She's my wife now."

Frank winced. "You tricked me into giving you Randall's plans. I thought you were my friend."

Frank's fingers drifted toward his holster, slow and deliberate, eyes locked on Thomas.

Thomas stepped back. "After all this time. I guess you're right. We're not friends. I tried to help you leave that way of life you seem to enjoy. You've betrayed me more times than I can count. I'm through with you." Thomas turned his back and walked to his horse. The click of a cocked gun stopped him cold. He shook his head. "Do what you want!"

A sudden blast shattered the silence.

Thomas hit the ground hard, rolled instinctively, and drew his weapon. Dust kicked up around him as he aimed toward the spot where Frank had stood. Only the echo of the shot remained.

He glanced down. The bullet had struck the dirt inches from his boot.

Breathing hard, Thomas climbed up and looked back once more.

Frank was gone.

When Thomas got home, he found Rebecca sleeping

peacefully in bed, with her favorite blue dress hanging from the door. His heart warmed. Just above where her heart would be, the crimson brooch her sister had given her was pinned in place. He had fastened it to that same spot on her wedding dress, on the wonderful day they were married. His smile grew.

CHAPTER SEVENTEEN
Party Time

The morning of the party arrived, and Rebecca was up before the sun. Light had barely crept through the window when she stepped into the kitchen, eager to start the day. She wanted everything to be perfect. Breakfast was ready, and Thomas hadn't awoken. Odd, she thought. She rushed into the bedroom. Thomas was breathing hard as he slept.

"Wake up, dear."

Thomas stirred, squinting as his eyes adjusted to the bright morning light.

Rebecca peered over the bed like a protective guardian.

He rasped, "You're up early."

"I'm so excited about the party."

A huge smile filled his face.

Rebecca smiled back, feeling a warmth in her chest that spread throughout her body. She reached down and gently touched Thomas's forehead, brushing away a few strands of hair that had fallen over his eyes during the night.

"I made breakfast for you," she said, gesturing towards the kitchen.

"The guests won't be here for hours." Thomas sat up, kissed her cheek, and went to the basin, splashing cold water on his face.

"Yes, I know. I just wanted everything to be perfect... including your breakfast. Come on, let's eat."

He followed Rebecca out of the bedroom and into the kitchen, where a delicious smell wafted through the air.

She placed a warm biscuit on his plate. "There's plenty more."

As they ate together at the small table in the corner of the room, they chatted about the upcoming party and all the preparations that needed to be made. Thomas listened intently as Rebecca outlined her plans for decorating the house, arranging the food, and making sure everyone had a good time.

"Elizabeth told me she invited the whole town. Alexander and

Martha are coming, too."

Thomas's fork paused midair. Joseph's warning about Alexander surged back into his mind. His gaze shot to Rebecca. "Why would you invite Alexander?"

"You two need to figure out how to get along. I like Martha, and those two are a pair. I hope she comes."

Thomas shook his head as he struggled to reclaim his fleeting good feelings.

"I asked that bank owner, Douglas, to come, too."

His chest tightened. He poked at his food. "Joseph saw you talking with Alexander yesterday. He said you two were laughing up a storm."

Rebecca's brows lifted as she kissed his cheek. "I love you and only you. No one in this world could ever take your place."

Thomas shifted in his chair. "I was a soulless scoundrel before I met you. I would disintegrate into darkness without you."

Rebecca smiled. "I'll always be with you. You're a wonderful person. You know that. Right?"

Rebecca's warm eyes melted Thomas's heart. A small smile found its way back to his face.

Thomas hugged her and then kissed her. "I love you."

She wrapped her arms tight around him and didn't let go right away. "Now sit and finish your breakfast while I go feed the chickens."

Rebecca disappeared out the back door.

When he was done, he took his dish to the basin. The caw of a crow outside brought his attention to the window. His lips curled at the sight of Rebecca. He watched the chickens scramble to her as she hummed, her dress stirring the morning breeze. His heart warmed and then tightened with guilt. He hadn't trusted her earlier. Not completely.

By noon, guests had begun arriving with food and gifts. Rebecca greeted each one warmly, her energy infectious. When Elizabeth and Joseph stepped down from their carriage, she rushed to meet them.

"Elizabeth! I'm happy you're here."

Elizabeth rushed to Rebecca. "You certainly have a lot of

energy today."

"Oh yes! I am so excited." Rebecca turned to Joseph. "Thomas is out back with the guests."

Joseph nodded. "I'll go park the carriage. I'll be right back."

Elizabeth and Rebecca went to the backyard and joined the festivities. The guests enjoyed the plentiful food and drink as they conversed with one another. Thomas, Rebecca, and Elizabeth sat together, sipping lemonade at a table near the kitchen window.

Rebecca placed her hand on her stomach. "I think I overate."

Elizabeth's eyes shot to Rebecca's middle, her brows furrowed, "Let's take a walk to the river. It'll settle your stomach."

Rebecca jumped to her feet. "That sounds like a great idea."

Thomas started to stand.

She leaned over and kissed Thomas's cheek. "Just us girls, honey. We'll be back shortly."

She straightened, then paused, her eyes fluttering shut as she steadied herself on Thomas's chair. "Oh my. I got up too quickly."

Elizabeth steadied Rebecca by taking her arm. "You okay?"

"Yes. I'm fine. I've just been sitting too long. Let's go."

Elizabeth turned to Thomas. "Joseph seems a bit distracted today. He told me not to worry, but you know me. Would you talk with him?"

"Sure."

Elizabeth and Rebecca sauntered toward the river, chatting as if they hadn't seen each other for months.

Thomas exhaled sharply as the pair disappeared down the trail. Something in Elizabeth's voice lingered in his mind—Joseph was distracted, and Rebecca... she'd seemed a little off. He stood and searched the yard for his pa, the hum of conversation suddenly distant.

Moments later, several crows watched silently from the trees as Elizabeth and Rebecca stopped near the riverbank below. Rebecca jumped onto a boulder jutting from the water.

Elizabeth gasped. "Be careful. Those rocks are slippery."

Rebecca giggled and then plopped down on the rock, careful to keep the bulk of her dress tucked under her legs. "Thomas was annoyed that I invited Alexander to the party. He thinks that

Alexander was flirting with me yesterday."

Elizabeth chuckled. "Thomas? Jealous? Alexander is respectable and devoted to his wife. You won't see anything inappropriate from him."

"I think Thomas is getting a little anxious about the baby."

"I suppose that makes sense," said Elizabeth as she tried and failed to jump up to the rock where Rebecca was.

Elizabeth gasped. "Oh dear! My dress! It's too muddy here. Let's go back."

"It's too beautiful here to leave. I'll go back in a minute. You go ahead."

Elizabeth looked down at her soiled dress. "Okay. I must get this stain cared for before it ruins this dress."

"I won't be long. I promise."

Elizabeth nodded, picked up her dress, and rushed away.

Rebecca's gaze lingered on Elizabeth, her lips curling into a smile as Elizabeth reached the crest and came face-to-face with Alexander. Elizabeth pointed at Rebecca and continued to the party. Alexander waved down to Rebecca and rushed toward her.

Rebecca called out, "Mr. Johnson!"

When Alexander reached her, he lent out a warm smile. "I just wanted to let you know that Martha sends her regards. She didn't want to leave the baby and asked me to thank you for the invitation."

"I understand," she said. "I'm glad you came. How soon can we expect to see Martha and your family?"

"I'm afraid that won't be for some time."

"Why not?"

"The doctor recommended my wife stay in bed for a little while longer, just to be safe."

Rebecca's eyes moistened. "That sounds serious. Martha told me about her rough time after arriving from New York. She said she almost died." Rebecca's gaze fell to the ground. "I'm sorry, I'm a bit emotional these days."

He reached for her arm to console her. Rebecca's lips trembled as their edge curled upward. He offered her his kerchief. She wiped her face. Her breath choked in her throat when she spotted Thomas and Joseph approaching, both with serious faces.

Joseph stopped, and Thomas rushed up from behind Alexander. "Take your hands off my wife!"

Thomas swung at Alexander, his fist slicing through empty air.

Alexander lunged and drove a punch into Thomas's jaw.

Thomas hit the ground hard, a grunt escaping as dust kicked up around him.

He scrambled to his feet, eyes blazing.

Rebecca's breath caught. She'd never seen Thomas like this— wild, unrecognizable. "Thomas! Stop!"

Thomas looked at Rebecca. Fear filled her eyes. He yelled at Alexander, "Get out of here, you scoundrel!"

Alexander cast a sideways, apologetic glance at Rebecca and then stomped away, shaking off the pain from his bloodied knuckles.

Rebecca rushed after Thomas. "What's wrong with you?" Her mouth fell open at the fire that filled Thomas's eyes. She was dumbfounded.

"Not another word," he snapped, his voice spiked with jealousy. He glared at her and then stormed away and rejoined Joseph. Rebecca, the air stuck in her throat, froze in disbelief at what had just happened. Her breath slowed as Thomas and Joseph disappeared up the trail. A wave of nausea and dizziness hit her. She staggered to the large boulder and sat, her eyes closed.

Light footsteps came from behind her. "Thomas?"

She spun around. John emerged from the trees, silent and deliberate in his approach.

He grinned. "Shouldn't you go back to your party?"

She wiped the tears from her face, and her voice deepened with rage. "Why are you here? You're not welcome."

"Why didn't you invite your sister to this? You keep pushing her away. You're hurting her over and over again."

She narrowed her eyes. "As long as she's with the likes of you, she has no place in my life."

John grabbed her arm, his eyes raging with fire. "I ought to teach you a lesson for treating my Charlotte like that after all she's done for you. She raised you after your ma died. You owe her your life."

"Let go of me, or I'll scream."

John's eyes flared as he tightened his grip.

A sudden burst of adrenaline fueled her rage.

Rebecca slapped him hard across the face. "Leave me alone!"

John recoiled, releasing her arm. His eyes widened, stunned. He rubbed his cheek, then let out a low chuckle.

"You're a feisty one. It runs in your family."

He turned, shaking his head, and strode up the trail toward Charlie.

Rebecca stood frozen, watching them until they disappeared from view.

Her heart racing, she ambled to the rock where she'd been sitting, tears welling as she sought to collect her composure. Once she talked to Thomas, everything would be okay. She loved Thomas with all of her being and found herself thinking about her sister, Charlotte. She should have invited her to the wedding, she thought.

She stepped on the rocks that jutted from the water to a large boulder a few feet away. The water gurgled beside her as she sat, careful not to wet her beautiful blue dress. She rubbed her fingers over the brooch that her sister had given her. "It was Ma's," Charlotte had told her.

Rebecca wore it proudly at the wedding. Thomas had helped her fasten it. Her eyes shut tight, she cried louder. The water rushed around her, the smaller birds chirped, and the murmurs of the party continued. A peaceful calm cradled her as she let out a torrent of tears. Her tears crept down her cheeks and fell into the river's serenity. Amidst her cries, she could hardly hear the beautiful sounds of the birds singing their hearts out, the leaves rustling, and the muted sounds of the celebration back at the house. An old crow watched silently from the tree that shaded her, tilting its head, puzzled by the grief etched across her face.

She didn't hear the approaching footsteps as they got louder and louder. Her face was nestled safely in her hands as she cried, oblivious to the world. She didn't even hear the warning cry of the crow, watching her and squawking sharply. Someone stopped behind her and held a rock high above and smashed it into the back of her head.

Suddenly, a crushing pain in her head interrupted her stillness. For an instant, she heard everything and then nothing. Her eyes reflexively opened wide as she fell face-first into the water. Her heart raced before she was able to take another breath. The water was cold on her face as her awareness left her. A minute or two later, her heart slowed and then stopped, as did the heart of the little one growing inside her.

The footsteps of someone running away, and the crow's flapping wings as it gave chase, faded into nothingness.

Face down in the water, her lifeless body bobbed gently as blood mingled with the river's calm.

Her cries had been silenced forever.

CHAPTER EIGHTEEN

Pretty Blue Dress

Elizabeth washed the mud from her dress at the cabin's kitchen sink when Thomas rushed in, his breathing forced.

She gasped. "You look terrible. What—"

Thomas, his eyes filled with fire, asked, "Why did Rebecca invite Alexander to the party? He was at the river, being inappropriate with her."

Elizabeth's head cocked back, her face etched with confusion. "What? That doesn't sound like him."

He stomped away out the door.

Elizabeth's breath caught in her throat. She turned to follow Thomas, but a movement outside the window stopped her cold. Douglas and Alexander were rushing toward Joseph. "That can't be good."

She leaned forward to get a better view. Not far from Joseph, Charlie shoved John hard. She shook her head. "I wonder what John did to deserve that," she muttered.

Just beyond them, a sullen-faced Thomas disappeared into the barn.

She raced out the door.

Outside, Douglas and Alexander approached Joseph.

Joseph's breathing slowed. "It's best you two leave."

Alexander glared and rubbed at his injured hand.

Joseph's brow narrowed at Alexander. He choked out, "You keep your distance from my son."

Douglas stepped between Joseph and Alexander. "Alexander, let's go."

Alexander locked eyes with Joseph. "I know you and Thomas are working with those robbers?"

Joseph's face exploded with fury. "You're crazy." His gaze shot to Alexander's knuckles, his eyes locking with him. "You flirt with

Rebecca, strike my son, and accuse me of working with criminals?" Joseph, his fists clenched tight, closed in on Alexander. "You stay away from my family!"

Douglas yanked Alexander's arm. "Let's go."

Joseph's breathing grew forced as he chased after them.

Douglas and Alexander jumped onto their wagon.

Joseph yelled, "You set foot in my town again, and you'll leave in a pine box!"

He tripped and fell as the wagon raced away. He got to his feet and brushed the dirt from his clothes. "Damn it!"

John, his eyes filled with suspicion, rushed to Joseph. "We need to talk."

Thomas was alone inside the barn, staring at his open pocket watch. A picture of Rebecca stared frozen back at him, moistening his eyes. The sounds of the guests and Joseph's loud outburst were muffled as they wafted toward him.

"Rebecca, what was I thinking? I know you love me. I love you, too."

His horse in the stall behind him whinnied and then looked expectantly at him.

He caught the horse's gaze, and a hint of a smile appeared on Thomas's lips. He saddled it quickly and raced out the barn door, headed to the river. Overhead, an old crow flapped its wings, slicing through the air—drawn to the familiar face below, silent and relentless.

When he reached the river's edge, Thomas yelled, "Rebecca." Only the gentle rustle of the wind through the trees answered him. The tree's branches hung high above him. He secured his horse, walked to where Alexander had knocked him down, and called out again, "Rebecca!"

A flicker of crimson light from the water distracted him, where bits of broken limbs and twigs floated. Something shiny beckoned, just a glint, but enough to draw him. His breath caught in his throat as he bolted toward the shimmer.

A dainty hand wearing a ring with a red stone protruded from the surface. The sun caught the gem's facet, sending a flash of light like a beacon calling to him.

"Rebecca!" he yelled.

He jumped into the water, grabbed her arm, and gently freed her lifeless body from the web of splintered wood and debris.

Her frilly blue dress clung to the ground as bits of it tore away when he dragged her cold body to the riverbank.

"My Rebecca!" He howled in pain as he carefully removed the twigs and leaves from her hair.

He stared into her vacant eyes. They met his, unmoving and hollow.

He was numb and surrounded by deafening silence. He screamed, "REBECCA!"

Back at the party, Charlie walked up next to John.

Joseph narrowed his eyes at John. "Why are you still here? You're supposed to be gone."

John grunted. "I came to have a chat with Charlie. I'm glad I did."

Joseph glared at Charlie.

Charlie's nose twitched as his upper lip tightened.

John glanced at the dust cloud left by Alexander's and Douglas's carriage. "I heard you were chatting with those two yesterday. And I saw you having words with them today. Did you tell them about us? Those two are working with the Law to put us away. And I know for damn sure that Alexander is responsible for killing some of my men."

"How many times do I have to tell you that I ain't gonna do that! I told them to keep away."

John narrowed his eyes. "I like you, Joseph, but don't cross us. Some of your brother's men aren't too happy with what you and your son did to Randall. If you betray us, there ain't no telling what—"

Charlie noticed Elizabeth running toward them from the house. He nudged John's arm. "I gotta go. I'm gonna go get a drink."

Elizabeth patted Charlie's arm as they crossed paths. He nodded politely and rushed away.

She ignored John and took Joseph's hand. "Joseph, where did Thomas go?"

John glared at her.

Joseph's eyes darted from John to her and then to the barn. He shifted uncomfortably. "Probably down to the river. He and Rebecca had a terrible fight, thanks to Alexander."

"I saw you chasing after Douglas's coach. Why?"

"Alexander struck Thomas."

Elizabeth gasped.

John pointed at the trail, grinning. "There's Thomas."

Thomas rode toward them, stiff-backed, reins loose in his hands. Something blue was draped in front of him.

Silence filled the air.

Elizabeth squinted as Thomas came closer, dread prickling her spine. Then she saw it. A scream tore from her throat. "Rebecca! No!"

It was Rebecca in her blue dress, lying face down, lifeless.

Elizabeth broke into a sprint, her legs numbed by panic, her voice still echoing through the trees.

CHAPTER NINETEEN

A Broken Man

Thomas sat at his kitchen table, dressed in a suit he hadn't worn since his wedding. He buried his face in his hands and muttered, "Today, my Rebecca will disappear into nothingness, into the earth."

He sniffed, wiped away his tears, and checked his watch. "Shoot!" Thomas jumped up, ran to his horse, and headed to the river, where he had discovered Rebecca's body.

He secured his horse near the spot where Alexander had knocked him down. His nose wrinkled with disgust. His gaze floated down to the water. Just a few feet away, it flowed smoothly over the rocks. The birds above chirped as if they had no cares in the world.

The sight of Rebecca's lifeless eyes, colored with terror, was indelibly etched into his mind.

A squirrel tiptoed near him and picked up a small nut. The creature inspected it and then returned to the safety of the oak tree, whose branches extended in all directions. One thick branch extended far over the water. Underneath it stood a large boulder jutting out like an island. Rebecca used to scramble up on that branch, crawl across, jump down to that boulder, and sit.

She had told him that it was her private island. From there, she could see their house and up and down the river.

He climbed up on the branch and went to Rebecca's little island. Above, the birds chirped noisily as they flew from branch to branch. Perhaps they were expecting Rebecca, not him.

He glanced back at the house; the barn partially obscured it, but not the back porch.

A crow squawked overhead, sharp and sudden. Leaves rustled in the breeze. Stillness settled over him as Rebecca's words returned, soft and steady.

"You are my rock," she had said.

He jumped up to the branch and started back to his horse. He gasped when he passed the spot where he had found her body. It was next to a large boulder. Nature had washed away Rebecca's blood that had stained it the day she died. He narrowed his eyes and stepped closer.

A crow was perched precariously on a floating branch, pecking at something in the water. The beady-eyed crow looked up at him. The crow's eyes weren't the usual black. In the dappled sunlight, they shimmered a deep chestnut brown—almost human, almost hers. It flew up into the tree and squawked at him.

He huffed. "Damn crow, what were you after?"

Thomas hopped over the muddy riverbank and landed on a large boulder slick with moss. He knelt, squinting at the spot where the crow had been. Sunlight danced across the rippling water. Then his eyes caught a glint of metal beneath the floating twigs.

As the ripples stilled, his breath stuck in his throat, and his eyes grew wide with horror. He reached for it.

Rebecca's brooch. Her mother's. The one he'd help pin to her dress on their wedding day.

He plucked it from its watery grave.

A galloping horse broke his despair. It was Joseph.

He pocketed the brooch as his father rode up.

"Thomas, how are you doing?"

"I'm okay," he said curtly.

"Elizabeth asked me to come by and bring you to the house. She was worried you might miss the service," said Joseph.

Thomas looked suspiciously at Joseph. "How'd you know I was here?"

"I could see you from your back porch."

Thomas glanced toward the house and then back at Joseph.

Joseph got down from his horse and secured it next to Thomas's. "You'll get through this. We'll help you. Family helps family. You know that."

"Thanks for taking care of all the arrangements."

"Son, Elizabeth did everything. We both would do anything for you."

Joseph reached into the saddlebag and pulled out an apple. As he stepped forward, Thomas gestured to the ground.

"Careful. It's slick with mud."

Joseph nodded, sliced the apple cleanly, and offered a half to each horse.

Thomas smiled. "I used to do that same thing with my friend —"

He froze. His eyes flicked to Joseph. "I mean, I always used to cut them into pieces for them."

Joseph's brow lifted. "It shows you care about them."

Thomas glanced at the river and then back at Joseph. "I can't do this. I can't handle the pain. How did you deal with losing Ma? It couldn't have been easy for you."

"A while back, I used whiskey as a medicine to get me through the day. Times like these make me want to go back to drinking. It helps me forget that kind of pain."

Thomas shot Joseph a sideways look. "Did you start on that whiskey again?"

Joseph shook his head. "I've been tempted."

Thomas leaned in. "I wouldn't want to forget Rebecca." He looked expectantly at his Pa.

Joseph cleared his throat. "I haven't touched a drop."

"You should be able to handle it now, don't you think?"

Joseph's gaze fell to the ground. "Maybe."

Thomas looked back at the house and then at Joseph. "I like it here. But..."

Joseph's eyes shot up to Thomas. "What's not to like?"

"I don't know how I can stay here without Rebecca. She's the one who wanted to move here."

Joseph's shoulders dropped, a gasp escaping his lips. "You love shooting, riding, and exploring that mine. I know you love this place."

Thomas perked up.

"That's true," said Thomas. "But when I lived in New York, I never felt this bad. Maybe going back wouldn't be the worst thing."

"Don't do anything yet. Give yourself some time," Joseph said, his voice cracking, his eyes moistening. "I need you here with me. I trust you."

Joseph looked away.

Thomas looked over his shoulder at the water. "I promised Rebecca I would keep her safe. I failed her."

Joseph took a breath. "You made her happy."

"Every time I have something special, someone steals it away." He gritted his teeth. Crimson filled his face. "I'm never going to let that happen again. I'm going to find Rebecca's killer and make him pay!"

Joseph's brows narrowed. "You sure it wasn't just... an accident?"

Thomas locked eyes with Joseph and shook his head. "I'll put a bullet in the man who took her from me."

Joseph's hand lingered on Thomas's shoulder, heavy with fear. He gulped and then gave it a gentle pat. "How about we head to the service?"

Thomas nodded, jaw tight. He glanced back at the water and left with Joseph for the service.

They rode side by side without saying a word.

When they arrived at the gravesite, they sat on either side of Elizabeth.

Thomas looked around. Most of the faces were strangers to him. His eyes drifted toward the minister, who was standing at the head of Rebecca's grave.

The minister said, "I met Rebecca years ago in Sacramento, shortly after I moved there. She was a beautiful spirit. Everyone loved her."

The minister's words faded away as thoughts of Rebecca gently pressed in on him.

He whispered, "I miss you, my darling."

He snapped out of his reminiscences when he felt a tap on his arm.

Elizabeth's eyes were locked onto his. "Everything is going to be okay."

A spark of warmth touched his heart. "I hope so."

Thomas's unease distracted him from the pain of losing his wife. The rest of the service blurred into the background. He shook his head as he thought of the cross words he'd spoken to Rebecca. Those were the last she'd heard him say.

A tap on his hand drew him back to the service.

"Thomas?" said Elizabeth.

He jumped, startled, and turned to her.

She said, "Why don't you come over to the house? We have plenty of food, and the neighbors are coming to wish you well."

He wrinkled his face. "I'd like to stay here a while longer."

She smiled softly and stood. "I understand. I'll come by tomorrow."

"Sure," he said.

Elizabeth left with Joseph.

He sat alone for a long time, staring at his wife's grave. Two people had shovels tamping the ground where an opening had been. He wondered how Rebecca could breathe under all that dirt.

After the two men left, Thomas examined the sizable, ornate tombstone. It had an inscription: "Here lies Mrs. Rebecca Pruitt, beloved wife of Thomas James Pruitt; She and her unborn child died."

Thomas fell to his knees, the weight of his grief showing in his eyes.

Joseph returned and patted Thomas's shoulder. "Let's go for a ride. It'll help clear your head."

Thomas nodded. He glanced hesitantly at the headstone and then followed Joseph.

They rode the winding trails that criss-crossed Joseph's land, saying little to each other. After an hour, they ended up at Thomas's cabin. Joseph went to the porch and sat in the chair opposite the swinging bench.

"I'll be right back," said Thomas as he disappeared into the house. He grabbed the whiskey bottle from the kitchen cabinet near the back door. He thought about Rebecca and stepped outside. He squinted to see through the trees to the river. He saw the spot where he'd been sitting earlier.

"Thomas?" asked Joseph, holding the back door open.

Thomas jumped. "Grab a couple of glasses."

Soon after the pair were on the porch, Thomas sat across from Joseph and poured whiskey from the jug into the two glasses. Thomas handed one to Joseph and took the other.

Thomas raised his glass. "To you, Pa."

Joseph reached for the glass, his hand slow, uncertain. "To

you."

He clinked it gently against Thomas's, then held the whiskey near his lips, hesitating.

Thomas said, "I'm sorry, Pa. I don't know what I was thinking, offering you this whiskey."

Joseph sniffed it like a fine wine, then took a sip.

"Son, this is the best medicine for dealing with stuff when life gets too complicated."

Thomas shifted in his seat. A drunken Frank had told him that before. "Complicated?" Thomas leaned forward. "Why is life complicated for you? Is it because of Randall? He ain't gonna mess with you anymore."

Joseph gave Thomas a sidelong glance. "I wouldn't be so sure about that."

"When I put a bullet through his shooting hand that day, I told him I wouldn't hesitate to kill him if he didn't keep his distance from you, me, and everyone I loved."

"I'm proud of you, son, for standing up to him. That took a lot of courage."

Thomas smiled. "Thanks, Pa."

Joseph's gaze fell to the ground.

"Did Elizabeth tell you it was my fault she fell?"

The smile faded from Thomas's face. "How was it your fault? She slipped. Didn't she?"

Joseph's jaw tightened. "We were arguing. She swung at me. I dodged. She lost her balance and hit the ground hard." He slammed his fist on the armrest. "I would never hurt her, but I did that day." His voice cracked. "I love her."

Thomas's heart skipped a beat. "She was in bad shape when the doctor examined her. And you were tore up when the doctor left."

Joseph shot an embarrassed glance at Thomas. "I'm glad she recovered, but it could have been so much worse. I don't know what I would have done if…"

Thomas shifted in his seat. "Sounds like an accident?"

Joseph cleared his throat and took a sip. "It was still my fault."

Thomas's face wrinkled, his gaze lingering on his father.

Joseph's face relaxed, his lips curled up slightly, and his gaze fixed on the whiskey. He took another sip. "I've missed how smooth the whiskey feels in my mouth." He paused and then smiled at Thomas. "Maybe it's time we become partners in my mining operation."

"Partners?"

"Yes! Pruitt and Son. I like the sound of that! You need something to distract you from your pain." Joseph drank the rest of his whiskey and poured himself and Thomas more, nearly spilling some.

Thomas stared at Joseph. "I don't want to forget Rebecca."

Joseph's face tightened. "No. Of course not. One day, you'll find comfort in the joy she gave you, just as I do when I think of your mother."

Thomas smiled. "In a lot of ways, she reminded me of Ma."

Joseph nodded. "You still interested in the mine?"

"Sure."

"It's got a lot more gold left in it. There's plenty for us to live a comfortable life. Someday, it'll be all yours."

Joseph took a drink and then stared at Thomas for several seconds.

Thomas moved uncomfortably. "What?"

"I'll let you in on a secret. There is another mine. It's smaller, and its entrance is hidden next to the barn, right behind that old table. Elizabeth doesn't know anything about that one. No one does."

Thomas leaned in. "Is there more gold there?"

Joseph grinned. "I use it for storage."

"Storage?"

"Remember when I asked you to be my deputy? I told you I wanted someone I could trust."

Thomas nodded. "I knew it! You rob stagecoaches. Rebecca didn't believe me."

Joseph recoiled, his voice sharp. "No! I don't rob stagecoaches!"

Thomas sat, confused.

"Randall brought dozens of men here. They were in a remote part of the property."

"They're here? Where?" asked Thomas, his face riddled with

concern.

"They're gone. I got them to move on. Randall and the other men were gone before you moved in."

"They were the robbers the Law thought you were harboring. Weren't they?"

Joseph shifted in his seat. "Yup. I didn't have much of a choice. There were too many of them. And they threatened to kill Elizabeth if I took action against them."

Thomas shook his head. "It was Randall who threatened her. Wasn't it?" Thomas grimaced. "I'm sure Elizabeth can take care of herself."

Joseph glanced away. "It was his fault your ma got shot. I learned my lesson. Besides, no wife of mine will live in fear of getting shot and having to always look over her shoulder, waiting for someone to shoot her dead."

"They're still robbing stagecoaches. Randall was with those robbers who attacked Martha and Alexander's place. I was there too when the same outlaws ambushed Martha's coach outside town, and then another group had Alexander's coach pinned down over by Auburn. Martha and I took care of them, too."

Joseph's ears perked up. "Sounds like you spent a lot of time with Martha. Why is that?"

Thomas's gaze fell to the ground. "I don't want to talk about her."

"Sorry. It's not my business."

"You should be working with the Law instead of those outlaws. You can't trust Randall or the rest of those men with him."

"He's not the only thing that concerns me." Joseph grimaced and huffed. He stared for several seconds at Thomas and then looked away. "Before leaving, those robbers left some boxes of gold next to my barn. They said it was a gift."

"What?!" Thomas gasped and stood abruptly, knocking his glass over. "What'd you do with it?"

Joseph grabbed at the glass and caught it before it fell to the floor. "I put it in that secret mine I told you about."

Thomas's upper lip tightened. "Why didn't you turn it in?"

"How could I? It would look like I was involved in the

robberies."

"But you are involved. The robbers were hiding on your property while they committed robberies. And now you're keeping their gold for them. You need to surrender those lockboxes."

Joseph's brow furrowed. "They would kill Elizabeth if they found out I handed it over to the Law."

Thomas's gaze darted away and then landed back on Joseph. "You're right. I understand now." He exhaled sharply and stood. "Let's go take a look at that gold." His voice was eager, but his eyes betrayed a hint of unease.

Joseph shook his head at Thomas. "Another time."

Thomas looked disappointed and sat. "Is that why you don't care for Douglas?"

"That man, and Alexander too, are out for blood. They rounded up a group of vigilantes, acting as if they were the Law. Those two are liable to get Elizabeth killed if those robbers think I'm working with the Law." Joseph's face grew dark with anger as he continued, "It's better for everyone if those two stay out of my town."

Thomas nodded, slow at first, as it all started to make sense: the outlaws, the lockboxes, Randall, and now Alexander.

Joseph huffed. "I got rid of those outlaws from my land. Now I need to figure out how to get rid of those lockboxes."

Thomas grimaced. "And, Alexander comes here, stirs things up, and sticks his nose where it shouldn't be."

Joseph's lips curled up at the edges. "Exactly!"

Thomas grimaced. "Alexander makes my skin crawl. I don't trust him at all. He said he'd kill me if I ever got near Martha. And the way he said it... It wasn't just talk. He meant it."

Joseph's breath caught in his throat. "He threatened to kill you? That's rich. You're the reason he and his wife survived those stagecoach robberies. That ungrateful snake is just like his pa."

Thomas's eyes darted to Joseph.

"If he intended to hurt you, killing someone you loved... yeah, that'd be the way."

Thomas leaned back, his voice low. "You think he had something to do with Rebecca's death?"

Joseph's upper lip wrinkled against his nose. "I don't trust him." He stood, eyes drifting to the trees. A crow let out a sharp cry above. "But it sure sounds like he wanted to hurt you."

Thomas's right cheek tightened. "She was crying the last time I saw them together."

Joseph sighed. "I shouldn't have said any of this." He patted Thomas's arm. "I'm sorry."

Thomas shrugged.

"Don't go tellin' Elizabeth I had a drink." He glanced back at the house. "Or about the mine. That's a mess we don't need stirred up."

"I won't."

Joseph got on his horse. "You okay?"

"Yup." Thomas's gaze hardened. "If Alexander had something to do with Rebecca's death, I'll make damn sure he pays."

Joseph's brows narrowed, his jaw slackened. "Don't do anything foolish."

Thomas exhaled in a huff. "It won't be foolish."

Joseph lent a hint of a smile—one that didn't reach his eyes—and then rode away.

Alone, Thomas glared at the crow screeching above. He hurled his glass at it. The crow vanished into the sky. The wind picked up, whispering through the trees like a warning.

At Joseph and Elizabeth's house, Elizabeth moved the stew to the edge of the stove to keep it warm. At the table, she'd set plates for herself and Joseph and thought about adding one for Thomas, but didn't. He wanted to be alone.

She took a cake from the cupboard and left for the front porch. She settled comfortably on the bench, the same one where she and Rebecca would often talk until the lanterns burned low, waiting for Joseph and Thomas to return.

Rebecca sat across from her the day before her death, wearing her pretty blue dress. She smiled as a pleasant memory surfaced.

"Won't it be lovely when I have my baby?" Rebecca asked.

"I can hardly wait."

Elizabeth wiped a tear from her cheek as the memory of Rebecca's voice dissolved into the faint whispers of time.

It was the same dress. Hours of cleaning and careful mending, and still the white lace at Rebecca's neckline held a faint, unshakable stain. Some marks, she thought, could never be entirely washed away. Thomas had insisted that she be buried in her favorite dress.

Elizabeth took a bite of her cake, the sweetness dulled by the ache in her chest. Her gaze slid to the road—still empty—and then to the door, thinking of the chicken, vegetables, and Joseph's favorite biscuits keeping warm on the stove.

Her face brightened as she imagined what life would be like for her and Joseph with a beautiful baby of their own. Rebecca had often told her that a child would inevitably come to them.

Elizabeth took a sip of tea.

"Joseph," she muttered. "Why are you worried about me?"

She noticed Joseph's attitude shift long before Thomas showed up. Joseph used to be relaxed and happy. Now, he was suddenly concerned for her safety.

She didn't need or want such a crutch. She preferred to meet her challenges head-on. She wished Rebecca were here to help her through her pain.

Her thoughts spilled out as she said, "Rebecca. I miss you so much." Elizabeth gazed up at the sky. The clouds floated by without a care.

"Why are you always cheerful?" Elizabeth once asked Rebecca.

"I always reach for the happiest thought I can think of," she had answered.

Elizabeth smiled.

A crow flew across and landed on the porch rail.

"Hello, my friend."

It squawked loudly.

Elizabeth took a small piece of cake and tossed it toward the bird. It cawed, snapped it up, and fixed her with its dark, unblinking eyes. She tossed another. This time, the bird didn't move. It just stared.

"I'm sorry I haven't fed you lately. I haven't felt much like relaxing at the river."

Her eyes flicked to the road, where a plume of dust curled behind Joseph's horse. The crow squawked, snatched the sugared delight, and winged past the wagon into the gray sky that had hung above her all afternoon.

She stepped quickly to the edge of the porch.

"Whoa!" Joseph called out, reining in.

He dismounted with a grin. He sniffed at the air. "My mouth is watering. What's for dinner?"

"It's your favorite," Elizabeth said. "Come in."

He climbed the steps and kissed her gently.

The warmth of his kiss faltered as she caught the scent of whiskey on his breath. Her welcome thinned, and her gaze drifted past him, haunted by memories of the reckless, nearly ruined, and dangerous man he'd been back then.

Joseph said, "Thomas says you're gonna stop by his place tomorrow... give him a hand with cleaning."

"Yup. I can only imagine the state of that cabin."

"Just make sure you take your gun." Joseph stepped inside.

Her right cheek clenched as she drew a shallow breath. She tossed the last piece of cake onto the bench and went inside.

A crow hesitated as its gaze lingered on the door. It flew down, looked at the door once more, and then snatched the cake away.

CHAPTER TWENTY

Help Is on the Way

A chill clung to the morning air as Elizabeth's carriage drew near Thomas's house. The cool breeze brushing her face reminded her of the last breakfast she'd shared with Rebecca — the two of them leaning in over their plates, laughing until tears warmed their cheeks.

She pulled back on the reins, and her coach came to a stop in front of Thomas's house.

Thomas sat on the porch and started toward her.

She gasped at his appearance. "Thomas! How are you doing?" His eyes were swollen, and his cheeks and nose were raw.

"I'm… I'm okay, considering." He offered his hand as she stepped down.

"You look like you've been wrestling with ghosts all night."

He shrugged. He secured the horse. He rushed up to the porch and held the door open. "Welcome."

Elizabeth stepped inside, her gaze dropping to the floor. Her breath stuck in her throat. A thick trail of muddy footsteps outlined the path to the kitchen. "It looks like a herd of cattle stampeded through here."

"I was cleaning out the chicken coop. Rebecca asked me to do that two weeks ago. I figured I might as well do that now."

A faint smile cracked her lips. She followed Thomas into the kitchen and glanced out the window at the coop. "Those chickens are living in luxury now."

Thomas nodded and let out a long breath. "I was about to get cleaned up."

"I hope you're hungry. I've got a picnic basket in the carriage. I'll get lunch ready after I straighten up this place."

"Sure. I'll go get it."

He was gone in a flash and returned with the food. He put it on the table and left to wash up.

"Thank you." Elizabeth stood in the front room, shaking her

head. Memories of Rebecca came flooding back to her. She thought about Rebecca's unborn child. It would have brought her and Thomas so much joy.

She wanted to be strong for him. She found the broom hiding in the corner and cried quietly while she swept the dirt (and her tears) away. The dried mud challenged the broom, but soon it crumbled away, leaving only the varnished, wooden floor behind. She froze when she came to the rocking chair next to the fireplace.

There, resting over its arm, was Rebecca's shawl. She rubbed her hand across the smooth folds and then picked it up. "I shouldn't have left you alone that day." She carefully folded it and returned it to the armrest. She surveyed the room and smiled. She let out a relaxed exhale and put the broom away.

She lit the stove, took the chicken and vegetables from the picnic basket, and poured them into a pot.

She went outside and chipped some ice from the large block still in the box sitting in the rear of the carriage. "Perfect for some refreshing, cold lemonade," she muttered.

As she was setting the table, she found Rebecca's brooch lying where Thomas usually sat. When she picked it up, the clasp pin pricked her finger.

"Ouch," she said as she dropped it. She sucked on her finger and then held it again, carefully examining it. Bits of long brown hair were tangled between the stones. Tears filled her eyes. Heavy footsteps from the porch stairs snapped her back. She hurriedly put the brooch down as Thomas walked in.

His gaze shot to the broach, then to her. She held his stare long enough to share the pain. Then he looked away and cleared his throat.

He let out a hard breath and then scanned the room. "What have you done here? This place is spotless."

Elizabeth smiled. She patted Thomas on the shoulder. "Let's eat." She went to the kitchen and returned with the pot of food. She looked where she'd left the brooch, and it was gone. She caught Thomas's gaze, and her brows bounced up. "You look refreshed." She served him a generous portion.

A relaxed smile filled his face. "This smells delicious."

As she poured Thomas a glass of lemonade, little chunks of ice fell out.

Thomas cocked his head back. "Ice?"

"Yes. There's a block in the back of the carriage," said Elizabeth as she served herself. "Perhaps after lunch, would you mind bringing it in?"

"I'll get it now before it melts," he said. He rushed out, and when he returned, he put the ice in the bottom of the icebox and went back to his seat.

"Thank the Lord for this food," said Elizabeth.

Thomas grimaced. "Where was He when Rebecca..."

A raspy gasp escaped Elizabeth's lips.

He exhaled sharply. "Rebecca used to make me feel like everything was going to be okay."

"Everything is going to work itself out."

Thomas shook his head. "She shouldn't be gone."

"It was a terrible accident."

"It wasn't an accident!"

"But Thomas, the rocks are slippery there."

"I know who killed her."

Elizabeth looked crooked at him, her face contorted in confusion. "What?"

"The back of her head was crushed."

"Maybe she hit her head on a rock as she fell."

"No!"

Elizabeth's jaw slackened. "No one would want to hurt her."

"I know of one person."

Elizabeth's face tightened.

Thomas said, his voice raised, "Alexander Johnson! He wanted to hurt me. And he did."

Elizabeth scoffed. "No! That's not possible. That man would never do any such thing."

"You weren't there."

"If she was murdered—"

Thomas interrupted. "Before she died, he was acting familiar with her. Had I not walked up to them at the river, who knows what else he might have done to her?"

Elizabeth gasped.

Thomas's eyes grew red and swollen. "I miss her."

Elizabeth reached for his hand and squeezed it. "I'm here for you. I miss Rebecca, too."

"She shouldn't be gone."

Her shoulders dropped as she leaned forward. "Thomas, sometimes accidents happen."

"I just told you that it wasn't an accident!"

Elizabeth let out a small breath. "The doctor thinks she might have fallen from the overhead branch and struck the rock below. The impact knocked her unconscious, and she landed face down in the water."

She paused. "That's what the doctor thinks, anyway."

"The doctor wasn't there when I picked her up. I saw her wound on the back of her head. It didn't happen from a fall."

"I would give anything for her to be here right now. Everybody loved Rebecca. Who would even think of doing such a heinous thing? It had to have been an accident!"

Thomas's cheeks tightened. "I'm telling you, it wasn't an accident!"

Elizabeth gasped. She blinked repeatedly. Her gaze lingered on Thomas for an instant longer and then went back to eating.

Neither of them said much for the rest of lunch. When it was over, Thomas glanced sheepishly at Elizabeth. "Thank you for lunch. It was delicious." He took his plate to the basin.

She smiled. "I'll take care of the dishes. Perhaps you could cool off outside."

Thomas nodded and left for the porch.

She cried softly as she washed the plates.

Thomas came back inside and stood beside Elizabeth. "It WAS Alexander Johnson," he said defiantly. Thomas's eyes were glazed over with rage. "He wanted to hurt me by taking her away from me. There's no one else who hates me that much."

"What about your uncle? Or that odd man, John? I saw him having words with Charlie at the party."

"Randall is more likely to want to kill Pa than Rebecca." He hesitated. "Alexander is the only person who threatened to kill me."

A plate slipped from her hands and crashed to the floor. Shards flew in all directions.

She burst into tears as she knelt to pick up the pieces.

"It slipped out of my hand."

He backed away and shook his head. "I'm sorry." He rushed out the front door.

"Thomas!" she yelled. She froze in thought, thinking about what to do. Perhaps Thomas was right about how Rebecca died. Maybe it wasn't an accident. But for sure, Alexander couldn't have had anything to do with her death. Thomas needs time to grieve. Indeed, Alexander should keep his distance. There's no telling what Thomas would do if he confronted Alexander now.

A moment of clarity surprised her. On the way home, I'll send Alexander a telegram with the sad news of Rebecca's passing and ask him to stay away. No, better to send it to Douglas, who could then warn Alexander.

She put the last of the dishes away and took her basket to the porch, where Thomas sat staring toward the river.

"Are you okay?" asked Elizabeth.

"You don't have to worry about me. I'll keep myself busy."

Elizabeth hugged Thomas and climbed up into the carriage with her basket. She turned back and smiled.

"Thomas, I'll always look out for you. Please don't let your grief cloud your judgment."

Thomas forced a smile. "Tell Pa that I'm okay."

She nodded and shook the reins. The horses obliged and took off.

Elizabeth glanced over her shoulder as she reached the road to the city. Thomas was still watching her from his porch.

Instead of turning right to her home, she turned left toward town.

Moments later, she pulled up in front of the Telegraph office. She rushed in and stood at the counter across from the clerk.

"I'd like to send a telegram to Douglas Holt in Sacramento."

He smiled and readied his pencil as he looked up at her.

She leaned in toward him as if she were telling him a secret. "It should say: My husband is in the clear; Rebecca died; Thomas blames Alexander."

"I'll return in a minute. I understand, ma'am. I'll handle this with discretion."

The clerk returned to his desk and sat at the telegraph,

clicking and clacking its arm with practiced ease. He waited a few seconds, and the machine whirred back to life—message received.

The door opened abruptly. In walked Thomas.

"I saw your cart outside. I thought you were headed home. What are you doing here?"

"I was letting Douglas know about the tragic news."

"It's none of his damn business!"

"He'll tell my Aunt Helen. She needs to know."

Elizabeth turned to the clerk and said, "Thank you."

When she turned back to Thomas, his eyes were narrowed and fixed on the clerk.

She led Thomas out the door.

CHAPTER TWENTY-ONE

Back in Sacramento

Alexander sat at his desk in the Sacramento bank, working on a ledger. He twiddled a pencil as he perused the page. It was difficult to focus after the ordeal he endured at the hands of Thomas and Joseph back in Auburn the previous day.

Douglas burst into his office, a piece of paper clutched in his hand. His usual composure was ruffled. "Alexander, Elizabeth sent a telegram. Thomas's wife is dead."

Alexander's hand froze on the pencil. The color drained from his face as the words sank in. "Rebecca is dead? But... we were just there. At her party."

"Yes. And the telegram also stated that Thomas thinks you killed her. Why in the world would he think that?" Douglas's voice was sharp with bewilderment and a hint of accusation.

Alexander pushed back from his desk, and his chair screeched against the floor. "That man is a lunatic! I was saying goodbye to Rebecca at the party. I told her Martha couldn't attend because she was still recuperating after having the baby. She suddenly looked frantic. When I apologized for upsetting her and turned to leave, he swung at me. Of course, I hit him back." A vein throbbed in his temple as he recalled the humiliation.

Douglas's expression tightened. "Well, perhaps you should make it a point to avoid Thomas when you travel to that town. There's no telling what a man in his state might do."

"He isn't much of a threat," Alexander retorted. He didn't like the idea of being seen as intimidated. The memory of Thomas's wild eyes lingered.

Douglas said, a half-smile playing on his lips, "Your wife is still recuperating. Why don't you go home and take a few days off?"

Alexander nodded. He collected his papers from the desk, his movements stiff, and stacked them in the top right-hand drawer. The accusation in the telegram stung, making Thomas's threats appear less like bluster and more like a sign of dangerous instability.

Douglas watched him, his half-smile fading. "Sheriff Pruitt was full of rage when he ran us off. And now that you're leaving, I need to say this: I think he's mixed up with those stagecoach robbers, even though Elizabeth... bless her heart... doesn't think so."

"It doesn't make sense," Alexander countered. "Sheriff Pruitt is a hero to that town, and he has so much wealth with that damn gold mine of his. Why would he care about helping robbers?"

"I've never trusted Joseph Pruitt. Not since our early days here." Douglas's eyes hardened, a flicker of an old, deep resentment visible. "Greed drives people to do many things."

Alexander picked up his satchel, slung it over his shoulder, and looked dead on at Douglas, the weight of the day's news pressing on him. "Even to kill?" he asked, the question lingering in the air.

Douglas held his gaze for a long moment, then nodded, his expression grim. "Especially to kill." He stepped aside, allowing Alexander to exit the office.

Alexander walked out of the bank into the bustling street. The news of Rebecca's death, coupled with Thomas's bizarre accusation, had left him reeling. He hurried through the crowds, his thoughts a jumble. Martha. He needed to get home to Martha.

As he neared their house, he saw her, standing on the small front porch, her gaze fixed on the street. She looked fragile but beautiful, the sunlight catching the soft waves of her hair. Relief washed over him, momentarily pushing away the day's grim tidings.

"Alexander!" Martha called out, a smile lighting her face as he approached. Her smile faded at the sight of his somber expression. "What's wrong? You look like you've seen a ghost."

He reached her, taking her hand. "Martha, I have some terrible news." He led her inside, closing the door behind them.

"What is it? Is it the bank? The stagecoaches?" she asked, her voice laced with anxiety.

"No. It's... Rebecca Pruitt, Thomas's wife. She's dead."

Martha gasped, her hand flying to her mouth. "Oh, no!

Rebecca? But... how? She was just at the party, so full of life." Her eyes welled instantly, tears brimming. "And her baby? Was it related to the baby?" She sat on the settee in the parlor.

Alexander sat next to her. "The telegram didn't say how. Only that she died, and that Thomas, in his grief, blames me." He recounted the confrontation at the river, the unprovoked punch, and his retaliatory blow. "He's lashing out because of that time I told him I'd kill him if he ever came near you."

Martha shook her head, tears now streaming down her cheeks. "That's preposterous! You would never hurt either one of them. And Thomas... he must be out of his mind with grief. But Rebecca... oh, Alexander, I feel awful. We barely knew each other, not truly, but she was so brave that day, us shooting those outlaws outside of Auburn."

Alexander nodded.

"And she was so funny!" Martha remembered, a faint, melancholic smile touching her lips through her tears. "Do you remember the time, long before she married Thomas, when she flirted with you at the restaurant? It was all in fun, of course. She loved to embarrass men, especially proper ones like you." Martha chuckled, a half-sob.

Alexander's cheeks colored slightly at the memory. "Yes, I recall. You made a joke out of it."

"She made everyone laugh," Martha murmured, then her expression turned solemn again. "Oh, Alexander, this is so sad. I was truly looking forward to visiting with her, especially after finding out she was going to have a baby. I wanted to share stories about our babies, offer her advice, and talk about motherhood. I'll never get that chance. It's so unfair."

She buried her face in his shoulder, sobbing.

Alexander held her close. The weight of the world, heavy on his shoulders. He was still trying to process the news, the irrational accusation, and now Martha's deep sorrow.

His heart ached for her. The grief was hitting her, not only for Rebecca, but also for their lost connection. Martha had been excited about their shared future as mothers.

"We'll visit her grave, Martha," he said, looking over her head at the quiet room. "When you're strong enough, we'll pay our respects."

She nodded.

"The other thing is that Douglas suspects Joseph's involvement with the stagecoach robbers."

She sniffed, pulling back. "Joseph? Do you think he's involved with those outlaws?" Her voice was laced with a fresh worry, as she remembered the tension she'd witnessed herself.

Alexander hesitated. "Douglas thinks so. He claims Joseph is greedy and that he's never trusted him." He didn't mention Douglas's chilling 'Even to kill' comment. "Regardless, Thomas's grief has made him unstable. Elizabeth warned Douglas that I should stay away from Thomas for now."

Martha looked at him with wide, tear-filled eyes. "Unstable? What do you mean?"

"He attacked me at the party, unprovoked. Just a wild swing. And now this accusation. Elizabeth said Thomas blames me. We need to be careful."

Martha shivered, clutching his arm. "This keeps getting worse. I wish we could help them, but... what can we do?"

Alexander sighed, rubbing his temple. "For now, we do as Douglas says. I stay here. And I'll continue to work to put a stop to these stagecoach robberies."

Martha nodded. Her face was tear-streaked, but a quiet determination was beginning to settle in her eyes. "Poor Rebecca. I truly hope she finds peace. And her baby, too."

A soft cry rose from the nursery. Martha glanced away. "I need to check on Marcus," she said, leaving for the nursery.

Alexander sat alone, his troubled thoughts weighing on him. He'd been focused before on eliminating the stagecoach robbers, but now he'd become entrenched in the Pruitt family drama. He recalled the first line of Elizabeth's telegram: 'My husband is in the clear.' In the clear from what? The question was its own answer. Joseph had been suspected. The puzzle pieces were falling into place, and the picture they formed was dark and disturbing.

CHAPTER TWENTY-TWO

Investigating

Elizabeth and Joseph sat at the table, lunch growing cold between them. Neither spoke.

Elizabeth cleared her throat.

Joseph shot a sideways glance at her. "What's wrong? You've been quieter than usual."

She put her napkin down. "Did you see Rebecca before she died?"

"Yeah. Alexander was being a bit too familiar with her. Mighty inappropriate of him, if you ask me."

Elizabeth frowned. "He was doing no such thing. I passed him on my way back to the house. He was telling her goodbye. That's all." She looked away.

Joseph narrowed his eyes. "Then why did Alexander have a bloody hand when he and Douglas left?"

Elizabeth blinked, confusion flickering across her face. "He didn't kill Rebecca." She leaned forward. "Why are you blaming him? Did you have anything to do with those stagecoach robberies he's investigating?"

"Of course not! I'd never get mixed up with those robbers?"

She shook her head and began clearing the dishes. "Douglas is sure you are."

"He's had it in for me since we all moved here from New York." His eyes flicked to hers. "You know that!"

"You two have been feuding for far too long."

Joseph rolled his eyes. "After your husband died, Douglas tried to convince you I was stealing your interests in the mine."

"Aunt Helen and I were satisfied with the settlement. That house and the money you gave us were more than fair."

"I'll never forgive him. It wasn't his business, and defending myself cost me plenty. He owes me."

"You more than recovered that money. In the end, it all

worked out."

Joseph looked away, jaw tight. "I need you to be safe."

"I am."

"Don't forget to carry your gun when you go into town."

Elizabeth met his gaze. "I've been carrying that six-shooter since the day you told me to."

The next morning, Thomas shuffled along the river's edge, stopping a few feet from the boulder where Rebecca had died. He picked up a large rock.

Climbing onto the boulder, he sat. Stared in the direction she would have faced. The rock bounced in his hand. He glanced down at the water where he had found her body.

Looking over his shoulder, he imagined someone creeping up behind her, striking her, sending her tumbling into the river.

A flicker of movement caught his eye: a trail, just beyond the brush. He hurried toward it. The path was narrow, half-swallowed by weeds, but along its center were several distinct impressions — footsteps, unmistakable.

A cacophony of birds urged him forward. He stopped beside a large oak as the wind rustled the leaves and the birds squawked wildly. The sound was deafening.

Rounding the tree, he froze. The pathway, concealed by brush, continued to his cabin.

"What are you doing here?" Joseph's voice rang out.

Thomas jolted, then turned. "I'm investigating," he said, tapping his badge. "That's what this is for, right?"

Joseph approached, his expression grim. "I guess so."

Thomas stared down the trail. "I've walked this way a hundred times... never saw this path before."

"It's a bit overgrown. Isn't it?"

Thomas pointed to the brush. "Enough to conceal footprints. Someone could use it to come here unnoticed."

Joseph shook his head. "I think you're reaching."

"Where did the robbers stay when they were here?"

Joseph gestured downriver to a wider trail. "A few hundred feet that way, there's a clearing."

"Let's go see it."

Joseph sighed. "Not much to see there." He glanced at Thomas, whose eyes didn't waver. He paused, took in a long breath, and then exhaled loudly. "It's this way."

Thomas followed him down the trail.

Ten minutes later, Thomas and Joseph reached a wide clearing.

Thomas slowed. A rock lay a few feet ahead—oddly placed, about the size of the one he'd held at the river. Its surface was mottled with dark, burnt-red stains.

He spat on his finger and then rubbed the stone. The smear turned rusty red.

"There's blood on here," he said, holding it out.

Joseph blinked, startled. He took the rock and turned it in his hands.

Thomas exhaled sharply. "Rebecca's killer was here. Must've been one of those robbers."

Joseph's brow furrowed. "The group was long gone when she died."

"One of 'em must have come back."

Joseph cleared his throat.

Thomas pressed on. "John was at the party. The man you spoke to in the church on my wedding day."

Joseph gasped. "You were there?"

"I was. I heard everything. Where's John now? I haven't seen him since."

Joseph's eyes widened. "I don't know."

"You said he threatened Elizabeth."

"No! That was Randall."

Joseph blinked, uneasy. He tossed the rock aside. "Let it go. John wouldn't have killed her."

"What about Randall?"

Joseph shook his head. "No."

Thomas's frustration grew, and he narrowed his eyes. "What if the killer was after Elizabeth?"

Joseph's breath caught. His jaw slackened.

Thomas grunted, picked up the rock again, and cast a sideways glance at Joseph—sharp, suspicious. Then he turned and walked away.

* * *

Joseph stood still, breath steady, watching as Thomas disappeared down the trail toward the river.

He exhaled sharply. "Damnit, Randall... if you killed her..."

Without hesitation, Joseph mounted his horse and rode hard toward town. He found Charlie at the saloon, hunched over a drink.

"Where's Randall?" Joseph demanded. "I know he's hiding out — and you know where."

Charlie's upper lip twitched. "Why would I tell you?"

Joseph leaned in. "He had something to do with Rebecca's death." He paused and narrowed his eyes. "Or... maybe you did."

Charlie's face darkened. "I didn't kill my sister. I would never..."

"Then where's Randall? He had reason enough to want her dead."

Charlie scoffed. "I doubt it. Thanks to your son, he ain't been in the killing mood lately."

Joseph stepped closer, voice low. "Where is he?"

Charlie chuckled. "If you're stupid enough to go looking, I won't stop you." He sipped his drink. "They're camped right outside Sacramento. I'm headed there now. You want to follow me, be my guest — just don't shoot me in the back."

The ride to the camp was long and silent. Dust kicked up behind them as the sun dipped low, casting long shadows across the trail. Joseph's grip on the reins tightened with every mile. He wasn't sure what he'd say when he saw Randall — only that he needed answers.

Joseph and Charlie rode up to Randall and John's camp. Two sentries stopped them.

Charlie said, "He's here to see Randall."

Joseph dismounted and stormed past the sentries.

"Let him through," said Randall as he limped toward Joseph. "What are you doing here? Trying to get yourself shot?"

Joseph yelled, "Why did you kill Rebecca?"

Randall cocked his head back. "I don't kill family. That's your thing."

Joseph's face burned red with rage. "I won't let you take

another life." He lunged, fists clenched. "Not Elizabeth. Not anyone."

"Cool down, little brother. I've been stuck here for the last few weeks, ever since your boy shot me."

Joseph glanced into the camp. Frank was peering from behind a tree.

"Who killed Rebecca? If you didn't, you must have had someone do it. That's your style."

"I told you, I didn't have anything to do with her death." Randall showed Joseph his bandaged hand. "I can't even hold a gun with this hand."

Joseph's eyes grew wide.

Randall inhaled long and then let it out all at once. "I tried talking to you that day she was killed. I've had plenty of time to think these last few weeks. I want us to be close like we used to."

Joseph wrinkled his face and tilted his head back. "After everything you've done? You expect me to believe that you've changed?"

"My whole life, I've prided myself on being the best at shooting and making things go my way. Now... thanks to your son, I can't shoot worth a damn." He held up his bandaged hand. "Thomas took everything that mattered to me away. I ain't got a purpose no more. I want to start over with you."

"Are you trying to make me feel sorry for you?"

Randall's head cocked back, and his jaw slackened. "I don't need your pity."

"You've always blamed everyone for your troubles. Why don't you make things right with your son?" Joseph's upper lip twitched. "It's about time Alexander learned the truth about you."

Randall's smile vanished, his eyes flaring with anger. "You leave him out of this." He growled. He lunged, teeth bared, and slammed a fist into Joseph's jaw.

Joseph stumbled back, steadied himself, and then lunged at Randall. He fell to the ground.

Joseph stood over Randall and drew his gun.

A crack from a gunshot rang out from the ridge.

John came running, gun drawn, and fired a warning shot into the dirt beside them.

"Knock it off!" he shouted.

Joseph backed away, panting, while Randall pushed himself upright and brushed the dust from his coat.

John walked up, eyes locked on Joseph. "I think it's best you leave. You reek of whiskey. I thought you said you were done with that."

Joseph hesitated, then holstered his six-shooter and scooped up his hat.

John turned to face them both. "I've got no interest in standing between you two. But this ain't your place to stir the pot, Joseph. You're a long way from home."

Still catching his breath, Joseph shot a final glare at Randall, then turned on his heel and stormed away.

CHAPTER TWENTY-THREE

Stirring Up Trouble

The morning clouds hung low over the town, thick and unmoving, like the question still hanging over Rebecca's murder.

Thomas walked into the sheriff's office.

The deputy dropped his boots from the desk, his eyes following Thomas as he approached.

"Morning," Thomas said. He glanced at the desk where the other deputy usually sat.

"Morning, Deputy Pruitt," the deputy replied. "Something I can help you with?"

"Where's the other deputy?"

"He went to get us something to eat."

"What do you know about Alexander Johnson?"

"Only that he works with the Law on those stagecoaches. The sheriff asked us to keep an eye out for him."

Thomas nodded slowly. "Did he say why?"

The deputy furrowed his brow. "No."

Thomas frowned. "Have you ever heard about any robbers holing up near my pa's place? Around the time Rebecca was killed?"

The deputy sat up taller. "Nope. The sheriff would surely tell us if there was. And I haven't seen many strangers around here."

Thomas folded his arms.

The deputy leaned forward. "Why are you asking about Mr. Johnson? Is he in some trouble?"

Thomas gave a half-shrug. "Just thinking out loud."

He stepped outside, the door thudding shut behind him. The street lay quiet. Those clouds hadn't lifted, and neither had his doubt.

Joseph was holding something back. Why tell the deputies to keep an eye out for Alexander? Why now? Maybe it's time to determine what else those outlaws were holding over him. It might be connected to Alexander.

Thomas rode to his Pa's barn, his mind tangled with thoughts of who might've killed Rebecca. Could it have been Alexander? Elizabeth was convinced it was John Walker. He dismounted. The horse's reins fell slack against the trough. He secured the reins, and the horse slurped the water. Thomas hiked to the far side of the barn to an area overgrown with brush and dead branches.

He went past the table where cans lay riddled with bullet holes. A few feet ahead, he stopped beside a four-foot-tall, loosely stacked pile of broken tree. The glint from a protruding metal rod caught his eye. It was clearly out of place. He tugged at it. The mound shifted, revealing part of a door.

His hands trembled as he cleared the brush and uncovered the door. When he opened it, a blanket of cold, damp air greeted him. He stepped inside, eyes scanning the darkness.

Joseph arrived at the house and grimaced. Thomas's horse was beside the barn, near the entrance to his secret mine. He gasped and walked cautiously to the barn. The entrance was exposed, the brush he'd used to conceal it was pushed aside, and the door was wide open.

Thomas walked out smiling. "Pa!"

Joseph, his face growing crimson, looked incredulously at Thomas. "What are you doing here?"

"Just exploring. I wanted to find out what those stagecoach robbers were holding over you."

Joseph cast a sideways glance at the house. "Did Elizabeth see you?"

"No! Of course not. You've got quite a stash in those boxes."

Joseph closed the makeshift door and moved the brush to hide the entrance.

Thomas cocked his head. "What the hell?"

Joseph rushed back to Thomas. "No one else knows about this place, not even Elizabeth. Don't ever come here again."

"Is this what those robbers are holding over you?"

"I told you already." Joseph rubbed his forehead. "I'm shielding Elizabeth. Suppose someone discovers this mine and its contents. They'd kill for it," Joseph said, voice low. "They'd kill

Elizabeth."

"Just like one of 'em killed Rebecca?"

Joseph locked eyes with Thomas. Things were unraveling too fast. He exhaled a drawn-out sigh. "My head's pounding. Let's go get a drink and talk this through."

Thomas offered a half-smile, though his eyes stayed sharp on Joseph. "I got something to take care of first," he said. "I'll catch up with you in a bit."

Joseph gave a slow, reluctant nod. "I'll wait for you at the saloon."

Thomas nodded and left.

Joseph's gaze lingered on Thomas as he rode off. The sound of hooves faded into the distance. Joseph stood still, the weight of the mine pressing heavier than ever.

Thirty minutes later, Thomas rode up to the sheriff's office and stepped inside with the bloodied rock he'd found earlier.

The deputy jumped up as Thomas approached.

"I've got proof my wife was murdered," Thomas said.

He set the rock down with a hard thud on the desk. A burnt crimson darkened one side.

The deputy stared at it, eyes narrowing. "Is that blood?"

Thomas didn't blink. "Sure as hell is."

"I knew it! Rebecca's death didn't look right. I told the sheriff that."

"It wasn't an accident."

"There ain't no one in this town that would hurt someone as respectable as your wife. She was a good-hearted woman."

"I have a suspicion of who killed her, but I want to talk with John Walker first. He might have had something to do with her death, too. He might even be the killer."

"The sheriff warned us to keep clear of Mr. Walker."

"I need to find out if that man knows something that could help. There's no harm in that."

The deputy stood frozen as if he expected Thomas to say more.

Thomas stared at the deputy.

The deputy jumped. "Oh, you want me to bring him in."

"Yes."

The deputy collected his gun and bolted out the door.

Thomas shook his head, walked to the sheriff's desk, and sat in Joseph's chair. He rested his hand on the desk, where Joseph's papers still lay. Rebecca's murderer was out there. He just had to keep digging to find him.

Joseph was fussing with his horse's straps outside the saloon when the deputy ran up to him.

The deputy, gasping for air, asked, "Do you know where John Walker is?"

Joseph's head cocked back, his brows narrowed. "Why?"

"Thomas wants to talk to him. He suspects he had something to do with his wife's death."

"Damnit! I told you…"

"I tried telling Thomas."

Where is he?"

"In the office."

"I'll go have a chat with him. I told you before to stay away from John Walker. I meant it!" He tossed the deputy a coin. "Go have a drink instead."

"Yes, sir!"

The deputy rushed into the saloon. Joseph took a deep breath and marched to his office.

He kicked the door open and strode inside, eyes blazing.

Thomas looked up at him calmly. "Pa! What are you doing here?"

"This is my office, damn it." Joseph took a breath. "And this is my desk."

"Yeah, I just thought—"

"Why in the hell are you sending my deputy out to arrest John Walker?"

"I just want to talk to him."

"We talked about this, son!"

"Rebecca was murdered. We have to search out her killer and bring him to justice. John must have had something to do with her death, or at least he knows something."

"My men are not going to go out and start arresting people just because you found a damn rock."

"I won't rest until I find out who killed her. If John Walker knows something, I gotta talk to him. No one said anything about arresting him."

"If anyone had reason to kill her, it would be Alexander Johnson. He looked mighty suspicious when I saw him leaving with Douglas Holt that day. Have you talked with him yet?"

"No. Elizabeth insists he had nothing to do with Rebecca's death."

"You're just too soft to see things as they are."

Thomas narrowed his eyes and stood.

"I ain't soft." His nose flared. "You're beginning to sound like Randall, calling me that."

Joseph's breath caught. He shook his head. "I asked you to be my deputy to help you out... to help me out. Next time, check with me before you go off half-cocked and start ordering my men to arrest people, especially that man. I don't want him back in this town. I've already told you why."

Thomas slammed his fist down hard on the sheriff's desk. "What if the killer thought he killed Elizabeth? She and Rebecca were both there together."

Joseph's face drained of color. His eyes went wide. The thought knocked the wind out of him. Without a word, he turned and walked out the door, heading back to the saloon.

CHAPTER TWENTY-FOUR

Arrest the Killer

The following day, Elizabeth walked out the front door. Joseph was asleep on the porch.

"Joseph! You've been drinking?"

He looked up groggily as the empty whiskey bottle fell to the floor. He wiped the sleep from his eyes.

"Thomas ordered my men to arrest John Walker for Rebecca's death."

Elizabeth shook her head, and her hand went to her chest. "That man is trouble. I saw him at Rebecca's party acting mighty suspicious. He was arguing with Charlie."

Joseph winced as he stood and said, "That doesn't mean anything."

Elizabeth said, "He's rotten!"

"It was Alexander Johnson. His hands were bloody that day when I chased him and that damn Douglas Holt away."

Elizabeth's eyes grew wide. "That's ridiculous. You know that's not true."

He glared at her. "Thomas has gone too far. He's turning reckless!"

"Thomas has helped you. Hasn't he?"

Joseph shook his head. "He's telling my men to do things they have no business doing—like arresting men that are better left gone. He doesn't appreciate what I've done for him."

"Joseph, he does appreciate you. You know that." She reached for his hand. "Why are you drinking again?"

Joseph shook his head and staggered to his horse.

"Joseph, don't go! Come back into the house."

He glanced back over his shoulder and then rode away in a huff.

Elizabeth brought her hand to her chest, her heart pounding. She took a deep gulp of air and let it out all at once. She rushed inside, got her bag with her gun, and went to the barn. A crow in a nearby tree watched silently. Dread crept toward her as she ran to her horse. A moment later, she was on her way to town to protect Joseph from himself, lest he might do something regrettable.

As Joseph arrived at the sheriff's office, his deputies were riding away. Thomas was on the porch watching them.

Joseph almost fell as he jumped down from his horse.

A crow watching from a distance flapped its wings in surprise.

"Where are my deputies going? Did you send them after John?"

"Nope. They'll be back soon. I sent them to check on the stagecoach."

"What the hell? They're my deputies!"

"Why don't you come inside and drink some coffee?"

Joseph staggered to his horse. "I'm going to go find my deputies," he said as he snapped the reins, and the horse took off in a gallop.

"Pa, come on back!"

Elizabeth rode up. "What happened?"

Thomas turned, surprised. "Elizabeth!"

"Where's Joseph going?"

"He's headed after his deputies."

"Why?"

"The stagecoach from Sacramento is long overdue. I sent the men to check on it. I'm sure it's nothing."

"I don't see why Joseph would be upset about that." Her brows bounced up, and her gaze flicked toward Joseph as he disappeared down the road.

"I tried to tell him," said Thomas. "Don't worry, once he sees those deputies doing their job, he'll come home."

Elizabeth turned back to Thomas and took out her kerchief, patting her face.

Thomas's face changed from one of frustration to concern as he gently touched Elizabeth's arm. "You okay? You look a bit flushed."

Elizabeth furrowed her brows. "I'm just a little warm. I'll stop at the doctor's office before I head home and ask Dr. Hammond for some of his feel-good tonic."

"That's a good idea."

She hesitated. "I'm worried about Joseph." She locked eyes with Thomas. "He's been running this town on his own for a long time. He's acting like he's losing control. Joseph is a proud man."

"I thought he wanted me to help him."

"You have." Elizabeth patted his arm, her voice soft. "I'll see you tomorrow."

Thomas smiled warmly, the warmth from her pat helping his unease abate. "See you then."

Elizabeth crossed the street and went into the Telegraph office.

The clerk handed her a telegram when she reached the counter.

As Elizabeth read it, her lips pressed together. Tears filled her eyes. She stood motionless, staring at the paper. Its words were stark: "YOUR AUNT HELEN PASSED EARLY THIS AM. DOUGLAS HOLT"

She blinked, once. The words didn't change. Aunt Helen was gone.

The clerk said, "I'm sorry for your loss, Mrs. Pruitt."

"Thank you."

She put the telegram in her bag and turned to leave. She glanced back, a smile painted on her face, and said, "She was a wonderful woman."

She walked out the door and headed to the doctor's office.

Thomas entered the sheriff's office and sat again at Joseph's desk. He surveyed the room. He smiled as he got comfortable in the chair, rubbing the armrests. He sat quietly, thinking for almost an hour.

He jumped as the deputy burst in through the front door.

"Thomas, you were right! The stagecoach was being robbed."

"Was anyone hurt?"

"Nope. We got there just in time. We surprised those robbers. They weren't expecting us to come in from the north."

"Did you see John Walker there?"

"No. As soon as we started shooting, those outlaws

scattered."

"Did my Pa catch up to you?"

"We ain't seen him. Shouldn't we let him know about that stagecoach getting attacked?"

"I'll tell him later. He's...." Thomas's fingers tightened on the armrest as thoughts of his Pa's drinking came to him. "I'll take care of it."

The Deputy shrugged. "Okay. You're the one keeping things together now."

"Were the passengers okay?"

"Yes. Mr. Johnson and Mr. Holt were mighty appreciative."

The color drained from Thomas's face.

The deputy glanced at the door and then back at Thomas. "They should be arriving any minute now."

"Thanks," said Thomas as he grabbed his hat and went outside.

Thomas stood on the sheriff's porch as a bullet-riddled stagecoach rattled to a halt in front of the hotel. Douglas and Alexander stepped out.

The driver set their luggage down. They each grabbed their bags in silence and started for the door.

Alexander held the door open for Douglas.

Douglas entered. "If everything is in order, the audit will be straightforward."

Alexander, his brows raised, lingered as his gaze swept from side to side and then settled on the coach. He shook his head and went inside.

The driver clicked to the horses, and the coach creaked, leaving a cloud of dust in its wake as it pulled away.

As the chalky haze settled, Thomas emerged, his face creased with suspicion. Eyes narrowed, he stared as the hotel door thudded shut behind Alexander.

That evening, Elizabeth was setting the table when Joseph stormed into the house. Elizabeth looked up, startled, and nearly dropped the plate she held. He slammed the door behind him.

Elizabeth put the plate down and looked sternly at him.

"What's wrong? Did something happen?"

"It's Thomas. He's lost his mind. He sent my men off to who knows where. He's up to something. I know it!"

"I'm sure it's nothing," said Elizabeth. She raised her hand to her nose, though the sudden bite of whiskey teased a memory she hadn't invited. It was a vow he made before they married, never to drink again. Back then, her trust in him strained against collapse, as his drinking dragged them both toward ruin.

"Damn it, Elizabeth."

"Come sit. I have some wonderful news, and some bad."

Joseph reluctantly sat at the table. Elizabeth served him and then herself and sat across from him.

He started eating. He glanced at her, annoyed. "What's the bad news?"

She painted a smile on her face and then cleared her throat. "I got word that my Aunt Helen died."

"Did she leave you anything?" he barked.

"She left me the house."

"Sell it!"

Elizabeth's face tightened. "No! How could you say that? It's a beautiful house, much bigger than this one. Perhaps we should consider moving there. It would be the perfect place to raise a child."

Joseph cocked his head back. "What! Are you joking?"

"Thomas could stay here to manage your interests. He'd make a fine sheriff, too."

Joseph jumped up.

"Sheriff? He's out of control and liable to get you killed!" he belted.

"You're getting upset about nothing!"

He flung the knife. Elizabeth shrieked as the blade grazed her arm, and blood splattered her sleeve and dress.

"Have you gone mad?" she screamed, grabbing her wound.

Joseph's eyes widened in shock. His breath hitched in his throat. "I'm sorry." He stood frozen.

She glared at him. "Maybe I need protection from you!"

His mouth fell open, his head shaking from side to side. He backed away and rushed out the door.

Elizabeth sat in disbelief at what had just happened.

"Something is very wrong," she muttered, examining her arm. The wound was minor. She went to the window in time to see Joseph ride away. She pressed her hand to the glass, the blood on her sleeve smearing faintly. Joseph was already a shadow in the distance.

CHAPTER TWENTY-FIVE

Worried About Joseph

Elizabeth woke early the next day, having tossed and turned for most of the night. Joseph hadn't come home.

She looked out the back window, and the muted light of dawn lit the yard. The cool morning air welcomed her as she hurried outside to gather eggs. A rooster flew up to the fence post and announced the start of a new day. She paused at the coop door, her hand trembling slightly. The chickens sensed something — or maybe she did. The hens clucked softly as she unlatched the door. When she went inside to collect their eggs, the chickens ran in all directions, squawking wildly.

"It's me. Everything is fine." She filled the basket.

The rooster screeched when Thomas rushed up, startling Elizabeth.

The chickens flapped frantically as they ran in all directions.

Thomas narrowed his eyes at the chickens. "Elizabeth! I heard a commotion out here. You okay?"

"Yes, I'm fine."

The early morning light cast shadows on the wrinkles around Thomas's eyes.

"How are you doing?" Her face was creased with concern.

"I couldn't sleep. I was worried about Pa."

"He didn't come home last night. I was up all night, filled with worry."

Thomas sighed.

Elizabeth patted his arm. "Let's get some breakfast. We can think better on a full stomach."

She carried the basket inside, her steps quick but uncertain.

Thomas followed.

She moved quickly in the kitchen. The scent of sizzling bacon and fried eggs curled through the air, warm and familiar. She served a plate for each and set them on the table.

She sliced a piece of fruit with steady hands, though her mind drifted to the knife from the night before—the way it cut through the air and nicked her arm. A few inches over, and it might've found her heart.

"What if—" she began, but stopped short of telling Thomas about the knife. The words caught in her throat.

His eyes snapped to her. "What if what?"

She blinked, pulled herself back. "What if we had bread?" She forced a smile. "I could toast it on the stove."

"That'd be tasty with butter." As Thomas sat, his holster snagged on the table leg, and with a quiet grunt, he unhooked it and set the gun aside next to his plate.

She added the fruit she'd cut to each of their plates. "Aunt Helen passed yesterday morning."

"Oh, that's a shame. I'm sorry." He paused. "Helen was very kind to me when I would visit Rebecca."

"She had a long, beautiful life. I'm content she's with Mother now. They were always close."

Thomas looked across into Elizabeth's eyes. "Like you and I have become."

She smiled. "Yes. We have." She inhaled deeply. "I was planning to travel down there, but..."

"But what?"

She cast a sideways glance. "I asked Joseph if he would move us to Aunt Helen's house."

Thomas's brows shot up, and his jaw dropped. "You did?"

"Yes. Aunt Helen reminded me often that she planned to leave the house to me. It's a mighty fine house. I never gave much thought to what I might do with it. But Joseph..."

Thomas leaned in. "What did he say?"

"He said no. When I insisted, he lost his temper. He started to rant about how angry he was with you." Her voice softened. "What's going on between you two?"

"Lately, he's been upset a lot. He's not been himself." Thomas's brows raised.

"He won't tell me what's bothering him. At supper, his eyes filled with fury when I asked him about moving to Aunt Helen's place. He threw a knife, and it grazed my arm."

Thomas gasped, and his voice cracked as he said, "Doggone it!"

"He didn't mean to do it."

"He was drunk when he chased after the deputies yesterday afternoon." Thomas looked away. His hands twisted against each other, knuckles pale. "He's out of control."

She exhaled loudly as a memory from before she and Joseph married startled her. Joseph had staggered into the Sacramento sheriff's office professing his love for her. "We've got to help him."

His shoulders dropped. "I was trying to make things easier for him. Those deputies thwarted a stagecoach attack. I thought he'd be proud." His face wrinkled as if he'd smelled something foul. "Alexander and Douglas arrived in that bullet-riddled stagecoach those deputies saved."

"They're here?"

Thomas nodded. "I want to talk to Alexander. He must know something about Rebecca's murder."

Elizabeth gasped. "Thomas, that man had nothing to do with Rebecca's death. I'm almost certain John Walker is responsible. He was acting mighty suspicious at the party."

Thomas stood up and walked to the window. He gazed toward the river and then back at Elizabeth.

"Alexander hasn't been here ever since the day she died."

Elizabeth looked away. "I asked him to stay away for a while."

"I figured you were protecting him."

Elizabeth rolled her eyes. "I need to tell you something else."

Thomas sat down across from her.

She continued, "Douglas Holt believes Joseph played some part in the stagecoach robberies."

Thomas's face remained expressionless. "Really?"

"He thinks Joseph aided the robbers by providing them with a haven on his land. And has a whole network of lawless men working with him."

Thomas shifted in his seat. "You don't think that's true, do you?"

"It's possible Joseph might somehow be involved with them. Perhaps trying to break them up or ridding them from this town."

Thomas shrugged.

She continued as her mind tried to make sense of Joseph's behavior. "He's done all sorts of things to keep this town safe. But I can't believe he would collude with them. Could it be that he's trying to get them to leave that life? He's done that before, too." The corner of her lips curved up slightly. "Do you know Howard?"

Thomas snickered. "The crazy man who hates crows?"

"Yes. Joseph helped that man turn his life around."

Thomas, red-faced, pushed his chair back. He took a deep breath and then stood as he exhaled loudly. "What if he doesn't have a choice but to work with them?" His gaze fell to the floor. "Or at least not expose them?"

Elizabeth reached for Thomas's arm. "He would never keep something like that from me."

Thomas glanced away. "What if it was to protect you?"

Elizabeth's head tilted, her eyes narrowing. "Do you know something about..."

Gunshots cracked from the riverbank.

They hurried to the window as shouting rose through the open frame.

Thomas's brows shot up. He turned to Elizabeth, eyes wide. "That's Pa!"

He sprinted to the door. "And he's not alone." The door slammed shut behind him.

She froze mid-step. His gun was still on the table.

"He's unarmed," she muttered.

CHAPTER TWENTY-SIX

Falling From Grace

Joseph sat on a boulder, drinking whiskey and waving his gun at the trees. He spotted Randall headed his way and said, "You again!"

Randall sauntered over to Joseph by the creek and stopped a short distance away.

"Joseph," he called out, voice steady. "I meant what I said. I'm here to talk. I want to make things right."

Joseph lurched to his feet, nearly stumbling. The whiskey clung to his thoughts like fog.

"Don't take another step," he snapped, raising the six-shooter. "I'll shoot you where you stand. You've made my life a living hell. I was happy here... until you showed up. Everything was going fine."

Joseph waved his six-shooter and fired into the trees. A thunderous crack split the air. Dozens of crows burst from the branches, squawking in a chaotic flurry. "Damn Crows," he muttered. "I spent years respecting them."

Randall didn't flinch. "That's not smart, shooting at them. Why don't you put that gun down and talk to me like family?"

Joseph staggered forward, eyes glassy. He didn't look at Randall... he looked past him, toward the trees. Squinting, he raised his weapon again.

Another shot rang out.

A lone crow dropped to the ground, limp and silent.

Randall's jaw slackened. "Why'd you go and do that?" he asked, eyes sweeping the treetops.

Silence settled over the creek, thick and sudden.

Joseph turned, his voice sharp. "Now... what did you want to discuss, brother?"

"I didn't bring a gun."

Joseph snorted. "Too bad for you!"

Randall took a breath, steadying himself.

"I've done you wrong. I know that. I wouldn't blame you if you shot me dead for how I treated you." He looked away, voice low. "And to your family." He inhaled sharply. "I'm sorry. I really am."

Joseph tilted his head, eyes narrowing. He'd never heard that word—sorry—from Randall's mouth. A glimmer of hope flickered in his chest. "You fooling with me?"

"Not this time," Randall said quietly. "I've had plenty of time to think." He raised his crippled hand. "Thomas did me a favor by wrecking my future. Without this hand... I ain't much."

Joseph let out a bitter chuckle. "There's nothing in this world that'll change you, except maybe a bullet through your cold heart."

Randall nodded. "Maybe so. But I'm sure as hell going to try." His voice cracked. "I need you, Joseph." He dropped to his knees. "Help me!"

Joseph's breath caught, thick in his throat.

"When I first got here, to California, I thought I escaped the likes of you. But it didn't take long for someone even darker than you to show up." He looked away. "I got rid of him. I paid him to stay away."

Randall cocked his head back, confused. "I ain't dark no more."

Joseph's right cheek tightened. "I got news that the circuit judge was murdered." He gripped his gun, his knuckles white. "Something's not right about the timing. This must be Gentry's move. I know it. This is how he comes back. He's a judge now." Joseph leaned in close, his voice a harsh rasp. "Gentry swore he'd return to take the badge, the gold mine, and the whole damn town. He wants everything Buchanan and I kept safe. I can't let him undo what it took years to keep buried." He shook his head. "I sent Buchanan a telegram."

Randall's head tilted. "I don't know what you're talking about."

Several crows returned to the trees, their squawking rising in a discordant chorus.

Joseph narrowed his eyes and raised his gun their way.

"Joseph!" Randall shouted. "Leave them be! They'll haunt you for the rest of your life."

Joseph froze. Then he turned the weapon on Randall. "You're still here? You come to kill my Elizabeth?"

"No!" Randall's voice cracked. "I was never going to hurt her."

Joseph shuffled closer, eyes burning. "Elizabeth is my life. You took Rose from me, and now you want my Elizabeth. I can't lose her."

Randall held his ground. "I swear, I'll help you anyway I can."

Joseph locked eyes with him. For the first time, he saw something unfamiliar in Randall's gaze—sincerity. "Really?"

Joseph caught sight of Thomas walking their way.

"My days of hurtin' family are over," Randall said, voice low. "I ain't got anybody who cares about me." He started to rise. "Even Frank's gone cold. But you—you've got Elizabeth and your son."

Joseph saw Thomas stop a short distance behind Randall.

"I love Elizabeth and Thomas," Joseph said, voice cracking. "But, I've disappointed them. I think Thomas is starting to hate me. Maybe you were right to keep him. I ruined everything— dragging him here, getting his wife killed. It's my fault!"

He looked past Randall. Thomas was shaking his head.

"No, it ain't," Randall said firmly. "We'll find her killer. You have my word—I'll help. I promise."

Thomas stepped forward, and the trail crackled beneath his boot.

Randall spun around.

A crow swooped low at Joseph just as Thomas walked up.

Joseph grinned and swiped at the bird. "Well, look who came to talk."

Thomas locked eyes with Randall. "What the hell are you doing here?"

Randall held up his hands. "I came to have a civil chat with your father. Then those damn crows started swooping down on us. The trees are thick with them."

Thomas spotted one on the ground behind Joseph. Its wings were twisted and lifeless.

Joseph followed Thomas's gaze, then laughed. "Those crows thought they could intimidate me."

"Why don't we go back to the house?" Thomas asked. "We can have some coffee and talk this out."

Joseph turned to him, grinning. "Randall says he's sorry. And I'm beginning to believe him. Ain't that crazy?"

Randall lifted his arms again, palms open. "No weapon. No tricks."

Thomas narrowed his eyes. "I suppose you came alone. Same as you did to Agnes's place."

Randall shook his head quickly. "No one's with me. I swear. I came to talk. I've changed."

Thomas said, "Did Alexander put you and your stagecoach robbers out of business? Is that why you're here?"

Joseph stiffened. His face twisted with rage. "That son-of-a-bitch! If Alexander were here now... He needs to answer for killing your wife."

Randall's eyes snapped to Joseph. "Leave my son out of this. He didn't kill her." He turned to Thomas, voice trembling. "I'm leaving that gang." He exhaled loudly, then choked on the words. "Just... give me a chance. I need my family."

Joseph raised his six-shooter and fired into the trees. The shot cracked through the air, and the crows exploded from the branches in a frenzy. He fired again. Click. Nothing. He lowered the gun and inspected it. "Damn thing jams when I don't clean it right."

Thomas stepped closer to Randall. "Do you know who killed Rebecca?"

Randall shook his head. "No! I only saw her once. I came to talk to Joseph... right after you got married. He shoved me in the water, and I left."

Joseph barked a laugh. "That's when she slapped him. He earned that."

Thomas gritted his teeth. "She told me she met you. She never mentioned slapping you. What did you do to her?"

"Nothing!" Randall's voice cracked. "She almost slipped, and I caught her. That's all. She slapped me after. Said you told her everything about me."

Thomas stepped closer, eyes blazing. "Did you kill her?"

"No!" Randall's gaze locked onto his. "I swear."

Joseph snickered. "It was Alexander, I tell you."

Thomas turned to him. "Are you protecting John Walker by blaming Alexander? Is that why you've kept me from bringing John back to town?"

Joseph's grip tightened on the gun, barrel pointed at the ground. He leaned in, face inches from Thomas. "I don't like your tone, son!"

The stench of whiskey hit Thomas like a slap. He recoiled and stepped back.

The crows squawked louder, their cries rising like a warning.

Joseph's gaze snapped to the trees. "I'm sorry," he shouted.

Silence fell. The crows stilled.

He turned back to Thomas, voice frayed. "I told you already. If you bring that man back here, you'll get Elizabeth killed."

Thomas huffed, defiant. "I'm not afraid of him like you are!"

Joseph's eyes locked onto his son's, steady and unflinching.

"I ain't afraid," he said, voice low and taut. "I'm just trying to keep my family safe."

Elizabeth's voice pierced the tension.

"Joseph!"

He turned and saw her sprinting toward him.

The glint of a rifle barrel caught his eye from the ridge behind Elizabeth.

His hands slashed downward in sharp, frantic arcs, driven by pure instinct and terror.

"Get down," he shouted, lunging forward, arms flailing in a chaotic rhythm.

A shot cracked from the ridge behind her.

The sound hit like a thunderclap.

His eyes shot wide as Elizabeth tumbled to the ground. The impact rocked his body, and roaring filled his ears. He dropped, the world going hazy and soft. He heard Thomas yell, "Pa!"

"Thomas!" Joseph gasped, his voice thin. "Take my gun. Go help Elizabeth."

He felt the weight of the six-shooter lift from his hand. He heard Randall drop beside him.

"Randall, keep Elizabeth safe."

"I promise."

He watched Elizabeth shove Randall aside, her face stricken. He felt her hand grasp his.

He coughed, the metallic taste of blood filling his mouth. He focused on her face. "You're so beautiful."

He looked at Randall, seeing the shock on his brother's face. He tried to gesture toward him.

Joseph's voice trembled. "This is my brother, Randall. He came here to make peace with me. I'm inclined to believe him. He promised to keep you safe."

Another gunshot cracked, and he flinched, his body tensing in a reflex he couldn't stop.

He watched Elizabeth reach into the satchel and then hand a pistol to Randall.

She said, "You make sure no one else shoots at us."

"Yes, Ma'am."

Joseph reached for Elizabeth.

"You need to get your gun," he rasped. "They killed Rebecca, and they're coming for you."

"I will," Elizabeth said.

He drew a deep breath. "Elizabeth, I've got to tell you something." He coughed up blood and cleared his throat.

She leaned in close, tears streaking her cheeks.

"What do you want to tell me?" she whispered.

His lips quivered. "I love you and Thomas." He paused, breath hitching. "I'm sorry I hurt you. I shouldn't have kept secrets from you."

"I suppose I kept a secret from you, too." Elizabeth's eyes shimmered with tears. "We're going to have a baby."

Joseph's lips curled into a faint smile as joy briefly eclipsed the pain. "If it's a boy... name him after Thomas." He saw the silent affirmation in her eyes.

Joseph turned his gaze to Randall.

"I forgive you," he said, voice barely audible.

He saw Randall's jaw slacken, and his eyes brimmed with tears.

Then, with his final breaths, he turned back to Elizabeth. "Alexander is Randall's son," he rasped. "He didn't kill Rebecca."

A loud gasp from Elizabeth startled him.

The darkest secret, long suppressed, clawed its way back into Joseph's fading mind. Not just the robbers, the gold, and his brother's—but the threat of the man he'd paid to stay away. Silas Gentry. He had to warn her now.

Joseph drew a deep breath and mustered all of his strength. His eyes stayed on Elizabeth's face—pained and beautiful. "Gentry… broken promise… Buchanan," he whispered, his voice fragile. "Protect the town from him."

He clung to her voice, her tears, her eyes as the rest of the world receded. Then even Elizabeth slipped beyond his reach.

CHAPTER TWENTY-SEVEN
Change Is Good

For the first time, Elizabeth struggled to focus. She'd faced the death of her loved ones before, but this was different. Joseph was her life, her everything. She took comfort in how Thomas swooped in and helped her with the arrangements for Joseph's burial. It couldn't have been easy for him either. Elizabeth remembered how broken Thomas was after Rebecca's death and appreciated how Thomas was there for her.

The morning of the funeral was cloudy and dark. The menacing clouds didn't keep the townsfolk away. He had been their sheriff for as long as most could remember. He cared for them and ensured their safety. And occasionally, he'd help them financially, telling them not to worry about repaying him.

Elizabeth received many well-wishers at her home, expressing their condolences.

At the burial, Elizabeth sat tall, her face solemn, displaying an air of strength. She wore a black, long-sleeved dress. It wrapped tight around her like grief itself—thick and unrelenting beneath the layers of mourning. She shifted in her seat, the damp fabric sticking to her. Now and then, a cool breeze would give her relief from the humid day.

Thoughts of Joseph whirled around in her head. What if she hadn't mentioned anything about moving to Sacramento? Is that what broke him? He was upset when he got home that day. Why did I say anything at all? We could have eaten in peace, and everything would have worked out. Her breath came in short, uneven bursts, as if grief had stolen her rhythms.

She chased the thoughts away and reached over to Thomas, taking hold of his hand. Thomas smiled at her.

The minister uttered prayers intermixed with words of consolation.

Her gaze drifted toward the casket. Her eyes, heavy with sorrow, closed. Echoes of his last words came to her. "I shouldn't have kept secrets from you." And his last words were about Silas Gentry, Buchanan, and a broken promise."

Elizabeth sniffled, a tear escaped her eyes, and she blurted out, "It was my fault, Joseph."

The minister paused, his gaze darting to Elizabeth.

Thomas leaned in close to her and whispered, "You okay?"

"I'm alright." Elizabeth wiped her tears and regained her composure. "I'm sorry."

She waved for the minister to continue.

Thomas sighed. "We should have delayed this service."

"Everyone has waited long enough."

His shoulders slumped as he exhaled.

Perhaps, she thought, she might benefit by traveling to Sacramento to settle her Aunt Helen's affairs.

"Caw!" the crows shouted.

Elizabeth fixated on the casket that held her love. This was the end, she thought. Joseph would want her to be strong and keep going.

Thomas patted her hand.

She straightened in her seat and felt her strength returning.

Elizabeth whispered to Thomas. "I appreciate all you've done for me. I couldn't have gotten through this without you."

Thomas smiled.

A ruckus erupted in the trees, and crows chattered loudly. Dozens of crows stared down from the trees.

The minister paused as more crows joined in the cacophony. He closed his book and spoke louder, saying some final words.

Two crows flew down at the group. Thomas felt the breeze ruffle his hair as one crow came close to him. "What the hell?"

In the last row, Howard Jackson jumped up from his seat and rushed away. Several crows chased after him.

The minister's eyes grew large with alarm. "Thank you, everyone, for coming."

The rest of the crows quieted down and flew to the trees.

A memory of Joseph's voice startled her, "Crows remember faces. They hold a grudge, and they never forget."

Elizabeth's gaze followed Howard as he left. "That poor man. He loved Joseph. And those crows won't even let him pay his respects." She looked up, shaking her head.

"You ready to go?" asked Thomas.

She nodded.

Douglas walked up. "I'm sorry for your loss."

Alexander stepped up. "My condolences."

Elizabeth smiled. "Thank you both. I'm so glad you came."

Thomas moved close to Alexander. "You can leave now. You've said your peace."

Elizabeth tugged Thomas's arm. "Thomas! Please!"

The edge of Douglas's lip curled up. "Elizabeth, let me know if you need anything."

"I will."

Thomas's gaze lingered on Douglas and Alexander as they walked away.

He helped Elizabeth into the carriage, his silence speaking volumes. The trip home felt longer than usual.

He pulled the reins, and the carriage stopped in front of Elizabeth's place.

Elizabeth stepped down. "Come in for a little while. We should be together during these difficult times."

Thomas briefly glanced toward town. "Okay. I'll be right there."

He jumped down and took an apple from his bag. He sliced it into quarters and gave the pieces to his horse.

A hint of a smile crossed Elizabeth's lips. She remembered how Joseph gave his horse a treat after arriving home. "I'll put some tea on," she said and then disappeared into the house.

Soon after, Thomas joined Elizabeth inside.

The table was laden with an array of bread, vegetables, and meats, a testament to the town's generosity.

"The townspeople cared a great deal for Joseph." His eyes shot to Elizabeth. "And for you, too."

"They most certainly did!" She smiled. "The town wants you to be the new sheriff."

Thomas's head cocked back, his eyes darting to hers. "What? Really?"

"Yes!"

"I couldn't do that. I wouldn't be able to fill Pa's shoes."

Elizabeth poured two cups of tea and brought them to the sitting room.

She reached into her pocket and handed him a polished sheriff's badge. It was Joseph's. "You'll be a great sheriff. Everyone in town likes you."

He hesitated. His brows narrowed, and then he took the badge. "You're always taking care of me." He fumbled with it, trying to attach it.

Elizabeth helped him affix it to the same spot where Joseph had worn it. "You wear it well."

"It's not something…" His voice trailed off. He looked at the badge and ran his fingers over the shiny surface. "It looked good on Pa."

She smiled.

"Being a deputy is one thing, but being a sheriff is a huge responsibility." His eyes met hers. "I never expected this."

"Your Pa always believed in you."

Thomas let out a soft breath. "I'll make him proud."

Elizabeth's lips curled into a broad smile. "I think Agnes will be proud of you, too."

"I'll have to go see her soon. So much has changed since I last saw her."

Elizabeth nodded. "I wish you could have had more time with him."

"I finally got the father I've always wanted." Thomas turned away and wiped his face. "And, now…"

"Perhaps you could come with me to Sacramento? I need to settle Aunt Helen's affairs. You could visit with Agnes, too."

Thomas shook his head. "I can't leave now."

"Getting out of town might do you some good. The time away could clear your head. The town can run itself for a few days. I'm sure the deputies would understand."

Thomas shook his head. "I think one of us should stay here."

"I suppose you're right." Elizabeth glanced away and smiled. "Aunt Helen was a bit of a hoarder. It'll be a challenge, but I'll see what I can do with her house."

"What about Pa's gold mine?"

"You can manage that for him."

"When do you plan to leave?" said Thomas.

"Tomorrow morning."

Thomas blinked, surprised. "That's perfect."

Just after noon, Thomas stepped into the sheriff's office and went to Joseph's desk. As he lowered himself into the chair, he picked up the nameplate. "Sheriff Joseph Pruitt" was ornately carved with elaborate letters. The word "Sheriff" was smaller, almost modest. "Who goes to all the trouble makin' these?" he muttered, then tucked it into the drawer.

He leaned back in his chair and smiled. He stayed there for a while, thinking, planning, and calculating what to do with his newfound power. He chuckled, picked up his hat, and strolled out of the office.

On the porch, he paused and grinned at the sight of two passengers next to the stagecoach. He reached down, patted his holstered gun, and started toward them.

Alexander stood next to the coach, shaking his head at Douglas.

"You've got to go. I can handle the rest myself," said Douglas.

Alexander rolled his eyes. "I don't understand why you don't want me to stay. It's not like you to shoo me off like this."

"Things are a bit unsettled here with Joseph's passing and such. After I conclude the bank business, I'll head home. If something changes, I'll let you know."

"It's Thomas. Isn't it?" Alexander paused. "Thomas is reckless and irrational. I certainly can handle him."

Douglas checked his timepiece. "He's unpredictable and likely to stir up trouble for you. You can come back here once things settle down."

Alexander narrowed his eyes when Thomas walked up.

Thomas smiled. "Running away again with your tail between your legs. Mighty suspicious that you're leaving town again after another murder."

Alexander stepped menacingly close to Thomas and gasped when the glint of light from the sheriff's badge hit his eyes. "You're the sheriff?"

Thomas grinned.

Alexander winced when the driver cleared his throat from above and shouted, "You gonna get in? We're on a timetable here!"

Alexander's eyes darted from Thomas to Douglas. "You knew about this?"

Douglas nodded. "Elizabeth told me this morning."

Alexander grimaced and climbed inside. The driver flung the reins, and the stagecoach left with a jolt.

Douglas turned to leave, eager to end the conversation, but flinched when Thomas tapped his arm.

Thomas said, "Things are about to change in my town."

Douglas's head cocked back, and his jaw slackened. "Joseph and I had an agreement—an understanding."

Thomas smirked. "How long will you be here in my town?"

"Until tomorrow."

Douglas stepped back as Thomas closed in.

"Elizabeth is leaving on the early morning coach to Sacramento. You'd be doing her a big favor if you accompanied her."

"I suppose I could," he said, his blood beginning to boil. "I've been wanting to discuss a matter about the stagecoach robberies."

"Great!" Thomas said, walking away. "You be sure and behave yourself in my town."

Douglas narrowed his eyes at Thomas.

CHAPTER TWENTY-EIGHT
The List

Elizabeth sat at her desk writing in her journal, where she recorded her thoughts and feelings that would someday fill the pages of a novel. It helped her to relax and sometimes make sense of the world around her. She paused and was about to resume writing when her eyes caught sight of Joseph's coat on the chair.

She sighed. As she reached for it, her hand caught on a corner of paper protruding from the pocket. She pulled out the small, folded note and opened it. Her breath caught. It held a list of names.

The names were as follows: John and Charlie; Zack Avery; L. Hamilton; Howard Jackson; A. Klein; Randall Pruitt; Frank Williams; Hank Flagg; Hayes; Will Chance; ... There were fifty in all. Some were circled. "Circled? That must be important," she muttered. She continued to peruse the list as her mind raced to interpret its meaning.

She recognized the names of John and Charlie. Howard Jackson was the drunk whom Joseph helped by giving him a place to live. Randall Pruitt was Joseph's brother.

She grabbed a blank sheet and copied each name in the same order as on Joseph's list. Afterward, she folded the paper and put it into an envelope. On the front of it, she wrote: 'Douglas Holt.'

She pulled her gun and a small pouch from the desk's side drawer. She tipped the pouch, bullets clinking onto the desk. She loaded her six-shooter and then looked out the window at the barn.

Moments later, she walked up to an old, dilapidated wooden table next to the barn. She set her six-shooter down on it and arranged several cans in a row along its edge. She took her weapon a few yards away and pointed it at her targets. The corner of her lips curled up as her gaze fell sharply on the target. She fired and missed. She took in a shallow breath and shook her head. She relaxed her arm and gripped her gun firmly. She aimed at the second can. A bittersweet memory tugged at her, distracting her.

She was a fourteen-year-old girl, and her father was with her as she practiced shooting.

She asked him, "When will I get a chance to shoot at something worth killing instead of these old tin cans?"

He replied, "One day that I hope will never come is when you will have to kill someone. But, if that time comes, you must be proficient at shooting."

The memory floated away as she focused on the remaining targets before her.

She stood, her feet firmly planted on the ground, the gun steady, facing the targets. She aimed and shot the targets one after another; the cans flew in different directions.

Her shooting was precise and deadly. Her father would have been proud. When she fired at the last one, it jerked back and crashed into something with a loud, metallic clank.

Her brows raised as she approached the source of the sound. Long branches and brush were arranged haphazardly. When she cleared much of it away, a wooden door was exposed. She shoved the rest of the dense shrubbery and found a metal rod leaning against a door. The can was lying on the ground at its base.

She pulled the rod away and opened the door. The scent of damp earth greeted her. She peered inside. It was too dark to see much. Without hesitation, she rushed to the barn and returned with a lit lantern.

Thomas sat sipping on a drink at the back table of the saloon. It was Joseph's favorite spot. A commotion came from the bar area where someone was shouting. He went to see what the ruckus was.

"Where's the sheriff?" yelled John Walker to the bartender.

Thomas walked up to John.

"You causing trouble in my town?"

John turned. "Well, if it ain't Thomas Pruitt, or rather, Sheriff Thomas Pruitt. I heard that you took over for your pa." John chuckled. "I used to do some important work with him."

"I know what you did for him. Or should I say – to him?"

"You sure about that?"

"Yeah. I know you or one of your men killed my wife."

John shook his head, chuckling. "I know who killed Rebecca. And it wasn't one of my own."

A muscle twitched in Thomas's jaw.

"I don't believe you. I heard you threatened to kill Elizabeth."

"That ain't true."

"Well then, who bludgeoned Rebecca to death?"

John stared at Thomas for a couple of seconds and blinked.

"I saw a man running from the river with a bloody hand. I walked down partway to get a better look, and there he was running away with a rock in his hand."

Thomas gulped. His breathing was shallow, and his eyes were wide in shock. "Why didn't you tell anyone?"

"I went to tell Joseph, but Elizabeth showed up. Then you came up ridin' with your... wife."

"Was it Alexander Johnson?"

The edge of John's lips trembled slightly.

"It's the fellow who works for that bank owner. Tall guy. Dressed sharply. He left the party in a hurry with a bloody hand."

Thomas shook with rage; his eyes filled with hate, and his pupils sharp with vengeance. His eyes darted from John to the bartender. "Two whiskeys."

In no time, the bartender poured them the two drinks.

Thomas slid one over to John and downed the other in one gulp.

John smiled and took a sip.

"I'm gonna need that gold that Joseph was keeping safe for me," said John. "I left it with him to keep him from double-crossing me. Seeing that he's not a threat anymore..."

Thomas scoffed. "I'll think about it."

John's face grew serious, the smile gone. "Don't think too long." He took a deep breath and let it out all at once, and then marched away.

Thomas chuckled and left for his office. When he walked inside, the two deputies jumped to their feet and stood silent. Thomas nodded and motioned for them to come to his desk. He sank into his chair.

"We've got two murders on our hands—Rebecca's, and now Joseph's," Thomas said, his voice low.

One deputy shifted his weight. "You think the same person killed them both?"

Thomas nodded. "I reckon so. And I've got a solid lead."

"There ain't no one in town that didn't like the sheriff…I mean Joseph. And your wife was the kindest woman I ever saw."

"Alexander Johnson, the bank manager, was here both when my wife was killed and when Joseph was shot."

"He don't seem like the killing type," said the deputy.

Thomas scoffed. "Killing's part of his job working on those stagecoaches!"

"Oh yeah. That's right."

"His hand was all bloody the day my wife was murdered. He left town just after she was killed. I saw him touching her at the river that day. Besides, I got a witness who said Alexander was holding a bloody rock."

The deputy's eyes grew wide. "Next time he's in town, we should bring Alexander in and chat with him," said the deputy.

"That scoundrel got away on the afternoon stagecoach. Just as he did after my wife's murder," said Thomas.

"You want us to ride after the coach and get him back here?"

"Nah, it's too far. I'll get him back here later. I have to go check up on Elizabeth. She ain't doing too well." Thomas turned to leave, a trace of a smirk tugging at his mouth.

Back at the ranch, Elizabeth held the lantern before her as she walked through the entrance she'd discovered. As she turned the corner, a glint of metal caught the light. She stepped closer. Two metal boxes sat side by side. She opened one and gasped. "Gold!"

Her breath hitched as a wave of disbelief washed over her, then anger, as her eyes confirmed what her heart had refused to believe: that her husband had been involved with the stagecoach robbers.

She walked outside and extinguished the lamp. She put the brush and branches back to conceal the entrance. She lined up the cans on the table and went back to her firing perch.

She loaded the gun with more bullets from her pouch and fired at the targets, hitting them one after the other.

Thomas rode up as she set the targets for another round. She stepped back farther than before, widening the distance, sharpening her aim. She shot at the cans, one after the other. Each one spun violently as it flew from the table. Thomas walked up to her. He remembered a time years ago when he visited Martha, and she was target practicing in her backyard. He brushed the memory of Alexander's wife away.

"That's some quality shootin'!"

"Thanks." Elizabeth raised a brow at Thomas. "Did you know about Joseph's secret mine and what he has in there?"

Thomas glanced at the entrance and then back at Elizabeth. "He warned me to stay away from there."

She shook her head. "You knew he was involved with those stagecoach robbers?"

"It's not like that."

Elizabeth stepped back, stunned.

"How could I have been blind to this place? I pass by here almost daily on the way to the barn."

"I only found out about it a few days ago. He asked me to keep my mouth shut. He said people would kill to get their hands on that stuff."

"I thought I knew everything that went on in this town," said Elizabeth.

"He had a talent for keeping secrets. Even from you."

Elizabeth stepped back. Her breath caught. "I don't—"

A shot erupted from the trail beyond the barn. Elizabeth dove behind a rusted trough as the bullet whistled past, close enough to scorch her skin.

Thomas scrambled for his weapon, fingers slipping on the grip.

Still crouched, she loaded rounds into the chamber—each click a stubborn heartbeat amidst the chaos. Her breath matched the rhythm—steady, defiant. Another shot hissed through the dust. She didn't flinch. Her gun snapped up, and she fired blindly toward the rising smoke.

Thomas swung toward the trail and fired. "This is Sheriff Pruitt! Come on out!"

Silence. And then the sound of a horse galloping away.

Elizabeth ran toward the road to see who it might have been. A trail of dust marking the rider's path was all that was left. "Whoever it was must not be interested in you. Why else would he bolt like a coward the moment you called? They're surely gunning for me," she said, her voice low. "And I won't be an easy target."

Thomas, his voice trembling, said, "You're doing the right thing by going to Sacramento."

"Better than moping around here waiting for someone to shoot me."

"I'll send a telegram to the Sacramento sheriff to tell him you'll be there tomorrow. He can look out for you while you're there."

"Thanks. I'll return once I've decided what to do with Aunt Helen's house."

"I spoke with Douglas Holt. He's heading back to Sacramento on the early morning coach."

"Oh?" asked Elizabeth, surprised. She thought about Joseph's list and the envelope she had prepared for Douglas. "I'll be ready."

"Make sure you take your gun," said Thomas.

"I'll take much more than that," she said, gesturing toward another gun, two rifles, and a shotgun nearby.

That evening, Thomas walked up to the counter at the telegraph office. The clerk looked up from his desk and smiled.

"I need to send a telegram for Elizabeth to Alexander Johnson in Sacramento. She says it's urgent."

"Of course. I'm sorry for your loss."

Thomas gave a hollow grin and handed over the note.

The clerk read it aloud, "Spoke with Douglas about the situation. Have vital information to share. Please return immediately." He glanced at Thomas. "I'll transmit it right away."

Thomas nodded and left. He walked into the saloon and scanned the tables. A smile tugged at his mouth when he saw Howard, a haggard, unshaven man, slumped at the corner table. Howard hadn't hit fifty, but looked seventy with his wrinkled, dried-up skin from years of sun and whiskey.

Thomas stopped at the bar. The obliging bartender sauntered over, grinning like a puppy dog expecting a treat.

"Give me a bottle of whiskey and two glasses," said Thomas.

The bartender slipped into his routine of retrieving the beverage, though this time with two glasses instead of the usual one.

Thomas tossed coins onto the counter and grabbed the whiskey and glasses. At Howard's table, he set them down without a word. Howard glanced at him, then at the bottle. Howard's eyes shot open, his mouth agape.

Thomas offered a smile, and his brows bounced up. "How are you doing?"

"I'm mighty thirsty," said Howard, eying the bottle with a grin.

Thomas poured a whiskey and slid the glass over. His brows lifted, then drew together as Howard raised the glass.

Without spilling a drop, Howard drank with reverence, as if it were water from the fountain of youth.

Thomas poured his own and took a sip. "I need your help on something."

"Sure. Anything. How about another drink?" Howard pushed his glass toward Thomas and looked up at him expectantly.

Thomas poured a little less than he had before, slid the glass back to Howard, and put the bottle down.

Howard squinted at the glass, then at Thomas, suspicion flickering behind his eyes. He grabbed the glass and drank it a little quicker than the first.

Thomas continued, "It's about apprehending a criminal."

Howard's brows narrowed, his mouth tightening. "Ain't you got deputies for that?"

"This is a delicate matter. I found the man who killed my wife. He works with the Law, so I want to handle this quietly."

"I see. What do you want with me? I ain't nobody."

"My pa trusted you."

Howard half-smiled, eyes distant. "I miss him. He looked out for me when no one else did."

Thomas leaned in and said, "I trust you, too. There's a bottle of whiskey waiting for you if you help me."

Howard sat up a little taller.

The edge of Thomas's lips curled up, his gaze locked on Howard. "Meet me on the ridge tomorrow afternoon at two o'clock. It's just a mile south of town along the one that overlooks the stagecoach trail."

"I know the place. Blind Man's Ridge. Those stagecoaches can't see anything but the road in front of them."

Thomas nodded. "That's the one. It's the perfect place to stay unseen. And bring a weapon. You might need it."

"I never go outside without my gun. Those damn crows are always out to get me."

Thomas chuckled. "I'll see you at two o'clock sharp."

Howard moved his glass closer to Thomas without uttering a word.

Thomas's lips curled into a smile and poured a little more whiskey for Howard.

Howard grabbed the glass as if it were a promise and said, "Yes, sir!"

CHAPTER TWENTY-NINE

Headed to Sacramento

The next day, Elizabeth was pacing on the hotel porch as the clerk loaded her luggage. Douglas was waiting inside for her. She glanced periodically up the road.

When the clerk finished, he stood by the door, offering his hand to Elizabeth. "Ma'am?"

"Can we wait a few more minutes?" she asked.

The clerk looked up at the driver.

The driver, perched high above, checked his timepiece and said, "We're on a schedule."

Douglas peeked out the window and said, "Elizabeth, we need to go!"

She shook her head, glanced once more down the road, and reluctantly stepped inside. The stagecoach lurched forward on its way to Sacramento.

Inside, Elizabeth turned toward the window as someone outside yelled, "Stop the coach!"

She grabbed the bench as the coach buckled to a stop, and Douglas fell forward.

Elizabeth's face lit up with a broad smile as she rushed out of the stagecoach.

Thomas jumped from his horse and ran toward her. "You didn't think I would let you leave without seeing you off. Did you?"

She hugged Thomas. "I waited as long as I could."

"Sorry about that. I sent a telegram to the Sacramento sheriff about your arrival."

"Elizabeth!" yelled Douglas from the coach.

She glanced at Douglas and then patted Thomas's arm. "You take care of yourself. Okay?"

"Will do," he promised.

She quickly boarded the stagecoach, and the coach lurched

forward. She peeked out the window. Thomas was standing alone, waving slowly. He looked sad and lonely, just as he had when Rebecca died.

Inside the coach, Elizabeth wiped away her tears. Her eyes flicked to Douglas and then looked out the window.

"I know you don't care for Thomas, but he's family. I promised Joseph I'd look after him. The responsibilities of being sheriff are demanding. He needs my help now more than ever."

Douglas's face tightened, and then he glanced at her. He pulled the curtain open and looked outside. "As a child, I used to love watching the countryside flash by from a window like this. Now and again, I imagined a bird would see images streak by, similarly as they flew through the trees."

"You love birds?" she asked.

"Yes. I always have."

"Do you keep them? In a cage, I mean?"

"I don't have the time or the patience. They can be quite demanding."

Elizabeth chuckled. "I do love the little ones. But those big crows are interesting creatures, too. They're intelligent and certain to cause grief if you cross them. Joseph didn't care for them much."

She glanced away. "There were so many crows up in the trees the day Joseph died." She pressed her hand on her stomach to quiet a dull pain.

Douglas shifted in his seat. "I'm sorry you lost your husband."

Elizabeth's brow furrowed at his attempt to console her.

"You didn't like him either," she said, her tone sarcastic.

Douglas frowned. He was about to say something when she suddenly reached into her satchel.

She took out an envelope and handed it to him. "I found a list with names in Joseph's belongings. I believe they are the ones who played a role in robbing the stagecoaches."

Douglas sat up taller. He tore it open and pulled the paper out. "What? I thought they..."

Douglas's voice faded as his eyes scanned the list. His jaw stiffened.

"I found the original list inside Joseph's coat pocket. I copied the names for you on that piece of paper."

Elizabeth glanced away as Douglas read the names aloud: "John and Charlie. Hmm. Avery, Hamilton, Jackson, Klein, Pruitt, Williams." He looked up at Elizabeth. "Pruitt?"

"That's Randall Pruitt, Joseph's brother."

"Oh my," he said. "Do you recognize any of the others?"

"Yes. I believe John is the man who dealt with Joseph. I wonder why Charlie's name is listed. I trust Charlie. He's a hardworking, courteous man." She glanced away. "Joseph treated him poorly. Howard Jackson is harmless. He's a bit off, and he drinks too much."

"There are many names here," said Douglas. He folded the paper and returned it to the envelope. "This list is going to help us catch those lawless men."

"I wish I had chatted with Charlie before I left. Maybe he could shed some light on this list. I want to ask him why his name is on there."

"Maybe it's a different Charlie?"

Elizabeth shook her head. "No. He was arguing with John at Rebecca's party. I'm sure it's him."

"I don't think it would be wise for you to involve yourself any more than you already are," said Douglas.

Her right cheek tightened. "I can take care of myself."

"I'm sure you can."

Elizabeth took a deep breath and exhaled all at once, her shoulders relaxing. "I need to tell you about Joseph's secret mine. It's—"

A booming shot rang out. Bits of wood splintered from the window frame, inches from Elizabeth.

The coach rocked violently.

Douglas's eyes widened, panic blooming across his face. "We must be at Blind Man's Ridge!"

Elizabeth yelled, "Get down!"

He dropped to the floor.

She reached under her seat and drew her weapons. She stowed the small handgun in her dress pocket, pushed the curtains away, and pointed the rifle out the window. She pulled the trigger, and the boom reverberated throughout the cabin.

Douglas shuddered as he crouched on the floor.

The coach abruptly stopped, and Elizabeth fell to the floor.

She recovered and jumped up. "Stay down!"

A wide-eyed Douglas nodded.

Elizabeth opened the door. There was only the silence of an ordinary countryside. The driver was hiding behind the rump of one of the horses.

"Go back inside," he rasped.

She shook her head and stepped out with her rifle pointed before her. Two men were riding toward her, about to shoot at her. A bullet almost hit her, putting a hole in the coach wall. She aimed and shot one of the men dead. The other stopped in his tracks and then raced away.

The man who was cowardly retreating had his face covered with a cloth.

Elizabeth ran to the man lying on the ground and stood over him. She yanked his mask, her brows knitting as she studied his face.

Douglas ran up behind her, his breath ragged. "Who's that?"

"That's Flagg. I recognize him. He had a run-in with Joseph a while back. Joseph ran him out of town, warned him never to show his face around here again."

Douglas, his hand shaking, pulled the list from his pocket. After a second or two, he said, "Hank Flagg."

"Yes. That's him." She glanced down the road where the other shooter rode away. "The man who got away is sure to be on that list, too."

"Those damn stagecoach robbers! Perhaps this list will help rid us of them once and for all." Douglas's fear curdled into rage, his voice low and dangerous. "Yes! Everyone on this list will be dead soon!"

Elizabeth looked with concern at Douglas and said, "Who wants me dead?" She gasped, choking on a gulp of air. "Someone took a shot at me yesterday, too. I could hear it whir past me, too close!"

Douglas's eyes widened with alarm. "What!? Someone shot at you yesterday?"

"Why would anyone be trying to kill me? It makes no sense."

Elizabeth shuddered and looked where the other shooter had gone.

The driver ran up. "We should go back to Auburn and get some help."

Elizabeth shook her head. "No." She turned to Douglas. "We'd be better off continuing to Sacramento. We need to get this list to Sheriff August as soon as possible."

"Agreed," said Douglas.

CHAPTER THIRTY

Stagecoach Ambush

Alexander left home early for work before his family woke up, a habit he was accustomed to. He usually stopped at the bank on his way out of town to check in with Douglas, but not today. Douglas was already in Auburn. He arrived at the hotel and waited on the porch bench for the stagecoach.

In the telegram, Douglas was insistent that he go there immediately. Why did Elizabeth and Douglas want him to return to that perilous town?

He should be spending more time with his wife and children instead of chasing after trouble in Auburn. Douglas must have found out something important. He shifted in his seat as he gazed down the road, his stomach filled with unease. He was fiddling with his six-shooter when the sound of marching horses wafted toward him. He stowed it and jumped to his feet as the coach approached.

He gathered his belongings. It stopped just a few feet from him. He checked the time and smiled, right on schedule. When he stepped inside, he sat down on the front bench. An older couple, George and Victoria Adams, sat across from him. Martha knew them better than he did. He exchanged the usual pleasantries with them as the coach drove off. He pulled his hat down over his face, leaned back, and drifted off to sleep.

The ride to the small town was uneventful.

Alexander woke up when the driver yelled, "Next stop, Auburn in twenty minutes!"

He checked the time and looked at his traveling companions. "It looks like we'll be arriving early."

Victoria nodded.

Alexander drew back the curtain and looked outside.

George said to Alexander, "Fine day we're having."

"Yup," said Alexander as he gazed out the window, trying to avoid any more conversation.

* * *

Frank Williams crouched low, waiting for the stagecoach carrying the man who had killed his father. Perched perilously near the canyon's edge, he narrowed his eyes at the road where the coach would soon appear. Yesterday's long day of drinking took its toll on him.

Barely a minute later, a stagecoach raising a plume of dust came around the bend, slow and steady. He readied himself, rifle in hand.

He wiped the sweat from his brow as the last words his father had spoken to him snapped at him: "Avenge my death. Kill Alexander!"

Frank's rage flared—face hot, breath sharp.

He aimed, waiting for the coach to enter a narrow stretch of road that was barely wide enough for the coach. A deep ravine was on the left side, and a canyon wall on the right.

He steadied his rifle as beads of sweat stung his eyes. Even expert hands faltered under whiskey and rage.

Hatred consumed him. He leveled the rifle and fired. The blast reverberated throughout the canyon.

Although he aimed for the head, the shot hit the driver's chest and knocked him off the stagecoach into the ravine. He grinned as the horses jumped, and the two closest to the gorge lost their footing and dragged the others off the road, pulling the coach over the edge. The horses broke free. A woman screamed as the coach plummeted down.

Frank raced down a small trail to get closer to the careening coach.

Inside the coach, Alexander held on to the door as Victoria screamed. She looked like a rag doll as she tumbled forward. Mr. Adams was holding on to the window and reaching for his wife. As Alexander pushed Victoria into her husband's arms, the door beneath him creaked. His breath caught.

After a loud crack, the door swung open behind him, and Alexander fell out. A low brush, the kind that hugged the canyon walls, broke his fall. He was lucky. He moaned in pain as he tried to stand. His brain went foggy, his head ached, as his eyes caught sight of the coach coming to a stop upright at the bottom of the canyon. Luggage, clothing, and papers were scattered everywhere. He tried to make sense of what he saw, and he couldn't.

Frank crept toward the stagecoach. A woman's moaning came from the still coach. Then a woman screamed, "George! Wake up!"

He held his gun in front of him as he approached. He stopped and peeked inside through the half-open door. He slowly opened the door. The sun, bright behind him, cast a dark shadow over a woman lying on the floor, wiping blood from her eyes.

She looked at him and said, her voice trembling, "My husband is having trouble breathing."

Frank leaned in, predatory and silent.

Victoria's mouth fell open, her eyes wide. "Who are you?" she said.

"Where's Alexander?" he yelled, pointing his gun at her.

She screamed as her head lurched back.

Frank pulled the trigger, silencing her.

Off in the corner, Frank noticed George's eyes flick open and turn to the woman.

Frank, his breath stuck in his throat, stepped back as a wave of dizziness from yesterday's whiskey overtook him.

George leaped up at him and kicked him.

He fell to the ground, turned, and shot. George fell back inside, and the door swung shut, sealing the couple inside.

Frank rose, brushing off dust from his clothes.

"Shoot! I just got these pants."

He climbed up top to get a better view. The air was still as he surveyed the area.

Debris littered the hillside. "Where the hell are you, Alexander?" He'd seen him get on that coach back in Sacramento.

He spotted the bank's lockbox and ran after it.

The sound of fast-approaching horses startled him. He dragged the lockbox away and hid it. His heart racing, he scrambled to his horse.

"Doggone it," he growled, eyes darting for any sign of Alexander. Then he took off, disappearing before the riders crested the hill.

Thomas arrived first at the scene of the stagecoach accident. He gasped when he saw the debris scattered along the side of the canyon.

Howard rode up, his eyes surveying the debris. "Looks like a robbery. Ain't no one going to survive that!"

"Keep an eye out. If there were robbers, they're long gone. I'm going to check it out."

Howard nodded.

Thomas jumped from his horse, grabbed his rifle, and rushed to the stagecoach. The couple inside was dead. With his rifle at the ready, he climbed up top. He looked from one side to the other. "Damnit! Where are you, Alexander?" He grimaced, disappointed, and started back.

Up above, Howard was panicking as he waited for Thomas. He looked over the edge, expecting to see him.

A thrashing sound from behind made him jolt. He stepped back from the ledge and turned. Something was moving toward him through the bushes.

He was cornered.

His breath caught as a man crawled out.

It was Alexander.

"Help me!" Alexander choked out. His face was bleeding, his clothes torn. He climbed to his feet and limped toward Howard.

Howard's jaw dropped.

"Mr. Johnson?"

Howard rushed to Alexander. Before he could reach him, Thomas struck Alexander hard on the back of his head with the butt of his rifle.

Alexander fell to the ground, unconscious.

Howard looked astonished at Thomas. "Why'd you do that?"

Thomas reached down, pulled a six-shooter from Alexander's hand, and showed it to Howard. "He was about to shoot you. There's a dead couple down there."

Howard's jaw dropped.

Thomas went to his horse and stowed Alexander's gun in the

pouch. "Let's get him back to town."

Howard's voice cracked with uncertainty. "Did he kill those people down there?"

"Sure looks like it." Thomas held his rifle pointed at Alexander. "This man will hang for killing those folks down there and robbing the coach."

Howard choked on his breath.

Thomas slid his rifle into its holder by the saddle and then went over to where Alexander was. "Let's get him on your horse."

Howard stood frozen, his eyes filled with worry.

Thomas said, "Aren't you gonna help me?"

Howard rushed over and helped Thomas lift Alexander onto his horse. Alexander was unconscious, slumped forward in the saddle. Howard climbed up behind him, steadying his weight, and waited for Thomas.

"You need to get him to the jail safe and sound. He needs to be fit for his hanging."

"Yes, sir."

Howard nodded and clicked to his horse to go.

Frank crouched behind the brush, watching Thomas stay behind as Howard rode off with Alexander. When he looked back, Thomas was still there, staring down the trail long after the riders had vanished.

Frank grinned. He took his rifle and lined up its bead on Thomas; his finger twitched on the trigger, itching to fire.

"Not yet," he said as he put his rifle down. "You haven't suffered enough."

Then, Thomas retrieved a gun from his saddle and fired two shots into the dirt. Next, he went back to his horse, stowed the weapon, and left.

"What are you up to, Thomas?" he muttered.

He waited for a few minutes until Thomas was gone. He sprang to his feet and hurried to the spot where he'd stashed the lockbox. He tied a rope to the box and dragged it away.

Thomas chuckled as he rode back to his office. "I finally got him," he said. He couldn't have planned a better end for Alexander.

"That fool is going to hang."

When Thomas arrived at the sheriff's office, Howard was standing by his horse, and Alexander was still unconscious. Thomas jumped down and went inside. A minute later, he returned with two deputies.

He pointed at Alexander, slouched forward on Howard's horse, and said, "He's responsible for killing a couple traveling on the inbound stagecoach. Get him locked up and get him a doctor."

"When you're done here, ride over to Blind Man's Ridge and take care of the stagecoach. It's just south of town. It's a mess. Make sure you take a cart. There are two bodies there. I couldn't find the driver, but judging from all the blood at his station, there ain't no way he's alive."

"Okay. We know where that is," said one of the deputies. "We'll stop at the bank. I'm certain one of their men will want to come with us."

"I'll head out there and join you after I have a chance to talk to the prisoner," said Thomas. Once the deputy left, Thomas went inside, where Alexander was lying on his cot in the jail cell.

Alexander sat up. He tried to stand, but then fell back onto his cot. "What happened?"

Thomas strolled up to the cell. "It's about time you woke up. You're locked up tight where you belong, you sorry excuse!"

Alexander stood, limped across to the bars, and locked eyes with Thomas.

"What happened to the stagecoach? Was it robbers?"

Thomas chuckled. "What did you do with the gold on that stagecoach?"

Alexander looked confused at Thomas.

"If you tell me what you did with it, the judge might take pity on you." Thomas laughed. "He'll be here tomorrow."

"But—" Alexander started.

Thomas cut him off. "I've gotta go. Someone will be by later with something to eat. Wouldn't want you starving before you get strung up."

Thomas strutted out of the office and slammed the door behind him.

* * *

Alexander hobbled back to his cot. He was rubbing his leg when he heard the front door open again. This time, it was Howard carrying a tray of food. He slid the food through the narrow opening in the door. Alexander stood once more. This time, he didn't fall back.

"What's happening? Why am I in here?"

Howard looked away. He didn't want to look Alexander in the eye.

"I don't know anything," said Howard, his eyes focused on the ground. "Did you kill that old couple in the stagecoach?"

Alexander shuddered. "What? They're dead?"

He rubbed at his temples and then looked up at Howard.

Howard was staring at him.

Alexander let out a breath. "Of course, I didn't. They were dear friends of my wife."

A grin appeared on Howard's face. "I didn't think so."

Alexander thought for a moment. "Do you know Elizabeth Pruitt?"

"Sure do. She's a mighty fine woman."

"Tell her what's happened. Tell her to come. Okay?"

Howard's gaze fell to the floor and then flicked back to Alexander. After a slight nod, he ran out the door.

Howard froze on the porch. He hadn't had a drink since the night before, and the withdrawal was clawing at him—sweat slicked his brow, thoughts tangled, hands trembling.

His gaze locked on the saloon.

A burn crawled up his throat. The tremor in his fingers worsened. Conscience urged him to turn away.

The horse, just a few feet away, whinnied.

He glanced back at the door.

Blood screamed for whiskey. Guilt screamed louder.

Thomas rode out to the stagecoach crash site and stopped next to the lone deputy there.

The deputy said, "The bank personnel said the lockbox was missing."

"Yeah. I didn't see it when I looked inside. That Alexander

Johnson is a crafty one. He probably hid it. I'll get him to talk. He comes up here, threatens me, and then leaves the next day."

"Mighty suspicious."

Thomas and the deputy walked over to the stagecoach and looked in.

"We took the old couple out of there already. They are messed up. The driver's dead, too."

Thomas shook his head. "I thought Alexander was supposed to protect these stagecoaches."

"Maybe he was working with someone. He couldn't have done this himself."

Thomas looked up at the deputy and nodded. "That makes sense. His accomplice probably shot the driver. And, Alexander killed the couple to keep them silent."

The deputy stepped back, about to walk away, and said, "I'm gonna get some folks to help get the stagecoach back to town. The horses seem okay."

"I'll stay here to see if I can figure out some things."

Thomas watched as the deputy rode away. He half-smiled. He was glad Elizabeth was in Sacramento.

CHAPTER THIRTY-ONE

Chance Encounter

Elizabeth and Douglas arrived in Sacramento later that morning. Sheriff August and his deputy greeted them as the coach stopped in front of the hotel.

Elizabeth's lips curled upward when she stepped out of the coach. "August, it's wonderful to see you."

Sheriff August's face filled with a giant smile. "And you are as beautiful as ever."

Elizabeth brushed his arm and nodded. "It's been far too long."

Douglas walked up and handed Elizabeth's list to the sheriff. "Elizabeth, tell the sheriff about this list and the secret mine."

"Can we talk about it tomorrow? I'm a little tired."

Douglas's smile faded as his eyes swung from Sheriff August to Elizabeth. "Of course."

Sheriff August led her to the cart parked between the coach and the porch. The deputy loaded Elizabeth's baggage. "We brought this cart from your aunt's house."

The deputy stepped toward Elizabeth. "When you're ready, I'd be happy to drive you home."

"That's kind of you," she said. "But, I'm used to handling those reins myself."

"Yes, Ma'am," he said. He looked at the sheriff.

Sheriff August nodded, and the deputy left.

The exchange between the two reminded her how loyal the Auburn deputies were to Joseph.

She smiled when she saw the horse. She walked up and rubbed its face. "This was my aunt's favorite horse, and mine too. He's not fond of pulling a cart."

The horse whinnied and nuzzled his head against her arm.

Douglas turned to Elizabeth. "May I stop by your house on my way home from the bank?"

"Of course. I should be there within the hour. I need to pick up some things at the store. I won't be long."

Sheriff August offered his hand to Elizabeth as she climbed into the cart. "Would you like to join me in the restaurant after you shop?"

"I'm not hungry," said Elizabeth. "I'm anxious to get to Aunt Helen's and see what state the house is in."

Sheriff August nodded. "When we heard you were coming, we made sure that the kitchen was ready for you. We even got you a block of ice for your ice box."

"Thank you. That's very kind of you. We'll talk tomorrow." She took the reins and drove to the general store. When she arrived, she stepped down and stopped next to the horse, patting its face.

"I won't be long. I'll get you an apple."

The horse whinnied. She tied the reins to the hitching post near the entrance.

She approached the store's door, smelling of fresh paint. Sam, the store owner, always kept his store neat. As she pushed the door open, a loud clang rang out from the bell atop the door. She rolled her eyes and grinned as she stepped inside.

The place was enormous and well-stocked. Sam had told her many times before, "If you don't see it on the shelf, I'm sure I can get it for you."

The comforting aroma that caressed her as she entered tickled her nose. There were soaps and sweet, aromatic botanicals right near the entrance. Sam, no doubt, had placed those fragrant things there to entice the women into the store.

Aunt Helen had said, "Sam doesn't care much for perfumes unless a pretty young woman is wearing them." The edge of Elizabeth's lips curled up slightly. Aunt Helen also said, "It's shameful for a married man to resort to such antics."

Elizabeth covered her mouth to stifle a chuckle as she walked past the aromas. Her heart warmed as memories of her aunt drifted in, summoned by the familiar scents that stirred them.

She sauntered to the counter, where Sam was handing a tall, slender woman her change.

"Please come again," said Sam.

Elizabeth gasped when the woman snatched the coins from his hands, wrinkled her nose, and stormed away.

Sam's face soured as the woman left.

Elizabeth cleared her throat. "Hello, Sam."

He jumped. His face softened when he turned to her.

"Elizabeth! What a pleasant surprise."

Elizabeth smiled.

She handed him Joseph's pocket watch. "Could you polish this? The crystal is all scratched up. I tried to do it myself, but only made it worse."

"Certainly." Sam examined the timepiece.

"It keeps perfect time. It was my husband's."

"It's a beauty," Sam said. "It'll take me less than five minutes."

"Wonderful."

"I'm sorry for your loss. Sheriff August told me about his passing. I was sorry to see your aunt go, too," he said. "She was here no more than six days ago. I swear, she looked fine to me. But you never know how good someone's ticker is."

"Thank you. My aunt had a wonderful, long life. I wish I'd been here for her more."

Sam pressed his lips together. "If there's anything I could do, please let me know."

Elizabeth nodded. "I'll be staying at her house for about a week or two."

"Mighty big house. I suppose it's yours now."

"Yes."

A broad smile crept onto his face. "I can help you sell it if you like."

"I'll keep that in mind."

The front entrance bell clanged. Elizabeth winced. She looked at the timepiece in Sam's hand and then at his face.

Sam was nodding, distracted by something behind her.

She followed his gaze. A woman at the front door was looking with narrowed eyes at the bell above the door.

Sam said, "My wife insisted I install that bell. She said it would alert me whenever a customer entered."

Elizabeth said, "It certainly does do that well."

His gaze returned to Elizabeth. "Would you excuse me. I'll be right back." Sam put the watch down on the counter, and he walked away.

"Take your time. I have to shop for a few things." She took the watch back from the counter and held it.

Sam rushed to the front door and stopped next to the woman. "Welcome. May I help you find something?"

The woman glared at him. "No, thank you. I'm looking for someone. I wasn't expecting that monstrosity," she said, pointing at the bell.

Sam closed the door and wrinkled his face as he narrowed his eyes at the ringer.

She grimaced. "It's deafening. Shouldn't you have a smaller one there instead?"

"I'm sorry, it—"

She bristled and brushed past him.

Sam winced as she moved swiftly away, heading toward Elizabeth.

Elizabeth was still at the counter holding the watch.

"That's a beautiful watch," said a woman who stopped next to her.

Elizabeth jumped. "Oh dear, you startled me."

"Pardon me, Mrs. Pruitt. I didn't mean to startle you."

A woman wearing a hat that covered part of her face stood beside her. The hat was worn low, like a man might wear it, obscuring her face and defying the custom for women. She remembered Aunt Helen's words: "A woman's face should be a beautiful centerpiece, and the hat a pleasant backdrop."

"Yes, I'm alright," Elizabeth was annoyed at the interruption, but held a painted smile on her face.

Sam walked up, cast a cursory glance at Charlotte, and then turned to Elizabeth. "May I have the watch, please?"

Elizabeth handed it to him, and then he rushed into the back room.

She turned back to the woman and smiled. "You have me at a disadvantage."

"My name is Charlotte."

"A pleasure to meet you, Charlotte." As Charlotte spoke, Elizabeth felt herself ease. Her voice carried a warm, familiar comfort.

"I feel like I know you already. I used to enjoy reading your articles in the newspaper when you lived here. Are you going to start writing them again?"

"Oh, heavens, no. I gave that up when I married and moved away," said Elizabeth.

"Most people didn't know a woman wrote that column."

A memory of the frustration she experienced working for the newspaper when they hid her identity behind the name "E. Roberts" because their readers had certain expectations. "I'm sorry to say, but it's true."

Charlotte said, "It's a man's world. Women are second-class citizens."

Elizabeth straightened, her head cocked back in surprise to find someone who shared her beliefs. "You'd think that today, people would give women the same opportunities men enjoy. We can't even vote."

Charlotte's head cocked back and nodded rapidly. "Yes! I agree. Can you imagine what women could accomplish if we were in charge?"

Elizabeth laughed. "You are delightful."

Charlotte rifled through her purse. "I almost forgot. Would you mind autographing my journal? It's a collection of your columns." She exhaled loudly and shook her head, her eyes shifting to Elizabeth. "I must have left it back at the hotel. I could get it right now. It won't take me long."

Charlotte removed her hat and used it to fan her face.

Elizabeth's eyes widened as Charlotte's eyes peered back at her. It was as if she were looking into Rebecca's eyes. The resemblance was remarkable.

Elizabeth stood silent, staring.

Charlotte stopped fanning herself. "Are you okay?"

Elizabeth nodded slowly and reached for Charlotte's arm. "It's just... your eyes are beautiful. They remind me of someone."

"Oh," said Charlotte, not smiling. "Who?"

Elizabeth gasped as she struggled to hide the feelings of loss she still held for her departed friend. She looked away and then turned back. "She passed away."

Charlotte's head tilted, her brows raised.

Elizabeth inhaled and let it out all at once. "Perhaps you could come to my home later today, and I'll be happy to sign your journal with an ink pen."

"That would be wonderful. I can be there at three, if that works for you."

Elizabeth smiled. "That's perfect. I'll be on the porch, and we can have afternoon tea. It'll be comforting to share the hour with you." Indeed, Douglas would be gone by then, she thought.

"Are you sure?" asked Charlotte.

"Yes, of course. Let me give you directions to my Aunt Helen's house." Elizabeth pulled a piece of paper from the counter and started writing.

"I know where that house is. That's where you used to live. Right?"

Elizabeth stopped writing, her hand frozen. She looked up, puzzled at Charlotte. "Yes."

Charlotte grinned. "You're a celebrity here. There are not many column writers in this town. I am one of your biggest fans here. You are an incredibly brilliant and gifted writer."

Elizabeth enjoyed the compliment. "Thank you, darling. That's nice of you to say. I'm looking forward to our afternoon tea party," she said as she glanced at the door.

Charlotte nodded.

Elizabeth thought again about her closest and dearest friend, Rebecca. Perhaps Charlotte was a cousin or a distant relative. Elizabeth was tempted to ask her about Rebecca, but decided against it. Maybe it was inappropriate since she had just met her. She could ask her when they were alone.

"It was a pleasure to meet you. I've got to get home."

"Mighty pleased chatting with you. I'm looking forward to seeing you later," said Charlotte.

"Me too."

Charlotte smiled and then sauntered over to the scented soaps. Elizabeth's gaze lingered on Charlotte as thoughts of Rebecca swirled in her head.

Elizabeth went to the fabrics. She and Aunt Helen always examined the types of fancy patterns available because, back in Auburn, there wasn't much variety. Sam motioned to her from the counter.

As she walked up, Sam held a broad grin as he handed her Joseph's watch.

Her mouth fell open as a quiet gasp escaped her lips.

The crystal was clear and bright. "It looks new."

"All it took was some superfine grit polish and a thorough buffing."

"Thank you. Joseph would have been pleased."

Sam smiled. "Anything else?"

"I need some writing paper, black ink, coffee, and bread."

"Sure thing." Sam collected the items into two boxes and then tallied the charges.

Charlotte marched up to the counter and hummed a delicate tune as she waited for Elizabeth to pay.

Elizabeth turned to Charlotte. "That sounds familiar."

"It's from a song my mother used to lull me to sleep when I was a baby."

Charlotte placed two small aromatic soaps on the counter and winked at Sam.

Sam smiled, and his cheeks blushed.

Elizabeth chuckled as Sam seemed to melt in front of Charlotte.

He said to Charlotte, "Ma'am, today is your lucky day. Buy one, and the second one is free."

Charlotte nodded as her eyes seemed to be studying Sam's face. "You are adorable." She handed Sam a few cents.

Elizabeth raised an eyebrow at the peculiar exchange.

Charlotte giggled and turned to Elizabeth. "It's so sweet to meet you, Elizabeth."

"The pleasure was all mine."

Charlotte chuckled. "Why, thank you."

"I'll see you at three," said Elizabeth as she picked up a box from the counter and was about to stack the second on top.

"Here, let me help you with that."

Elizabeth turned back to Charlotte.

"Thank you, you are very kind."

Elizabeth and Charlotte walked to the exit. Charlotte hesitated and looked up before opening the door. She looked at Elizabeth and chuckled.

"That bell is about to accost us," said Charlotte as she pulled the door hard.

The clang reverberated throughout the store.

"After you," said Charlotte.

Elizabeth laughed. "It's louder on the way out."

Elizabeth led Charlotte to her cart and placed the box into the back. She turned to Charlotte, whose face held a wide grin. "I can take that."

"Please, let me," Charlotte said, placing the second box beside the first.

"Thank you again," said Elizabeth. She climbed up to the seat and took the reins in her hands.

Charlotte stood on the porch, smiling at Elizabeth. A tinge of hope warmed her heart. It may have been better to ask her for the money outright.

"I'll see you soon," said Elizabeth as she flicked the reins and left for Aunt Helen's place.

"Have a safe trip," shouted Charlotte, smiling and waving until Elizabeth was far away. As Elizabeth's cart disappeared behind a trail of dust, Charlotte lowered her arm.

She strolled over to where John Walker waited. "She's not as bad as I thought."

John chuckled.

Charlotte kissed his cheek. "She's on her way to her aunt's house. I told her I'd be there at three."

CHAPTER THIRTY-TWO

Aunt Helen's House

Elizabeth pulled away from the store in her wagon. She was curious about Charlotte, who bore a striking resemblance to Rebecca. She smiled and nodded softly. "What a lovely woman."

The horse slowed as it approached the sheriff's office. She didn't notice, absorbed in her thoughts. Why did Joseph's life spiral out of control? Maybe he would still be alive if he hadn't kept so much from her—the list, the lockboxes, the hidden spot near the barn. Tears brimmed in her eyes.

"Elizabeth!" Sheriff August waved excitedly from the restaurant porch, too far to see her tears.

She regained her composure. "See you tomorrow," she yelled, flicking the reins. Not here. Not now.

Once she was a distance away, more thoughts distracted her.

The horse whinnied again, slowing down in front of the turnoff leading to Aunt Helen's house. "Oh dear. Thank you. I'm glad you know the way home."

As the wagon crested the hill, the house came into full view. She loved how the house sat back on the property. Off to the side stood the barn, and beyond that, the creek ran quietly through the trees.

Before marrying Joseph, she lived in this house and spent most of her time with her best friend, Rebecca, and her Aunt Helen.

The thought of Rebecca triggered a memory. Maybe Thomas was right about Rebecca being murdered. After seeing Joseph's list, only one man could have murdered her, she thought.

The cart stood motionless in front of Elizabeth's new house. The horse whinnied, snapping her out of her memories. She shook her head, forcing herself back to the task at hand.

She stepped down from the wagon and tied the horse next to the water trough, the reins taut against the hitching post. A soft breeze stirred as she rounded to the back and caught a whiff of a floral scent.

"Oh, my!" Charlotte's aromatic bundle was tucked between the boxes.

"I'd better make sure I get that back to her," she murmured.

She took the items to the porch. The horse turned, his mouth dripping.

"Let's get something to eat."

She led the horse into the barn and emerged a few minutes later, smiling. The gurgling water from the creek triggered a memory of when she and Rebecca would sit there, talking for hours.

Rebecca was ecstatic when she married Thomas. Elizabeth sighed. She'd still be alive if she and Thomas had stayed here in Sacramento.

Elizabeth cried softly as she walked into the house, carrying her belongings. The scent of Aunt Helen's favorite perfume greeted her. A barrage of memories warmed her heart. She exhaled loudly as they played tug-of-war within her. She smiled as she went from room to room. She put the clothes she'd brought into the bedroom, locked Joseph's list in the desk there, and stowed her gun in the desk by the kitchen.

She walked into a spotless kitchen. No doubt, Aunt Helen's friends had cleaned it. She sat at the table as her gaze darted around the room. Soon, the memories of her life with Joseph, Rebecca, and Aunt Helen, and their deaths came rushing at her. The memories were relentless, and the tears came without resistance. She buried her face in her hands and cried.

The tears liberated her from her pent-up grief. She put on her aunt's apron and prepared a modest lunch. She savored the fresh eggs from the henhouse and the bread she'd bought. A calmness washed over her. Everything was going to be all right, just as Rebecca preached to her when things weren't going well. The clock chimed. Douglas would arrive soon. She tidied up the kitchen and glanced out the front window—no sign of him.

She smiled, the fine lines around her eyes betraying the sorrow still clinging to her. She had known sadness before, but joy had always carried her through.

Elizabeth walked into the parlor and surveyed the room. It was neat and orderly. She swiped her fingers along the table that held Aunt Helen's favorite lamp. There was not a speck of dust.

The sound of something resembling horses' hooves wafted into the house. "Douglas," she said, and then peeked out the front door. Nope. She went into the kitchen and made lemonade. She checked the icebox for ice and found more than enough. As she poured the sugar, she thought about Thomas. He lost both the love of his life and his father.

"So much loss," she muttered.

Joseph told her after her first husband died, "Nothing brings a family together more than a tragedy does." She'd written that in her journal.

She loved those times when Joseph shared stories from his life. She had notebooks filled with them. Now and then, he would utter some pearl of wisdom or saying, like: "Family takes care of family." He had told her that it was something his brother often muttered. Joseph's favorite was: "There's always a sliver of good in people. Even the worst of them."

She glanced at the parlor clock, which had stood like a sentinel for as long as she could remember. It was a quarter past one.

She hung her apron where she had found it (a hook above the kitchen sink). She pulled Joseph's watch from her pocket. She grabbed her keys, which were next to Joseph's gun in the desk drawer outside the kitchen.

When she went into the bedroom, the curtains were gently swaying in the breeze. That's odd, she thought. She didn't like to sleep with the window open. Too easy for someone to find their way in. She pushed the curtain aside and looked outside. Douglas was rounding the corner and heading her way. She shut the window. She unlocked the center drawer, placed the freshly polished watch beside Joseph's list, and secured it.

She took one last look around and went to the porch to greet Douglas.

CHAPTER THIRTY-THREE

Unwelcomed Guest

Elizabeth was on the porch as Douglas approached her house. He stopped a few feet from her next to the trough.

"Welcome," she said.

Douglas secured his horse to the post and patted its cheek. "I'll get you a treat."

The horse's gaze swung toward him.

He pulled an apple from his pocket, cut it into quarters, and gave one to his horse. He put the rest of them on the edge of the porch within easy reach of his animal.

Elizabeth remembered Joseph doing the same.

"Did you find everything okay?" he asked.

"Yes. It brought back beautiful, heart-filled memories." She held the door open. "Please come inside."

"It's a beautiful house," he said as he entered. "My wife sends her regards. She hopes to meet you while you are in town. I'm sure you two would have many things in common."

"Perhaps, once I'm settled, you two could come over for some tea and cake."

"Her name is Mary. I thought you might have met her before when you lived here. Mrs. Mary Holt."

"I do remember a Mary McDonnell from years ago."

Douglas smiled. "Yes! That's her."

"It's been years since I last saw her."

"She's a loving woman and quite patient with me," he chuckled. "Although she says I travel too much."

His face grew serious. "I wanted to ask you more about the 'secret' mine," he said. "You didn't tell me what you plan to do with its contents." He paused. "Perhaps return it to the bank?"

Her eyes darted away. "I hadn't thought about it." Her gaze flicked back to Douglas. "Maybe some of that gold in there could fund additional stagecoach protection."

A huge smile filled Douglas's face. "That's a marvelous idea. I hadn't thought of that. Turning that ill-gotten treasure into something worthwhile. I'm sure the rightful owners would have no problem investing in that."

She continued, "Of course, I'll also contribute some of Joseph's wealth to help with that."

The edge of his lips curled upward.

"Alexander, Sheriff August, and I will put together the right men. With your funding and that gold, we can make that happen."

"Yes. That would be great."

"Perhaps we can meet tomorrow with Sheriff August to discuss the details," said Douglas.

"That sounds like a wonderful idea."

"Well, I'd better get home. You be sure—"

The sound of heavy footsteps came from the hallway.

Dread filled Elizabeth's heart as her eyes darted toward the sound.

A short man crept out of the shadows of the hallway, pointing a gun at Elizabeth and Douglas. The man had dark brown, almost black hair and a well-groomed mustache.

"Sorry to intrude," said John.

Elizabeth's breath choked in her throat.

Douglas gasped loudly. "What the hell?"

"Mrs. Pruitt," said John.

John smiled and glanced over his shoulder while keeping his gun on Elizabeth and said, "Come on out, Charlie."

A tall, thin man walked up from behind John. Charlie took his hat off, revealing a large bald spot on the top of his head, surrounded by tufts of hair pointing in all directions. His face was rough with a prickly smattering of whiskers. He glanced at Douglas and then turned to Elizabeth, smiling. "Hello, Mrs. Pruitt."

Elizabeth, her brows narrow, held disappointment in her eyes. "Charlie? What are you doing?"

"I came to make sure he doesn't hurt you," said Charlie. "That's the only reason I'm here."

John rolled his eyes. "No one is going to get hurt." He exhaled sharply. "Why don't you introduce us to your friend?"

Elizabeth's gaze flicked past Douglas and landed, barbed with contempt, on John. "I was hoping you were dead by now."

John didn't flinch; he chuckled instead.

"Who are you?" Douglas said, his voice cracking.

Elizabeth pointed at John and then grimaced. "John led the men who robbed your stagecoaches. Charlie is Rebecca's brother. And..." she paused. "John here killed Rebecca."

Douglas stepped back, closer to Elizabeth.

Charlie blinked and turned to John. "You told me that wasn't you—"

John cleared his throat and glared at Charlie. "That ain't true. I didn't kill her. I would never hurt her."

The edge of John's lip curled up. "What's your wife's name, Mr. Holt? Mary? I think that's what she said."

Douglas shook his head and took a step toward John. "How do you know that?"

Elizabeth's gaze shifted between Douglas and John as she crept backward toward the desk that held her gun.

John held a devilish grin and said, "We have men waiting in Auburn. No one gets hurt if you give us what rightly belongs to us."

Douglas's voice trembled as he said, "If you dare harm my wife..."

Elizabeth reached into the drawer behind her, unnoticed.

"Mrs. Pruitt!" John yelled.

Elizabeth froze. She assumed she'd been caught going after her gun.

John, his voice steady, said, "All you have to do is tell us where Joseph hid our gold. I know it's on your property. You wouldn't want us to tear up your place searching for it."

Charlie said, "Gold? What gold?"

Elizabeth's eyes sharpened at John. "None of that ill-gotten bounty is yours."

Charlie said to Elizabeth, "We came here to ask you for some money. I don't know anything about any gold."

John said, "Shut up." He turned to Elizabeth. "I paid a visit to Thomas."

Elizabeth flinched. "Did you hurt him?"

John snickered, "No! Of course not."

Charlie pulled away from John. "I told John I'd come with him to ask you for that money so his group could head back East. With that generous heart of yours, I knew you'd help him. But I didn't know anything about any gold." He turned to John. "Is that why you got men waiting in Auburn?"

Elizabeth gasped.

John yelled at Charlie, "You stupid fool. What the hell are you doing? Shut up!"

Charlie stepped back and holstered his six-shooter. He narrowed his eyes at John. "Don't call me stupid! Let's go. You tricked me. I don't take kindly to being used. It's over."

John's eyes widened. "Damn it! Are you crazy?"

John, his face flushed with anger, glared at Elizabeth and aimed his gun at her. "Joseph was keeping the gold safe for me. It's mine!"

Elizabeth, her eyes filled with fire, said, "So that's it. You gave him that gold so he would keep his mouth shut. You knew he couldn't rid himself of you as long as he had that ill-gotten bounty."

Charlie jerked towards John. "Is that true? Those men of yours were struggling to make ends meet. You could have used that wealth and disappeared with your men weeks back. You didn't want Elizabeth's help. You were after the gold from the start."

She spotted beads of sweat rolling down John's forehead. He seemed to be losing control.

John's face creased. "Joseph needed to keep his trap shut just a few days longer. I was going to take it off his hands and leave him free. I liked him. How was I to know he was going to go off and get killed?"

Charlie shook his head at John. "You lied to me."

John's eyes flared, and he shoved him hard. "Shut up!"

Charlie lunged at him. John's gun fell to the floor, and Elizabeth fired.

John fell, knocking Aunt Helen's favorite lamp to the floor. Charlie froze.

Elizabeth stared through the smoke, her breathing hard and short.

Charlie turned to Elizabeth in shock.

Douglas grabbed John's gun and pointed it at Charlie.

Charlie, his face void of emotion, knelt next to John. He picked up John's limp hand and patted it.

Douglas stepped back and shouted at Charlie, "Slide your gun over here!"

Charlie's gaze rose to him, then slid the weapon over.

Douglas kept his gun on Charlie as he grabbed the gun.

Still holding John's hand, Charlie's gaze drifted from John to Elizabeth. "Sorry, Mrs. Pruitt. I thought he was going to ask you for some money. John threatened to kill you if I didn't go along with him. He knows I like you."

Elizabeth lowered her gun to her side. "He tricked you."

Douglas's breath choked in his throat. He kept his gun pointed at Charlie.

Elizabeth walked over and put her hand on Charlie's shoulder.

He winced. His gaze rose and caught Elizabeth's.

She felt sorry for him. When she saw him coming up the hallway, she was almost glad to see him. He was always polite and respectful to her. He was thoughtful and hard-working. She admired those qualities in him.

Charlie let John's hand rest on his blood-splattered chest.

Elizabeth gasped when John's hand slid limply to the floor.

Douglas waved the gun at Charlie, "What about my wife? Is she safe?"

Charlie turned to Douglas. "She's safe. We didn't know anything about her until we heard you say her name a few minutes ago." He turned to Elizabeth. "He has two men at the telegraph office in Auburn waiting to hear from him. Now I understand why."

"Then what?" asked Elizabeth.

Charlie's gaze fell back to John. "I guess they'd head to your place and get the gold," he said. "Why didn't he tell me about the gold?"

"How many men did John have?" said Douglas.

"At least forty. I'm not sure exactly." He glanced at Elizabeth. "He used to have more."

Charlie shook his head at John, "Sorry, John. We never should have come here. I should have known you were up to something."

Elizabeth stepped toward Charlie.

"Were you two close? I know what it's like to lose someone you care about."

Charlie shrugged. "His wife ain't gonna like this."

Elizabeth's jaw dropped. "He has a wife?"

"Yeah. He was my brother-in-law."

Elizabeth gasped.

Charlie rose to his feet.

Douglas stepped back, his gun pointed squarely at Charlie.

Elizabeth shot a disapproving glance at Douglas.

Charlie held his hands up. "I'm not armed. There's nothing I can do."

Elizabeth stowed her weapon in her pocket.

"Both of you go sit at the kitchen table. I'll get you something to drink, and we can all calm down."

Douglas frowned. "I won't put this gun down."

Elizabeth pointed to the chair that faced away from John's body. "Charlie, you sit there."

Charlie glanced over his shoulder at John and then sat down.

Douglas nodded and then glanced down at John's face. "He smells of death. He looks as if he's going to rise from the dead and shoot us." Douglas half-smiled and then grimaced.

"Douglas!" said Elizabeth.

His eyes shot to her. "Forgive me."

He walked into the kitchen and sat across from Charlie.

Elizabeth stood between them, watching both with quiet dread. John had forty men waiting. The local authorities couldn't handle a crew that large. But Charlie, a familiar face with knowledge of their tactics, could. It was the fastest, perhaps the only, way to turn John's threat into the town's protection.

"Douglas, you're going to need some men to care for the safety of your stagecoaches, aren't you?" asked Elizabeth. "Charlie has the men you need."

Douglas laughed. "You can't be serious?"

Charlie leaned forward.

Elizabeth put two glasses on the table. She poured lemonade into each. She gave one to Douglas and the other to Charlie.

"It's not that cold," said Elizabeth.

Charlie took a sip. "It's delicious. Thank you, ma'am."

"Okay, let's hear it," said Douglas after taking a drink.

"Charlie, can you organize John's men to protect the stagecoaches?" asked Elizabeth. "You said they'd expect you to lead them."

Charlie took a deep breath and glanced back at John for an instant. "I'm a ranch hand, not someone who leads a band of criminals."

"You know them, don't you? It sounds like they know you," said Elizabeth.

Charlie straightened up and shook his head. "I know them all. I'm certain they'll listen to me," said Charlie. "Most of them barely have enough to live on from John. I guess that's why he wanted that gold. Some of them have a wife."

Charlie's gaze darted away.

"But these are thieves, robbers, and murderers," said Douglas.

Charlie sat up taller. "They're not killers."

Elizabeth winced. She knew that wasn't true. "Douglas, you'll need men with grit. Some might be convinced to come over to the right side of the law. You and Alexander can pay them to protect the stagecoach lines."

"Mr. Johnson is a fine man," said Charlie. "I did some work for him when he first moved here."

Douglas stared at Charlie for a few seconds.

Charlie shifted in his chair. "What?" Charlie asked as a bead of sweat rolled into his eye.

"Is that something you could do? Or that you would want to do?" snarled Douglas.

Charlie wiped his forehead with his sleeve. "To earn an honest living? Yes! I have spent years working as a handyman, doing legitimate work," said Charlie. "I know those men are tired of running and hiding from the law. That's why they were headed east – going to start over with some help from you."

Elizabeth poured more lemonade, her hand steady as she filled the glasses and took the last for herself. She caught sight of the parlor floor. Blood, thick and dark, was pooling beneath John's body.

She drank her lemonade, set her glass down, and reached for a bundle of rags.

"I'll leave you two to iron out the details. I'll be right back with Sheriff August. He'll know how to handle this mess," she said, her voice clear.

Charlie flinched. "I'm sorry. I thought—"

"Don't worry, Charlie." Her tone softened. "You'll be okay. Sheriff August is a trusted friend. You and he will work together to keep the stagecoach lines safe. We'll explain it all to him."

Charlie exhaled, his breath evening out as his pulse calmed.

Elizabeth tossed the rags into the pool of blood.

She shut the doors to the back rooms and cracked open the windows, letting fresh air into the parlor.

John lay still. His body gave no trouble now, but he brought a storm of trouble she couldn't ignore. Tragedy had come for her again, and now she was cleaning up the mess.

She stared at Douglas, glassy-eyed, the pain momentarily slipping away.

"You okay?" Douglas asked.

Elizabeth blinked out of her haze. "Yes." She brushed a tear from her cheek. "Everything is going to be okay."

Charlie cleared his throat. "Mrs. Pruitt... would you like us to move John outside? It's getting a little smelly in here."

"That would be great. There's a cart in the barn."

"We'll take care of it," said Douglas.

"Thank you. Thank you both."

As she stepped toward the door, she felt it. Her strength was beginning to fray.

"I'll be back soon."

CHAPTER THIRTY-FOUR

Something Terrible Happened

Elizabeth stepped out onto the porch, where the fresh air welcomed her, a respite from the smell of death and two sweaty men.

Douglas's horse stood quietly, eyes on the front door, waiting for Douglas.

"Good boy," she said as she continued to the barn.

It flicked its head, eyes steady on the door.

Elizabeth glanced back at him. "You're a magnificent creature."

Joseph once told her, "They embody strength, endurance, and power as they carry a rider back and forth." She envied those traits that came so naturally to them.

She bore the world's weight on her shoulders as she entered the barn. Just when everything got settled, life came crashing down again. Weakness crept into her legs.

A tear rolled down her face. "It's not fair!"

Her horse's gaze darted toward her as she walked up.

"Sorry, I didn't mean to startle you." She wiped her cheek and cleared her throat. "I've got to be strong."

He let out a soft nicker. It nuzzled her arm.

"I love you, too."

She hitched him to her buggy.

"We have to get to Sheriff August."

It dropped its head, submitting to the reins.

Soon after, Elizabeth was on her way.

She enjoyed driving her aunt's buggy. The fresh air hitting her face and the scenery flowing smoothly beside her felt rejuvenating. A sense of calmness settled over her. Her tears dried quickly. She flicked the reins. A rush of freedom washed over her as the horse galloped faster.

Within minutes, she was outside his office, barely two miles from the house. She stepped down, pulled the straps around the hitching post, and gently patted her horse's head.

It whinnied.

She climbed onto the porch and almost tripped on a loose plank. Someone could trip and fall, she thought.

She rushed inside. The deputy, who was sitting and reading a paper, jumped.

Her face was creased with worry.

"Hello, Mrs. Pruitt. Is everything okay?"

Elizabeth's eyes flicked to the empty chair at the sheriff's desk and then to the deputy. She was tempted to tell the deputy about the dead body lying on her parlor floor, but decided against it. "Yes."

He rose to his feet. "Great," he said hesitantly.

"Where's Sheriff August?"

"He's likely having lunch in the restaurant."

She nodded and walked swiftly to the door, and then glanced back. "You've got a loose plank on the porch."

The deputy chuckled. "Yeah. That happened today. It's getting repaired tomorrow."

She half-smiled and then left before he could explain why the plank was loose. He liked to talk.

Rushing to the restaurant across the street, she stopped at the large picture window and saw her reflection. Her hair was disheveled, and her dress was rumpled and dusty from the ride. She fixed her hair, straightened her dress, and brushed the dust off her clothes.

When everything was in place, she went inside. Before the woman behind the counter could help her, Elizabeth saw the sheriff seated at a secluded table at the back of the restaurant.

She rushed over to him. "August, I need your help!"

He looked up, surprised. "What's wrong?"

"Something terrible has happened." Her voice was strained.

August set his fork down and pulled out a chair for her. She glanced at him and noticed him nod and smile at someone behind her.

"Elizabeth, what is it?" he asked, returning to his seat.

"A dead man is lying on the floor of my parlor."

"What?" he said, his voice raised. He jumped to his feet, nearly knocking his chair over.

Fifteen minutes earlier, Charlotte stood outside the restaurant, peering through the picture window and searching for the sheriff. He was sitting alone. She noticed an isolated table next to the sheriff's, separated by a gaudy four-foot partition.

"Perfect," she muttered.

She walked into the restaurant. A woman from behind the counter smiled at her.

"Can I sit at that table?" asked Charlotte, pointing to the one closest to the sheriff's.

"Certainly."

The woman followed Charlotte to the table.

Most of the other patrons were seated toward the front of the restaurant. She smiled at the woman and took a seat. The woman took her order and headed to the kitchen.

Charlotte leaned back and made herself comfortable. She faced the partition of crisscrossing wooden slats that separated her from the sheriff. Slivers of his face peeked through the gaps between the slats. A minute later, a woman walked by with a plate of food and paused on the other side of the partition.

"Thank you," said Sheriff August.

"My pleasure," said the woman.

The woman returned to the kitchen.

Charlotte's stomach growled. She rubbed her middle, feeling relieved that Sheriff August had decided to get something to eat. This way, she could have lunch while keeping an eye on him. She straightened, smiling as the woman set her plate of chicken and vegetables before her. It was steaming, and the gently spiced aroma wafted toward her. With her fork in hand, she cut into the tender meat and took a bite. The flavor melted in her mouth, and a sense of calm washed over her.

Thoughts of her husband floated into her mind. "Meet me at the hotel at two-thirty," he told her. There was plenty of time to pay Elizabeth a quick visit afterward.

Charlotte smiled as she remembered her first meeting with John. At the time, she was nearly fourteen. He embodied everything she wanted in life: independence, excitement, and true love. His boyish charm was captivating. She dreamed of running away with him someday.

Her mother disapproved of him. "He's making you into a tomboy," she had said. "A proper young lady should be wearing fancy dresses instead of those disgusting pants." Her mother was a beautiful, elegant, and charming woman who worried Charlotte might end up a lonely spinster.

Her father, the town's sheriff, on the other hand, was proud of the woman she was becoming. He taught her respect, how to handle a gun, and how to stand up for herself. Her father beamed with pride when his daughter single-handedly protected her mother from a robber. Charlotte had beaten the misguided young delinquent. She was fourteen at the time.

Charlotte smiled at the memory and took another bite of her chicken.

Her life with John was truly exciting. He was a short, thin, highly reactive man who dressed perfectly. He was careful with his money and sometimes bought her a fashionable dress. She enjoyed dressing up for him in those lovely clothes. Her favorite outfits were more masculine, as they were better for riding a horse.

She looked at the clock adorning the restaurant entrance. She and her husband would be leaving town in a few hours. Two years after her mother passed away, John proposed, and he whisked her away to the life she had always dreamed of. That marked the moment her passion for life ignited. She loved the excitement (and the mischief) her husband often got into.

Charlotte snapped out of her trance as the tempting aroma of chicken called to her. She took another bite of the tender meat. She closed her eyes with pleasure as she savored the flavor. Her eyes flicked open when a woman's voice spoke from behind the partition. Sheriff August's head appeared over the barrier and locked eyes with hers. She tried to smile, but her mouth was full of food, so she covered it. With a nod and a smile, he disappeared behind the partition.

It was Elizabeth Pruitt. Charlotte's face flushed crimson. Elizabeth was supposed to be at home.

Charlotte moved closer to the partition to hear their conversation. She took a drink and listened.

"What? Are you okay?" Sheriff August asked, his voice cracking with incredulity.

Charlotte jumped.

"As you can see, I'm fine," said Elizabeth with a snap, her voice raised.

He took a deep breath and let it out slowly. "Who is it?"

"He was a man who led the stagecoach robbers."

Charlotte gasped and lowered her glass to the table.

"He surprised Douglas and me. Charlie was with him."

"Where's Douglas? Is he…"

"He's fine and has everything under control at the house."

"That's good. Then what happened?"

"Well, Douglas was getting ready to leave when John came out of the hallway, pointing a gun at us. He demanded I give him the location of Joseph's secret mine that held the gold."

Sheriff August grimaced. "Secret mine? Gold?"

"Yes. Joseph had two bank lockboxes full of gold in a mine near the house in Auburn. John wanted to know where it was so he could take it."

"Who is lying dead in your parlor?"

Charlotte's eyes moistened. Dread filled her heart.

"John Walker," said Elizabeth. "I shot him!"

Charlotte's breath caught in her throat, and her fork fell from her hand. It clanged against the plate. Her eyes reddened, and a tear slowly rolled down her cheek. She pulled a kerchief from her pocket and wiped her eyes. She shook her head, and her gaze dropped. She picked up her fork and stabbed at her food.

"I had a friend named Rebecca," Elizabeth continued.

Charlotte blinked, her eyes sharpened.

"Yes," said Sheriff August. "I remember Rebecca when she lived here."

"I loved Rebecca. She was the sister I never had. I'm certain John Walker killed her. The last time I saw him was the day Rebecca died."

Charlotte slammed her fork down on the table. The sound echoed loudly. She had wondered why John was so eager to leave that small town. But she refused to believe her husband would kill Rebecca, even though he disliked her.

Sheriff August's narrowed eyes aimed at her through the slats. "We'd better go."

"It's my fault," Elizabeth said, remaining seated.

"Let's go!" He stood.

She continued, "Wait. I have to tell you the rest."

He settled back into his seat. "What else?"

"I've asked Charlie and his men to work with Douglas and Alexander to protect the stagecoach lines."

"What? You can't trust someone who came into your home with guns blazing, probably ready and willing to kill you," he said, his voice laced with skepticism. "They were there for the gold."

"Charlie claimed they wanted money to help them move on. I would have been happy to give it to them, especially if it meant getting rid of that awful man, John Walker," said Elizabeth. "But then John demanded I turn over the gold in Joseph's mine. Charlie didn't know anything about that."

Charlotte's fist hit the table. "What gold?" she whispered.

After a brief silence, the sheriff spoke in a hushed voice. "Elizabeth, let's go. I'll bring the deputies."

When Elizabeth stood, Charlotte leaned down.

Elizabeth and the sheriff rushed away, neither noticing Charlotte.

Charlotte peeked out. Elizabeth and Sheriff August were walking out the door. She left some coins and followed them. She stepped onto the porch. Outside the sheriff's office, the pair stood together, his hand in hers.

Charlotte stood rigid, her hands clenched. The shock of grief gave way to cold fury. She watched as Elizabeth got into her carriage and drove away. Sheriff August shook his head and walked inside. Charlotte stood silent, every muscle tense, her vengeance focused on the trail where Elizabeth had gone.

CHAPTER THIRTY-FIVE

He's My Husband

Elizabeth stood next to Sheriff August on the front porch of Aunt Helen's house as the deputies loaded the dead body of John Walker onto a wagon. Douglas and Charlie were on the stairs below, watching.

"Can we give him a proper burial?" asked Charlie.

Elizabeth stepped down. August instinctively reached for Elizabeth's arm.

She smiled at him, then turned to Charlie. "Charlie, don't worry. We'll make sure he does."

"We're headed back," said one of the deputies to Sheriff August.

Sheriff August said, "I'll be there shortly."

Charlie's eyes remained fixed on the wagon with his dead brother-in-law as it pulled away onto the main road.

Douglas said, "We'd better get going." He turned to Elizabeth. "Are you going to be okay?"

"I'll be fine." She glanced back at the door to the house. "I have my work cut out for me inside."

August said, "I checked the house, and all the windows and doors are secure."

Charlie abruptly turned to the sheriff. "No one else is coming; it was only John and me. I promise."

Douglas tapped Charlie's arm. "You ready to go?"

Charlie nodded and turned to Elizabeth, his eyes never meeting hers. "Goodbye, Mrs. Pruitt."

Elizabeth's smile flickered. "Goodbye."

Douglas and Charlie got on their horses and rode away after the wagon.

August stood with Elizabeth on the porch.

She handed August a small pouch. "Here's a bit of money to help Charlie's men until Douglas can put them on a payroll."

He hesitated. "I'll see he gets it."

"Thank you."

The corner of his lips bent upward. "I'll be back later to check up on you."

"I would appreciate that."

"Will you be alright?"

Elizabeth cast a sideways glance over her shoulder at the front door behind her. "Yes, I'll be fine. I'm anxious to start cleaning that bloody mess inside before it permanently stains the floor."

"It's too late for that. There was a lot of blood, and it's been pooling there for way too long." He thought about the blood-stained floor near the jail cells.

"I've got to try."

August smiled and then walked to his horse. He mounted and then turned back. "You be sure and keep your door locked."

Elizabeth nodded.

He waved and rode off.

She remained on the porch, watching him disappear down the trail. Only when he was gone did her shoulders loosen. She buried her face in her hands and broke into tears. She couldn't hold them back any longer.

A lone crow watched from the tree that shaded her porch, unnoticed, and quietly observed her.

She pulled a kerchief from her pocket, wiped away the pain, and thought about the anguish the day had put on her.

A few minutes before, Charlotte had followed Sheriff August to Elizabeth's house and hid behind the far corner of the barn. From there, she could see the front porch. Charlotte saw the deputies load her dead husband and then leave. She waited a bit longer until the rest of them left, and Elizabeth was alone.

Charlotte was surprised to see her so emotional. She had heard from Charlie that Elizabeth was a resilient and sturdy woman. Moreover, Elizabeth was a woman of few tears.

"Hmm." She shook her head. Elizabeth was no pillar of strength as her brother had told her.

Charlotte thought it would be too strange to approach Elizabeth in her state. She wanted to confront Elizabeth, the woman who killed her husband, not a woman who was broken.

She checked the time. It was a quarter past two. Elizabeth was expecting her at three. She glanced down at the creek below and thought that sitting in the cool breeze for a little while would help her unwind and clear her mind. Her gaze flicked to the shell of a woman still standing on the porch and then back to the peace and tranquility of the water.

She walked down the trail and settled on a large rock near the water's edge. The water moved steadily, its surface gliding downstream in effortless motion. The quiet surrounded her, soothing in its simplicity. She thought about her husband, and the tears came at first silent, then full. She lingered in her sorrow until the tears ran dry.

A family of ducks passed through the water. The mother led the way, five tiny ducklings paddling close behind. Charlotte wiped her cheeks and watched them.

"You'd best keep those little ones close," she said softly. "There are all kinds of critters out here."

One duckling strayed, and the mother let out a sharp quack. Charlotte nodded.

"You're a good mother. You protect them."

She watched as they waddled up the grassy bank, the ripples in the water fading behind them. Reflections of the sky, clouds, and trees shimmered across the stream.

The calm of the woods wrapped gently around her. A soft breeze cooled her face while cawing birds rustled in the trees above. She turned her gaze back toward the house. Her smile faded. She retrieved her pocket watch and checked the time.

Back at the house, Elizabeth went inside and noticed a trail of blood leading to where the corpse once lay. Douglas and Charlie must have carried it through the front door. The trail stopped at the pool of blood, which had spread evenly on top of the wooden floor. The blood had thickened along the edges and had seeped between the slats. She filled a pail with water from the well in the backyard. She got some rags and began to clean.

Elizabeth scrubbed away at the blood-red ooze that stained the floor. There was a lot of blood. Thoughts of what had happened earlier flooded through her mind. She shuddered at the thought of the man who had been lying there. She scrubbed harder. A nauseous knot settled in her stomach. This was the man who had killed Rebecca.

She wiped a tear from her cheek. The last time she'd seen him was the day of her dear friend's death. And, today, here he was in her living room, pointing a gun at her and Douglas, an hour or so before. She threw the once-pristine white rag into the pail of blood-red water and went to fetch some fresh water. It took three bucketfuls to clean up the mess. She dried the floor with a fresh white rag. It was pink when she was done.

"Enough!" she muttered.

She took the bucket and the mop outside one last time. She went back to the parlor and stood over where the pool of blood had been. She didn't move for a long time, lost in thought. The dread loosened its grip on her. A faint reminiscence of a smile grew as Rebecca's words returned to her. "Things can only get better."

A knock at her front door interrupted her solitude. Her face wrinkled. It was too early for it to be the sheriff. There was another knock. She went to the door and opened it.

Charlotte stood there, smiling. "Hello, Elizabeth!"

At first, Elizabeth didn't recognize the woman standing before her. Then, the realization hit her. She gasped. "I forgot. Right now is not the best time for me."

Elizabeth wiped her face.

Charlotte's gaze fell to Elizabeth's apron.

"Is that blood?"

Elizabeth fumbled with her apron and put it on the table next to the door. She glanced at the broken lamp, walked out to the porch, and closed the door behind her.

"There was an accident," said Elizabeth. "Please..."

Charlotte stepped forward, her eyes sharp as daggers with no trace of a smile. "Did he die quickly? Did he suffer?"

Elizabeth's brows rose, her mouth agape. "What? He..."

"I saw them carting him away."

Elizabeth's gasp caught in her throat. She stepped back and choked out, "Did you know him?"

Charlotte forced a smile.

"Yes. His name is…" She hesitated and then continued, "or rather, was John Walker."

Elizabeth gasped.

"How do you know him?"

"He was my husband," she said firmly.

Elizabeth fell back against the porch wall, "No!"

CHAPTER THIRTY-SIX

All Is Good

Douglas and Charlie arrived at the sheriff's office. They led their horses to a post next to the watering trough.

Douglas cast a sideways glance at Charlie. "It's tough losing someone."

Charlie nodded.

"I was young when my mother died, and I still miss her."

Douglas patted his horse and turned to Charlie, his curiosity piqued. "Was that recent?"

"No. It was a long time ago."

Douglas hesitated. "Did you know Joseph well?"

"Yup, although he liked John better. He was generous to us both."

"I'm sorry about John."

"Me too." Charlie glanced down. "I'm going to miss him. I should never have let him talk me into any of this."

"Let's head to the telegraph office and send that message to your two men in Auburn. We'll meet up with the sheriff later."

"Sure thing."

They were crossing the road when Sheriff August rode up between them.

Charlie jumped out of the way, annoyed.

Sheriff August chuckled. "Douglas, I'll be back in a bit. I have to chat with the coroner."

Douglas nodded as the sheriff took off and then pointed up the road. "The telegraph office is about a hundred feet that way, just this side of the train tracks."

Charlie looked from side to side. "I'm not used to this many strangers. You never know if someone is going to jump out at you."

Douglas's brows raised. "These are good people here."

"I guess."

"Where will they go?" Douglas asked, wondering about the outlaws waiting in Auburn for Charlie's telegram.

Charlie glanced at the crowds around them. "Who?"

"Your men in Auburn."

"They'll head back to the camp a few miles northeast of here."

There was a commotion outside the telegraph office as they approached. People were laughing and cheering.

Charlie stopped abruptly. "What's going on?"

Douglas stepped onto the porch and asked one of the men who was cheering. "What happened?"

"We got news that General Robert E. Lee surrendered. It looks like the War is ending," said the man. "Hooray!"

The crowd continued to cheer loudly.

Douglas smiled. "I don't understand why those Southerners can't..." He glanced at Charlie. His face was wrinkled tight, and he was covering his ears. "Let's go inside where it's quieter."

Charlie followed Douglas into the telegraph office.

The room was small. Behind the counter was a desk holding a gadget, which clicked and clacked away. The clerk at the desk wrote something down as the rhythmic device continued. When he was done, he walked to the counter. "May I help you?"

Douglas said, "We need to send a telegram to Auburn."

"What's the message?" he asked. He pulled a pencil from its perch above his ear and slid a pad of paper in front of him, ready to write.

Charlie said, "Williams, all is okay. Come home now. Walker." He turned to Douglas. "That should do it."

Douglas smiled as the clerk wrote down the message. Everything was working out. This deal with Charlie and his men may work out well for the bank.

The clerk touched his pencil to each word. "That's seven words."

He pointed up at the sign above the desks. It held the prices for sending telegrams.

Charlie turned to Douglas. "I don't have any money, Mr. Holt."

Douglas reached into his pocket and tossed a shiny fifty-cent piece onto the counter.

The clerk locked eyes with Douglas and then adjusted his glasses. "Are you Mr. Douglas Holt? The bank owner?"

"Yes, sir."

"I didn't recognize you. Put your money away. My wife and I are so grateful to you for helping us buy our house. We owe you our lives!"

Douglas nodded rapidly. "I appreciate that, but please, send that message now. It's urgent."

The clerk rushed to his desk. "I won't be a minute."

Charlie eyed the coin still sitting on the counter.

Douglas slid it over to Charlie.

"You need this more than I do."

Charlie quickly picked it up.

Douglas blinked at Charlie's eagerness to take the coin.

The clerk sat before the contraption and transmitted the message. He was swift. There was a brief silence, and then the machine returned to life. The clerk wrote something on the paper. "They got it."

Charlie's head bobbed up and down quickly. "You should be receiving a telegram for Walker from Williams shortly."

The clerk went back to the telegraph machine. Suddenly, it sprang to life.

He scribbled something on a paper and handed it to Charlie.

Charlie read it aloud, "John Walker, heading home, Frank Williams."

Douglas nodded to the clerk and started for the door. He glanced at Charlie. "Let's go see the sheriff."

Charlie hurriedly followed, twiddling the coin between his fingers as they passed the saloon. Douglas noticed Charlie peeking inside through the swinging doors.

Douglas smiled as they walked up to the Sheriff's office.

Sheriff August was sitting on the porch bench.

Douglas winked at the sheriff. "Charlie's men in Auburn are headed back to their camp."

"That's good to hear."

"I have to get to my wife. I'm sure Mary is worried sick by now."

August nodded and glanced at Charlie. "Charlie and I will discuss the arrangements you and Elizabeth made with him. You go home, and we'll contact you if something changes."

"You, gentlemen, have a great day." Douglas extended his hand to Charlie and shook it firmly, and then left.

August thought it was curious that Charlie's gaze had followed Douglas as he rode away.

"Charlie, let's go in and talk for a while. I've just talked with the coroner. John's in capable hands."

Charlie turned to the sheriff. "Yes, sir."

Inside, Sheriff August lowered himself into his chair behind the desk and gestured to the one across from him. Charlie shuffled over and sat, the chair's back to the door. He glanced over his shoulder, uneasy.

"Where's your camp?"

"It's a few miles northeast of here. That's where the men waiting in Auburn went."

"Good." The sheriff settled into his seat. "How do you know Elizabeth?"

"I mostly worked for her and her husband, Joseph, doing chores at their place. Joseph was a real fine man. I miss him."

"Douglas told me he was drunk when he died. I thought he gave up drinking a long time ago."

Charlie shrugged. "I wasn't there. I wouldn't know." His voice trailed off, and he shifted in his seat.

"You hungry?"

"I'm starving. I haven't eaten all day."

The sheriff chuckled. "Come on. Let's go. I didn't finish my lunch earlier."

"Sure, but all I got is this fifty-cent piece."

"Don't worry about it. I'll pay." He walked to the desk across from his. "The deputy is probably still at the coroner's office. I'd better let him know where I'm at." The sheriff scribbled a note for him. "That restaurant has the best food around." He turned to Charlie. "Let's go."

Charlie jumped up and rushed to the door. Sheriff August followed him out and shut the door behind him.

"Aren't you going to lock the door?" asked Charlie.

"I trust these folks. The deputy will be back in a few minutes."

When they got to the restaurant, the sheriff went to his favorite table. This was the same one where he and Elizabeth sat earlier. He glanced at the table on the other side of the partition, where he'd seen a woman before. It was empty.

"Welcome back, Sheriff," said the woman.

She hesitated when she saw Charlie. She studied his face and then leaned in toward the sheriff. "What can I get you two?"

"I'll have the usual."

Charlie's eyes widened. "I'll have the same."

"It'll be a few minutes. We have to fire up the stove." She left and yelled to the kitchen, "Two Steak and Potato plates."

"I didn't like the way she stared at me."

Sheriff August chuckled. "I guess she's never met you before. She likes to size up people. See if they're the type to cause trouble in her place."

"I ain't gonna cause trouble."

The sheriff smiled. "We have some time to chat. Tell me about John."

"There's not much to tell. John had a short temper, and I worried it might get the better of him someday."

"You seem more subdued and level-headed than he was. I'm guessing John was more of an aggressive, irrational kind of man."

Charlie raised an eyebrow. "How would you know what kind of man John was?"

"Well, you're still alive. John isn't. No one ever would survive against Elizabeth if she saw you as a threat." Sheriff August paused, his gaze drifting toward the restaurant window, though all he saw was his own reflection. "She's already had to survive one outlaw."

Charlie grinned. "She's quite lethal with that weapon of hers."

"Years ago, she could outshoot the best of them. I guess she still has it in her."

"Yup, I got that," said Charlie, his hand twitching.

Sheriff August's eyes darted to his hand.

Charlie pulled his hand back. "When I was younger, my hand was steady. Now it makes it hard to shoot straight."

Sheriff August's eyes fell back to Charlie's hand. The tremor was gone.

The woman walked up with their food and set it on the table.

Charlie's eyes lit up, and his grin widened. "This smells great."

He didn't wait for the sheriff. He cut into his steak, stabbed the slice with his fork, and dabbed it with gravy on the way to his mouth. The taste was familiar, almost forgotten, and it hit as soon as the meat touched his tongue. He closed his eyes as he savored the flavor.

The sheriff cocked his head back, surprised to see Charlie's eyes shut. It was only for a few seconds, long enough to see that Charlie was not used to eating such a meal.

The sheriff cut a piece of meat. It was juicier and more tender than the one he had started on earlier. "I told you this food is delicious."

Charlie spoke with a full mouth. "It sure is. I ain't eaten like this in forever."

"What do you usually eat?"

"Beans, potatoes, and sometimes chicken. That's why I'm so skinny," laughed Charlie. He felt more festive with a full stomach.

"Now that you'll be working for the bank, you'll enjoy this kind of food a lot more."

"I'm glad about that."

"So, what are your ideas about protecting the bank's interests?" asked the sheriff. He was starting to feel a little more comfortable with Charlie.

"I told Douglas I've got at least forty men."

"I thought they worked for John."

Charlie chuckled. "They did. But now, I guess they work for me."

Charlie took a sip of the lemonade and then puckered his lips. He added more sugar.

"This isn't as tasty as Mrs. Pruitt's."

Sheriff August chuckled. "She must put something special in it." He took another bite and sipped his lemonade. "Elizabeth trusts you."

Charlie nodded. "My men can help ensure the stagecoach lines are safe. Now that the trains are starting to take over, I think you would want us to work those lines, too."

"I didn't realize how quickly the railroad would be finished across the continent. The rails from here to Utah are almost completed. We got word that we'll soon have tracks from the East to Utah, too."

"When will we be able to travel to the East Coast by train?" asked Charlie.

"We're a few years away from that day. However, you could go part of the way by rail and partway by stagecoach today. Why do you ask? Do you want to go back East?"

"Maybe I will someday. I've never been to New York. That's where I think my Pa left to. Maybe I'll visit him." He locked eyes with the sheriff. "Assuming he's still alive."

"You don't know if he's living?" asked Sheriff August.

"Nope." He shrugged. "He's been gone a long time."

"You can send a telegram from here to New York now."

"That costs a lot of money. And it's been way too long since I've seen him."

"If you want to message him, I'll pay for it."

Charlie's brows bounced. "I'll let you know." He took another bite.

"Elizabeth told me she would've been glad to help John and your men." Sheriff August hesitated. "I almost forgot." He pulled a pouch from his pocket.

Charlie squinted at the small bag in Sheriff August's hand.

The sheriff handed it to Charlie.

"Elizabeth asked me to give you this money."

Charlie smiled and straightened up.

"Really?"

"Once we make the arrangements with Douglas, we can arrange a proper payroll for you and your men."

"Thanks. I think this arrangement will work out well."

Sheriff August glanced at Charlie's plate. It was wiped clean.

Charlie pushed his plate away. "I have to go. I want to get back to camp before it gets late."

"Where's that at?"

"Northeast of here, right outside of town. I already told Douglas about it."

The sheriff stood, an inkling of trust for Charlie growing. "I'm glad we got to chat."

Charlie rose to his feet and grinned. "Me too. I'd better stop at the hotel and tell Charlotte what happened before I head out."

"Who's Charlotte?"

"Charlotte is John's wife and my older sister," said Charlie, his voice calm.

The sheriff tensed. "Wait. Your sister? And the wife of the man Elizabeth just shot?"

Charlie nodded slowly.

Sheriff August's eyes grew wide, his heart thumping against his chest. He jumped to his feet. "I'll go with you! She'll probably be upset when she finds out her husband is dead."

The sheriff led the way out the door.

Charlie chuckled.

The sheriff looked over his shoulder at Charlie as they crossed to the hotel. "What's funny?"

"Oh no. I didn't mean anything by that. It's just that this whole thing was her idea."

Charlie stepped inside the hotel first and stopped at the room directly across from the front desk. The sheriff pushed past him and knocked on the door.

The clerk yelled out to them, "She's gone. She left earlier to visit Elizabeth Pruitt."

The sheriff checked his watch. Quarter past four. Dread filled his heart. "Let's go. We need to get to Elizabeth's."

The sheriff rushed outside and then to his horse.

Charlie lagged. "I should get back to my men and tell them about John. News spreads fast. And I want to tell them about our arrangement."

"Good idea." The sheriff mounted.

Sheriff August nodded, snapped the reins, and bolted to Elizabeth's house.

He glanced back. Charlie hadn't moved, a grim little smile on his face.

CHAPTER THIRTY-SEVEN

I Wanted to Kill You

Elizabeth stood chatting with Charlotte next to the front door. A lone crow watched from a distance high above.

Charlotte leaned in toward Elizabeth. "I was sitting in the restaurant in the booth adjoining your table when you told Sheriff August about John. I heard everything."

Elizabeth gasped, her eyes fixed on Charlotte's.

"At first, I was angry. I wanted to come over and kill you right then and there."

Elizabeth's head jerked back, and she grabbed her chest.

Charlotte's brows raised, her head tilted slightly. "I didn't mean to frighten you. I tend to say whatever is on my mind without giving it much thought. John told me I shouldn't do that."

Elizabeth stood taller, puzzled by the woman's behavior. "Do you plan to kill me now?"

Charlotte chuckled. "Heavens no." Her brows bounced. "Although I initially wanted to."

Elizabeth's mouth fell open.

"I'm just kidding," said Charlotte, grinning.

"It's not funny."

Charlotte continued. "I arrived early enough to see John's body carted away. I watched for a little while afterward. After your guests left, I decided to head down to the creek and give you time to cool off." Charlotte's gaze drifted to the trail leading to the river. "It was peaceful there. I cried for a little while and cleared my head. I had a chance to think things through."

Charlotte turned abruptly.

Elizabeth's head jerked back.

Charlotte said, her brows narrowed. "I realized you couldn't have meant to kill him."

Elizabeth shook her head rapidly. "I didn't have much of a choice."

"I figured." Charlotte leaned in, a smile forming. "Can I tell you something in confidence?"

Elizabeth nodded.

"John told me he wanted to settle down somewhere and start a family. Your husband had something to do with that."

"He did?" Elizabeth glanced away. Her hand fell to her stomach.

"Are you okay?"

Elizabeth took a quick, shallow breath. "A family?"

A smile crept back onto Charlotte's face. "Yes. John loved me. We both thought it was time for a change." She rolled her eyes. "Even though I think he loved money a bit more. But he treated me well. And, we did have a fine time together."

Elizabeth's heart had begun to settle, her calm returning.

"I'm gonna miss him." Charlotte locked eyes with Elizabeth. "At the very least, you could talk to me for a while. Maybe, offer me some words of consolation."

Elizabeth studied Charlotte's brown eyes. A memory of Rebecca flashed through her mind.

"I was going to head back to the General Store, but I can go tomorrow," said Elizabeth. "You might as well come inside and have some tea."

Charlotte's face lit up with a smile. "You're very trusting."

"If you wanted to kill me, you would've done it by now. Instead, you waited for the sheriff and everyone to leave, went to the creek, and then came to chat with me. There's something about you that..."

Charlotte laughed. "I'm beginning to like you."

Elizabeth opened the door. "Come inside."

Charlotte stopped in the parlor, where a faint dark stain marked the floor. She pointed to the spot on the floor. "Is this where it happened?"

Elizabeth closed the door. "Yes. There was a lot of blood." She looked at it for a few seconds and then shook her head.

"The floor looks immaculate. You've wiped away almost all traces of him," said Charlotte, her voice cracking. She sighed. "I'm going to miss him."

Elizabeth's gaze fell to the floor and then back to Charlotte, her eyes wide, her expression still.

Elizabeth gasped. "Come sit in the kitchen. We can talk. I have a kettle going."

Charlotte sat in the chair nearest to the parlor. The same one Charlie had sat at earlier.

Elizabeth prepared the tea, her heart steady despite the tremor. She placed the teapot, cups, and two Queen Cakes on the table and then sat.

Charlotte moved her bag to one side and slid one cake toward her.

"This smells wonderful. Did you bake this?"

Elizabeth nodded and added sugar and milk to her tea.

Charlotte did the same and took a sip. "Oh my, I've never tasted anything this delicious."

Elizabeth smiled as Charlotte took a bite of the cake.

"This cake is heavenly," said Charlotte.

"It's my favorite dessert."

Charlotte smiled. "Look at us. We're having tea and cake, just like the British."

Elizabeth chuckled. Her anxiety had lifted. She felt a calmness descending, much like the one she and Rebecca had shared during their afternoon tea.

Elizabeth leaned in. "Where do you live?"

"John and I were staying at the camp northeast, just a few miles from town. We were staying with Charlie's men."

"Charlie's men? I thought they were John's men."

Charlotte laughed. "Charlie will take over for sure."

Elizabeth shook her head and said, "All this time, I didn't know Charlie was part of a gang."

"He wasn't. He hardly spent any time with us. Most of the time, he worked as a ranch hand here and in Auburn. He likes that kind of work," said Charlotte. "Anyhow, it was my idea for John to ask you for some money to help us get out of town."

Charlotte looked over her shoulder at the parlor floor where John's body had been. "I guess you must have said no to John." She took a sip of her tea, her eyes trained on Elizabeth.

"That's not how it happened. I would have gladly helped John's…I mean…Charlie's group."

"Really?"

"But, he wasn't asking for money. He was demanding I turn over the gold."

Charlotte's head cocked back, her brow narrowed. "I don't know anything about any gold."

Elizabeth paused as she studied Charlotte's face.

"Tell me then, why did you need the money?"

Charlotte took a deep breath. "We needed money to help us move East. He gave up robbing stagecoaches, so I told him to ask your husband for some money. When your husband passed, John seemed more determined to ask for the money."

Elizabeth shifted in her seat. "And then?"

"He asked Thomas, and he said no. When he returned, he said you were arriving on the morning coach. He told me he was going to ask you directly."

"He was using that ill-gotten gold to blackmail my husband."

Charlotte gasped, the breath stuck in her throat. "I didn't know anything about any gold." She shook her head, and her eyes moistened. "He's made a terrible mess of things."

Elizabeth hesitated. "My husband kept it a secret from me, too." Her eyes warmed. "We'll put part of that gold, along with some of mine, to good use."

Charlotte exhaled a loud puff of air and relaxed her shoulders. "At least something good could come from it."

"Douglas Holt, who owns the bank, is making a deal with Charlie. He's planning to hire Charlie and his men to protect the stagecoach lines."

Charlotte winced, took a sip of tea, and put the cup down. "Charlie doesn't care much for me. With John gone, I don't know what I'll do."

Elizabeth tilted her head. "I'm an only child, but I'm beginning to learn that siblings aren't always kind to each other."

"Or grateful!" Charlotte looked around. "You're here alone?"

"Yes," Elizabeth said. "Now that Aunt Helen is gone... She just passed... I came here to figure out what to do with the place."

"Were you close?"

"Yes. She and I lived here together before I married Joseph. Aunt Helen had a wonderful, long life."

Charlotte nodded. "It's tough losing loved ones."

"Yes, too many."

Charlotte shuddered. She tapped her finger on the edge of her bag and said, "You should keep a gun handy when you're alone here or out and about."

Elizabeth shifted in her seat, her gaze snapped to Charlotte's bag and then back to Charlotte. "I know how to fire one."

The edge of Charlotte's lips curved upward. "I'm sure you do. I always keep mine close."

"I keep mine stowed away until I need it."

Charlotte chuckled. "It isn't handy if it's always stuck in a drawer somewhere."

"I can assure you I can get to it fast enough if necessary."

Charlotte reached for her bag and pulled out her six-shooter.

Elizabeth leaned back, her eyes wide with alarm.

"Here's mine."

She handed Elizabeth the weapon. Elizabeth took it.

Charlotte flinched. "Don't touch the trigger. It's … sensitive."

"Oh my, it's hefty," Elizabeth said, handing it back to Charlotte. "Violence is never the answer. Believe me, it's taken too many of my loved ones from me."

"I understand," said Charlotte as her gaze darted to the dark spot on the floor.

Charlotte put the weapon next to her bag. "I have another one strapped to my leg. It's much smaller. Would you like to see it?"

"No." Her eyes darted for an instant to Charlotte's leg. "Thank you."

"We should practice together sometime. It would be fun." Joseph had also mentioned Elizabeth was a skilled shooter, possibly even better than he was.

Elizabeth grimaced. "My husband wanted me to carry a gun when I rode into town. He was concerned someone was going to kill me. I never needed it until now."

Charlotte pushed her gun aside and leaned in toward Elizabeth. "But I heard you shot Joseph."

"No!" Elizabeth's hand covered her mouth. A lone tear trickled down her cheek. "That's not true. I loved him." She paused. "He was shot right in front of me and died in my arms. I didn't shoot him."

"But only you, Joseph, and Thomas were there."

Elizabeth wiped her cheeks and shook her head. "Joseph's brother was there, too."

Charlotte's eyes widened. "Randall was there?" She reached for Elizabeth's hand. "Randall killed his brother?"

"No! He didn't kill Joseph. I couldn't see who the shooter was." Elizabeth's eyes welled with tears.

"Shoot," said Charlotte. "I didn't mean to upset you?"

Elizabeth dabbed her face with a kerchief. "I still get emotional. I'm not usually like this."

"Think nothing of it," said Charlotte. "Joseph was a good man."

Elizabeth nodded.

"A stranger once got too forward with me, and Joseph set him straight. My brother was right there in the saloon with me and did nothing to help me."

Elizabeth shifted in her seat. "Is it possible that we've met before?"

"I wish we had. We probably would have become close friends. In fact, that's what your husband told me not that long ago."

Outside, Sheriff August pulled back on the reins. His horse slowed and came to a stop a hundred feet from the house, where Elizabeth was surely in danger.

He dismounted and tied his horse to the fence post. A blood-stained cart sat beside Elizabeth's porch, no movement, no sign of anyone. He crept toward the front door. At the base of the steps, he stopped, drew his gun, and moved upward, slow and quiet. A wooden plank creaked beneath his boot as he stepped onto the porch. He hesitated, then crossed to the door and leaned in. Voices.

Inside, Elizabeth laughed loudly with her new friend and drank tea. She thought about her friend Rebecca. Now that she was sitting comfortably across from Charlotte, she saw more similarities between her and Rebecca, especially in her eyes.

"Charlotte, I wanted to ask you something this morning, but I couldn't bring myself to do it."

"Sure, what is it?"

"You look so much like someone I was very close to. Do you by chance know Rebec—"

Sheriff August burst in through the front door.

CHAPTER THIRTY-EIGHT
Put Your Gun Down

Both Elizabeth and Charlotte sprang to their feet. Elizabeth's eyes darted to the table. Charlotte's six-shooter wasn't there anymore. Sheriff August held his weapon pointed squarely at Charlotte.

Elizabeth choked out, "August, put that thing down. We're having afternoon tea."

He didn't lower his weapon. "Charlotte sent John here to kill you."

Charlotte's face cocked back, her nose wrinkling tightly as if she'd smelled something terrible. "That's a barefaced lie!" Her gaze darted from the sheriff to Elizabeth. "That's not true."

He smirked. "Charlie said so."

"What?" said Charlotte. "Why would he say that?"

"He said it was your idea for John and Charlie to come here."

"Yes, but only to ask Elizabeth for some money, not to rob her or kill her." She turned to Elizabeth and said, "I promise."

He continued, "Is that why you told your husband this morning you wanted him dead?"

"What? That's ridiculous. Is Charlie with you? He'll tell you I didn't say that." She glanced at the front door. "I loved my husband."

August narrowed his eyes at Charlotte.

"Listen, Sheriff, you must have misunderstood Charlie. I told Elizabeth everything."

"From where I stand, it's quite clear." He took a step forward.

Charlotte rolled her eyes. "You're not going to believe me, no matter what I say. This conversation is pointless."

The sheriff said, "I think you'd better come with me. We can talk this over in my office."

"Right! You expect me to go with you so you can lock me up in a cage."

Charlotte showed the sheriff her gun. She had it pointed at

Elizabeth.

He gasped.

Elizabeth felt the icy cold barrel pressing against her side. It was the gun with the sensitive trigger, loaded and ready to fire.

"Don't hurt her," said August as he turned his six-shooter sideways and raised his hands high.

"Charlotte, please," said Elizabeth.

Charlotte pulled Elizabeth backward toward the door. "Sorry, Lizzie."

A blink of an eye later, she pushed Elizabeth into the sheriff and rushed out the door.

He started after her.

Elizabeth grabbed August's arm.

"Let her go."

"But..."

Elizabeth pointed to the chair. "Sit down. Let's talk."

He glanced at the door and then back at Elizabeth. He holstered his gun and sat where Charlotte had been moments before. The seat was still warm.

Charlotte tore out the back door and sprinted to the side of the barn, where her mare waited. She swung into the saddle and kicked her horse toward the road. She looked back. There was no sign of Sheriff August. She slowed as she turned onto the path leading to the creek and followed it down. She crossed at its lowest spot and continued for a few minutes. She glanced over her shoulder—she was alone.

After another half hour, she found a cove hidden from the main trail. It was the perfect spot to see if someone was approaching and make a quick exit if needed. She climbed down from her horse and tied the straps to a tree beside a massive rock wall. Her mare looked expectantly at her.

"I think I've got something for you," she said as she rifled through her pockets.

She found two pieces of candy, gave one to her horse, and then popped the other in her mouth.

Charlotte's heart pounded as Elizabeth's words echoed in her mind. She paced along the rock wall, then stopped, shaking her head.

"I thought we'd built something real, some kind of trust."

Her mare flicked an ear, then shook her head.

"I told Elizabeth I wouldn't hurt her. I thought she believed me." She exhaled in a huff. "I don't understand. I was honest with her."

Her horse whinnied.

Charlotte stared at her mare. "Everything was going well until that sheriff showed up. He poisoned her with lies."

She patted her horse's face, and then it occurred to her who had filled that sheriff's head with those lies. "Charlie!"

Back at the house, Elizabeth leaned in closer to August.

"Charlotte wasn't going to kill me."

She glanced at the door and wondered where Charlotte had gone, perhaps to see Charlie.

He shook his head slowly. "You don't know that."

Elizabeth took a deep breath and let it out all at once. "Where's Charlie?"

"He went to join his men and tell them about John and the deal we've made. He's coming to the bank tomorrow to meet with Douglas."

"Did you give him the money?"

"Yes."

"It wasn't much," she said as her thoughts wandered back to Charlotte.

August grimaced. "I don't trust Charlotte."

"She told me it was her idea to ask me for some money. John and his men would have used that money to head east. I certainly would've helped them with that."

"Why? They're thieves. I don't trust Charlie all that much either."

"I felt sorry for those men when I gave Joseph's list of names to Douglas. Some of them have wives. Who knows? Maybe some have children, too."

"They should have thought of that when they resorted to a life of crime."

Elizabeth looked warmly into his eyes. "Some people get

backed into a corner and do what they need to do to survive."

"There is never a proper excuse for robbing and killing."

"John Walker is the true criminal. I still think he killed Rebecca. Although…" She turned away.

"Did you know she sat next to us in the restaurant this morning? She was on the other side of the partition. I saw her when you arrived. She heard everything we said. She was still sitting there when we left."

"Yes. She told me."

August shifted in his chair. "She was stalking us."

Elizabeth cleared her throat. "It does sound suspicious. I'll admit. But I trust Charlotte had her reasons. She came straight here afterward. She was here when your men left with John's body."

His eyes widened. "She was here all afternoon?"

"Yes."

"Did she tell you she had a hotel room and was waiting for John to return? She sure looks guilty to me."

"I spoke to her earlier, when I first arrived. I told her to come by. She wanted my autograph."

"Oh, she's clever. She was stalking you this morning, too," said August, his blood boiling.

"Don't mock me." She glared at him and then looked away. "Something isn't right."

"I'm sorry. I'm looking out for you."

"I know," she said, "I'd like to talk with Charlie."

"He's meeting with Douglas at ten tomorrow. Charlie said he'd stop by my office at eleven-thirty."

Elizabeth said, "You, me, and Charlie can lunch at the restaurant."

"What about Douglas?"

"I want to learn more about Charlotte. I don't want to discuss any of this in front of him. I'm sure he's a bit shaken about me shooting John."

"I'll be at your place in a wagon or a cart at eleven," he said, his calm returning.

"I'd rather ride into town on my own."

His shoulders slumped. "For your safety, I insist on

accompanying you."

Elizabeth took a deep breath and rolled her eyes. "Okay. We can go together. I'll be ready."

"Please make sure you lock up this place tight tonight. I don't trust that woman. If she returns, don't let her back in. Promise me."

"I promise. Don't worry. I'll stay inside. I'll write for a little while and then go to bed."

He noticed an empty leather bag sitting in front of him. He reached for it.

Elizabeth's eyes shot to Charlotte's pouch.

August brought the bag to his nose.

"This smells like gunpowder."

He looked astonished at Elizabeth and said, "This is hers. Did you know Charlotte had a weapon?"

"Yes. She let me see it earlier."

August's face grew bright red. "What! She could have killed you."

She grimaced.

"You're lucky she decided to play this game of hers. Once you finished your afternoon tea, she would have pulled out her six-shooter and shot you dead."

Elizabeth rolled her eyes, her shoulders sagging. "That's absurd. She suggested we go outside and practice with it."

His eyes narrowed, and his jaw dropped. "Exactly! Once she drew you out in the open, she would have put a bullet in you. You're seeing friendship where none exists."

At the hidden cove, Charlotte paced back and forth, not far from Elizabeth's house, still replaying her conversation with Elizabeth as the daylight faded.

A sound came from behind her.

Her horse was lying down, staring up at her.

"Okay, Misty. I suppose I should get some rest, too."

Her mare stared at her for a few minutes longer, beckoning Charlotte to come over.

Charlotte smiled and walked beside her. She sat and leaned against the rock jutting from the ground. Closing her eyes, she shifted, trying to find a comfortable position.

She couldn't sleep. If she did, a predator might find her exposed. As the night wore on, the howls and screams of wild animals blurred into fragments of her conversation with Elizabeth, both conspiring to keep her awake. She fell asleep anyway, only to wake briefly before daybreak to a cacophony of birds. But soon, she fell back to sleep, dreaming of Elizabeth.

CHAPTER THIRTY-NINE

Vengeance and Doubt

The next morning, Elizabeth awoke after a night of tossing and turning. The clock in the living room chimed, its sound sharp against the quiet house. The day had started without her, leaving her hours behind.

She went into the parlor, her gaze falling on the faint, ghostly stain still etched into the floorboards where the body had once lain.

She thought about how relieved she was that John was finally gone and muttered, "That dreadful man is dead and buried!"

The edge of her lips curled upward as she recalled the surprise in his eyes when she pulled the trigger. Her smile widened, warm and wicked, as the truth settled in: Rebecca had been avenged.

A torrent of emotion overwhelmed her. Her smile faltered. Hatred and revenge had taken root in her heart. She covered her mouth to keep from crying. She set her glass down and stood quietly, waiting for her warmth to return.

She opened the windows in the parlor. A cool cross-breeze traveled from the front of the house to the back.

She closed her eyes and took a deep breath. She smiled as the fresh air replaced the stale, foul air that had settled into her lungs. Her eyes shot open when her stomach grumbled.

She quickly prepared breakfast. As she sat to eat, she glanced back at the parlor room floor. She shook her head and then went back to her meal.

As she took a bite, the back door screeched behind her. She froze, then spun around, heart pounding, half expecting Charlotte to be standing there with her gun with the hair-fire trigger. But the doorway was empty. She crept closer, peeked out front and back, and saw only the beauty she'd admired a few minutes earlier. A breeze nudged the door wider, the hinges shrieking once more. She let out a breath and chuckled, then placed a doorstop to keep it still.

When she returned to her meal, the eggs were cold. She ate them anyway. Soon after, she had the kitchen back in order and then got ready for the important lunch with Charlie.

The clock chimed 10:00 am. She put on her favorite dress. She usually wore pants when she went riding, but there was no need today. In no time, she was ready and waiting in the study for August to arrive. Charlotte had drifted into her thoughts. She looked out the window at the trail that led to the creek and wondered where her new friend might be

Meanwhile, not far from Elizabeth's home, Charlotte felt something push her arm. She opened her eyes and jumped to her feet. She pulled her six-shooter as her mare whinnied and stepped back.

"Sorry, Misty."

She put her gun away as the horse nuzzled against her shoulder. Charlotte smiled as she stroked Misty's head.

"I bet you're hungry. Let's go see if Lizzie is home."

She looked at her watch and then grimaced. It was late.

She got on her horse and rode out of the cove and followed the path back to Elizabeth's house. When she reached the water's edge. Misty leaned over and drank.

"There you go, girl."

Charlotte looked across the creek at the trail leading to Elizabeth's house with a sense of urgency.

"Hurry. Let's go, Misty. It's almost eleven."

She quickly arrived at Elizabeth's house and hid behind the barn, deciding whether she should go see Elizabeth.

Elizabeth was at her desk in the study, overlooking the porch, when she heard the hooves of a horse landing outside. She stowed her pen and leaned toward the window. It was August. "I'll be right out," she yelled.

"Okay. Take your time."

She glanced at the mirror by the door and then put on a hat. A minute later, she stepped out in a lovely dress, a cute hat, and two-tone lace-up boots.

August was on the bench.

The clock chimed 10:30 am.

"Right on time," she said.

She thought she caught sight of someone peeking out from behind the barn. But when she took a second look, no one was there.

"Elizabeth, you look beautiful," said August.

"Thank you. Why on earth did you bring a stagecoach?"

"I was at the bank, and Douglas offered it to us. I told him you were coming to the town center. And I wanted to ensure you were safe on our way there."

Elizabeth shook her head, laughed, and then stepped into the coach. She settled into the back and glanced around the cabin. It was fresh and clean.

Sheriff August climbed in and yelled to the deputy above, "Okay, let's go."

The stagecoach jerked forward as they began their journey.

Charlotte lingered behind the barn, watching until the coach disappeared down the trail. Then she turned to her horse and said, "Well, Misty. Let's get something for you to eat."

She took her mare to the barn and got her some hay from the stall. Elizabeth's horse quietly stared at her.

"I'm a friend of Lizzie's," whispered Charlotte.

A pail of water on the front porch caught her eye. She brought it over for Misty.

As she stepped onto the porch, the parlor-room curtains gently swaying through the open window caught her eye. The deliciously sweet smell of those Queen Cakes lingered—a mixture of roses and sugar. Elizabeth had offered them last night. The curtains seemed to be waving her in.

She slipped through the window and crept to the kitchen cabinet, where she found three cakes. She took two and left the third for Elizabeth. On her way out, she gazed at the parlor floor. "Oh my. You've done an excellent job getting rid of John's blood."

She turned toward the window and then froze. The front door hung ajar. "Lizzie, you should know better than to leave that unlocked."

Once outside, she secured the door.

A few minutes later, Charlotte left for Charlie's camp.

"Maybe Charlie can help sort this mess," she muttered, her voice tight with hope and fury.

Her mare whinnied.

Elizabeth glanced out the stagecoach window. "That was fast."

The stagecoach slowed.

"Charlie is waiting for us at the restaurant," he said.

"Did he and Douglas have a fruitful meeting?" asked Elizabeth.

"Absolutely! Douglas is thrilled with the prospect of practically having a standing army to safeguard the stagecoaches. He wanted them to protect the rail lines, too."

"That's great!" Her eyes glazed over as she remembered Joseph doing something similar when he became the sheriff, but with only a handful of men.

August looked at Elizabeth. "You okay?"

"I'm fine. I'm wondering how Charlotte fits into this puzzle."

"As soon as she's captured, we can figure that out."

Elizabeth looked at him. His eyes were narrowed and fixed straight ahead.

As the coach came to a stop, she looked out the window and said, "There's Charlie."

Charlie was sitting on a bench outside the restaurant.

August stepped outside and held the door for her.

Charlie approached with a broad smile. "Mrs. Pruitt, beautiful as always."

"Thank you, Charlie. That's kind of you to say."

He turned to Sheriff August and said, "Sheriff, it's good to see you."

Sheriff August nodded.

Barely two minutes later, the three of them entered the restaurant. August led Elizabeth and Charlie to his favorite table. Charlie seated himself. August gently pushed Elizabeth's chair in as she sat next to Charlie. August settled into the chair beside Elizabeth.

Elizabeth's gaze lingered on Charlie's freshly shaven face. For as long as she'd known him, his cheeks were always shadowed with stubble, and his chin bore a scraggly tuft of thin hair. "You've shaved, Charlie? You look dashing,"

"Thank you. I figured I'd better get cleaned up for my new job."

The woman who was standing behind the counter walked up.

"I'll pay for today's lunch," said Charlie.

Elizabeth's brows raised slightly. Douglas must have advanced Charlie some money.

"What can I get for you?" said the woman.

Elizabeth's mouth opened, about to speak.

Charlie spoke right up. "That steak I had yesterday was so tender. I'd like that with the potatoes."

August glared at Charlie, annoyed that he hadn't waited for Elizabeth to order.

"Something wrong?" Charlie asked.

August said, "Perhaps next time you could let Elizabeth order first." He turned to Elizabeth. "What would you like?"

Charlie's nose twitched.

"That's okay, Charlie." Elizabeth turned to the woman and said, "I'll have the Chicken and Vegetables."

The woman pointed to the sheriff. "The usual for you? Steak, potatoes, and greens?"

A broad grin filled his face. "Yes."

"Can you bring us some lemonade?" Elizabeth asked the woman.

Charlie chuckled. "I hope it's as tasty as yours this time."

The woman winced at Charlie's comment and then went off to the kitchen.

Elizabeth leaned toward Charlie. "Could you tell me about John and Charlotte?"

Charlie spoke in a lowered voice. "John told Joseph he would kill you if you got in his way."

"Why?" Elizabeth cocked her head in disbelief.

"John and Randall's men were hiding out on your property. And…"

Elizabeth's head jerked back, "They what? Did Joseph know?"

Charlie blinked repeatedly. "Yes, of course, he knew. They were there up until right before Thomas got married."

Elizabeth shook her head. "I suppose that's why the cabin we gave Thomas and Rebecca was in such sad shape."

Charlie continued, "Right before they left, Joseph gave some of the men some money to convince them to leave the group."

August said, "Did they?"

"Some did right away. But the rest of them went to the camp northeast of here. They were supposed to leave later with John." His gaze darted to Elizabeth. "But John got himself killed."

Elizabeth drew a sharp breath.

August tapped Elizabeth's hand affectionately. Elizabeth smiled at August and then turned back to Charlie.

August locked eyes with Charlie. "It sounds like you've left something out."

Charlie's eyes opened wide, and he shook his head. His eyes flicked around the room, searching for a way out.

Elizabeth took note of his odd reaction. "When was the last time Joseph and John talked?"

Charlie exhaled slowly and said, "Just before Joseph died, he showed up at the camp here. He was drunk. He marched into the camp demanding to see his brother."

His eyes flicked to the sheriff and then back to Elizabeth. "Joseph and Randall fought. Then Joseph pulled a gun on Randall and was about to shoot him, but John ran up and shot a bullet a few inches from Joseph's feet. The next thing I see is John chasing him away."

Charlie glanced away. "John and Charlotte said it was your fault Joseph and Randall fought."

August's eyes shot to Charlie. "Why didn't you tell us this before?"

Charlie shrugged. "That was a while back. Surely, Charlotte would have gotten over that by now."

August shook his head. He turned to Elizabeth. "See. Her husband's death must have ignited her long-dormant feelings against you."

The corner of Charlie's lips twitched upward slightly.

Elizabeth shifted, her calm fraying under the weight of Charlie's words.

Charlie leaned in. "She and John fought now and then.

Yesterday morning was the worst fight of them all. She told John she hoped you'd kill him, like you gunned down Joseph."

August's eyes darted to Charlie and then settled on Elizabeth.

"Oh my!" Elizabeth gasped. "She said she thought I killed Joseph."

A woman carrying three plates of food, expertly balanced on a large tray, stopped at their table.

"Let me know if you need anything," said the woman as she placed the plates in front of them.

"Thank you," said Elizabeth.

The woman nodded and left for the kitchen.

"This smells great," said Charlie, ignoring Elizabeth's distress.

Charlie sliced into his steak, glancing toward the sheriff and Elizabeth.

August reached for her hand, resting on the table. She squeezed his fingers but let go the moment she caught Charlie's gaze.

Charlie's brows lifted, and a half-smile was tugging at his mouth.

The three of them ate in near silence, the air thick with everything unsaid.

Charlie abruptly pushed his plate back and stood. "Sheriff, Mrs. Pruitt, I have to go make arrangements with my men regarding the bank contract." He nodded curtly.

August said, "Very well, Charlie. We'll be here a while yet. Good luck with the arrangements."

Charlie nodded again, glanced briefly at Elizabeth, and marched quickly out of the restaurant.

Elizabeth watched him go. "That was quick. Did you notice how anxious he got when you said he left something out?"

August smiled. "I did. But now that he's gone, we can talk about those revelations." August settled back into his chair, signaling they would be chatting for a while.

CHAPTER FORTY

Where's Charlie?

Meanwhile, back at the camp, not long after Charlie left the lunch meeting, the mood had changed.

Charlotte rode into Charlie's camp, having taken the longer route to avoid running into that sheriff.

One man was guarding the well-hidden entrance.

"Where's Charlie?" she asked the guard.

The edge of his lip curled up. "He should be back soon. He's in town finishing up a big meeting with the Law."

Charlotte studied his face. Did that hint of a smile mean she could trust him?

"Could you tell Charlie I'll wait in John's tent?"

"Sure thing."

"Thank you," said Charlotte as she marched to the place she and her husband had called home for the last few weeks.

The room, with its canvas walls, had ample space for two people to sleep and was tall enough for them to stand up. It had one door that closed with two heavy canvases overlapped at the entrance. Heavy stones kept the canvas wall firmly in place against the ground.

Charlotte stepped inside. The memories of her life, together with her love, came rushing at her. She wiped a tear from her face. But now he was dead. She sniffled as more tears snuck from her eyes.

It was as tidy as she and John had left it, although a bit dusty. She put some of her clothes into her bag. She found John's gun, which he had hidden near the head of the makeshift bed. He always kept it ready in case someone surprised them while they slept. She slipped it into her bag. She shook her head. It wasn't the same without him here. She curled up in bed and dozed off, imagining that John would return, as he always had in the past.

A rustle outside stirred her awake. She sprang to her feet, grabbed her bag, and scrambled out. Three men were marching toward her.

She smiled. "Hello, gentlemen, it's great to see you."

"We heard you were here," said Jack, the man standing in front of the others.

"Something terrible has happened. John is dead."

Jack leaned in and patted her arm. "We know, Charlie told us last night."

Charlotte's gaze fell to the ground and then lifted to Jack.

Jack cast a sideways glance at the others and then locked eyes with her. "Let us know if there is anything we can do for you."

Her lips curled upward. Jack had always been kind to her. "Thank you. You're good people. You stood by John when it mattered, and I know you'll stand by me, too."

Jack's face lit up with warmth. He shot a sideways glance at the others and then leaned in toward her and said, "That Mrs. Pruitt has some nerve. She…"

Charlie walked up behind the men and pushed Jack aside.

"Charlotte, what are you doing here?" asked a stone-faced Charlie, his tone much different than when he talked with Elizabeth and Sheriff August.

Charlotte flinched; her gaze snapped to Charlie. "Charlie! I need to talk to you."

He leaned forward and reached for Charlotte's arm.

He glared at Jack.

Jack's jaw tightened.

Charlie tugged at Charlotte's hand and pulled her away. "Let's go for a walk."

She saw Jack wink at her as she left.

Charlie, his eyes wide with suspicion, led her to the camp's entrance.

She wondered what Jack was about to say to her. She had a soft spot for Jack and liked him. She followed a step behind Charlie and almost collided with him when he stopped.

Charlie faced her. "What are you doing here?"

Charlotte ignored the question. "What happened yesterday? What went wrong?"

"John pulled out his gun and waved it around, demanding the location of Joseph's secret mine with his gold."

"Secret mine? Gold?"

"He even threatened the bank owner's wife."

"I don't understand."

Charlie shook his head. "Sheriff August thinks you sent John to rob Elizabeth and then put a bullet in her."

Her head cocked back, her brows narrowed. "Where did he get that idea?" Charlotte glanced away, confused.

She turned back in time to see Charlie stifle a grin. "I told him you were upset Elizabeth killed Joseph."

"I wasn't upset, and Elizabeth didn't kill Joseph."

His brow furrowed as he blinked. "She didn't?"

"She and Thomas were with Joseph when he was shot. Randall was with them, too."

Charlie drew a shallow breath and asked, "Randall was there?"

"Yes," she said.

He glanced away for a moment, then offered a dry chuckle. "I'm glad Joseph's gone."

Charlotte's eyes flared. "He was a respectable man. I miss him. I would imagine his wife, Elizabeth, is as devastated about her loss as I am about losing John. Joseph was a good-hearted man. I could count on him to look out for me better than you ever did."

"That ain't true. I took care of you plenty."

His gaze flicked away briefly, then hardened as it shifted back to Charlotte. "You should turn yourself in."

"What? Are you kidding me? I didn't do anything wrong. That sheriff's got it in for me. I wish I'd gone to see Lizzie myself to ask her for the money. We'd be miles away by now if I'd done that."

"Lizzie?" Charlie laughed. "You think you and Elizabeth are friends?"

"Something's not right." She exhaled sharply. "I'll stay here until I can sort this out."

"You can't! Sheriff August could show up anytime, now that we're working with the Law."

Charlotte shook her head, then locked eyes with Charlie. "What did you tell Sheriff August about me?"

"You should turn yourself in."

Her eyes bore into Charlie. "You're my brother. Doesn't that mean anything to you?"

Charlie's eyes fixed on Charlotte with a cold stare. "You're in my way."

Charlotte's mouth fell open. She leaned in toward Charlie. A devious grin filled her face. "You know about that list containing the names of all the men in this camp. Joseph's list. I'm sure Elizabeth has it now."

Charlie stepped back and lowered his hand to his holster.

She snarled, "Oh, are you going to shoot me? Go ahead!"

"It's best you be going now."

Charlotte narrowed her eyes. "You didn't know about that list, did you? Looks like John wasn't the only one standing in your way anymore to lead those men. Once Lizzie turns it over to the Law, your lawless plans, whatever they are, are poof."

Charlie flinched. "Like I said, you'd best be going now."

She half-smiled. She sauntered over to her horse and affixed her bag to the saddle. She stepped up with her left foot and swung her right leg over Misty's back to the other side. She imitated a ballerina performing an intricate dance move as she turned to leave.

She grinned as Charlie narrowed his eyes and clenched his teeth.

He said, "Sheriff August will take care of you. I just had lunch with him and Elizabeth."

"See you around," she said as she left, headed to see Elizabeth.

She glanced back. Charlie had his gun drawn and pointed at her. His hand shook slightly. She held his gaze, knowing his weakness. She smiled, then rode on.

CHAPTER FORTY-ONE
Charlotte and Lizzie

Later that afternoon, Charlotte arrived in town and hid her horse not far from the General Store's back door. She snuck to the restaurant window and saw Elizabeth and the sheriff inside. She waited in the nearby alley for almost thirty minutes until August and Elizabeth emerged from the restaurant. The pair walked out together, and after speaking a little longer, they went their separate ways—the sheriff to his office, and Elizabeth to the store.

Charlotte checked the time. "Perfect. The old bear's gone."

She waited a few more minutes and waited for Elizabeth to enter the store.

She took one last peek. Sheriff August was nowhere in sight. She stepped onto the porch and peered inside through the window.

Elizabeth was examining a bolt of fabric. The tall piles of cloth would hide them from view while she and Elizabeth talked. She pushed the door open enough to squeeze through. The annoying ringer didn't announce her arrival like it did the last time.

She glanced up at the doorframe and saw that the bell was missing. She smiled and closed the door. She walked around several women who were chatting next to the soap display. One of them flinched and coughed. Another raised a gloved hand to her scrunched nose. She ignored them all. The owner was talking with a customer to her right. And to her left, Elizabeth was perusing the fabrics. Charlotte rushed to Elizabeth.

"Lizzie," whispered Charlotte.

Elizabeth jumped.

"Are you going to put a bullet in me now with all these people to witness?"

Charlotte rolled her eyes as she shook her head. "No, of course not."

"You did send John to rob and kill me!"

Charlotte shook her head rapidly. "No! It wasn't supposed to happen like that. I already told you!"

"He broke into my house and pointed a gun at Douglas and me. If he were there to ask for money, he would have knocked at the front door."

"I don't know what happened. I don't know why he and Charlie did what they did. And I, for sure, knew nothing about any gold!"

"You said John didn't take orders from you."

"I didn't order him to do anything. John had a mind of his own. Maybe he panicked when he saw the bank owner there. I don't know. When he left the hotel, he thought you were alone."

Elizabeth gasped and clutched her hand to her chest. "Oh, so you admit you were in on this."

Charlotte rolled her eyes, took a deep breath, and then let it out in a huff. "You killed my husband. I did love him. I've loved him since I was a youngster. I didn't send him to hurt you."

Elizabeth frowned. "You've hated me probably as much or worse than John did. He would have shot me dead yesterday if I had been alone. It's good that Douglas was there. I'm glad I shot John! He was the dreadful man who killed my dearest friend, Rebecca. Justice was served."

Charlotte stepped back in shock, her breath stuck in her throat, and her mouth hanging open.

Tears gathered in Elizabeth's eyes as she pulled a kerchief to her face.

Charlotte gasped. A stranger stood before her. One that was consumed with vengeance and grief. Lizzie had a breaking point, and here it was, gushing from her through tears. She gently reached for Elizabeth's arm.

"Rebecca was my sister," Charlotte said. "I never had a chance to…"

Elizabeth's tear-filled eyes snapped to Charlotte.

"I don't believe you." She took a shallow breath. "You would say anything to get me to trust you."

"Rebecca disapproved of my rough lifestyle and my friends. She asked me to stay away, and I did. John and Charlie both knew that."

Elizabeth shifted her weight to her other foot and sniffled.

Charlotte's patience was waning. With fire in her teary eyes, she said, "I tried talking to her right before she got married. She ran me off. At least I got to give her our mother's crimson jewel brooch."

Elizabeth gasped. "You gave her that? She was wearing it when she…"

Charlotte wiped the errant tears from her cheeks that had escaped her eyes. "Our mother died wearing that, too," said Charlotte, shaking her head. "It's cursed."

Elizabeth said, "No. I'm sure it's not." Her face softened. "Why did John kill Rebecca?"

"He didn't! He wouldn't have killed her. He knew I loved her and wanted her to forgive me for disappointing her."

Elizabeth pulled a kerchief and handed it to Charlotte.

"You do bear a remarkable resemblance, especially your eyes."

"It doesn't matter much now, does it?"

"You should turn yourself in. I'll help you to clear this whole thing up."

Charlotte wrinkled her nose. "You can't be serious. That's a terrible idea."

Elizabeth's eyes shot toward the front of the store, where a large picture window looked out to the street. Charlotte followed her gaze.

The sheriff was coming toward the store. "Here comes Sheriff August. Let's talk to him together."

Charlotte shook her head. Sheriff August and Charlie were stepping up onto the porch.

"Charlie is not what he seems. He's fooling you," Charlotte snapped. "I gotta go."

"I don't know if I trust you," said Elizabeth.

"You'd better watch your step. You'll end up dead if you're not careful."

Elizabeth's eyes widened. She stepped back and grabbed her chest.

Charlotte spotted Sheriff August coming inside. Her eyes darted to the back door.

She rushed to the back and vaulted the counter there with

practiced ease. She continued past a row of crates lining the pathway to an open door to the outside. She flew out the door, easily sprinting toward the dense trees where her horse waited.

"Stop," yelled August.

His hoarse gasp faded behind her.

She was much too fast for him. She turned back and saw the sheriff leaning over, gasping for air. Once a safe distance away, she stopped. Sheriff August was retreating into the store.

He turned back.

Charlie stood next to Elizabeth by the store's back door.

"She's as slippery as a bar of soap," said Charlie, looking in the direction where Charlotte had gone.

August nodded, catching his breath, "Elizabeth, are you okay?"

"Yes. I'm all right."

Elizabeth glanced at Charlie and then back at Sheriff August.

"She said she wanted to talk."

August's breath stuck in his throat. He stared incredulously at her, his face showing disbelief. "She's a killer, plain and simple!"

"Actually," she said sarcastically, "I asked her if she was there to kill me, and she said no."

Sheriff August chuckled. "And I suppose you believed her?"

Her brows bounced up as she locked eyes with August. "Some of the things she said got me thinking."

Charlie flinched. "Like what?"

Elizabeth's gaze darted to Charlie. "May I chat with some of your men?"

Charlie turned expectantly to the sheriff.

August cleared his throat. "Charlie here said that Charlotte visited his camp. She caused quite a disturbance up there, and he had to ask her to leave."

Charlie nodded. "I found her making some arrangements with three of my men. She asked me what went wrong with the plan."

"What did you tell her?" Elizabeth asked suspiciously.

Charlie shrugged. "I didn't know what to say."

August shook his head. "Elizabeth, we can meet with Charlie's men tomorrow."

Elizabeth stepped back.

August asked Charlie. "What time can we go up there?"

"I'm meeting with Douglas at nine. We can head up there right after, about ten."

Elizabeth nodded. "That'll be great. We can meet at the sheriff's office." She turned to August, grinning. "I'll ride my horse there in the morning."

August said, "I'll pick you up." He nodded. "I insist!"

Elizabeth shook her head, her grin fading to a half-smile. "You win. But don't bring a stagecoach this time. That was awkward. Just come over on your horse."

August laughed. "I'll ride over!"

Charlie cleared his throat. "I need to head back. I'll see you both at ten."

August said, "Good, Charlie. We'll see you then."

Charlie waved awkwardly and then left. August wondered about Charlie's odd wave and turned to Elizabeth.

Elizabeth's gaze lingered on Charlie, and then she leaned in toward August. "I'd like to know what plans Charlotte was making with his men."

"I guess we'll find out tomorrow," said August. "He's an odd fellow."

"I'm a little tired. I didn't sleep well last night. Would you mind taking me home?"

He nodded, and soon, after they arrived at her home.

She started to get down. She shook her head as August hurried over to her side and offered his hand. She grinned and took it.

"Wait right here," he said as he pulled his gun and went inside.

Elizabeth rolled her eyes and waited patiently for his return.

He peeked out of the door an instant later. "It's all clear." He opened the door wide.

Elizabeth stepped inside. "I'd ask you in, but I'm going straight to bed."

"Have a pleasant nap," he said as he climbed up onto the carriage.

CHAPTER FORTY-TWO

Hangman's Noose

Meanwhile, in the small town of Auburn, the day had come crawling in like a cat stalking its prey for Alexander.

Alexander was half asleep in his makeshift bed, a flat wooden board covered with tattered rags and scattered feathers, some fine linens incongruously mixed in. He rubbed his temples and struggled to open his eyes against the early morning light.

Sheriff Thomas Pruitt stormed toward Alexander's jail cell, eyes blazing. "We've got a new judge coming to town," he said, voice sharp. "He's on his way. It looks like we're gonna have a hanging today."

Alexander reached for his tin cup, sloshing with stale brew, and glared at Thomas through the bars. Without a word, he hurled it, and cold coffee sprayed across Thomas's face.

Snarling, eyes wide with fury, he drew his gun and pointed it at Alexander. "I should shoot you right now for what you've done!"

The sheriff's eyes blazed, his shooting hand trembling with restraint.

Alexander limped toward the edge of the cell. "Go ahead and shoot you lying bastard. I had nothing to do with that gold, and I sure as hell didn't kill Rebecca."

A smile cracked through Thomas's coffee-stained teeth. He uncocked his gun and holstered it. "You're as stupid as you look."

He walked to the front door and glanced back at Alexander. "You told me to stay away from your Martha. You said you'd kill me if I came near her. I knew you wouldn't have hesitated to kill me in cold blood. I stayed away, and then you went and took my Rebecca from me, to hurt me."

Alexander fell back into his bunk. "You'll never get away with this!" he said, his voice hoarse. "I wouldn't have killed you."

The door slammed shut behind Thomas.

Not ten minutes later, a commotion outside startled Alexander. The office door flung open, and Sheriff Thomas Pruitt marched to the cell, followed by his two deputies. The sheriff unlocked the door, turned to the men, and said, "He's all yours. I'll be next door talking with the judge."

Thomas grinned and left.

Thomas stepped onto the courthouse porch. Six townsmen, loyal to him, waited to see justice done. He nodded at them as he walked past and went inside.

Thomas froze when his eyes landed on the bench. Judges in this town were usually worn men, softened by the trail. But this one was different. He was older, lean, his black suit crisp, his silver hair combed back. The calculating eyes and thin smile made Thomas's stomach tighten with unease.

"Sheriff Pruitt," the man said smoothly. "I'm Judge Silas Gentry."

Thomas extended a hand. "Didn't expect a new judge for our little town. Welcome."

The man's grip was firmer than Thomas expected.

Judge Gentry's lips curled. Just slightly. "I've been meaning to return for some time. Your father made sure I never set foot in Auburn. But times change, Sheriff."

Thomas blinked. "You knew my father?"

"Oh yes," Gentry said. "Joseph was a man of conviction. He preferred to keep things local. Independent." His gaze tightened. "And I believe Auburn is ready for a more... structured approach to justice."

Thomas blinked again as he tried reading the judge's features. His tone was steady, unbending. "Well, we've got a man in custody. Alexander Johnson. He threatened to kill me. I want him tried and hanged."

Gentry's smile widened just slightly. "Swift justice. I admire that. I'll review the charges and see that the process moves forward."

Thomas's gaze lingered on the judge, a coolness seeping into him.

The judge nodded to the clerk. "Seat the jury." The man hurried to the side door and opened it. Six men, their eyes narrowed, their faces glum, marched inside the courtroom.

Thomas watched as the men took their seats in the jury box. He turned back to the judge. "My deputies are bringing Mr. Johnson in now."

"One more thing," Gentry said, his voice low. "I intend to make Auburn my permanent post. I'll be working closely with you, Sheriff. Together, we'll bring order to this town."

Thomas felt an unease creep in. Working together? "Fine by me. We could use the help."

Judge Gentry's smile faded.

Thomas turned toward the window, eyes narrowing as the sound of boots and shouting echoed from outside.

"Help," the judge said. "For now."

Thomas turned back to the judge, puzzled by his last words.

Thomas jumped as the front doors burst open, and the two deputies dragged Alexander inside.

"Get your hands off of me," Alexander yelled as they seated him in the front.

Thomas's heart raced as he took a seat not far behind Alexander. His eyes bounced from Judge Gentry to Alexander and back. The judge reflected the cold, hard justice he wanted to mete out to Alexander. But it was darker than any cold he'd ever felt.

Judge Gentry turned to the clerk. "Let the record show that court is now in session. The matter before us concerns Mr. Alexander Johnson, accused of murder, attempted murder, and robbery."

Thomas's stomach began to ache as Judge Gentry adjusted his papers and looked toward the accused.

Alexander yelled to the judge, "I didn't shoot that couple! I didn't do it!"

The deputies pushed Alexander down hard into his chair.

The judge cast an annoyed glance at Alexander and then looked at Thomas. His gaze lingered on Thomas for a few seconds and then returned to Alexander. "What say you, Mr. Johnson?"

Thomas held his breath for an instant.

Alexander stood and rasped, "I'm innocent! I didn't kill Mr. Adams or his wife."

"How is it you escaped the tragedy that befell them? I can see with my own eyes that you suffered a few cuts and scrapes."

"I don't know. I fell out of the stagecoach after I heard a shot. Next thing I know, I'm back on the road."

Thomas noticed the judge's face turning crimson.

The judge said, "Can you explain why two bullets were missing from your six-shooter?"

Alexander gasped and then glanced over his shoulder at Thomas. "I never fired my gun."

Thomas stifled a chuckle.

The judge made brief eye contact with Thomas and said, "Mr. Johnson, I understand you recently threatened to kill Sheriff Pruitt. Is that true?"

Alexander's eyes shot to Thomas, his face burning red. He jumped from his seat and charged toward the judge. "I'm innocent! I protect stagecoaches. That's my job."

Thomas gasped as the judge lurched backward as if avoiding a blow.

"Settle down!" yelled the judge, his face turning a dark crimson.

The deputies forcefully brought Alexander back to his seat.

"It's evident you participated in some manner to down that stagecoach holding my dear friend, Mr. George Adams, and his lovely wife."

Alexander shot to his feet. "Your Honor…"

Thomas gasped, expecting Alexander to come at the judge again.

The judge continued, "I've heard enough."

Judge Gentry cleared his throat and addressed the jury. "Gentlemen of the jury," he said, voice steady. "You've heard the charges. You've seen the evidence. You may confer."

The jurors leaned in, whispering. None looked toward Alexander. One scratched his neck, another shifted in his seat. It didn't take long.

One of the jurors stood, his eyes briefly darting to Thomas.

Thomas held his breath.

The juror said, "Guilty, Your Honor. For the deaths on the stagecoach line."

The others nodded in agreement, murmuring assent.

Thomas exhaled sharply, his eyes steady on the judge.

A murmur of unease rippled through the room.

Gentry nodded solemnly. "Then it is the judgment of this court, by jury and law, that Alexander Johnson be hanged by the neck until dead. The execution shall take place tomorrow at noon."

Alexander said, his voice weak, "You're making a mistake! I didn't do it."

Thomas stood. "Your Honor, I request that the hanging happen this afternoon."

"No!" said the judge. "That'll have to wait till tomorrow at noon. The hangman won't be back in time. He's taking care of another hanging," Judge Gentry said, eyes narrowing. "One that didn't take nearly as long to decide." His eyes darted to Alexander. "Justice moves faster when the guilty don't scream."

Thomas grimaced.

The corner of Judge Gentry's lips curled as he presided over the case. Returning to the town of his birth had taken far longer than he ever intended. His gaze settled on Thomas. His father, Joseph, had helped drive him out once—alongside that self-righteous Sheriff Buchanan.

But Gentry had come back. He'd brought men with him, enough to put Buchanan on the ground and close to death. The sheriff hadn't recovered from that beating; he'd handed the badge to Joseph before fleeing for his life.

Joseph had seemed like a problem at first, but he'd proven more reasonable than Buchanan. A deal was struck. Gentry would leave town and stop hunting the fallen sheriff—so long as Joseph paid him well for the courtesy. Gentry had taken the money, sworn his oath, and let Buchanan run all the way to New York, abandoning his children to Sheriff Pruitt's protection.

The gold had served him well. It had bought him time, men, and influence—everything he needed to rebuild his power under the respectable cloak of Justice.

Now, at last, it was his time to return home.

Joseph's son, Thomas, had let him back in. And Alexander was the first to pay the price for his return.

The judge rose, his eyes lingered on the jury, then on Thomas.

"I'll return in two weeks. We can talk about this town's future then."

Thomas blinked several times. "Yes, your Honor."

The judge pulled out his pocket watch. "Almost nine." He had enough time to get to the ten o'clock stagecoach.

He turned to the deputies and pointed at Alexander. "Get that man out of my courtroom."

Alexander sat frozen, disbelief etched across his face. Two deputies gripped his arms and dragged him away, the echo of their boots trailing behind.

CHAPTER FORTY-THREE

He's in Auburn

Elizabeth was sound asleep in bed when a loud knocking boomed from the front door.

She jumped, shocked. A piercing dread crept over her. She leaped to her feet and quickly dressed. The knocks grew louder and faster. She grabbed her six-shooter. She'd heeded August's advice and kept the gun close. She cautiously moved to the door and stopped in front of it, her weapon drawn.

"Who's there?" she shouted.

"It's August!"

She lowered her weapon and opened the door wide.

August stood next to Martha Johnson, her eyes filled with a sense of urgency.

"Come inside! What's wrong?"

Martha's voice rasped with worry. "Something terrible has happened."

August nodded, his gaze lingering on the weapon in Elizabeth's hand.

She tucked her gun into the small desk beside the kitchen, then rushed back to them.

Martha continued. "Howard Jackson came to my house. He told me Thomas has gone crazy and that Alexander is going to be hanged tomorrow at noon."

Elizabeth's eyes opened wide with shock. "What? I thought your husband was at home."

August exhaled sharply. "He's in Auburn."

Martha rasped, "He left on the coach early yesterday morning."

Elizabeth turned to the sheriff. "We have to go there now. Thomas will listen to me, I'm sure."

August shook his head. "It's already getting dark. It'll be too dangerous on a moonless night. I've arranged for a coach to depart at 6:00 a.m. tomorrow. That'll get us there well before noon."

With pangs of guilt and anger etched in her face, Elizabeth asked, "What in the heck is Thomas thinking?"

"I don't know." August patted her arm. "Douglas will stay behind to handle things with Charlie, and my men and I will accompany you."

Martha said, "I'm going with you. Gertrude will take care of my children while I'm gone."

CHAPTER FORTY-FOUR

Hurry

The following morning, Thomas slid a tray of food into Alexander's cell. He froze, startled, as Alexander lay moaning in bed in the throes of a nightmare, muttering, "I'm sorry!"

Thomas shuddered as a sense of weakness, or perhaps guilt, crept over him at the spectacle. Who was he apologizing to?

He snatched his gun from the desk and bolted out the door. At his horse, he paused for a breath, then swung into the saddle and rode. He pushed hard, not slowing until he reached the river where Joseph had died.

He'd barely arrived when a crow swooped down.

"What the hell?"

He pulled his gun and remembered his father's warning: "Let them be."

Another crow flew at him.

He shot at the crow and missed it. The loud blast from his six-shooter reverberated through the trees. Hundreds of crows burst from the trees, fleeing the safety they'd trusted. The crows didn't scatter from fear; they scattered from knowing.

He watched in amazement as a storm of birds darkened the sky. He fired again, defiant against the swarm.

"Damn!" he roared with renewed vigor. "Damn them all!" The crows feared him. The echo of his father's warning faded.

Thomas checked his timepiece, and a cruel smile touched his lips. Gone was the weakness that had threatened to undermine his plans to rid himself of Alexander.

Back at the jail, Alexander awoke with a start. He wobbled as he sat up in bed. A tray with food sat next to the cell door, containing a small piece of bread, a scrambled egg, and coffee. As he went to get it, he looked across at the sheriff's desk.

"Anyone there?"

No one answered.

He took a sip. The coffee was cold, but he drank it anyway. He was still expecting Elizabeth to come and free him from this nightmare. Undoubtedly, Howard had told her about Thomas's plot.

Alexander picked at his egg. His stomach growled as he tasted it. It was delicious. But as he tried swallowing, it stuck in his throat. He doubled over and fell to the floor, choking. The walls closed in on him as his imminent death was just hours away. He would never see Martha's face again. Never hear his sons' laughter. Nausea rose in his throat, curling through him like grief.

At Aunt Helen's house in Sacramento, the birds chirped loudly outside Elizabeth's window. Elizabeth woke abruptly from the raucous cacophony. She'd been baking cakes long after the sun had settled the night before. She sprang from bed and rushed to get ready, tend to the chickens, and have breakfast before Sheriff August and Martha arrived. The chickens were happy to escape the cage that kept them safe at night. She took care of the rest of the animals and left some food for the birds as well. They weren't as friendly with her as the ones back home in Auburn. They were noisier and more intense. These watched her with their beady, chestnut-brown eyes. She went back into the house with a small basket of eggs. She locked the back door on the way to the kitchen.

She sat down to eat the hearty breakfast she had prepared. Within minutes, she scraped the precious last morsels from her plate and gobbled them down. When she was done, she pulled the cakes from the cabinet and put them into a pouch.

"Where is August? We should leave as soon as we get to town!" she muttered.

The sound of galloping horses echoed into her house. She jumped from her chair, raced to the parlor, and peeked out the window. It was August.

"Good! The sooner we get there, the sooner we end Thomas's vengeful madness."

She grabbed her bag and the cakes and rushed out the front door. She waved to August, her face set with determination, and hurried to the barn. A minute later, she was on her horse and racing toward him.

He said, "Martha will meet us at the stagecoach. She said she'd bring her guns."

"Great! All I got is my six-shooter," Elizabeth said. "We gotta get going. There's no sense in taking a chance and getting there late."

She shook the reins, and her horse took off at a gallop.

He looked at her in disbelief. "Wait for me. The coach doesn't leave for another half-hour," he yelled as he clicked for his horse to go.

"There's not a moment to spare. Hurry!" yelled Elizabeth. "The coach needs to leave as soon as we get there!"

"Slow down! We've got plenty of time!"

The sheriff's office was in her sights.

"We're almost there. Hurry up!" she yelled back to him.

Elizabeth leaned forward and shook the reins hard. "Go!"

Her horse leaped forward at lightning speed.

A gunshot split the air like a scream.

Elizabeth fell to the ground, her body crumpling in a cloud of dust.

CHAPTER FORTY-FIVE

What About Charlotte?

The bullet tore through Elizabeth's jacket and gashed her skin as it flew past her. She thought of Joseph, who'd always warned her to keep her gun close. He'd tried protecting her from this moment. But he was gone. More than her life was at stake: the child growing inside of her, Alexander awaiting the noose, and the soul of Joseph's misguided son, Thomas.

Instinct took over. Before she ever held a gun, her father taught her how to leap from a moving horse without breaking bones. She yanked the reins and twisted as she fell, her heels landing first. She let go of the reins and leaned into a roll to avoid breaking anything. She absorbed it, gritted her teeth, and lay still on the ground.

"Elizabeth!" Sheriff August called out, his voice tense and filled with fear.

He leaped from his horse and drew his six-shooter. He sprinted toward her, his feet pounding the ground, while his eyes searched for the danger. A fleeting movement caught his eye. It was Charlotte, running away with a gun.

He dropped to his knees beside Elizabeth. His face was drained of color, his breathing fast.

Elizabeth sat up. "What's all this fuss?" She inspected her arm. "Doggonit!"

Charlie and Douglas rushed up.

"How is she?" asked Charlie. Worry was etched into his face.

The sheriff's eyes darted to Charlie. "Get Dr. Martin. He's in his hotel office."

"Sure thing."

Charlie hesitated briefly and then ran through the growing crowd to the hotel.

Sheriff August offered his hand to Elizabeth.

She pushed it away. "Is my horse okay?"

Douglas nodded, pointing behind her. "Yes. He's right here."

Her horse stood quietly, ears tilted forward, eyes locked on her.

"I'm okay," she called out, her voice cracking.

She rubbed her eyes and then her temples. "My head is pounding. I haven't done that in a while."

She brushed the bloodied dirt from her sleeves. A section of one of them was stained with a small patch of blood.

Douglas, his face creased with worry, said, "You're bleeding, Elizabeth! The doctor will be here soon."

She examined her arm. "This jacket is ruined! It was practically new. This is only the second time I've worn it."

Her waist-length leather jacket had a fancy braid trim around the collar.

The doctor ran up out of breath and knelt next to her.

Elizabeth rolled her eyes. "Doctor, it's not that bad."

"Let me be the judge of that," said the impatient doctor.

The doctor put his bag down and inspected her arm. "You're lucky. The bullet grazed you."

The doctor tore away part of the sleeve and cleaned the wound. He wrapped her arm in a bandage. "There, good as new."

Elizabeth grimaced at the doctor. Shredded remnants of her once beautiful sleeve hung lifeless below her bandaged arm. "If only that were true for my jacket."

The doctor turned to Sheriff August and stood. "Let's get her to my office. I want to make sure nothing is broken."

"Oh, please! Stop making such a fuss. Help me up," said Elizabeth as she stood. "We have to get going."

August frowned. "The coach won't leave without us. I saw to that."

Elizabeth exhaled sharply. "Has Martha arrived?"

Douglas checked his timepiece. "She won't be here for another ten minutes at least."

She nodded at Douglas and then brushed herself off.

The doctor grabbed his bag. "Elizabeth, come inside. We can have some privacy while I examine you."

Elizabeth rolled her eyes. "Okay. But make it fast!" She turned to Douglas. "When she gets here, ask her to join me at the doctor's office."

"Certainly."

August reached for her arm.

Elizabeth pushed his arm away and smiled at him. "I'm okay!"

"We'll wait out here for Martha," said August.

The doctor picked up his bag and then extended his arm for Elizabeth.

She grimaced and strode off, her steps uneven but determined.

She glanced over her shoulder. "Hurry up, doctor. I don't have all day!"

He caught up to her. "Why are you limping? Is that leg hurting you?"

She shook her foot. "No. My foot fell asleep. It's fine."

She took several more steps. "See, Doctor, no more limp."

The doctor half-smiled.

Once inside, Elizabeth rinsed off her arm and wiped clean the blood that had splattered her jacket. Then she sat across from the doctor.

"Other than my sore arm and foot, I'm fine."

The doctor examined her. "You fell from a horse! I would have expected you to have suffered a few more injuries than any soreness."

"I fell gracefully. When I was younger, I could do that easily."

He looked at her with disbelieving eyes, listened to her heart with his stethoscope, and then took her temperature.

"Are you…"

She straightened up. "I'm going to have a baby. Yes! I feel fine, and I'm certain my baby is fine."

He stepped back, shocked. "Why in the world were you riding a horse? You could have lost the child growing inside of you. You need rest. And stop riding horses!"

Elizabeth grimaced.

He hesitated, embarrassed to have lost his bedside manner. His calm returned. "Sorry," he muttered, barely loud enough for her to hear. He opened a nearby drawer and pulled out a giant scarf. He folded it in half to form a large triangle.

"Here's a sling to keep your arm somewhat stable."

He carefully affixed it around her arm and tied it loosely at the top behind her neck. He tucked the shredded sleeve inside and then stood back, his brow bouncing twice, and chuckled. "Better?"

A smile creased her lips. "Thank you, doctor. It works perfectly."

"You were lucky this time. The fall could have been terrible for you and your..."

"The bullet missed me, and I'm fine now. I'll be more careful in the future. I promise."

The doctor tilted his head down, his eyes locked with hers. "It grazed your arm. Could have been worse."

Elizabeth rolled her eyes. She winked at him and then rushed away, stopping at the mirror by the door. Elizabeth had washed away any remnants of the attack from her dress. Even the tiny bits of blood splatter that had found their way to her clothes were gone. She hurriedly made a few adjustments to her hair. She combed her hair until every strand was back in place. She turned slightly to acknowledge the doctor. Then she left and raced to her horse.

"How are you doing?" said Elizabeth to her horse.

The horse whinnied with delight.

August rushed up. "Is anything broken?"

Elizabeth shook her head. "Just some bumps and bruises, that's all. I'm all right."

He exhaled, his shoulders relaxed, and said, "I'm glad."

"I want to take my horse back with us instead of leaving him at the stable," said Elizabeth. "I may have to stay there a while."

"I can arrange that. My deputies will be accompanying us on horseback. I'm sure one of them wouldn't mind bringing your horse." Then he grinned and added, "Maybe they can tie him to the back of the stagecoach."

Elizabeth's head cocked back, her eyes flared. "Heavens, no! That's a terrible idea."

He smiled. "I was kidding. Don't worry about your horse. We'll get him there safe and sound. I'll ask Douglas to take care of that."

"Thank you."

Her eyes drifted to the General Store, where Charlotte had vanished. "I saw Charlotte before I fell."

"I did, too."

Elizabeth took a deep breath and let it out all at once. "We need to get to the bottom of this and figure out what's going on here."

Charlie approached quietly from behind as Elizabeth spoke.

"I want to review Joseph's list of John's men," she told Sheriff August.

The sheriff caught Charlie's startled expression and said to Elizabeth, "We can talk more about it on the stagecoach."

Elizabeth turned, surprised. "Charlie! I didn't see you there. I'll be back in a few days. I trust you and Douglas can keep things moving without me?"

Charlie nodded. "Where are you going?"

"I have to settle a matter in Auburn."

Charlie shifted uneasily. "What about Charlotte?"

She glanced at the General Store. "I can't think about her now."

August spotted Douglas chatting with the doctor on the bank's porch. "I'll be right back. I'll ask Douglas about your horse," he said, taking the reins and leading it away.

Charlie followed Elizabeth's gaze to the horizon, where the stagecoach kicked up a cloud of dust as it approached. He turned to her. "Have a safe trip."

Elizabeth gave a faint nod, her eyes fixed on the road, waiting for Martha.

As the coach rolled to a stop, August returned.

Charlie gave Sheriff August a curt nod and strode off without a word.

A buggy thundered in behind the coach, its wheels skidding slightly as it came to a halt.

Elizabeth smiled as Martha stepped down and rushed over to her.

Martha turned to Sheriff August. "Could you help me load my things into the stagecoach?"

"Certainly." He stepped over to her buggy and grasped the edge of the canvas cover. With a tug, he peeled it back and then froze.

Beneath the tarp lay a small arsenal: rifles, revolvers, boxes of ammunition, even a knife tucked beside a coil of rope.

He exhaled sharply. "Why are you bringing all of these weapons?"

Martha chuckled. "I'm not going to ride in a stagecoach without my guns. And besides, if Thomas gives us any trouble, I want to be ready. He won't stand a chance." Martha winked at Elizabeth and then looked expectantly at Sheriff August. "Time's a-wasting. Let's go save my husband."

CHAPTER FORTY-SIX

What's He Planning?

Minutes before Elizabeth was shot, Charlotte was alone behind the General Store, her gaze locked on the bank's front door. Charlie disappeared into the bank immediately after he arrived in town. "What are you up to, Charlie? I've got to tell Lizzie what he told me."

Half an hour later, a cloud of dust was rising from the road leading into town.

Two horse riders were approaching the town center. It was Elizabeth on horseback racing much too fast.

Charlotte gasped when a glint of metal caught her eye from the second-floor window of the building across the street. It was a man pointing a gun at her friend. Her gaze darted from the gunman to Elizabeth and then back to him. She squinted hard to get a good look at him. A mouthful of air stuck in her throat. "Frank!" she whispered.

Charlotte pulled her six-shooter and pointed it at him.

"Frank! Stop!" she shouted.

Her finger twitched on the trigger as the gunman glanced at her and then fired at Elizabeth. Frank bolted. Charlotte froze, stunned as Elizabeth hit the ground.

Sheriff August was rushing to Elizabeth. Charlotte gasped, flinching when the sheriff looked in her direction. Then Elizabeth looked her way.

"She'll be okay," she muttered.

As she turned to leave, Charlie and the bank owner were running to Elizabeth. She exhaled sharply and muttered, "I gotta get to the camp ahead of Charlie. I need help." She fled to her horse and raced away.

When she arrived at the camp, a lone sentry sat at the entrance. It was Smith. He was the kind of man who didn't care who was in charge. He was loyal to John. However, after John died, he followed the instructions he was given and didn't bother anyone.

Charlotte slowed as she rode up. "Where's Charlie?"

"He's not happy with you," said Smith.

"I know. It's not the first time."

"Yup. He has a vindictive, mean streak. I'd be careful if I were you."

"He's my brother, he's not going to shoot me. Is he here?"

"Nope. He went into town."

She glanced around. "Did he go alone?"

"Yes. But Hamilton left with that drunk Frank not long after Charlie."

Charlotte's brows jumped, her eyes blinked. "Did Charlie know they followed him?"

"I don't know. Frank told me to mind my own business when I asked him what he was up to."

"I'd ask Jack over there," said Smith as he pointed behind Charlotte. "I saw Frank talking to him right before he left." He shook his head. "You'd better make your stay brief. Charlie doesn't want you here."

She nodded and then hurried to Jack. Along the way, she felt the eyes of the men follow her. Some of the men glared at her as she went by. Jack was facing away from her as she walked up.

"Jack, can we talk?"

He turned around, his eye wild with fire. His gaze darted about and then fell on Charlotte. "What are you doing here? It's not safe!"

"What were you and Frank talking about before he left today?"

Jack narrowed his eyes at the sentry. Smith shrugged.

Charlotte asked, "Jack, are you hiding something from me?"

Jack shook his head. "Of course not. He was tight-lipped about where he was going when I asked him. He asked me to look in on Randall. They had another fight, I guess."

"Smith said Frank was drunk. I didn't know he drank much."

"He's been acting crazy lately, drinking a lot more than he usually does."

"He tried killing Elizabeth Pruitt earlier." She wrinkled her nose. "He always claimed to be the best shooter around. He missed."

"He missed? He must be losing his edge with all that drinking."

"I bet Charlie put him up to it."

"Is that such a bad thing to get rid of her? She killed John. I think every single one of these men feels the same way about her."

"She was defending herself."

"She killed Joseph, too," said Jack.

"She didn't kill Joseph."

"Charlie told us she did."

"No. Elizabeth Pruitt didn't kill her husband!" Charlotte insisted.

Jack shook his head. "It never did make sense that she would. Joseph was so protective of her."

"It was her idea to make this deal with Sheriff August. She's using her own money to pay for it."

"Really?" asked Jack.

Charlotte nodded. "I need some men."

Jack hesitated. He led her to a clearing a short distance from the others.

"Charlie is mad at you. He said you tried sabotaging him."

"I would never do that!"

"Some of the men here are calling you a traitor."

"That's ridiculous! You know me better than anyone does. These men have been through some tough times. We all have. That deal means they'll finally be able to settle down on the right side of the law."

"I know you would never betray us. John trusted you."

She grimaced. "Of course, he trusted me. I was his wife!"

Jack winced. "Sorry. I meant to say John was a trusting man."

Charlotte nodded and then hesitated. "Can you round up some men loyal to John? We need to stop Charlie."

Jack cast a sideways glance at Smith and then leaned in closer to Charlotte. "Charlie's been meeting with some of the men here privately. It's been making the other men a little nervous. When John ran things here, he never kept anything from us."

Charlotte shook her head. "That doesn't sound good."

"I don't know what he's planning, but some men want out. They're worried the deal he's made with the bank owner doesn't include those who were loyal to John. Not everyone trusts Charlie."

"Now that John's gone, Charlie is out for blood."

Jack nodded. "Some of them are planning to leave. Especially now that Elizabeth is going back to Auburn."

Charlotte wrinkled her face. "Why is she going there?"

"I don't know. Howard was at the saloon last night spouting off about the Auburn sheriff going crazy and about to get someone hung."

"What? That doesn't make any sense. That's Joseph's son. Thomas."

Jack shrugged. "Charlie's going there too – along with the men he's been meeting with in secret."

Charlotte glanced away. Her mouth fell open. The threat from Charlie was worse than she'd imagined. "There's no time to waste. You need to gather the men you trust and go somewhere safe."

"That's what we were planning to do."

Randall walked up from behind Charlotte and said, "What are you talking about, all hush-hush?"

Charlotte jumped and pulled her gun. Her breath caught, and her eyes narrowed, sharp as blades.

Randall chuckled. "I'm here to help."

Her head cocked back, and her jaw dropped. Her gaze darted to Jack.

Jack said to Randall, "She wants to work with us. She said someone shot at Joseph's wife."

Randall glanced at Charlotte's gun. "I guess things are getting out of hand faster than I figured." He turned to Charlotte. "I know you don't care much for me. But it's time to put those feelings aside for now. We've got a plan to peel away those men who were loyal to John."

Her eyes softened. She cast a sideways glance at Jack.

Jack said, "He's on our side."

Charlotte, her eyes locked with Randall's, exhaled sharply. "What in the hell makes you think I'd ever trust you?"

Jack cleared his throat. "Today, Randall and I had a long chat.

Turns out Randall's on the same page as us."

Randall grinned. "Yup."

Charlotte kept her gun steady.

Randall let out a sharp exhale. "I promised my brother I'd be there for Elizabeth and ensure she's safe. Ask Elizabeth. She'll tell you I'm telling the truth."

"What's Charlie up to. He would have told you something," she asked.

"That boy ain't no leader. He's acting like he's in charge, but he's not. He's in way over his head."

Her head cocked back, surprised, and she holstered her gun. "You got that right. But if you double-cross us, I'll..."

Randall grinned. "I don't blame you, but we ain't got much time. This won't work unless we're together on this."

She gritted her teeth and nodded.

Randall said, "We should stay on Joseph's property. At a place not far from the camp where we stayed before. That'll get our men out of Charlie's grasp and get us near Elizabeth."

Charlotte said, "That's good! I've got to make sure she's okay." She glanced at Jack and nodded.

Randall continued, "Not far from Joseph's cabin, a trail leads down to the creek. When you get to the water, you'll continue to the other side. If you follow the path for half an hour, you'll find a large, well-hidden cove. It's a few hundred feet past our old camp. I'll meet you there."

Jack nodded. "It won't take long to tell the men. We'll leave soon."

Charlotte exhaled hard, her calm returning. "Thank you, Jack. You might want to bring a few supplies just in case."

Jack winked at Charlotte. "Supplies won't be a problem."

Smith walked up. "Charlotte, you have to go now," he urged. "A trail of dust is kicking up behind some riders. I'm guessing it's Charlie."

"Sure," she said. Her eyes shot to Randall. She nodded.

Jack said, "I'll walk you out." He turned to Smith. "After we get Charlotte out of here, we need to gather the men. We'll be heading out soon."

Charlotte blinked. "Smith's with you?"

Randall chuckled.

The edge of Jack's lips curled up. "I trust Smith with my life. He's a trustworthy man."

Smith smiled. "It's time for you to leave."

Jack and Charlotte rushed to the exit. She jumped on her horse and locked eyes with Jack. They were warm and caring. Her heart warmed.

"Hurry up, time's a-wasting," said Smith.

Charlotte leaned forward in her saddle. The horse obediently took off like the wind.

CHAPTER FORTY-SEVEN

But He's the Sheriff

Elizabeth and Martha sat on the bench facing forward in the stagecoach across from Sheriff August on their way to Auburn.

"I'm glad I'm off my feet," said Elizabeth.

Martha moved closer to Elizabeth. "Sheriff August said you took a terrible tumble. Are you sure you're okay?"

"I'm fine. I didn't fall off the horse. It was more like I jumped."

The sheriff let out a huff. "You were going much too fast. I should have insisted on taking the buggy or a wagon."

His voice cracked as he said, "I was worried about you."

Martha suppressed a smile as her gaze danced from Elizabeth to August.

Elizabeth removed her sling. "I'm a little sore here and there." She wrinkled her face as she stretched out her arm.

August's eyes widened. "Shouldn't you keep that thing on?"

Elizabeth shook her head and winked at Martha, and then smiled at August. "It was a fashion accessory to hide my damaged sleeve. There wasn't enough time to go home and change."

He chuckled. "Elizabeth, you're a fashionably dressed, strong woman."

Elizabeth grinned and straightened up. "That's a delightful compliment. But let's not waste any more time with pleasantries. Let's take a look at Joseph's list."

Martha cocked her head to one side. "What list? And what does it have to do with Alexander and Thomas?"

Elizabeth gasped, a sudden realization tightening her chest.

August cleared his throat. "Perhaps we should discuss Thomas first. What's going on with him? He's the sheriff now. Why would he do this?"

Martha sighed. "Those two are like oil and water. I don't blame Alexander for threatening Thomas. But Thomas using his

284

position as sheriff to hang Alexander is a different story."

August's head cocked back. "Alexander threatened to kill Thomas?"

Martha took a deep breath and exhaled quickly. "I'm sorry to say he did."

He shook his head. "That's out of character for him. We've been working together for a while now, and that's not something I would have expected from him. Why did he threaten Thomas?"

Martha shifted in her seat. "I have to admit, I wanted him dead, too." Her gaze darted to Elizabeth and then back to August. "But not anymore."

August grimaced. "But why?"

Elizabeth rested her hand on Martha's and then leaned toward August. "They had a good reason. Let's leave it at that."

His brow furrowed. "Maybe Thomas had a good reason for what he's doing, too!"

Elizabeth shook her head. "Those two... Before Joseph passed, he shared something important about Randall and Alexander."

Martha, her cheeks tight, said, "Alexander is Randall's son. Alexander and Thomas are cousins."

August rolled his eyes and muttered, "Family!"

Elizabeth nearly choked as she turned to Martha. "You knew?"

Martha nodded. "Gertrude told me this morning. It turns out Agnes has known for a while, and this trouble between Thomas and Alexander somehow convinced her to reveal that secret. She thought it might help bring peace between those two." She glanced away. "That is, assuming we get there in time."

August said, "Don't worry. We've got plenty of time."

Elizabeth turned to Martha. "Are you okay?"

"Perhaps we should tell the driver to go faster," said Martha.

August's gaze shot to Elizabeth. "I told the driver to take the road carefully because..."

Elizabeth rolled her eyes. "For goodness' sake! I'm not as delicate as a basket of eggs. You yell up to that driver and tell him to make haste! If you don't, I'll do it."

August grimaced. He pounded on the ceiling and yelled up to

the driver. "Get those horses moving. We're in a hurry."

August dropped into his seat, bracing himself as the stagecoach jolted forward.

Elizabeth steadied herself as the coach shook more intensely. She grinned at August. "You talked to the doctor when you took my horse over to Douglas, didn't you?"

He nodded.

She turned to Martha. "The doctor told him about the baby. But before you say anything, I'm fine. We can chat about my baby later. We have a pressing matter to attend to first."

Martha patted Elizabeth's arm. "I understand. I'm here for you."

Elizabeth smiled and locked eyes with August. "Let's take a look at the list, now."

She unfolded the paper and handed it to Martha. "Every man who worked for John is written on this list."

Martha looked closer, the list shaking in her hand. "There are about fifty names there." She brought it down to her lap and shut her eyes for a second.

August objected. "The coach is shaking too much to read anything right now. Once we get further on, the road gets smoother."

Elizabeth nodded. "We can look at the list later when everything has settled down. I'll share what I've found."

Martha nodded.

"I discovered that list in Joseph's jacket. I believe it holds the names of all the men in Charlie's group. It used to be John Walker's group until I shot him."

Martha's head jerked back.

"I'll tell you that story later. Anyhow, I believe that Joseph might have been using this list to help some of them. He's done something like that before, where he helped people, down on their luck, turn their lives around."

"Those men on that list are criminals," said August.

Elizabeth shot August a disapproving glance, then turned to Martha. "While I can't imagine the list directly explains the feud between Thomas and Alexander, I do think at least one of the people listed murdered Rebecca and Joseph."

August said, "And the identity of the person shooting at you, Elizabeth!"

Martha's mouth fell open. "What? Someone is trying to kill you?"

Elizabeth nodded. "They tried when I was on the stagecoach headed to Auburn a few days ago, and again this morning right before we departed. The bullets missed me each time."

Martha glanced at the sheriff and then back at Elizabeth. "Oh dear."

Elizabeth shrugged. "At first, I blamed John Walker for killing Rebecca. And Thomas insisted Alexander had killed her. Both Thomas and Joseph said Alexander left the party, the day of Rebecca's death, with bloody knuckles."

Martha gasped.

Elizabeth continued, "I don't think John Walker killed Joseph or Rebecca. Yes, John and his men were inflicting havoc on the stagecoach lines. But he didn't kill them, or shoot at me."

August snickered. "Charlotte shot at you this morning."

Elizabeth rolled her eyes.

"Whose Charlotte?" asked Martha.

"Charlotte is Rebecca's older sister."

Martha's eyes opened wide, a smile growing on her face. "Rebecca had a sister? I can hardly wait to meet her."

Elizabeth chuckled. "The sheriff thinks she's after me. She calls me Lizzie."

Martha's brows went up. "I like that name, 'Lizzie.' She must like you."

Elizabeth chuckled. "I like her, too."

August half-smiled. "Once we capture her, she can answer to a judge."

Elizabeth rolled her eyes and shook her head. "Let's get back to the list."

He nodded. "When Douglas gave me a copy of that list, I knew it would help us to capture those stagecoach robbers."

"I'm still unsure how Joseph was involved in all of this," said Elizabeth. She glanced at the list in Martha's hand. "Now that the shaking isn't as bad, let's continue with the list."

Martha held the list so everyone could see it.

August leaned awkwardly forward to get a better look.

"It's still readable, although the edges of the paper are a bit frayed," said August.

"The writing is elegant," said Martha.

August asked, "Is that Joseph's writing?"

"No. His strokes weren't this refined," Elizabeth said, pointing to the top of the list. "John's and Charlie's names are listed together. All of the others are listed on separate lines."

"That makes sense since they were the leaders of the group," said August, leaning in. "Did you know the names of Joseph's deputies?"

"Yes, of course. Their names aren't on here."

Martha's brows bounced up. "Some of the names are circled."

"I don't know why," said Elizabeth, puzzled.

Martha ran her finger down the list, stopping at each circled name. "John and Charlie's names aren't circled. Zack Avery, L. Hamilton, Howard Jackson, A. Klein, Randall Pruitt, Frank Williams, Hank Flagg, Hayes, Will Chance, and …"

Martha grimaced. "That figures we'd find Randall on this list."

"And, it's circled…" Elizabeth squinted as she examined the bottom. "I can't make out the last name." She turned to Martha. "Can you read it?"

"It's faint, and the paper is frayed." Martha brought the list closer. "I can't tell what it says, but there are letters there."

Elizabeth rubbed her eyes. "The circled names are probably important."

August said, "Elizabeth, when you asked me about the list earlier, Charlie was more than surprised. His eyes narrowed, and his jaw tightened. He seemed threatened by it."

Elizabeth's brows raised. "I didn't see him standing behind me." She hesitated. "Some of his men's names are likely on this list. That doesn't bode well for the arrangement between him and Douglas."

August exhaled sharply. "That makes sense."

Elizabeth looked at August. "Could Charlie have shot me this morning?"

"No. He was with Douglas. He said Charlie seemed shocked that you'd been shot. Douglas said Charlie told him he was concerned Charlotte would ruin everything for him. And she won't stop until she's killed you."

Martha glanced up from the list at August and then returned to perusing it.

Elizabeth sat stunned, her thoughts racing as the implications settled in. "What does Douglas think?"

"He said Charlie is worried we'll back out of our deal with him and lose out on that money."

Elizabeth's brows narrowed. "We have no reason to back out. Right?"

"Right. Charlie knows each of his men will be paid a generous salary."

Elizabeth took a deep breath and then exhaled slowly.

August was nodding. "We can talk to him when we get back."

Elizabeth straightened up. "I have to admit these last two days have been exhilarating."

August grimaced. "You don't need this kind of excitement."

"At least now I have some interesting material for a novel."

Martha looked up from the list. "Are you a writer? I love books."

"I enjoy writing. I've always kept a journal. I have plenty to write about."

Martha said, "Are you going to include these last few days in your book?"

Elizabeth chuckled. "A lot more than that!"

"How exciting! I've never met a writer before. I must have an autographed copy of your novel once it's published."

The memory of Charlotte wanting her autograph came to her, and the aromatic soap that Charlotte had left in her cart.

"She used to write for the paper, too," said August. "I looked forward to reading those articles."

"You read them?"

"Of course I did. I was disappointed when you stopped writing them and moved away."

She smiled, her gaze catching the warmth in his eyes, the same blue she'd fallen for years ago. "I didn't know that."

A hint of a smile cracked on Martha's face as she glanced from August to Elizabeth.

Elizabeth caught Martha's smile. "Let's change the subject." She locked eyes with August. "We were supposed to talk with some of Charlie's men this morning."

August nodded. "We can do that when we get back."

Elizabeth cast a taunting smile in August's direction. "I'd also like to chat with my friend Charlotte about the list. I bet she knows plenty."

The sheriff shifted in his seat, avoiding her gaze. He shrugged and checked the time. "We should be there well before noon."

Martha nodded. "We can finally put an end to Thomas's despicable act of revenge once and for all."

Elizabeth glanced away. "I think Joseph's death broke him. It was bad enough that he lost Rebecca, the love of his life. And then he lost his Pa, too."

August said, "But he's a sheriff. And a sheriff doesn't falsely accuse an innocent man of murder."

"It's a good thing a judge has to get involved to sentence a man to a hanging," said Elizabeth. "He would see through Thomas's thinly veiled scheme of revenge. I'm sure of it."

CHAPTER FORTY-EIGHT

Just in Time

"Wake up, you sorry excuse!" yelled Sheriff Thomas Pruitt.

Alexander jolted awake, heart pounding.

The sheriff laughed. "Let's go for a walk." He turned to the two deputies behind him. "He's all yours."

They picked Alexander up and dragged him down a dark, seemingly endless corridor. His adrenaline was pumping, and his breathing turned shallow and erratic. The pathway led out back to an open area.

As the group walked out of the door leading to the gallows, the sun blasted them with its rays.

Alexander squinted as he tried to make sense of the scene before him. His breath stuck in his throat, the sweat stinging his eyes. He stopped abruptly. A sharp pain shot up his leg.

Ahead stood a tall, wooden structure with rickety stairs that climbed up to a platform where a rope swung gently. He'd never seen a gallows before.

"Keep moving, damn it!" scowled Thomas.

"You can't get away with this. Elizabeth won't stand for it."

The deputies dragged Alexander up the stairs.

The sheriff followed close behind. He leaned in toward Alexander and whispered, "You shouldn't have touched my beloved Rebecca. A life for a life."

The others didn't hear those icy words. Alexander's body tensed with rage. He broke free and charged at Thomas, knocking him to the ground. Alexander pummeled Thomas. The two deputies struggled to pull Alexander off.

The red-faced sheriff jumped and planted his clenched fist on Alexander's face. Blood rushed from his nose.

The deputies hauled Alexander onto the gallows, his boots scraping against the wooden planks.

Before him, the noose dangled, gently swaying. He muttered, "Why?" But the answer hung heavier than the noose before him.

Sheriff Thomas Pruitt shoved him hard and shouted, "Hang that bastard! He's out of his mind! He tried to kill me! String him up now!"

One deputy looped the coarse rope around Alexander's neck. It was damp and sour, reeking of mildew and finality.

Alexander recoiled, nostrils flared, his chest tight. A tremor ran up his thigh as his foot pressed against the loosely closed trap door. He gasped as nausea threatened to overtake him. His breath caught in his throat.

Crowds of people, unbearably loud, were gathered. Alexander couldn't hear them over his throbbing heart. His mind wandered to images of his family—Martha and his two boys, Alex and Marcus. His mouth moved, but no words came out as he tried to speak.

But then, something caught his eye off to his left. His pupils shrank to pinpoints. A half dozen riders were fast approaching. A glimmer of hope helped him catch his breath. He closed his eyes and tried to shake the hallucination away.

The sheriff turned to see what had distracted Alexander. "Damn it! Who the hell is that?"

As he rushed down the stairs, he shouted to the deputies, "Hurry up! Get this done!"

The deputy who'd placed the noose glanced at the posse. He recognized them. He yelled to the sheriff, who was already halfway to his horse. "That's the Sacramento deputies!"

The deputy removed the noose from Alexander's neck.

"Let's wait to see what's going on," said the deputy to the other. "Something ain't right."

A glimmer of hope crossed Alexander's face.

When Sheriff Thomas Pruitt reached his horse, he quickly mounted.

Crows cawed at him from the tree above the hitching post. They began swooping at him relentlessly.

He swung his pistol at them and shouted, "Damn, birds!"

He raced away. A lone crow chased after him for a few seconds and then returned to the others.

Thomas stopped a short distance from the Sacramento

deputies.

"What do you men want here?" He yelled. He recognized them. He'd worked with them for a short time when he lived in Sacramento.

"You're hanging an innocent man!" said one of the deputies.

Thomas narrowed his eyes. "He robbed a stagecoach and killed the passengers."

Howard rode up from behind the deputies.

Thomas's eyes bulged from their sockets. "Howard, what the hell have you gone and done?"

Howard ducked.

Thomas pulled his six-shooter and shot. Howard fell from his horse.

The deputies fired back, and one bullet grazed Thomas's side, while the second struck his horse's saddle. He howled as the bullet seared his skin, and paralyzing nausea overcame him. His horse jumped. He crumpled, and his head hit the ground. Flat on his back, eyes wide with shock, he twisted in agony. Crimson blood covered his side. Each breath he took came shallow and bubbling in pain.

One of the deputies kept his gun aimed at the downed sheriff.

Howard got up and brushed the dirt from his clothes. He grimaced at the ruined sheriff as he walked past him. "I need a drink," he said as he shuffled toward the saloon.

The stagecoach stopped near them. Elizabeth, Martha, and Sheriff August jumped out. Elizabeth ran to Thomas. Without hesitation, Martha and Sheriff August seized two of the deputies' horses and sped off toward Alexander.

Elizabeth knelt next to Thomas. "Why, Thomas? Why?"

His breath choked in his throat. "I captured Alexander Johnson. He killed Rebecca."

Elizabeth winced and then shook her head. "No! He didn't."

"Yes. John Walker told me."

"He lied to you. I put a bullet in that disgusting man."

Thomas's eyes filled with confusion.

Sheriff August, Martha, and Alexander walked up.

Alexander glared at Thomas and rasped, "I didn't kill Rebecca." He cleared his throat. "And I didn't shoot anyone on that stagecoach, either."

Thomas's eyes widened with rage, gasping for air. With a sudden blast of adrenaline, he jumped up and lunged at Alexander.

Sheriff August grabbed Thomas's arm and knocked him down.

Martha ran up to Thomas. "What's wrong with you, Thomas? I thought you changed."

Thomas's mouth fell open, his eyes wide with shame.

Elizabeth turned to August and said, "Joseph wasn't working with them. He was trying to protect me from them."

Sheriff August signaled for his deputies to take the disgraced sheriff away.

August walked next to Elizabeth, Alexander, and Martha.

A rumbling thunder of horses' hooves shattered the silence.

Martha pointed at the road. "What's that?"

Two dozen riders kicked up a plume of dust as they charged straight toward them. The group halted. Two men peeled off from the rear and rode away, while two at the front kept coming.

Sheriff August stepped in front of Elizabeth, gun drawn.

"That's Charlie leading them," she said.

Sheriff August holstered his weapon.

Charlie and Douglas rode up, while the rest of them kept their distance. Douglas, astride Elizabeth's horse, grinned.

Elizabeth's smile grew as she ran to her horse, patting its cheek. She looked up at Douglas. "What are you doing here?"

She went round and helped Douglas down.

His legs wobbled as he stood. "Charlie and I thought we might be able to help," he replied, catching his breath.

"Take a moment," she said.

"I brought your horse; I thought you'd appreciate it." He took a breath. "Didn't realize the trip would be so taxing. I much prefer riding by stagecoach."

Elizabeth smiled, and Douglas handed her the reins. "Thank you, Douglas."

Douglas shuffled to Alexander. "You look dreadful!"

Alexander shrugged. "Come join Martha and me for a walk. I'll fill you in on all of the details."

Martha hugged Elizabeth. "We did it."

Alexander said, "Thanks."

"Alexander and I will stay here for a few days at the hotel," Martha said. "We'll stop by your place tomorrow."

Elizabeth's shoulders eased as she exhaled. "Perfect."

She watched Martha and Alexander walk away, hand-in-hand, a quiet smile settling on her face."

Douglas tapped Elizabeth's shoulder. "I'll be heading out on the morning coach. I'll make sure your house in Sacramento is cared for while you're gone."

"I appreciate that."

Douglas nodded and then caught up to Alexander and Martha.

Sheriff August turned to Elizabeth. "I'll send my deputies back to Sacramento in the morning. I'll stay here until this town can get a new sheriff."

"Is Thomas going to be okay?" she asked, a frown of worry creasing her brow.

"Yes. The doctor will fix him up after he's locked up tight in jail."

Confusion etched Elizabeth's face. "I should go talk to him."

"No! Give him some time to cool off. Maybe stop by tomorrow."

Charlie walked up. "Sheriff, my men came out to help."

Sheriff August half-smiled. "Thanks. You and your men can check into the hotel."

Charlie shook his head. "We found a spot on the way here where my men can camp."

"Good," said Sheriff August.

Charlie smiled and then pointed across the road to the restaurant. "That place serves great steak and potatoes. I think it's better than the one in Sacramento. Do you all want to go eat?"

Elizabeth patted Charlie's arm. "I'm exhausted. Maybe we could have lunch tomorrow."

"Sure," said Charlie, his smile fading as he left.

Elizabeth watched him walk away, the dust rising behind his boots. Tomorrow would bring answers—but tonight, she needed rest.

CHAPTER FORTY-NINE

Back in Auburn

Sheriff August and Elizabeth arrived at her Auburn house. She followed him as he checked all the rooms.

"I think you should be careful. I don't see why you don't stay at the hotel. I'll be staying there, and it'll be easier to keep you safe."

"I would feel much safer here in my home," she said as she plopped her bag onto the kitchen table.

"I see," said Sheriff August.

"Perhaps I can convince Charlotte to move in here with me."

"Elizabeth!"

"There is nothing to worry about," she said as they stepped outside onto the porch. "As soon as you leave, I'll go inside and lock the door behind me. I'll be okay."

"I'll stop by a little later to check up on you," said August as he walked to his horse.

Elizabeth smiled. "That'll be wonderful."

August mounted and turned back to Elizabeth. "Be safe."

"Thank you for a lovely day," said Elizabeth, grinning.

August looked crooked at her. "Elizabeth! You could've been killed this morning." He shook his head. "And Thomas with his crazy revenge plot."

"You worry too much. Think happy thoughts."

August grimaced.

She smiled warmly. "I'm glad Thomas is okay, considering."

"He'll spend time in jail for what he did. And I plan to have a chat with that judge who let him get away with this!"

"It doesn't make sense that a judge would allow this," she said, turning to the door.

"It was a new judge. Silas Gentry. Took the morning coach. Won't be back for two weeks."

She hesitated. "I haven't heard that name in years. Met him

once. He came to the house right after Joseph and I were married. He wasn't a judge. Joseph ran him off with a shotgun. I don't think he cared much for him."

August shrugged. "Joseph didn't care much for me either." He mounted his horse. "I'll see you later."

Elizabeth's gaze lingered on August as he rode away. For a moment, she considered walking down to the creek, where it was peaceful. But as the sound of hooves faded into the distance, she turned and stepped inside and closed the door behind her.

The solid thud of the bolt sliding home echoed through the quiet house. That sound made her think she was safe.

She picked up her bag, withdrew Joseph's list, and found a few cakes left. She went to the kitchen and stowed them in the cabinet.

She took the list to the study and sat at the desk by the window that looked out onto the front yard. She loved this spot for writing. The outside light illuminated her pages perfectly. She pulled her journal from the center drawer and placed it alongside the list on the desk.

She read the names aloud as she ran her finger across each one. She looked out the window as she digested the conversation she'd had with August and Martha earlier in the stagecoach.

She had told August, "Charlie's men are better off working with the law than reverting to their old habit of robbing stagecoaches or worse. Surely, Charlie would understand that."

She thought about Charlotte. Perhaps she would listen to reason. On the other hand, Charlotte might put a bullet in her.

She set the list aside, then took the pen and scribbled on a blank journal page, "Who is trying to kill me?"

She looked out the window again and thought how pleasant it would be to sit by the creek.

"I need to clear my head. I'll never figure this out sitting here," she muttered.

She placed the list inside the journal and then returned it to her desk drawer. Peace and tranquility waited for her outside.

She hesitated and then exhaled sharply. "I'll be fine!"

She walked out the back door, past the barn, to the creek. She smiled softly as she reached the water's edge, the quiet wrapping around her like a shawl. She sat beside a large tree. She felt safe; no one could sneak up on her.

She picked up a stone and tossed it into the serene water. The surface broke, and rings spread out from where it fell. She smiled as they rode out in all directions, quiet and steady. It was beautiful, she thought. She looked up as the wind whispered through the leaves, a gentle hum that matched the slow rhythm of the water.

A soothing calm enveloped her as her thoughts bonded into answers. She closed her eyes as some of them gathered into images. A horse was fast approaching from the other side of the creek. Her eyes shot open. She jumped to her feet and ran behind the tree. She covered her mouth in shock. It was Charlotte.

Charlotte rode out from the trail across the creek, crossed it at its lowest spot, and continued to Elizabeth's house.

Elizabeth watched.

Charlotte stopped beside the barn. She dismounted, went to the porch, and knocked on the door. She leaned over and yelled into the window, "Lizzie, are you there?"

After a minute or two, Charlotte tried the door and then went around to the back door. She called out again, her voice filled with disappointment, "Elizabeth?"

Elizabeth cringed. She'd left the back door unlocked.

Her mouth fell open when Charlotte disappeared into her house through the back door.

A minute later, Charlotte walked out, eating one of her cakes.

Elizabeth instantly knew Charlotte had been in her Sacramento house the day before. She gasped loudly.

Charlotte looked Elizabeth's way. Then she shrugged and continued to enjoy the cake on her way to her horse. She gave Misty a small piece. She took one last look and left the way she'd come. Elizabeth moved from the back of the barn to the side. She peeked around the corner as Charlotte rode away.

Elizabeth slipped quietly down to the creek and saw Charlotte disappear down the trail.

She walked to the stream's edge and stood there for a long time, looking at the trail where Charlotte had disappeared.

"How did you know I was here in Auburn?"

CHAPTER FIFTY

Watching Out for Her

Elizabeth walked back to the tree that had hidden her from Charlotte. She couldn't imagine how Charlotte knew she had returned. Indeed, Charlie wouldn't have told her. Perhaps she thought August was right to believe Charlotte was stalking her to kill her.

She sat quietly for several minutes, trying to relax. She closed her eyes and strained to reach the calm from before. She jumped when she heard her name being called. It was Sheriff August.

"Elizabeth," yelled Sheriff August, his voice full of panic.

"I'm over here," she yelled back.

She glanced back to where Charlotte had gone, shook her head, and then rushed toward August.

August was marching toward her, his face etched with anxiety.

"What are you doing out here?" he asked, his voice filled with angst.

"I needed to relax; this is the best place for that."

She didn't mention Charlotte. Not until she could figure out why Charlotte was there.

"It's too dangerous for you."

A faint smile graced her lips. "I can't stay cooped up in the house."

August said, "I'm worried about you. That's all."

"I know. I appreciate it very much."

"You don't even have your gun with you."

She let out a long sigh. "Let's go have some cakes." She started toward the house, silently praying Charlotte hadn't taken them all, and shot a sideways glance at the barn as she stepped onto the porch.

August's gaze shot to the barn and then back to Elizabeth. "What's wrong?" he said suspiciously.

She cast him a sideways glance, her voice cracking, and said,

"Nothing."

He glanced once more at the barn and then followed Elizabeth inside. "I spoke with Alexander, and I suggested he and his wife stay with you for a few days. Would that be okay with you?"

"That's a marvelous idea. I should have thought of that myself. I'll prepare the guest room for them. I feel terrible about what Thomas did to Alexander. Is he alright?"

"Yes. He'll be fine. He's angry with Thomas, but he's blaming himself, at least in part. He says he regrets threatening to kill Thomas."

Elizabeth shook her head. "They have a history. That's too bad. I guess Thomas becoming sheriff tipped the power in his favor."

August shrugged. "Thomas did help Alexander and Martha stop those robbers outside of Sacramento. Even so, I'm not sure how either of them could use their position of authority to justify killing the other."

He sat at the kitchen table, his leg tapping on the floor. "Thomas will have to stay in jail for now."

Elizabeth opened the cabinet where she kept the Queen Cakes, small and fragrant with currants. Only one was gone. She chose two and placed them, one by one, on waiting plates.

"Here is your cake," said Elizabeth. "Do you want some tea?"

"No thanks. Water is fine." He took a bite. "You make the best cakes." His floor tapping stopped.

Elizabeth smiled and then bit into hers.

August cleared his throat. "I think it's crystal clear Charlotte is trying to kill you."

Elizabeth's face wrinkled as she cocked her head back. "No, it's not! Why do you think that?"

August looked at her, astonished. "She shot at you this morning. You and I both saw her."

"You're jumping to conclusions, just like Thomas accusing Alexander of killing his dear wife. I want to chat with Charlotte before you go off and hang her."

"When I return to Sacramento, I'll round her up and talk to her myself. In the meantime, you'll be safer if you stay here."

Elizabeth grimaced.

August continued, "I don't want you to worry about anything. Promise me you'll let me handle this."

Elizabeth said, "But…"

"Promise me!"

She rolled her eyes and exhaled sharply.

"Okay, I promise."

Sheriff August stood. "I need to get back to town. I told my deputy I wouldn't be gone long. He'll send a posse after me if I don't return soon."

"I'm glad you came by."

She watched from her doorway as August rushed to his horse. He waved at her as he rode off. He was gone within minutes. A dissipating trail of dust was all that was left of his visit. She stood there for a few minutes and then looked toward the creek.

She felt an urgency to talk with Charlotte. Eventually, August would discover Charlotte had followed her here. However, she wanted Charlotte to help her sort out some things before that happened.

She glanced at the road and thought about her promise to August to let him handle Charlotte.

Charlotte hadn't seemed hostile earlier, she thought. She shook her head when she remembered Charlotte had "stolen" one of her cakes.

Her brows raised. "Charlotte seemed disappointed when she called out to me as Elizabeth instead of Lizzie," she muttered. "But, I promised August!"

The promise she made to August weighed heavily on her.

She closed her eyes, drew in a breath, and released it slowly, as if shedding the weight of her promise.

"I'm sorry, August. I'm going after her," she said, smiling.

Elizabeth strolled toward the barn, looking here and there for anything suspicious. She opened the door and peeked inside. She rushed to her horse and patted him on his head.

"We're going to have a chat with Charlotte. If you don't want to go, we can stay," she said, trying to justify the visit.

The horse whinnied.

"Let's go find some answers," she whispered, more to herself than the horse.

She mounted her horse and rode down the trail toward the creek. She guided the horse to the spot where a trickle of water crossed the bed.

Her horse hesitated at the water's edge.

"It's alright. You can do it. Trust me."

He whinnied, stepped into the water, and continued across to the other side, following the path Charlotte had taken.

"See, that wasn't so bad. I could tell you enjoyed that. We'll need to come back here again. It's a beautiful place to cool off."

The horse relaxed.

"Let's go a little faster. We don't have a lot of time."

She leaned in as the horse started to gallop. After about half an hour, she pulled back.

"Whoa! Slow down. There's no telling what's ahead."

Her horse moved along the curved trail toward a densely rocky area. Some of the stones were twice the size of her house.

"This is heavenly."

The horse whinnied as he came to a stop.

She got down, led her horse down the trail, and then turned onto a narrow trail. Water was trickling off to her right. Then, as she rode, a twig broke behind her.

She looked over her shoulder.

A man had a rifle trained on her. "What business do you have here?"

Elizabeth narrowed her eyes at the man. "I'm here to see Charlotte."

"And, who are you?"

"I'm Elizabeth Pruitt. I own this land!"

The man cocked his head back and gripped his weapon.

Elizabeth gasped.

Charlotte rushed up. "Lower your rifle, Jack."

"She's Joseph's wife!"

Charlotte glared at him. "She's a friend!"

Jack lowered his rifle with a huff. "I sure hope you know what you're doing," said Jack as he walked away.

"Are you looking to get shot?" asked Charlotte.

"You stole my cake!"

Charlotte burst out laughing. "You saw me?"

"Yes, I was relaxing by the creek when you came by."

"I love those cakes. I couldn't help myself. You can't blame me. Can you?"

Elizabeth's shoulders relaxed slightly. "Why did you come here?"

"I stopped by to check on you. I wanted to make sure you were okay."

A smile tugged at Elizabeth's lips. "I'm fine. How did you know I came back home?"

"Charlie told his men, and Jack, the man who greeted you, told me."

"Greeted?"

Charlotte pointed to an open space a few feet away.

"Let's go talk in private."

Elizabeth nodded and glanced at Jack, and noticed three other men had joined him.

They walked to the far side of the path near the main trail that led to Elizabeth's house.

"This morning, I saw you right before I was shot. Did you shoot at me?"

"Of course not. I was following Charlie. I did see the man who shot at you."

Elizabeth looked around. "Is he here now?"

"No. That man is not wanted here!" She paused. "His name is Frank. I don't trust him, never have. John didn't either."

Elizabeth gulped a breath and let it out hard. "Frank Williams?"

"Yes. I didn't see Hamilton, but he was with him, too. Frank and Hamilton followed after Charlie into town this morning."

"How did you know they followed him? Charlie was with Douglas when I got shot," said Elizabeth, her brows raised.

"I went to Charlie's camp this morning. My friend Jack told me," said Charlotte as a smile crossed her lips.

Elizabeth snickered. "Your friend?"

She caught the slight lift at the corner of Charlotte's lip before adding, "Charlie and some of his men are here in town."

"I know. That's why I'm here – to keep Charlie from killing you."

Elizabeth grimaced. "I've known Charlie a long time. He hasn't given me the impression he's trying to kill me."

Charlotte shrugged.

Elizabeth continued, "Who are these men here with you?"

"They are not very sympathetic to Charlie. They were loyal to John. They needed someplace to go for a while."

"I would imagine Charlie won't be thrilled about this."

Charlotte shrugged. "Someone shot at me this morning, too."

"Who?" asked Elizabeth suspiciously.

"I don't know. I didn't see anyone and didn't stick around to find out. I rode into town, and I saw Frank shoot at you. I yelled out to him, spooking him. I think that's why he missed you. He's a sharpshooter. It's not like him to miss."

"I see," said Elizabeth. "He keeps missing me, so there must be something more."

"I hear he's been hitting the whiskey hard over the last few days."

"That would explain it, but is he the only one trying to kill me?"

"Someone's trying to kill me, too."

Elizabeth steadied her breath. "Sheriff August can help you."

"No! He'll lock me up. He's not going to solve this. You and I have to. Whoever it is, they won't stop until we're both dead."

Elizabeth shook her head. "I don't know what to think. I'm —"

She was cut off when a loud boom came from the main trail, and wood splinters showered Elizabeth and Charlotte.

"Get down," yelled Charlotte.

Elizabeth and Charlotte ran behind a large boulder next to the splintered tree.

Charlotte pulled her gun.

"Is this how you trick me? Get me alone so your men can shoot me?" asked Elizabeth.

"You're the one who came here unarmed, looking for trouble. Anyhow, those people shooting at us must have followed you. They sure as hell didn't follow us."

Charlotte peered out from the safety of the boulder and saw the shooter exposed and vulnerable. She aimed and fired into the man's chest. The man was dead before he hit the ground.

Elizabeth flinched at Charlotte's calm precision. It wasn't the shot; it was the ease.

Charlotte turned to Elizabeth. "Do you still think I'm trying to kill you? That was Avery." She shook her head. "It's a good thing you weren't at home alone having to face those two!"

Several men from the camp jumped on their horses and gave chase after the second man, who had raced away on his horse.

"Are you okay?" asked Charlotte.

"Yes. I…" Elizabeth caught her breath. "Do you know the name of the man who got away?"

"It looked like Frank Williams, the same man who shot at you this morning."

Elizabeth narrowed her brows and shook her head. "Twice in one day. Someone really wants me gone." She bolted to her horse. "I promised the sheriff I would let him handle this."

Charlotte grimaced and followed Elizabeth.

"Lizzie, let's talk about this."

Elizabeth mounted and looked back at Charlotte. "We can talk about that at my house over tea. I have some more of those cakes you like so much."

Charlotte smiled. "That's a marvelous idea!"

CHAPTER FIFTY-ONE

Captured

Charlotte rode beside Elizabeth along the trail, brush lining both sides like a quiet escort. The sound of water gurgling over rocks caught Elizabeth's horse's attention. Its ears perked, and without warning, it broke into a gallop, splashing eagerly into the creek. It stomped through the water, tail flicking, clearly delighted.

Charlotte caught up and pulled alongside, laughing. "Misty loves the water too."

Elizabeth grinned. "This is the second time he's been in the water." She gave a gentle snap of the reins. "Alright, let's go."

Her horse obeyed, climbing the trail ahead. But as they reached the rise, Elizabeth's smile faded.

"Do you think that man who shot at us is still nearby?"

Charlotte scanned the trees. "I doubt it. He's long gone by now."

Elizabeth exhaled. "Good!" She turned to Charlotte. "Sheriff August is going to be stopping by later, so you can't stay long."

Charlotte shook her head. "That sheriff should be protecting you from that man who just shot at us. Not from me."

When they reached the barn, Charlotte jumped down. "I'll tie my horse to this post. I wouldn't want the sheriff to see my horse in front of your house and sneak up on me."

Elizabeth got down and led her horse inside. "I'll be right back. Let's go, Augie."

"Your horse's name is Augie?" asked Charlotte as she followed Elizabeth.

Elizabeth blushed, embarrassed that she'd said the name. No one, not even Joseph, knew she'd named him that. "Yes."

"You named him after Sheriff August?"

Elizabeth grinned. "It's an odd story."

"I like stories, especially odd ones," said Charlotte with a smirk.

"Sheriff August gave me and my aunt that horse after my first husband passed. It was long before Joseph and I were married. I promised August I'd name it after him."

"Why did he give it to you? Was he interested in you?"

"We received gifts from many neighbors after my first husband died. August was a trusted friend of Aunt Helen and me, and he helped us a great deal when we first moved to Sacramento. Over time, I think he developed a romantic interest in me, though he never said so outright. It was too soon after my husband's death, so I didn't pay much attention to his gentle hints."

Charlotte laughed. "How did you end up with Joseph?"

Elizabeth half-smiled. "About fifteen years ago, my first husband, Aunt Helen, and I traveled here from New York. He died not long after we arrived. Joseph came on that same wagon train. He helped my aunt and me secure the house in Sacramento —the one my husband had bought just days before he passed. Later, Joseph bought out the rest of my husband's share in this property, including the mines."

"Sounds like Joseph. He was always generous," said Charlotte. "The first time I met him was in Auburn. It was a while back. He wasn't married then. What happened next?"

"It took me a while to get over the loss of my husband. August seemed to be showing an interest in me, and I told him I couldn't."

"That's sad," said Charlotte.

Elizabeth nodded. "Eventually, I moved on. Then, one day, Joseph staggered into the sheriff's office where August and I were chatting. That's when Joseph, as drunk as he was, professed his love for me."

"Sounds romantic," said Charlotte with a chuckle.

Elizabeth said warmly. "The next week, and for several weeks later, he brought me gifts and candies, accompanied by romantic letters. He swore off drinking. I eventually married him."

Charlotte remembered the day she'd first met John. He had kept calling on her, buying her things, and making a spectacle of himself. Eventually, she relented and fell in love with him. She brushed the thought aside and said, "My horse's name is Misty."

"She's a lovely mare," said Elizabeth as she walked out of the barn.

Charlotte laughed as she followed Elizabeth. "I love—" She stopped abruptly in the doorway when she heard the click of metal at her head.

Elizabeth looked over her shoulder and gasped. There was a six-shooter pointed inches from the side of Charlotte's head.

Charlotte reached for her weapon.

"Drop your gun," shouted the man.

Elizabeth stood stunned.

Charlotte dropped her gun.

"Alexander!" said Elizabeth. "What are you doing?"

Alexander didn't take his eyes off Charlotte as he picked up her gun.

Elizabeth moved beside Alexander.

Charlotte furrowed her brows. "You lured me here, Elizabeth. You tricked me."

"No!"

"Sheriff!" Alexander yelled, keeping his eyes locked on Charlotte. "Elizabeth, go get the sheriff, he's in the house."

Elizabeth said, "Don't hurt her. I'll get him, and we can discuss this."

"The sheriff said he was looking for her," said Alexander. "He said she's been trying to kill you."

Elizabeth exhaled sharply. "I'll be right back. Everything will be fine." She ran to the house.

Charlotte trembled with anger.

"Turn around so I can see you," said Alexander.

As she turned, the sunlight caught her face.

Alexander stepped back, surprised. "Rebecca?"

Charlotte half-smiled and locked eyes with Alexander. "She was my sister."

He cleared his throat.

She exhaled loudly, her shoulders relaxed. "I won't give you any trouble."

Alexander smirked. "I heard you tried to kill Elizabeth this morning."

Charlotte took a deep breath and then let it out in a huff. "No, I didn't. Like I told Elizabeth, I saw the man who shot at her.

Someone tried killing me, too."

"Well then, you won't mind going with Sheriff August and telling him your story."

Charlotte chuckled. "You mean to put me in jail."

"It's the right thing to do."

She rolled her eyes. Her gaze stopped on Alexander. He was leaning awkwardly against the door. With one swift kick, she kicked the door. It didn't give.

Alexander chuckled.

"Don't try that again! Please!"

Charlotte squared her shoulders, her eyes sharp with defiance. She hesitated, weighing her options. She rolled her eyes and let out a huff. "Okay, you got me. This is ridiculous."

Sheriff August came running up. "She's been trying to kill Elizabeth and needs to be locked up."

He reached for Charlotte's arm. Charlotte jerked it back and stood as she glared at the sheriff.

Martha rushed up and said, "Rebecca?"

Charlotte chuckled and shook her head. She glanced at Alexander and then back at Martha. "Did everyone know my sister? Who are you?"

Martha stepped back, surprised. "Remarkable. I'm Martha. What's going on here?"

Charlotte snickered. "These two gentlemen want to arrest me for something I didn't do."

Elizabeth came running up, out of breath. "Sheriff, can't we all sit down and talk this out?"

August shook his head. "We can discuss this with the judge tomorrow, or when he returns."

Alexander's eyes shot to the sheriff. "Is this the same judge who sentenced me to be hanged?"

Sheriff August shrugged. "I think so."

Alexander grimaced.

Elizabeth turned to Charlotte and said, "Please go with them. We'll get to the bottom of this. I promise."

Charlotte tilted her head, a smirk tugging at her lips despite the tension. "Yeah, right!"

"Let's go," said the sheriff, grabbing her arm.

Alexander turned to Martha. "I'll be back a little later."

Elizabeth yelled to Charlotte, "I'll take care of Misty."

Charlotte didn't respond. Her silence was louder than any protest.

Soon after, Sheriff August and Alexander left with Charlotte for the town jail.

Martha watched as the cart disappeared down the road. "She's furious."

Elizabeth exhaled sharply. "She has every reason to be angry with me. I hope she forgives me. She's not trying to kill me; she's been working hard to protect me. August won't believe that."

Martha's gaze lingered on the road where the cart was. "We'll figure it out."

Elizabeth walked over to Misty. "My, aren't you beautiful," she said as she patted the horse's face.

Martha joined Elizabeth. "Charlotte will be okay. The worst that will happen to her tonight is she'll get a meal and maybe a good night's rest."

"I don't know. She'll be stewing all night, I bet." Elizabeth led Misty to a stall inside the barn.

Martha got some hay for the horse, then touched Elizabeth's arm. "I think you need a distraction. Let's go over the list you showed me this morning."

CHAPTER FIFTY-TWO

You Could Have Been Killed

Elizabeth and Martha sat side by side at the desk in the study, with Joseph's list spread out in front of them.

Martha leaned forward, peering out the window. "No sign of Alexander yet."

Elizabeth joined her gaze. "It's too soon. He won't be back for another hour."

Martha nodded, then turned back to the list. "What's Charlotte like? She looks so much like her sister."

A soft smile tugged at Elizabeth's lips. "When we talk, it's like I'm with Rebecca again. She shares so many of her sister's mannerisms."

Martha smiled. "I know what you mean. When I looked into her eyes, I could've sworn Rebecca was staring back at me."

Elizabeth's smile faded. "Charlotte's a bit more rugged than Rebecca ever was. She was married to an outlaw—he led a gang of stagecoach robbers."

Martha's eyes widened. "Oh my!"

Elizabeth looked away. "He's dead now."

Martha hesitated. "What happened?"

Elizabeth met her eyes. A pause hung between them. "I killed him."

Martha gasped.

"It's a story for another time. Let's get started on that list." Elizabeth reached for her pencil and paper. "Charlotte mentioned a few names earlier: Hamilton, Avery, and Frank Williams." She wrote each name down.

"Frank Williams supposedly shot at me this morning. Hamilton accompanied him. Then, later, Charlotte killed Avery. Frank Williams got away."

A crackling noise came from outside. Elizabeth stopped writing.

Martha's breath caught in her throat. Her eyes darted to the window. "What was that?"

Elizabeth followed her gaze. "No one's there." She looked back at the list.

"Jack," said Elizabeth, and added the name. "He was pointing a gun at me when I arrived at Charlotte's camp."

Martha's eyes flicked to Elizabeth. "You went to a place filled with outlaws? Alone?"

"Yes. Several people were standing behind Jack, and others were farther back in the cove. Charlotte appeared to be in charge. She told them not to shoot me."

Martha shook her head. "That sounds like something I'd do." She hesitated. "Any idea what Charlotte is planning to do with those men?"

"I don't know."

Elizabeth lined up Joseph's list next to the new one.

A fast-approaching horse startled them.

Martha jumped to her feet and peeked out the window. "It's Alexander. I'll go get him."

Elizabeth hesitated, glanced at the two lists, and then followed Martha.

Alexander walked in the front door. "Are you two okay? The front door was open."

Elizabeth said, "Heavens, I thought I locked it. We've been in the study. Everything is fine. Come with us. I want to show you something."

Alexander secured the front door, then followed Elizabeth and Martha to the study. The two women sat at the desk, Martha to Elizabeth's right.

Alexander grabbed a chair and sat on Elizabeth's left. "Is that Joseph's list? Douglas told me about it."

Alexander leaned in. "There are quite a few names there."

"Yes. All these men worked for John when…"

Alexander brought the paper closer to him. "Frank Williams? That name sounds familiar."

"He's the sharpshooter that's supposedly trying to kill me."

"Hmm," said Alexander. "Why are some of the names circled?"

Martha said, "We're not sure."

Alexander glanced at Elizabeth. "Why were you with that woman earlier?"

"I had a feeling she would be able to help me figure out what was going on."

"She tried to kill you," said Alexander through gritted teeth.

Elizabeth shook her head. "No. I don't believe that."

Martha said, "I know I met her briefly, but I doubt she wants Elizabeth dead." She turned to Elizabeth. "She's had many opportunities to do you in, and she didn't. If anything, she's looking out for you."

Elizabeth nodded. "I followed Charlotte to her camp, where she and her men were hiding—"

Alexander gasped. "What? You could have been killed!"

Elizabeth took a deep breath and exhaled slowly. "In retrospect, I guess it was not a wise thing for me to do. I didn't know all those men would be there with her."

Alexander sat back, astonished. Then he leaned forward. "How many men were there?"

Elizabeth offered a half-hearted grin. "Six people were standing behind the man who greeted me with a gun, but I'm sure there's more."

Alexander's head cocked back, his jaw slackened. "Elizabeth! That man could have shot you."

"He was guarding their camp." She chuckled. "He didn't like me."

Martha's lips curled into a slight smile. "How could anyone not like you?"

Alexander's jaw slackened. "Martha!"

"Elizabeth can take care of herself. This sounds similar to the time when I apprehended those bank robbers on my own. Remember? And you later told me I could have been killed."

"Oh dear!" said Elizabeth.

Alexander's eyes turned back to the list, shaking his head. "By now, all of the men here know you've turned it over to the Law."

Elizabeth nodded. "I'm sure you're right. When I locked eyes with Jack's, I saw his rage."

"Who is Jack?" asked Martha.

"He was the sentry who was guarding Charlotte's camp."

Alexander bit his lip. "Charlotte's camp?"

"Well, they took direction from her," she said.

Alexander gave Elizabeth a sideways look.

"I can see now why Charlie was upset. He told Douglas that some of his men were missing when he returned to his camp."

"Alexander, Charlotte is not trying to kill me. If anything, she's been helpful."

Martha said, "That's what it looks like to me. Everything you've said about her supports that. If she's skilled with a gun, I'm sure she would have had plenty of opportunities to shoot you."

Elizabeth smiled. "The first day I met her, she brought a heavy six-shooter with a hair-fire trigger. She held it to my ribs when she escaped."

Alexander choked on his breath. "What?"

"August had his gun on her and wasn't listening to reason. I admit I was worried about the sensitive trigger, but I understand why she did it."

Alexander shook his head. "She's up to something. Looks like she's gathering an army large enough to worry the Law. Douglas told me Charlie came here with about twenty riders. What was she planning to do next? Start a civil war? Charlotte's men against Charlie's."

Elizabeth said, "All of them were once loyal to John, or at least most of them anyway. And they all know by now I killed John. So I can understand why they don't like me."

Martha pointed to the list. "And now, some of these men listed here think it would be better if you were dead."

Elizabeth shrugged. She added Hamilton's name to the new list and wrote a check mark beside Hamilton's and Zack Avery's names.

Martha asked, "Elizabeth, what are you thinking?"

"Charlotte told me Hamilton and another man, Frank Williams, rode into town after Charlie this morning. That's when Frank shot at me. She didn't mention anything else about Hamilton, but he must be working with Frank."

She put a check mark next to Frank's name.

Martha said, "Both Hamilton and Frank's names are circled in

Joseph's list."

Alexander's forehead was riddled with creases as he strained to keep up. Martha leaned in as if she'd soaked up everything Elizabeth said and was ready for more.

Elizabeth continued, "This evening, Frank or Avery shot at us. I'm not sure which because Charlotte says someone shot at her early this morning before they shot at me."

Alexander gasped. "You believe someone is trying to kill her, too?"

"There's more."

Alexander glanced at Martha and then took a deep breath. Martha was silently examining Joseph's original list and the new one Elizabeth had created.

"What happened next?" said Alexander as he exhaled loudly.

"Well, Charlotte killed Avery. Then Frank Williams got away, and Charlotte's men chased after him."

Martha interrupted, "Avery's name is also circled on Joseph's list."

Elizabeth said, "Interesting."

Alexander said, "Did you come home right after you left Charlotte's camp?"

"Yes. If I hadn't been at Charlotte's camp, those outlaws would have ambushed me here while I was all alone."

Alexander's face tightened with worry. "You are smack in the middle of all this mess."

"I know."

Alexander's stomach growled. "I'm beginning to understand why you both think that Charlotte is innocent."

Elizabeth's shoulders relaxed.

Alexander said, "Twice in one day, someone has tried to kill you."

Elizabeth smiled. "And they failed. Now, let's get something to eat."

Martha glanced up at Elizabeth. "I'll be right there." Martha continued to scrutinize the two lists.

Elizabeth nodded. "It'll be ready in fifteen minutes."

"Okay," said Martha.

Alexander followed Elizabeth as she hurried into the kitchen to prepare something for them to eat. Alexander sat at the table as she took some plates from the cupboard.

Elizabeth glanced at him. His face was creased with concern.

"What did you think about Charlotte?" she asked as she sliced the apples.

"Other than she might be trying to kill you?"

She ignored his sarcasm. "She bears quite a likeness to Rebecca."

Alexander hesitated. "When I saw her face, I thought it was her."

Elizabeth placed a plate of food before Alexander, then prepared two more plates for herself and Martha.

Elizabeth said, "At first, I saw Rebecca in her eyes. But as I got to know her, her mannerisms, her speech... I knew she was related to her."

Alexander said, "Do you believe her?"

"She can't be lying about her features."

He took a quick sip of water. "I don't trust her."

Elizabeth smiled again. "I want to see Charlotte tomorrow. I need to talk to her. I think she knows more than she's letting on."

CHAPTER FIFTY-THREE

Powerful Enough?

The following day, Elizabeth walked past the guest room. The door was open.

"Martha? Alexander?"

When she went into the kitchen, a breeze rushed at her. The back door was open.

She peered out the window. Martha was feeding the chickens, while the horses grazed on the grass next to the barn. Charlotte's horse stood near the fence, ears pricked toward the trail that led to the creek.

"Poor thing. She's looking for Charlotte," she muttered.

She reached for her egg basket by the back door to collect eggs. It was heavy with fresh eggs. Smiling, she took them and placed them in a bowl she kept on the counter. She lit the stove and laid out the ingredients for making Queen Cakes. Then, with practiced ease, she whipped up the cake batter, poured it into her muffin pan with nine rounded wells, and slid it into the hot oven.

She leaned out the door and called out, "Breakfast will be ready soon."

"Okay. We'll be right there," Martha yelled back. "Would you like some help?"

"No. Enjoy the sun." She rushed into the kitchen and worked quickly on breakfast.

Alexander walked in behind Martha. "Something smells delicious."

"It's almost done."

"When did you want to go to the sheriff's office?" asked Alexander reluctantly. "I don't think it's wise to go there."

"Perhaps we could be there at eleven," said Elizabeth. "I'd like to talk with Thomas, too."

Martha's eyes shot to Alexander. His nose was wrinkled, and creases of disgust painted his face.

Elizabeth said, "Let's have breakfast. Then, I'd like to get some target practice in."

Martha's face lit up bright. "I'd love to join you."

Elizabeth smiled. "I've heard stories about your epic shooting skills, Martha."

Alexander said, "No doubt you've heard she's a better shot than I am."

Elizabeth chuckled. She served up the food. "There's plenty if you want seconds."

They all sat and ate.

Elizabeth's gaze danced from Alexander to Martha. "I'm glad to have your company."

"Me too," said Martha with a mouthful of food.

"Elizabeth, how can you be so cheerful amid all this trouble?" asked Alexander.

Elizabeth saw the bruises on Alexander's arm and his face. She imagined the horror Thomas had put him through. "Soon, we'll get to the bottom of this and put this whole thing behind us."

Alexander scraped the last bit of food from his plate. "This was delicious."

Elizabeth smiled and said, "Are you doing okay?"

Alexander glanced at Martha. "I'm fine. I'm glad it's over. Let's focus on you and who is taking shots at you."

Elizabeth said, "Agreed. I think it's one of those people on Joseph's list. Probably Frank Williams."

Martha said, "I'm curious about the circled names. I think that's important. John's name wasn't circled."

Elizabeth hesitated. "Neither was Charlie's."

Alexander said, "Another thing that's important is that his men aren't pleased you shot John."

"I'm not happy with them either." She took the cakes out of the oven and set them aside to cool. The sweet smell of roses from the cakes filled the air.

Martha laughed. "Is it time to shoot some cans?"

Elizabeth nodded. "I'll be right back." She smiled and then rushed to her bedroom. She closed the door behind her. She walked to the closet on the far side of the room and opened its door.

She caught sight of two pouches, one big, the other smaller, on the top shelf. "There you are."

She stepped up on her tiptoes and brought them down. She stuffed the smaller one into her pocket and took the other to the kitchen, where she set it on the table.

"I used to tell Joseph violence was never the answer," said Elizabeth. "Now I'm not so sure. There are shades to this I never wanted to see. And now that I do, I'm ready to stand for justice."

Martha opened the pouch and pulled out the six-shooter. "This one's a beauty!"

"Let's take turns shooting with it."

Martha smiled, raising her brows, and left for her bedroom. She returned, grinning, a minute later, brandishing her weapon. "I never leave home without my gun."

Alexander sat dumbfounded.

"Really? You two are a lot alike."

Martha laughed.

"I have more bullets," said Elizabeth as she reached into her pocket and pulled out another pouch. "I take this gun out every so often and keep it oiled up. I keep it clean. It was Joseph's. I have mine, too, but I'd like to get comfortable shooting with his gun. It's a bit heavier than mine is."

Alexander smiled. "That's smart."

Elizabeth took her gun and the pouch of bullets, then stopped by the back door. "Let's go practice some."

Alexander said, grinning, "Do you mind if I get a little shut-eye? I'm still a little tired from the hanging and all."

"Put some pillows over your ears if the noise bothers you," said Martha.

A few minutes later, Martha joined Elizabeth outside.

Elizabeth asked, "Is Alexander okay? He seemed more subdued than usual."

"He was thrashing in bed for part of the night."

Elizabeth's face creased with worry. "It's his first night in a regular bed."

Martha cast a sideways glance at the house, then back at Elizabeth. "He'll be fine. He needs to work some things out. He wants us to focus on you for now." She nodded softly. "Okay? Let's start practicing!"

Elizabeth fired, her stance unshaken, as the tin cans toppled and dropped to the ground.

Martha cast a sideways glance at Elizabeth. "I thought you hadn't shot in a while."

Elizabeth shrugged. "I was quite the tomboy when I was younger. Back then, I always carried a gun. I was the best shooter among all of my friends. No one could outshoot me, not even my Pa." Her gaze fell momentarily to the ground. "For a time, I gave it up. However, after I married Joseph, he encouraged me to take up shooting again. He and I used to practice often."

Martha said, "My word! We're not that different. Growing up in New York, I was a tomboy, too. I used to wear pants and pretend I was the fastest draw in town. My mother disapproved. She preferred I wear fancy dresses. It's funny, though, she had more of an issue with me wearing pants than firing a gun. Anyhow, after my parents died, I took up shooting again." A memory of her parents' death came to her. Thomas had participated in the stagecoach robbery where her parents were killed. And, Thomas's uncle, Randall, had killed them.

Martha continued. "It's difficult to imagine you as a tomboy. You're always dressed in the latest fashions. And your hair is always delicately placed and smelling of roses."

Elizabeth smiled. "My father taught me to shoot as a young girl."

"My father taught me, too! Why did you stop shooting?"

She hesitated and turned to Martha. "I've not spoken about my father for years. I'm ashamed of what I did."

"You know you can tell me anything. I'll always love you. No matter what."

Elizabeth took a deep breath and exhaled all at once.

"The older I got, the cockier I was with that gun."

"The power the gun yields can be intoxicating," said Martha.

"One day, my father and I were arguing. I pulled my six-shooter to shoot some cans."

"Yes."

"He insisted I give him my gun, and I refused. My father tried to wrestle the gun away from me, and it went off."

Martha gasped. "Did you shoot him?"

Elizabeth offered Martha a warm smile. "Yes. He died a few days later. I was horrified and angry at myself for what I had done. After that, I stopped shooting for a long time until I met Joseph."

"I'm sure your Pa would have forgiven you."

Elizabeth smiled at Martha as she held Joseph's gun. She turned back to the cans and fired mercilessly at them. Each fell as the bullet pierced their thin metal bodies.

Alexander walked up. "It's almost ten, we should get going soon."

Martha kissed his cheek. "Did you rest well?"

"Yes. Thank you," said Alexander. He yawned.

Elizabeth nodded and leveled her six-shooter at the target and shot. It didn't have a chance.

"My turn," said Martha. She aimed and pulled the trigger. A dirty, red liquid exploded from the can. "That's disgusting!"

Elizabeth laughed. "I loaded it with some rusty-red water."

"Yuck. It looks like blood."

Alexander grinned. "We'd better go if you want to get there by eleven."

Elizabeth nodded. "I have to put a few things in a basket for Charlotte and Thomas."

Alexander's face soured, "Are you sure you want to go. It's gonna be hard to keep someone from shooting at you out in the open. Maybe we should wait a few days."

Martha cast a sideways glance at Alexander. "What's wrong? Your face went from laughter to glum."

Elizabeth gasped. "It's that judge. Isn't it?"

Alexander rolled his eyes. "I keep replaying that day that he sentenced me to hanging. He was brutal and didn't give me a chance to plead my case. How many other folks did he do this to?"

Martha hugged Alexander.

Elizabeth rested her hand on Alexander's arm. "I'm sorry. I should have realized the gravity. If you'd rather stay, Martha and I could go."

Alexander straightened up. "No! I'll work out my issues with that judge, and it won't interfere with my duty to protect and serve the public. Let's go!"

They went back to the house, and Elizabeth quickly put the gun back in the bedroom. She planned to clean it when she returned.

Alexander and Martha were sitting at the table when Elizabeth came rushing into the kitchen.

She loaded the picnic basket with some tasty food and the Queen Cakes, Charlotte's favorite.

"I wish you were more careful with Charlotte. I don't trust that woman," said Alexander.

"Don't worry. I don't want to talk about Charlotte now. Please tell me how Gertrude and your two boys are doing while I finish packing lunch. We haven't had much of a chance to chat about them."

Alexander and Martha smiled.

Martha said, "I miss them all, especially my two little boys."

"I bet they're anxious to see you."

Alexander said, "We sent Gertrude a telegram saying all was well and we would return in a few days."

Elizabeth covered the basket with a towel. "I look forward to seeing them."

"Those cakes smell delicious," said Alexander.

"Would you like one? I made plenty."

"Maybe later," he said.

Elizabeth nodded. "I'm ready to go."

"I'll bring the wagon around front," said Alexander.

Ten minutes later, Elizabeth, Martha, and Alexander were on their way to see Charlotte and Thomas.

CHAPTER FIFTY-FOUR
Caged Animal

Elizabeth walked into the sheriff's office carrying her basket. Alexander and Martha followed close behind.

Sheriff August jumped to his feet, surprised. "Elizabeth, what are you doing here?"

"I brought lunch for Thomas and Charlotte."

He let out a short breath of disapproval and then pointed at the cells. "They're right there. Thomas is in the cell on the left, across from Charlotte."

Thomas looked up at her from his cot and then looked away. He went back to facing the wall.

Elizabeth hurriedly took out some cakes and wrapped them in a cloth. "Alexander, would you please take this to Thomas?"

Alexander stood frozen, his face cocked back, looking at her as if she were crazy.

"Oh dear. I'm sorry, Alexander. Forgive me." She turned to Sheriff August. "Would you mind?"

August grimaced and took the dessert to the disgraced sheriff.

Charlotte watched Thomas curiously as Sheriff August placed the cake inside Thomas's cell. Thomas didn't move.

"Martha and I need to chat with Charlotte," Elizabeth said firmly.

August returned to his desk. "Are you sure that's a good idea?"

"Yes."

He shrugged in surrender and let out a long breath. "Okay."

Alexander sat in the guest chair as August followed Elizabeth and Martha to the cell where Charlotte sat on her bed.

"What do you want?" snarled Charlotte. She looked suspiciously at Martha. "Are the two of you going to gang up on me?"

Elizabeth shook her head. "We're here to talk."

Charlotte's cheek twitched into a half-smile.

Elizabeth showed Charlotte the basket. "I've brought you some lunch and some of those cakes you like so much."

Charlotte narrowed her eyes.

The sheriff stepped in front of Elizabeth, blocking her sight of Charlotte. "Elizabeth, this is a bad idea."

"Nonsense! Please move aside and open the door so we can talk comfortably with my friend."

Charlotte grinned. "I'll be good, Sheriff. I promise."

The sheriff looked menacingly at Charlotte and then unlocked the door. "I'll stand right here."

Martha followed Elizabeth into the cell.

Elizabeth furrowed her brows. "I'll let you know when I need you. Now leave us alone to talk."

Charlotte stifled a grin and then sat down on the cot.

The sheriff glared at Charlotte and then closed the cell door. He jiggled the keys next to the lock, pretending to secure the door. He didn't trust Charlotte, and he wanted to be able to jump in quickly if something went wrong.

"Alexander and I will be at my desk, where I can watch you both."

Elizabeth turned back to Charlotte and took three cakes from her basket. She handed a cake each to Charlotte and Martha, keeping one for herself. "I baked them this morning."

Martha took a quick bite. "I love these."

A hint of a smile crawled onto Charlotte's face. "I'm still mad at you for tricking me."

Elizabeth exhaled through her nose, her patience waning. "Sometimes things happen. Get over it."

Charlotte laughed. "Our first fight!"

Elizabeth rolled her eyes and then glanced at August. His eyes were narrowed and locked on Charlotte.

"Sheriff, I thought you were going to chat with Alexander."

August snapped out of his obsessed glare. He cleared his throat and straightened. He smiled at Elizabeth and then turned to Alexander.

Charlotte grinned. "Okay, what do you want to talk about?" She took a bite of her cake. "I feel like a caged animal in here. The sheriff watches me like a hawk." She pointed to Thomas.

"And he sits in there and sulks, staring at the wall."

Martha and Elizabeth glanced at Thomas and then settled on Charlotte.

Elizabeth said, "You're safe here."

Charlotte coughed out a chuckle. "That's not true. Anyone could walk in and shoot me when the sheriff and his deputies are gone. They probably don't lock the front door." Charlotte snickered. "Heck, he didn't lock the cell door."

Martha walked over to the cell door and pushed it gently. It creaked open. She chuckled softly.

Elizabeth rolled her eyes and shook her head. "He's convinced you're behind this whole mess. Honestly, I think you could help us figure out what's going on here."

Charlotte rolled her eyes. "I told you someone is trying to kill us. Both of us!"

Elizabeth stared at Charlotte.

Charlotte took a deep breath and let out a huff. "Now, what do you want to talk about?"

Elizabeth reached into her bag and retrieved the list she'd been obsessing over. She handed it to Charlotte.

Charlotte smiled. "This is the list I wrote for Joseph."

Martha's eyes shot to Charlotte.

Charlotte caught sight of Thomas as he stirred. She blinked in surprise at Thomas's interest in the list or perhaps the mention of his father.

Elizabeth turned to Thomas in time to see him turn back to the wall.

Charlotte continued her examination.

Martha asked, "You created this for Joseph?"

Charlotte nodded and then focused on the list for a few seconds.

She cast a sideways glance at Elizabeth. "Is this the list you gave Sheriff August?"

"I copied the names to a new list for him."

Charlotte let out a dry laugh. "You used this against us." She blew out a puff of air. "Joseph would most certainly have been disappointed. He wanted to do good with this!"

Elizabeth gasped.

Charlotte winced. "Sorry. I shouldn't have said that."

"I understand."

Charlotte perused the list and then smiled.

"What? Why are you smiling?" asked Elizabeth.

"See, there I am." Charlotte pointed to the list.

Elizabeth leaned in for a closer look. "Where?"

Martha's right brow lifted, and then she took another bite of her cake.

Charlotte showed Elizabeth the line with "John and Charlie" written on it. "Right there."

Elizabeth shook her head. "But Charlie is your brother."

Charlotte rolled her eyes and let out a breath. "Yeah, he is. Look down here."

She passed her finger over each name down the list and stopped at the bottom of the page.

The edge of the paper was crushed. Charlotte carefully used her fingernail to flatten the edge. It was faded from the crease marks.

"It spells C-H-A-R-L-E-S. Then B-U-C-H. There is a little tear after the H. It doesn't matter. That is Charles Buchanan listed there. That's his given name. Most everyone calls him Charlie."

"Really?" Elizabeth blinked at the revelation.

"Yes." Charlotte straightened up and shifted on the bumpy bed where they were seated. "Joseph always referred to my brother as Charles. Charlie hated that. Several times, Charlie asked him to call him 'Charlie' instead. But Joseph stuck to Charles."

Elizabeth's brow furrowed. "Why'd you write: 'John and Charlie' for you and John?"

"Because I'd like for people to call me 'Charlie' because Charlotte is too dainty. If people called me Charlie, they'd treat me with respect."

"That's probably true. But, I think you have a beautiful name."

Charlotte shrugged.

Elizabeth paused as she studied Charlotte's face, wondering how a powerful woman like her would care much what others thought of her. She brushed the thought away and went back to the reason they were there. "Why did you create the list for Joseph?"

"Joseph asked me to write down everyone's names in the camp, including Randall's and John's men. He told John he wanted to pay each man himself."

"Really?"

"Yes." Charlotte looked at the list, puzzled. "Why are some of the names circled?"

Elizabeth shrugged. "I thought you circled them."

"Nope. Joseph must have." Charlotte's eyes shifted upward in thought. She smiled. "Frank Williams shot at you yesterday morning. Avery and Frank Williams shot at us last evening."

Charlotte cast a sideways glance at Elizabeth. "They shot at both of us."

Elizabeth grinned. "Yes, they did. Please go on."

Charlotte smiled as she turned back to the list. "Notice their names are circled."

Elizabeth felt encouraged. "Are any of your men's names circled?"

"Those men are not mine. They're good people. Jack told me several men wanted to escape Charlie's control. And Randall told them they could hide out at the cove at the edge of Joseph's property."

Martha gasped. "Randall?"

Charlotte nodded. "Yes. He's helping us." She looked at the list. "Of all the men at the cove, only Randall's is circled." She paused. "Hmm. Smith's name isn't circled. Anyhow, he was one of Randall's men, but he's with us now."

Martha glanced at Alexander by the sheriff's desk and then back at Charlotte. "That's hard to believe that Randall would be helping anyone but himself."

Elizabeth let out a soft breath. "Randall and I had a long chat the day Joseph was shot. He's not trying to kill me."

Martha asked, "What did he tell you?"

Elizabeth shook her head and remained tight-lipped.

Charlotte shot Elizabeth a puzzled look and then turned to Martha. "He said that he made a promise to Joseph to look out for her. I didn't believe it myself, but he's changed."

Elizabeth's eyes bore into Charlotte. "That's true. I asked Randall for a little time before we met again. Suffice it to say that whenever that list was created, Randall's name deserved to be circled, but not anymore."

Charlotte half-smiled. "If Joseph circled these names, maybe he knew who was loyal... and who was dangerous. Someone inside the camp must have told him which was which."

Martha's brows narrowed. "What puzzles me is why Howard Jackson's name is circled. I met him briefly. He does drink too much, sure." Her gaze flicked upward for a moment. "Still, he came across as amicable and polite. Claimed he'd never killed anyone."

Charlotte smiled. "He's a lovely man. I think he's lonely and maybe a little off. He thinks the crows are out to get him."

Martha's mind was working to solve this part of the puzzle. "Hmm. And yet his name is circled."

Charlotte turned to Martha. "One thing that angered John was when Howard showed up at the camp and handed out envelopes from Joseph to some of the men. He didn't give an envelope to everyone. When Howard gave John and me one of those envelopes, John got angry. He went and talked with Joseph about it, and Joseph said he was hoping to help out the men so they could quit robbing stagecoaches."

Elizabeth smiled. "That sounds like something Joseph would do." She glanced away and wiped an errant tear from her face.

Charlotte grinned as she pointed to the top of the list. "John's and my names are not circled. See, I'm one of the good ones!" She glanced away. "John was, too."

Elizabeth's face held a soft smile. "I'm sorry about your husband."

"I miss him. We had some wonderful times together. Believe it or not, he liked Joseph. John was upset when he died. That's when Charlie started acting like he was in charge."

"John was okay with that?" asked Elizabeth.

"He wanted out. He was tired of the life we led. He said it was time to settle down and go back east. He was done with always running from the Law."

Martha crossed her arms and then uncrossed them, clasping her hands together. "What did Charlie think of John?"

"I don't know why, but Charlie was a little uneasy with John, kinda like how a younger brother might be with his older brother. But I know Charlie looked up to John. Charlie and John argued about Joseph quite a bit when Joseph was alive. John wanted Charlie to apologize to Joseph and try to make amends. Charlie wanted nothing to do with Joseph."

Elizabeth remembered the day Rebecca was killed when she'd seen Charlie arguing with John. "I was aware Joseph didn't care for Charlie. But Charlie was always polite to me."

Charlotte's nose wrinkled. "Something occurred to me. John told me that Randall once bragged that Frank Williams was a sharpshooter. Randall claimed Frank was a better shot than anyone, including me. If he's so great, then why does he keep missing you?"

Elizabeth hesitated. "You told me you shouted to him as he was about to shoot me when I was riding into town. Maybe that was enough to distract him."

"Jack told me that Frank is hitting the whiskey hard these days. He probably gets easily distracted," she said. "Randall used to be close with Frank, but not lately."

Charlotte hesitated when Thomas glanced at her and then quickly turned back.

Martha turned to Elizabeth. "If Joseph trusted Howard to deliver those envelopes of money to John's camp, then that must mean Joseph trusted Howard."

Elizabeth nodded. "Joseph bought a little shack for Howard, and Howard was appreciative."

Charlotte said, "Maybe you should ask Howard. Seems like he'd tell you about those circled names. From what I saw, he didn't give any of those envelopes to any of the men whose names are circled."

Elizabeth's face filled with a broad smile. "That would explain why Howard's name was circled. Why deliver an envelope to himself?"

Martha said, "I wonder if Charlie knows that some of those 'bad' guys are working for him?"

Elizabeth said, "Or against him?"

August walked up. "Elizabeth, let's get to lunch. Charlie is going to meet us there."

Elizabeth turned to Charlotte. "Please have a little patience. We'll get this all sorted out soon. I'll be back tomorrow."

Charlotte rose, looming over Elizabeth with a flash of irritation. "My patience has its limits!"

Elizabeth chuckled. "I can see that."

Charlotte rolled her eyes and sat back down.

Elizabeth exhaled softly. "Enjoy the cakes and the hearty lunch I brought you."

"Ask Charlie about those names on that list."

Elizabeth's brows lifted. "I plan to."

Martha patted Charlotte's arm. "I'm glad we talked. Thanks to you, I think we have enough to figure out what's going on here. I hope we can be friends too. I cared for your sister."

Charlotte's breath choked in her throat as her eyes moistened. She nodded at Martha.

Elizabeth's eyes shot to Thomas when he peeked over at them briefly and then turned back to the wall.

Martha walked out of the cell and cast a sideways glance at Thomas as she rushed to Alexander.

Elizabeth hugged Charlotte and then walked out of the cell, stopped next to Thomas's cell, and said, "I love you. I'm sorry I wasn't there for you when you needed me most. I should have believed you about Rebecca's death. I'm here for you now."

Thomas's head moved slightly.

CHAPTER FIFTY-FIVE

Do You Know?

Alexander, Martha, Elizabeth, and Sheriff August stepped out onto the sheriff's office porch.

Elizabeth took Martha's arm. "What a beautiful day."

"It certainly is," said Martha. "It's unfortunate Charlotte is stuck inside and can't enjoy this day with us."

Sheriff August exhaled sharply. "That woman is dangerous."

"Guffaw!" said Elizabeth.

He rolled his eyes and muttered to Alexander, "Elizabeth is too trusting." He grinned at her. "You know that's true."

Elizabeth chuckled.

Alexander turned to Elizabeth. "Did Charlotte tell you what you needed to know?"

"She told us quite a bit. Things are coming together. Maybe Charlie will give a few more answers. He reacted strangely when I mentioned the list." She glanced at Martha. "What do you think about Charlotte?"

Martha said, "Charlotte is an exceptional woman. She's very open, and I believe we have a lot of information that can help us figure out who's responsible for killing our loved ones. I think Charlie and Howard might provide some of the missing pieces we need to solve this serious mystery."

August said, "I haven't seen Howard today. Charlie should be at the restaurant." He shook his head. "Charlie is probably going to order that same steak and potatoes he likes so much."

"Isn't that what you usually get?" asked Elizabeth.

He glanced at her and smiled.

"Yes. The last time Charlie and I ate at the restaurant in Sacramento, he asked for his usual. When it was my turn, I ordered my usual as well. That woman taking my order had no idea what that was."

Elizabeth laughed.

As they stepped up on the restaurant porch.

August opened the door. "After you."

Elizabeth and Martha marched inside, followed by Alexander and August.

Charlie jumped to his feet when the group walked up. "Hello, Mrs. Pruitt." He blinked several times. "Mrs. Johnson."

"It's good to see you, Charlie. It's been a while," said Martha as she settled into her seat.

Elizabeth sat across from Charlie. "You know Martha?"

"Yes. Douglas had hired me to take care of their home before they arrived in California."

Alexander sat next to Martha. "He did a great job. He had a block of ice waiting for us in the icebox when we got there. That was considerate of you."

Elizabeth nodded. "He helped Joseph and me on our property, too."

"Thank you, Mrs. Pruitt."

"Charlie, how many years have we known each other, and in that time, how many times have I asked you to call me Elizabeth?"

"I'm sorry, Mrs.—I mean—Elizabeth," said Charlie.

Elizabeth chuckled.

Sheriff August asked, "Have you ordered yet?"

"Nope, I thought I should wait for you all."

Sheriff August waved at the woman coming out of the kitchen.

"Can we order?" asked the sheriff.

The woman approached and fixed her eyes on Sheriff August with quiet anticipation.

Charlie perked up and said, "I'll have the—"

Sheriff August interrupted.

"Elizabeth, Martha, what would you like to order?"

Elizabeth offered a polite smile. "I'll have the chicken...no, I'll have the Steak and Potatoes."

"Same," said Martha.

Sheriff August winked at Charlie and said, "Steak and Potatoes, please."

"I'll have my usual," said Charlie.

"What's that?" asked the woman.

"Steak and Potatoes," a flustered Charlie said.

"And you, sir," said the woman to Alexander.

"I'll have the Steak and Potatoes, too," said Alexander.

The woman nodded and rushed away to the kitchen.

Charlie offered a wry grin and looked at Elizabeth. "So... now that Charlotte is locked up, would you say you feel a little safer?"

"It's already past noon, and no one has shot at me since last night. I guess that's a positive sign."

"Somebody shot at you last night?" asked Charlie, his face etched with surprise.

"Yes, and I'm here to tell you they missed their target."

Charlie didn't laugh. "Do you know who shot at you? Was it Charlotte?"

Elizabeth fixed her gaze on Charlie. "There were two men. One of them was named Avery."

Charlie's eyes widened. "What? That's one of my men. No one has seen him since yesterday. Avery and more than a dozen men left the camp after Charlotte arrived. You should ask Charlotte about them."

Elizabeth continued, "Avery is dead. The other one got away."

Charlie's gaze fell away and then shot back to Elizabeth, his brows raised.

"Those men who have gone rogue are causing trouble. I spoke with my men this morning, and they are all committed to pledging their loyalty to our agreement."

Sheriff August cleared his throat. "Charlie, don't worry. We'll catch those rogue men and get things back to normal here. We need you and your men to provide safety for our stagecoach lines."

Alexander said, "Douglas is ready to start."

"I am, too," said Charlie.

Elizabeth studied Charlie's face, watching as his eyes lit up with excitement.

Alexander smiled. "Charlie, Sheriff August here says you have some ideas to help us get started."

"Yes. We should have one or two men ride with the driver on the stagecoaches. It would be helpful to get them familiar with the routes. Some could stay at the way stations, too."

Alexander nodded, his eyes focused intently on Charlie. "That sounds like a great idea now that you have fewer men."

Charlie winced, the weight of his thinning ranks clearly pressing on him.

Sheriff August's breath caught. "We can recruit more men later if needed."

Charlie's lips edged into a faint smile. "Trains will soon replace the stagecoaches."

"That won't happen for a long time," said Sheriff August.

Elizabeth's brows lifted in surprise, and she turned to August. "These days, progress moves quickly."

Sheriff August nodded. "I'm just saying that we should focus on the stagecoach robberies for now."

"Of course," said Elizabeth, scratching her arm, as her gaze fell back to Charlie.

Charlie's eyes darted to her. "Is that where you were wounded?"

"Yes. The doctor made such a fuss. The bullet barely grazed me."

"I'm glad you're okay," said Charlie. "I was worried."

The corner of Elizabeth's lips curled up at his sincerity.

Just then, a serving girl came over, balancing five plates of steak and potatoes. She set them down one by one, lingering as she placed the last plate before Alexander, her smile hinting at mischief.

Alexander shifted in his seat.

Martha straightened, her eyes locking on the woman's.

Elizabeth's eyes lit with a playful fire. "Excuse me. I'll have you know he's happily married to this beautiful woman." She pointed to Martha.

Martha fluttered her fingers at her.

The woman frowned, then rushed away.

Alexander chuckled.

They went silent for a few minutes as they ate.

Alexander spoke up first. "This is delicious."

"It's superb," said Elizabeth.

Elizabeth's gaze lifted from her half-eaten meal to Charlie. He was focused on his food, gobbling it down quickly as if he had somewhere else to be. "Charlie, do you have a man named Williams working for you? A Frank Williams?"

Charlie stopped chewing, his eyes shot to Elizabeth, and then he swallowed. "Williams?" he choked out.

"Yes. Frank Williams."

Charlie slumped, his eyes darting from Elizabeth to Sheriff August and back to her as he swallowed again. His breathing went shallow. "He does work for me."

"Have you seen him?" she asked, her voice steady without a hint of accusation.

"He hasn't been around since yesterday."

Charlie drank some water. "Why do you ask?"

"He shot at me yesterday morning."

Charlie's breath caught in his throat.

Sheriff August suddenly turned to Elizabeth. "I saw Charlotte holding a gun when you were shot."

Charlie leaned closer to Elizabeth. "He wouldn't have fired at you. I trust Frank; he's loyal. He understands how important this deal is, and it's because of you that we have it."

Martha kept her gaze steady on Charlie for a few seconds.

Elizabeth pulled a piece of paper from her bag.

"Charlie, this is the list Charlotte created for Joseph."

Charlie's breath stuck in his throat. His eyes flared open, his pupils narrowing to pinpoints.

Elizabeth handed Charlie the list.

Charlie took it and examined it closely. "Flagg was killed a while back. And Pruitt…"

"Why is Randall Pruitt's name on there? Was that my husband's brother?" She already knew it was.

"Yes. He came out here from New York at the same time Alexander did. He brought several men with him, but most of them are dead." His eyes flicked for an instant to Alexander and Martha.

Alexander nodded.

Charlie continued. "He used to be a force to reckon with, but ever since his hand got shot, he's lost his edge. I was counting on him to keep the men together. But…"

"Is he a member of your group?"

Charlie sighed. "He was gone along with those other men Charlotte stole."

Elizabeth asked, "Do you know why some of the men's names are circled? It's mighty suspicious."

Charlie began at the top of the list, his eyes flicking down each name. He paused, set the paper on the table, and unfolded the crease at the bottom. The color drained from his face as he read the final name.

Elizabeth cast a sideways glance at Martha, who raised her brows in quiet acknowledgment.

"I'm not sure. There's Zack Avery, Hamilton, and Howard Jackson." He glanced at Elizabeth and said, "Howard Jackson isn't dangerous. He's a harmless drunk." He went back to the list.

"Frank Williams is circled, too," Martha added.

Charlie gasped and said, "I…"

Sheriff August huffed and then snatched the list from Charlie. He handed it back to Elizabeth. "Now that Charlotte is locked up, stop worrying about nothing."

"I guess you're right." Elizabeth cast a sideways glance at Martha and took the list.

Charlie's eyes tracked the list as she put it back in her bag.

Sheriff August smiled at Elizabeth. "We're looking out for you."

"Perhaps we should be going," said Elizabeth. "Thank you, Charlie. I'm glad we talked."

Martha nodded to Charlie with a painted smile. Elizabeth's questions had undone him with ease.

Charlie awkwardly jumped to his feet, bumping the edge of the table with his holstered gun.

"It was great to see you, Mrs. Johnson and Mrs. Pruitt," said Charlie.

Martha's gaze shot to Charlie and then to Elizabeth. Elizabeth didn't correct him this time to address her as 'Elizabeth.'

Alexander, Elizabeth, and Martha started for the door.

Sheriff August turned to Charlie and waited a few seconds for them to walk out of earshot.

"Charlie, we'll catch those outlaws and get things under control. You focus on getting your men ready to start work. We've got a lot riding on this. It's got to be a success."

Charlie nodded, and Sheriff August left to join the others.

His gaze stayed fixed on Elizabeth as the group disappeared through the door.

"Damnit, Frank!"

CHAPTER FIFTY-SIX

Let's Chat with...

After arriving home from lunch, Elizabeth and Martha sat on the porch, chatting about what had happened at their meeting with Charlie. Alexander walked up and sat down next to Martha.

Elizabeth said, "I enjoyed our visit with Charlotte. I wish we could have gone back and asked her a few more questions."

"Like what?" asked Martha.

"I would have liked to have asked Charlotte what more she knew about Frank Williams. Maybe she would know more about why he's after me. And, I'm wondering about Charlie."

Martha nodded. "When you showed Charlie the list, I thought he was going to fall out of his seat."

"The color drained from his face when he read the names, especially the last one," said Elizabeth.

"He's hiding something. That's for sure," said Alexander.

Elizabeth half-smiled and said, "I'm thinking the list holds the names of the men who would be better off in jail than protecting stagecoaches. And some of them are his men."

Martha's brows raised. "His name on there must make him nervous." She looked away. "I bet Howard could help us. If he gave out those envelopes, then he could tell us a lot."

Alexander chuckled. "That poor man hasn't been seen since Thomas shot at him. Howard's afraid Thomas is going to kill him for spoiling his plans." Alexander shook his head. "Once he learns Thomas is locked up, he'll find his way back to the saloon."

Elizabeth half-smiled. "I'm guessing Howard will be able to explain why his name is circled on that list, too. For now, I'm sure he's one of the good ones because Joseph trusted him."

Martha smiled. "Agreed."

Elizabeth reached for her purse. "Would you both help me go over the list again. I want to mull over what Charlotte and Charlie told us."

"Of course," said Martha.

Alexander nodded. "I'll join you after I take the horse to the barn and get him fed."

Martha and Elizabeth hurried to the study and sat at the desk. Elizabeth took Joseph's list from her purse and then withdrew a paper from the drawer. It held the names —Avery, Williams, Jack, and Hamilton. All of the names had check marks except for Jack's name.

She picked up the pencil and a new sheet, speaking as she wrote: "Hamilton and Frank Williams left camp after Charlie yesterday morning. And Frank Williams shot at me."

"How do you know Frank Williams shot at you?" asked Martha.

"Charlotte told me," Elizabeth said as she finished writing.

"Do you believe her?"

Elizabeth nodded. "Let's assume everyone is telling the truth, including Charlie."

"That's a good idea." The edge of her lips curled up. "Did Charlie know that Hamilton and Williams left after him?"

"I didn't ask him. I wish I had."

Elizabeth began a new line and wrote, "Frank Williams shot at Elizabeth yesterday morning."

On the third line, she wrote: "Avery or Frank Williams shot at Elizabeth yesterday evening."

She glanced at Martha. "It was probably Avery since he was closest to us when he shot at us. Charlotte shot him dead!"

Martha said, "She sounds like she's an expert with her gun."

"She's both skilled and lethal!"

Alexander walked in and pulled up a chair next to Elizabeth.

"Good, you're here." Elizabeth went back to the paper, left some space below what she had written, started a new line, and wrote, "Zack Avery was killed by Charlotte yesterday evening."

Martha looked crooked at Elizabeth. "Why did you leave a blank line between those two entries?"

Elizabeth chuckled. "I wanted room for another name in case someone else tries to shoot at me again."

Alexander caught his breath. "That's not funny."

Martha grinned

Elizabeth shrugged. "I'm kidding. It'll be easier to solve this if we're level-headed and relaxed. And there's no better way to relax than with humor."

Alexander shooed away the thought of Elizabeth getting shot and then half-smiled. Martha cast a sideways glance at Alexander and winked.

His shoulders eased, a slight smile forming on his lips.

Elizabeth continued, "Frank Williams got away yesterday evening."

Alexander's head cocked back. "Wait a second. That name sounds vaguely familiar. You all brought it up earlier, and it's been bothering me."

Martha said, "Is it someone from the bank?"

"I don't know. I'm terrible with names. It would help if I saw him. I'm good with faces."

Elizabeth patted Alexander's hand. "I wish I could describe him, but I never got a good look at him." She turned back to the paper. "Let's continue with our suspects."

On a new line, she wrote, "Jack pointed a gun at me yesterday evening."

She grinned. "He doesn't like me. None of them do. Except for Charlotte."

Alexander asked, "Why don't they like you?"

Elizabeth let out a sigh, her face softened. "It's either because I killed John, their much-loved leader. Or, because they think I killed Joseph, their beloved benefactor."

Martha shook her head. "That's their loss. Charlotte does indeed like you. I can tell."

A smile returned to Elizabeth's face. "I like her too. She reminds me a lot of Rebecca. She's fiercely independent and self-sufficient."

Martha cast a sideways glance at Alexander. "Sounds like me, huh?"

Alexander rolled his eyes and chuckled. "You're not a criminal."

Elizabeth smiled. "You two are a lovely couple." She took a deep breath. "Okay, let's focus on the circled names. It appears Joseph considered the circled names to be important for some reason, probably because the names were those of dangerous men.

Except, of course, for Howard."

She left more space on the paper, drew a line across the sheet, and wrote 'Circled Names' above the line.

She looked at Joseph's list and started copying each circled name.

"Avery, Hamilton, Howard Jackson, Klein, Randall Pruitt, Frank Williams, Flagg, Hayes, and Chance," she said as she wrote each one on a separate line.

"There's one more," said Martha as she pointed to the bottom.

She pulled her magnifying glass from the drawer and scrutinized the document.

"That's Charlie's name, and it IS circled," said Elizabeth as she added 'Charles Buchanan' to the list.

"What about Randall?" asked Alexander.

She cast a sideways glance at him and said, "He's not a threat."

Alexander winced. "I should have realized Randall and his men were involved with John's group."

Martha took a deep breath and let it out quickly. "Alexander, there's something you should know."

Alexander leaned forward, expectant, fixing his gaze on Martha.

Elizabeth said, "Martha, now is not the time. We need to focus on this list. Lives are at stake. Mine, for example."

Martha's breath caught. "But…"

Elizabeth locked eyes with Martha and narrowed her gaze.

Alexander's face filled with confusion. "What's going on?"

Martha relaxed her shoulders and exhaled loudly. "I'm sorry. I misspoke. It was something Gertrude heard from Agnes."

Alexander chuckled. "You know I can't stand to hear gossip. It's so hard to keep track of what's true and what's hearsay from those two."

"Sorry," said Martha.

Elizabeth nodded with a comforting, small smile. "Let's get back to this list. Howard Jackson came to Sacramento to tell us about Thomas. He's a friend. That's for sure."

Alexander smiled. "I haven't thanked him for riding to Sacramento to tell you. I'd be dead right now if he hadn't done that."

Martha hugged Alexander.

Elizabeth drew a line through Howard Jackson's name. "Joseph was fond of Howard."

Alexander shook his head and chuckled. "Howard and his crows!"

A hint of a smile crossed Elizabeth's lips. "Howard had been living here in Auburn in a small, makeshift cabin not far from here. Joseph gave it to him a while back. I used to hear him shooting his shotgun at those crows until Joseph got him to stop. I'd be surprised if he's still involved with any of the men on this list, but we should still talk to him. He might know something important."

Martha said, "He told us he stayed with the gang because some of them were his friends."

Elizabeth said, "I suppose that's the reason he knew so much about them." She pointed to the list. "Anyhow, Frank Williams shot at me yesterday morning."

Alexander cleared his throat. "At least that's what Charlotte said."

Elizabeth glanced at Alexander. "I think it was him."

Martha said, "I think so, too."

Elizabeth nodded. "Frank Williams was in the same direction as Charlotte, across the street from her."

She put the pen back in its holder and then sat back.

She exhaled sharply. "Okay, let's examine the list more closely."

This is what it showed:

Hamilton and Frank Williams – Left Charlie's camp yesterday morning. Did Charlie know?

Frank Williams – Shot at Elizabeth yesterday morning (According to Charlotte).

Avery/Williams Group – Shot at Elizabeth yesterday evening.

[Blank line]

Zack Avery – Killed by Charlotte yesterday evening (No longer a threat).

Frank Williams – Escaped yesterday evening.

Jack – Pointed a gun at Elizabeth; appears loyal to Charlotte.

Flagg - Died a while back.

Randall Pruitt - Joseph's brother (Not a threat).

"We can cross off Avery, Flagg, Randall Pruitt, and Howard. That leaves Frank Williams, Charlie Buchanan, and three other names we don't know much about yet: Klein, Hayes, and Chance. That's our list of primary suspects."

Martha's gaze lingered on the list. "Charlie's head jerked back, surprised when I asked him about Frank Williams."

Elizabeth glanced at Martha and then back at the list. "What if Charlie is wrong about Frank Williams? Charlie said he trusted him with his life, but he hadn't seen him since yesterday morning. I think Frank has an agenda independent of Charlie's."

Martha nodded. "That would explain why Charlie seemed so upset when you mentioned Frank's name. He's trying to make this deal happen, but he's losing control of his men."

Alexander let out a small gasp. "And for him to say Frank is his right-hand man tells me he must not have known about Frank's agenda."

"I think Charlie's backed into a corner and doesn't even know it." Elizabeth let out a sharp exhale. "What will Charlie do when he finds out what Frank's up to?"

"Poor guy," said Alexander.

Elizabeth gritted her teeth. "In any case, I think we've proven none of this is Charlotte's fault."

Alexander nodded hesitantly.

A small smile crept onto Elizabeth's lips. "She said something that got me thinking. She said Joseph didn't like Charlie. He'd call him Charles even though he preferred to be called Charlie. Joseph didn't like Charlie. And, Charlie didn't like Joseph either."

"Could Charlie have been the one who shot Joseph?"

Martha shook her head. "I don't think so." Martha gasped. "Could you have been the intended target?"

Elizabeth's brows furrowed. "No!"

Martha took Elizabeth's hand. "Would you tell us what happened?"

Elizabeth hesitated and then nodded slowly. "It all happened so fast. I was running toward Joseph. Randall and Thomas were arguing next to him. And then all of a sudden, Joseph looked at me with a crazed, desperate look on his face. He'd been drinking, so I thought that's what it was. He turned and yelled something at me. His eyes were wild, and he was waving his arms frantically at me. Like…"

Alexander leaned in close. "Like what?"

Her gaze fell to the floor, and her eyes welled up with tears. "Like he was signaling for me to get down. I started to look over my shoulder, and that's when I heard the shot and felt the bullet whiz past me. Oh my God!"

Martha gasped.

Elizabeth sniffled. "That bullet was intended for me, not for Joseph." She closed her eyes and covered her mouth.

Martha said, "I'm sorry."

Elizabeth opened her eyes and exhaled sharply. "Even at the end, he was trying to protect me." She paused and then looked from Martha to Alexander and back. "I think we should chat with Frank Williams and Howard."

"Howard is probably at the saloon by now," said Alexander. "For now, we need to steer clear of Frank Williams. I'll notify Sheriff August about him. Let him handle Williams. What about Charlie?"

Elizabeth said, "I'm beginning to think Charlie might be in over his head. If he's being fooled and is worried about losing everything, we might need to step in and help him before he does something…stupid."

Elizabeth narrowed her eyes as the satisfaction of a solved mystery came into view. "I think this mystery might be unraveling. The only thing left is to find out what Frank's hidden agenda is."

Elizabeth brought Joseph's list closer to her and pointed to Frank Williams's circled name.

"Mr. Williams, I believe you should have killed me when you had the chance."

Alexander gasped. "Elizabeth!"

"I'm being melodramatic," she said with a chuckle. "Let's go see the sheriff."

"No. I think it's better if you two stay here. I think you both will be safer here than out on the road. I'll get Sheriff August, and then we'll see if Howard is in the saloon. I'll be back as soon as I can."

Elizabeth smiled at Martha.

Martha left for her room and quickly returned with her gun.

"Just do me a favor and lock up tight. And, please keep your guns close," said Alexander.

"Even inside the house? That sounds silly," said Elizabeth.

Alexander pointed to his holster.

Martha chuckled. "That must be uncomfortable to have on all the time."

"I don't think anyone has a chance with either of you."

"You're right." Elizabeth opened the drawer, pulled out Joseph's six-shooter, and put it beside her on the desk.

"Okay. Hurry back. Martha and I will protect this fortress," said Elizabeth as she grinned.

CHAPTER FIFTY-SEVEN

Freedom

Charlotte sat in her cell as she ate the last of her food. The office was empty. Sheriff August and the deputies had left almost an hour before.

She glanced across the way. Thomas was staring at her.

She narrowed her eyes at him. "I hope they hang you."

"You look so much like Rebecca."

"You kept me from seeing her. She was my sister."

"She didn't want to see you. She knew you hated her," said Thomas.

"I didn't hate her. I resented her having all the opportunities I never had," said Charlotte. "I wanted to be there for her wedding. I begged and pleaded with her."

Thomas's gaze fell to the floor, and he was quiet for a few seconds.

Charlotte took a deep breath and let it out all at once. "Did she really hate me?"

Thomas's gaze lifted, and he shook his head. "She was feeling guilty that she told you to stay away. She often said she missed you. She said you took care of her growing up, especially after your Pa left."

Charlotte's mouth fell open. Her eyes moistened. She held back the tears. "She told me she wanted nothing to do with me as long as I was with John and his people. But I've loved John ever since I was a young girl. I couldn't leave him."

"I'm sorry."

"If my sister loved you, then you must have some goodness in you. She was always a skilled judge of character." She glanced away and sniffled. "Maybe you're not all bad."

The edge of his lips curled up slightly. "Rebecca told me I needed to focus only on the good inside me." He sighed. "I guess my grief got the better of me, and I took it out on Alexander."

"Were you going to go through with the hanging?"

He shrugged. "It's a long story. He and I go way back."

"Were you friends?"

Thomas's face grew tight. "No! Never!" The corner of his lips curled up slightly as he remembered the secret Frank had told him about Randall. "Do you know Randall Pruitt?"

"Sure, I do. He's helping us."

"What?" The devious hint of a smile gave way to astonishment. "Randall Pruitt?"

"Yes. Joseph's brother. You shot his shooting hand. Didn't you?"

Thomas's head jerked back. "Randall is helping you?"

She nodded. "He's a changed man. Just about every one of John's men hated Randall until you crippled his hand. For a while, they felt sorry for him because he'd mope around the camp, complaining his life was over. He went from being this self-centered, jackass to a recluse."

"That doesn't sound like the Randall I know."

Charlotte shrugged. "I heard him arguing with one of his men, Frank Williams, one day."

Thomas took a quick breath.

She continued, "Frank told him, 'You've gotten soft ever since you got your hand shot.' Then, Randall started shouting at Frank. It was awful. I'd say the whole place witnessed the take-down. Randall was brutal. I'd swear Frank was crying afterward. Frank disappeared for several days after that. He deserved it."

"He was my friend at one time." Thomas shook his head as his gaze fell to the floor.

"Really? I can't imagine him having any friends."

"He was my best friend."

"If you're not his friend anymore, then he's liable to want you dead."

"No. He wouldn't."

"Well, he shot at Elizabeth in Sacramento and again at her place here. I think he's trying to shoot us both."

"No!" His breath caught in his throat as a realization struck him. He reached for the bars. "We've got to get out of here."

"I agree." She eyed the basket Elizabeth had brought earlier. She reached in and pulled out a cake.

"These are delightful. That was sweet of Lizzie to bring me these cakes," she said.

She took a bite and chewed slowly.

"She knows I love these cakes." She turned to Thomas. "You and Alexander need to work things out."

He sneered and then sat back down on the cot. The smile crept back onto his face. "He doesn't know it, but he's Randall's son."

She gulped and almost choked. "What! And, he doesn't know? Boy, is he in for a rude awakening."

She took another bite and stopped when she heard the front door open. She couldn't see the door from her cell.

"Sheriff, are you back already?" yelled Charlotte.

There was no answer.

The sound of light footsteps came from around the corner.

"Sheriff August!" she called out.

"Be quiet, it's me," whispered Charlie as he walked toward her cell.

Thomas sat quietly, unnoticed by Charlie.

"Charlie, what are you doing here? Are you going to kill me?"

"Hush! I'm here to get you out of here."

Charlotte tilted her head, her brows furrowed. "What? Why would you do that?"

"I need your help."

"Why don't you ask Sheriff August? He's your close friend now," snarled Charlotte.

"I can't go to him with this. You know all of John's men."

"Now you're calling them John's men. I thought they were your men."

"Look, Charlotte, this deal with the bank means a lot of money for us. And a handful of the men are causing trouble for the rest of us."

"Like your men trying to kill Elizabeth. And me, too."

"That's what the problem is. When I told them that Elizabeth gave the list with their names to the Law, some wanted to shoot Elizabeth dead right then and there."

"Well, what did you expect? I wanted to kill her, too, when I found out," said Charlotte. "But I didn't mean it literally."

"I didn't believe there was a list until Elizabeth showed it to me."

Charlotte shook her head. "You shouldn't have told the men about it."

"You're right. I thought that wouldn't have mattered much to them."

Charlotte huffed.

Charlie cleared his throat. "Some of the men have gone missing, including those you took yesterday."

"I didn't take any of those men. Jack told me those men were concerned that you were plotting with a small group. They were worried you would exclude them from the deal you made with the bank."

Charlie rolled his eyes. "I was. The bank owner doesn't need forty men. He only wanted twenty or so."

Charlotte gasped. "Really?"

"Yes, but a small group of men wanted nothing to do with the deal as long as Elizabeth was involved."

"That's ridiculous. It's Elizabeth's money that's funding the operation."

"They don't care about that. I'm guessing Frank Williams is behind the whole thing. Avery and Hamilton are with him," said Charlie.

Charlotte was stunned.

"I trusted Frank. He's always been loyal to me, even when John was around," said Charlie. "He went crazy after he and Randall had that falling out."

"When was the last time you saw them?" asked Charlotte.

"I haven't seen them since yesterday morning, before Elizabeth was shot."

"Hmm," said Charlotte.

"We should leave now. Sheriff August might show up soon."

Charlie rushed to the sheriff's desk and grabbed the keys to Charlotte's cell. He hurried back and released her.

"We're lucky the sheriff left the front door unlocked," said Charlie.

Charlotte still had half of a cake in her hand. She picked up the basket as she walked out of the cell. She took two quick bites.

"Let's go," said Charlie.

While Charlie closed and locked the cell door, she sneakily pulled her gun from the shelf next to the desk. She hid it inside the basket and followed Charlie to the front door.

"What about me? You gonna break me out, too?" asked Thomas.

Charlie stopped abruptly. "What the hell? I didn't see you there."

Charlotte rushed up. "Don't let him out. He tried to kill Alexander."

Thomas grinned. "Is that such a bad thing?"

Charlie laughed. "Charlotte, the men are north of town, just off the road to Sacramento. I'll meet you later. You'll be safe there. We all will."

Charlotte gasped. "Someone's coming."

"You go on ahead. It's probably Sheriff August. I'll talk to him to give you a few extra minutes to get away. There's a horse for you in the back."

"Okay. Thanks, Charlie. I had you figured wrong."

Charlie rushed out the front door.

Charlotte ran out the back door and then watched Charlie from a distance. She saw Alexander walk up to Charlie. She pressed herself against the wall, straining to hear every word of their exchange.

"Hello, Alexander," said Charlie.

"Is the sheriff inside?"

"Nope, I was looking for him. I think he's still in the restaurant having his Steak and Potatoes."

Alexander glanced at the restaurant across the way. "Have you seen Frank Williams or Howard Jackson lately?"

"No." Charlie's eyes flicked to his horse, as if measuring how fast he could leave. "I have to get back to camp. My men are expecting me. We're going to go over the work assignments. Could you tell the sheriff I stopped by?"

"Sure." Alexander hesitated, his voice low. "If you ever want to talk."

Charlie tilted his head, a flicker of unease crossing his face.

"Okay. Have a good night."

Alexander nodded. "You too." He turned and sprinted away.

Charlotte kept her eyes on them as Alexander headed toward the restaurant. Charlie stayed on the porch, watching him go. When Alexander disappeared inside, Charlie went back into the sheriff's office.

She took the gun out of the basket, ran to the horse waiting for her, and raced away. Several minutes later, she came to a fork in the road. Charlie had told her to go north to his camp. She thought she might be safer going south to the men in "her" campsite. She smiled and then turned south.

After riding for a while longer, a shot rang out. Charlotte's horse jumped, and she fell to the ground. She scrambled to a nearby tree. A bullet splintered the wood inches above her head.

"Give it up," Frank called out.

She recognized his voice and yelled, "I know about your plans to kill Elizabeth! Charlie told me."

"Those are his plans, you dumb fool. I had my reasons for wanting her dead. But I'll let Charlie take care of her now that he and I have an understanding. He's already on his way to put a bullet in that woman."

Charlotte's eyes widened in shock. Her brother had played her for a fool. "I'll stop my brother from killing her, even if I have to kill him."

Charlotte crawled through the tall weeds to where she could easily see Frank.

He yelled out to her. "Charlotte, come on out. It's over. Now that you don't have John protecting you, I'm going to kill you."

Charlotte held her gun steady. She pointed it squarely at Frank's chest. "Not if I kill you first."

Frank spun around toward her voice. "You ain't as skilled as me. You might as well give up."

Charlotte half-smiled, a sinister curve of her lips in the dust-choked air. Her aim was true, the bead of the sight settling on Frank's outstretched gun hand. She fired.

A sickening thud immediately followed the crack of her shot as the bullet found its mark. Frank's wrist exploded in a crimson spray, a geyser of blood and pulverized bone erupting into the twilight. His gun, still clutched in a hand that was no longer whole, bucked and fired as the force of the impact ripped it from his grasp. A guttural cry, more animal than human, tore from Frank's throat as his body, suddenly unbalanced, toppled from the saddle. He hit the ground with a gruesome thud, writhing in agony beside his terrified, whinnying horse.

Frank screamed. He grabbed his hand as he howled in pain. "You monster. You shot me!"

CHAPTER FIFTY-EIGHT

Family Takes Care of Family

Thomas rode in the direction Charlie had told his sister, his eyes darting from one side to the other. Loud, angry shouts came from ahead, followed by gunshots that reverberated through the trees. He pulled his gun, which he'd taken from the sheriff's office, and raced toward the commotion.

His eyes grew wide when he saw Frank fall from his horse and Charlotte on the ground. He jumped down and ran to Charlotte.

"Well, look who finally arrived," she said, springing to her feet. She pointed to the man who'd claimed to be a better shooter than her. "There's that man who's been trying to kill Lizzie." A dark smile crept onto her face. "I shot his shooting hand."

Thomas gulped, surprised. Frank was lying on the ground, wrapping a rag of sorts around his hand.

"I gotta get to Elizabeth before Charlie does."

"Go," he said. "I'll take care of him."

Charlotte sprinted to her horse and took off in a gallop.

Thomas trained his gun ahead of him and inched slowly toward Frank.

Frank was crouched over on his knees, facing away.

Thomas kept his distance, else Frank was likely to spring up and shoot him.

"You need to turn yourself in. I came to help you with that."

Frank choked out, "You're about as stupid as they come." He spun around and fired. "I'm just as good with my left."

Thomas dropped. The bullet cracked in the tree behind him. "I thought we were friends," he said, breathless.

"Friends? That's a stretch. You double-crossed me. You betrayed Randall. You're dead to me."

"Is that why you murdered Rebecca?"

"I killed your pa, too." He sneered. "Wasn't meant for him. The damn fool got in the way—trying to protect his wife."

A wave of nausea hit Thomas. "Why?"

Frank laughed. "Because you ruined Randall. You shattered the one thing that made him great when you shot his hand. There was no one better. You crippled him. You destroyed his life."

"He was headed toward rock bottom anyway. If it hadn't been me, someone else would've set him straight." Thomas paused. "I tried to help you."

Frank's face went red with rage. "You tried changing me into something I'm not. I tried to make you understand, but being righteous, you thought you knew better. Where's it got you?"

"It's what made me the sheriff of this town."

"You ain't got what it takes to be a sheriff! The first thing you do is string up Alexander."

"I made mistakes." Thomas's gaze drifted away. "...lots of 'em."

Frank scoffed. "Yeah. You made some big mistakes, like trying to hang Randall's son and hiding behind the law to do it."

Thomas's face grew crimson. "You wanted him dead as much as I did, maybe even more, since he put a bullet in your pa's chest."

Frank glanced down, and his shoulders dropped. "Before you took Randall's dignity away, I would have done anything for him. He warned me to keep away from Alexander, and I did. But after you messed up his shooting hand, he went soft. I spent day after day taking care of him while he howled in pain, drowning himself in whiskey night after night. You left him a shell of a man."

"Randall can take care of himself. He's responsible for whatever happened to him."

An enraged Frank pointed his gun at Thomas's chest. "No! It's your fault. How could you have shot your uncle? He's your blood."

"I'd put that gun down if I were you."

"I'm a better shot than you any day of the week."

Thomas's eyes narrowed, and he kept his eyes locked on Frank's. "Why did you have to kill Rebecca?"

"She never saw me coming. One blow. That was satisfying. I knew how much it would hurt you."

Thomas's breath stuck in his throat. His heart pounded hard in his chest. "My dearest Rebecca, love of my life."

"And then there was your Pa, didn't mean to kill him. I had Elizabeth in my sights. The bullet got him by accident."

"You should have just killed me. That would have been easier."

"I wasn't looking for easy. I wanted revenge for what you did to Randall and for betraying me. The killings were intoxicating. I wanted more."

Thomas paused. He took a deep breath and let it out slowly. He remembered Rebecca's words: 'Be good for me.' Calm surged through him like adrenaline, steadying his aim. He narrowed his eyes at Frank, the bead of his six-shooter locked on Frank's chest. "Your hand must be getting tired. Your other one is bleeding badly. Looks like Charlotte's a better shot than you after all."

Frank stomped his foot. "That witch! She got lucky."

"Put your gun down. Let's talk this over like we used to when we were friends."

Frank's shooting hand twitched. "I ain't your friend." He winced in pain.

Thomas saw his chance. Frank's gaze snapped to the road. A galloping horse was fast approaching. Thomas pulled the trigger. The bullet nicked the edge of Frank's hand.

Frank fired back but missed Thomas. Before Frank could shoot again, Thomas, gun in hand, lunged at Frank and knocked him to the ground. Thomas's weapon fell out of reach.

They fought fiercely until Frank took control. He tightened his grip around Thomas's throat. Frank welcomed the pain in his shattered hand as Thomas clawed at Frank's arms, vision blurring. The world narrowed to the pressure at his throat, the weight of failure pressing harder than Frank's grip.

A primal hunger for violence gripped Frank. He wanted to see the light fade from Thomas's eyes—to feel his last breath tremble beneath his fingers as he choked the life out of him.

Frank, his eyes wide with rage, roared, "Why did you betray me?"

When it was over, Thomas lay still, and a flicker of a grin crossed Frank's face, revealing a twisted sense of triumph. He savored the victory.

His breath caught, his eyes wide with despair as he pulled his hands from Thomas's throat. "Thomas?"

Thomas's neck was mottled with blood and bruises, the skin darkened where Frank's fingers had pressed hardest.

Frank fell back in horror. He had become a monster, consumed by hatred and violence.

Kneeling over Thomas, Frank didn't hear the pounding footsteps rushing toward him.

Randall rushed up and stopped suddenly. His nephew Thomas was lying motionless on the ground next to Frank. Randall's eyes locked on Frank in horror. "What have you done?"

Frank, his eyes brimming with tears, rose to his feet and stood there, trembling, facing Randall. The silence between them was louder than any scream.

Randall's gaze fell to Thomas's face. "Thomas." His eyes darted to Frank. "You killed them all, my brother Joseph, and even Thomas, your best friend!" he rasped, his voice barely above a whisper.

Frank nodded, feeling the weight of his actions settle on his shoulders like a heavy stone. "He deserved it," he muttered defensively. "He destroyed you! You should hate him as much as I do."

Randall shook his head sadly. "No one deserves this, Frank— especially not Thomas. I was proud of you once. I saw a better man in you, but that man is gone. You've become just as much of a monster as I was. You're dead to me."

"But, you were like an uncle to me."

Randall winced. "I ain't your uncle. You ain't even family. Not anymore. I ought to kill you for what you've done." His face etched with regret, Randall turned away from Frank.

"But I did it for you. Thomas destroyed your life by crippling your shooting hand."

"You ain't nothing but a sniveling coward. That boy there, Thomas, has more integrity, more worth than you will ever have. He did me right by shooting my hand. That boy saved me from myself." Randall shook his head and then pointed to Thomas. "He could have saved you, too."

Frank, filled with guilt and despair, raised his gun, intending to end it all and join the souls he had condemned to eternal rest. But before he could pull the trigger, Randall spun around and grabbed the weapon from his hand.

"You've taken all of my family from me, Frank," Randall said, staring into Frank's eyes with a mixture of sadness and anger. "I can't let you hurt anyone else, not even yourself. You're going to rot in hell for what you did."

Randall raised his six-shooter, held it in his shaky left hand, and pointed it at Frank. "My left hand is good enough to shoot at this distance."

Frank's eyes grew wide with shock.

Randall pulled the trigger and then sent a bullet into Frank. As he fell to the ground, gasping for breath, he looked up at Randall in disbelief.

"Why?" Frank croaked, his voice splintering to speak through the pain that tore through his body.

Randall shook his head. "Because I cared for you," he whispered. "And because I couldn't let you go on being the monster I made. There ain't no good left in you."

A moan broke the stillness behind him.

He turned. Thomas was on his knees, bloodied and shaking.

Randall froze.

Frank crawled toward his gun and leveled it at Thomas. But Randall was faster. He spun and fired. This time, the bullet struck Frank square in the chest.

As Frank lay there on the ground, his lifeblood seeping out of him, he realized with a jolt of horror that he had failed in his mission for revenge. He hadn't saved Randall from Thomas or anyone else.

His last thoughts were filled with regret and self-loathing as he watched Randall rush to Thomas, embrace him tightly, and whisper words of forgiveness into his ear.

Randall and Thomas shared a tearful moment of reconciliation before Thomas finally stood up, his face pale but determined.

"I heard what you told Frank." He glanced at Randall's shooting hand. "I'm sorry I shot your hand, Uncle Randall."

Randall shrugged. "That's the past."

Thomas nodded. "You know that thing you always say, 'Family takes care of family.'" He paused. "You were right about that."

His gaze fell to Frank's body, and then they suddenly darted back to Randall when he remembered about the danger that was headed Elizabeth's way. "Charlie... Frank said Charlie's riding to kill Elizabeth. Right now!"

Randall gasped, his eyes blazing. "Let's ride! If we don't stop him, Elizabeth's done for."

CHAPTER FIFTY-NINE

Surprise

Back at Elizabeth's house, she and Martha sat in the study, each with their guns on the desk in front of them. Elizabeth pointed to the sheet of paper lying between the guns. At the bottom, two names were scrawled out next to each other: Charles Buchanan and Frank Williams. Elizabeth drew a double-underline under Frank's name, then leaned back in her chair.

"He's the one who's been trying to kill me," Elizabeth murmured.

Martha asked, "Do you think it was Frank who shot at your stagecoach headed to Sacramento?"

"Yes. Either it was Frank or one of those other two men, Avery or Hamilton."

Martha scribbled a note on the paper. "Is it possible Frank shot your husband, too?"

Elizabeth nodded, her shoulders slumping. "I should have believed Charlotte from the start."

"Could Frank have shot Rebecca, too?"

Elizabeth inhaled deeply and exhaled all at once. "She wasn't shot. Thomas found the blood-stained rock that struck her."

Martha nodded. "I'm beginning to see a pattern." She glanced at the list and then back at Elizabeth. "Has anyone tried to kill Thomas?"

A guilty smile crept onto Elizabeth's lips. "Only Alexander."

Martha let out a nervous chuckle. "That's bad. Really bad."

"Are you thinking Frank killed them all?"

Martha nodded. "Frank or one of his men." She examined the crumpled bottom edge of Joseph's list. "And, now that Charlie knows all about this list with the circled names, it changes everything."

"When you showed Charlie that list. I'm betting that made him nervous. When you told him Frank shot at you yesterday, I saw him gasp. I don't think he knew Frank was trying to kill you until then," said Martha. "Charlie strikes me as the kind of man who might act irrationally if pushed too far."

"Charlie is worried we might cancel the deal with him and his men. I don't think he would like that. But he wouldn't kill me. Would he?"

Martha took a deep breath and let it out all at once. "You are the only one standing in the way of that deal. Since he said that he trusts Frank Williams with his life, it seems like he'd want to get rid of you rather than turn on Frank."

Elizabeth leaned forward and drew a larger circle around both Charlie's and Frank's names. "Do you think that those men that we've been calling Charlie's men aren't his at all? Do you think they're Frank's men?"

Martha nodded. "I was about to say that exact thing! I think that Charlie is Frank's puppet. Charlie can't do anything without Frank!"

"I think you and I make a great team," said Elizabeth.

"We do." Martha stood up.

Elizabeth gazed out the window. "Yesterday at lunch, what would Charlie have said had Sheriff August not interjected that Charlotte was the shooter? That's when Charlie said Frank was his loyal and trusted friend."

She chuckled and said, "Charlie, you're not as innocent as you purport to be."

Martha gasped. "Did you hear that? Alexander must be back."

"Probably the wind. I doubt Alexander would be back this soon."

Martha grabbed her gun. "I'll go check."

"You want me to come?"

Martha shook her head. "I'm sure it's nothing, but no sense in taking a chance. I'll be right back."

Martha walked out of the room, her gun in hand.

Elizabeth gathered the papers and put them into a neat pile.

"Mrs. Pruitt, you figured it out, didn't you?" asked Charlie as he stood outside the study room window.

Elizabeth gasped. Charlie's piercing blue eyes stared back at her, unblinking and wild.

"Yes, I did," she said, her eyes locked on Charlie's as her hand crept toward Joseph's six-shooter. In an instant, she grabbed it and raced out into the hallway.

Charlie fired into the room. Shards of glass exploded across the desk and onto the floor. He climbed inside and onto the desk. His hand landed on Joseph's list, pressing it against the desk. His blood boiled as he lifted his sweaty hand. The paper and tiny bits of glass were stuck to his bleeding palm. He pushed against the slippery surface and fell to the floor with a thud.

"Damn it," yelled Charlie as he brushed the glass and paper from his hand.

Elizabeth yelled as she ran toward Martha, "Let's go. Charlie's coming in behind me."

A gunshot and a raucous crash came from the study.

Elizabeth led the way out the back door. "We'll take cover by the barn. There's no telling if he's got Frank with him."

They were almost to the barn when a loud shot came from behind. Charlotte shot Charlie when he exited the back door.

Charlie grabbed his left arm and ran behind the chicken coop. He shot back. The gunshot sent the chickens squawking and scattering into the nearby fields.

Charlotte charged into the barn, shielding Misty from the gunfire. Then she bolted toward Elizabeth and Martha. "I got him in the arm. I heard he was coming here to kill you."

"And Frank Williams, too," said Elizabeth.

"Nope." Charlotte grimaced. "Charlie helped me escape from jail and then sent me to my death. Frank was waiting for me and tried to kill me. I got him first. Thomas is taking care of him. I hope he finishes him off."

She grabbed the reins and rushed the horse into the barn, then returned. "Tell me you both have guns?"

Martha nodded. "Of course. I got more in the barn if we need them."

Elizabeth showed Charlotte her gun. "This was Joseph's."

Charlotte smiled. She glanced toward the chicken coop. "He's mighty quiet over there."

Elizabeth yelled, "Charlie, it's over. I know the truth. The circled names on Joseph's list are men he didn't trust. And that last name on there was Charles Buchanan, and it was circled."

Charlie croaked, "Joseph was weak. He tried to bribe some of the men to leave the group."

Elizabeth laughed sharply.

Charlie yelled, "After you killed John, Frank and I took over. We did what John couldn't do."

Elizabeth laughed. "You mean Frank took over. You were working for him."

Charlie rasped, "We were partners."

Charlotte glanced at Elizabeth. "Charlie's not thinking straight. He's in way over his head."

"Charles, throw down your gun and come on out. We can talk about this," yelled Elizabeth. "I can help you."

"My name is Charlie, don't call me Charles!"

Charlotte's brows raised. "Elizabeth, he won't listen to reason. He's not right in the head. He's never been ever since he shot our ma when he was a boy."

Charlie yelled. "I'm going to kill you just like Frank killed Joseph. Turns out he's been killing everyone close to Thomas. Who knows why?"

Elizabeth yelled, "Is that why he killed Rebecca?"

Charlie was quiet.

Elizabeth's gaze went from Charlotte to Martha.

"He shouldn't have killed her. I found out the day after he tried killing Alexander when he was on that stagecoach with that rich couple. Said he couldn't find them, so he killed that couple."

Charlotte yelled, "She was our sister, Charlie. How could you let him do that?"

Charlie sobbed as he shouted, "He shouldn't have done that."

Elizabeth's jaw dropped. She was horrified. Suddenly, everything made sense. She turned to Martha. "You were right."

Martha said, "This is a revenge plot against Thomas."

Charlotte said, "Thomas told me he and Frank were best friends, but they had a falling out." Her brows narrowed. "That explains why Frank was trying to kill you. But why is my brother trying to kill you now?"

Martha shook her head. "He wants to kill all three of us now."

Elizabeth's smile was tight. "We're in his way."

Charlotte said, "That's what he told me when I went to his

camp. He said I was in his way."

Elizabeth called out to Charlie. "It's time to end this, Charlie. We've known each other a long time."

"Mrs. Pruitt, I did like you until Charlotte turned you against me."

Charlie was silent for a few seconds and then shouted, "Charlotte, you're supposed to be dead."

"Sorry to disappoint you. You stupid fool," said Charlotte mockingly.

"I'm not stupid! Stop calling me stupid!" Charlie fired a shot.

His bullet splintered the wood above the spot where Charlotte, Martha, and Elizabeth hid.

"You were always a lousy shot. I'm surprised you even know how to pull a trigger with that twitch in your hand," Charlotte taunted.

Charlie fired another shot, but it missed again.

A thunder of approaching hooves echoed down the road as the riders rounded the corner. A dozen of them appeared, kicking up a cloud of dust.

Martha squinted. "Now we're in for a real gunfight! I'm glad I'm not wearing a dress."

Elizabeth grinned. "No time like the present to teach these men a lesson."

Charlotte looked cock-eyed at the other two women. "You two seem awfully cheerful for what's coming."

Martha dashed into the barn and returned with a cache of weapons.

The ground trembled beneath them as the riders closed in, dust curling like smoke around the barn.

Charlie shouted, "Here come my friends!"

CHAPTER SIXTY

Howard

Sheriff August was in the restaurant, enjoying his usual meal. He savored each bite of his steak. His fork, on its way to his mouth with a juicy piece of meat, stopped short.

Alexander slid into the seat across from him. "Sheriff!"

The sheriff put down his fork and sat taller. "Aren't you supposed to be at Elizabeth's? Is she okay?"

"Yes. She's fine. She wants us to chat with Howard Jackson."

Sheriff August let out a long breath, his shoulders relaxing. He looked crooked at Alexander. "Why would you want to talk with that drunk?" He went back to eating.

"He used to work for John Walker. Elizabeth thinks he knows something about the list. She said Joseph trusted Howard."

"I bet he's in the saloon." The sheriff glanced at his half-eaten steak and then stood. He tossed some coins on the table. "Let's go."

A few minutes later, the pair entered the saloon and spotted Howard sitting slumped over at the corner table. They walked over and sat on either side of him. Howard, his knuckles white, tightly clenched a partially filled glass. An empty bottle lay tipped over.

The wheezing man was still, a stark contrast between his friendly spirit and the sour, pungent smell of sweat and whiskey that clung to him.

The stench made Alexander's nose wrinkle, but he pushed past it, his focus on the urgency of their mission. "Howard," said Alexander.

Howard continued to breathe with a rasping rhythm that never faltered.

Sheriff August grimaced.

Alexander tapped Howard's shoulder.

Howard jumped up, almost falling back in his chair. He gasped, eyes shooting open. He squinted as he looked from one to the other and settled on Alexander. "Alexander!" he cried, spittle flying from his mouth as he slurred. "I'm glad you're okay." A huge grin filled his face, exposing his yellowed teeth. His once-sharp features were now blurred by years of drink, and his eyes, though open, seemed to gaze through a perpetual fog.

Howard's words tumbled out, thick and garbled. Alexander leaned in closer to catch them.

Alexander winced as Howard's breath accosted his nose. "It's great to see you again, Howard."

The sheriff huffed and shook his head. "Where's Frank Williams?" he asked, his voice raised.

Howard's face soured. "Are you the sheriff of this town now?"

Sheriff August scowled. "No," he said curtly.

Alexander put his hand on Howard's shoulder. "Howard, do you know where Frank Williams is?"

Howard turned to Alexander, wrinkled his nose, and shuddered. For a moment, a glimmer of the old Howard, the one Joseph must have trusted, shone through the haze of his intoxication. "I told them to leave Elizabeth alone. They laughed at me. They wouldn't listen to me. They never pay attention to me."

"We'll listen to you. Now tell us. Who did you tell?" asked Alexander.

"Frank and Charlie. Ever since John passed, those two have been inseparable. They took over, and most of us didn't like that one bit. I used to like Charlie, but he's changed. I think Frank corrupted him."

Sheriff August's breath stuck in his throat. His brows furrowed, and a dawning unease replaced his earlier dismissal of Howard. "This doesn't make any sense," he muttered to himself.

Howard raised his glass, taking a long sip of his whiskey before speaking. "A little while ago, Frank wanted me to go with him to kill Charlotte. I never killed anyone. I told him to leave me alone. I ain't no killer. Besides, I like Charlotte. I like Mrs. Pruitt, too. Frank told Charlie he would take care of Charlotte, and he had to shoot Mrs. Pruitt."

A cold dread seized Sheriff August. "No!" he choked, his hand instinctively going to the gun on his hip.

"I saw Charlie outside your office, not long ago," said Alexander. "He said he was headed to his camp. He's probably going to Elizabeth's instead."

The sheriff jumped to his feet. "Let's go!" He bolted toward the door. "We've gotta get to Elizabeth."

"Thanks, Howard," said Alexander. "One more thing. What does Frank look like?"

"He knows you. I thought you knew him." Howard pulled his glass close. "He was always hanging around Randall." He chuckled as his head sank toward the table, landing with a dull thump.

Alexander's breath caught as the memory hit him. It was the shootout at his place in Sacramento several months before. He and Martha fought off Randall's outlaws there. It was Frank Williams who helped Randall escape.

Sheriff August yelled from the door, "Alexander, we gotta go!"

They burst into the sheriff's office moments later, urgency in every step.

Sheriff August held his gun at the ready as he entered. Only quiet met him. He crept past his desk to the cell where Charlotte was being held. "She's gone! Charlie must have let her out."

Alexander shook his head. "Thomas's cell is empty, too."

Sheriff August slammed his hand against the iron-barred door. The clang echoed like a church bell struck in fury. "Damnit!"

The deputy walked in.

Sheriff August marched over to him. "Where have you been?"

The deputy wore a sheepish look, blind to the weight of what was unraveling. "I was right next door."

Sheriff August grimaced. "You need to come with us. We might have some trouble at the Pruitt place."

"Yes, sir," said the deputy.

Sheriff August rushed to the door. "Let's go."

Within minutes, the trio was on their way to Elizabeth's house. Sheriff August was in front, then Alexander, and then the deputy. When they reached the fork in the road, they slowed. A man was lying dead ahead of them on the right. Alexander, his gun drawn, rode past the sheriff, expecting to see Thomas there.

He dismounted, six-shooter in hand, and crept toward the man lying face down in the dust. He stepped closer. One of the man's hands was a bloody stump, and the other clenched tight. He hooked the toe of his boot under the body and flipped it. The corpse's eyes stuck open. A dark, spreading stain bloomed in the middle of his shirt. He studied the face, searching for confirmation.

Alexander breathed out in relief when he saw it wasn't Thomas. He crouched beside the body, touched the skin, then called to Sheriff August. "Dead less than a few minutes. Still warm. No stiffness in the limbs, and the blood hasn't crusted."

The sheriff rode alongside Alexander. "Who is it?"

"Frank Williams," Alexander said. "That's him, alright."

Sheriff August looked closer. His eyes shot open wider. "I remember him from the shootout at your place. Thomas wanted me to let him go free."

The sheriff motioned to the deputy. "Take care of this. Alexander and I will continue to Elizabeth's house."

The deputy said, "Sure thing."

Sheriff August turned to Alexander. "Charlotte must've killed him when she escaped. Didn't Howard say Frank was going to kill her?"

"Yup. She must have got the better of him. Sounds like she might have been on the right side of the law after all."

"I think you're right."

Alexander jumped on his horse and said, "We gotta go! Elizabeth is in trouble."

"Damnit, Charlie played us!" said Sheriff August as he pulled hard on the reins, his horse charging toward Elizabeth's place.

CHAPTER SIXTY-ONE

Used to Like You

Charlie crouched, hiding behind the chicken coop, while Martha, Charlotte, and Elizabeth peered out from behind the barn.

Six figures emerged from the tree line beyond Charlie, fanning out with rifles glinting in the morning light.

"Is that all the friends you got, Charlie?" Elizabeth yelled, her voice betraying no fear.

A flash of movement caught Charlie's eye as Martha emerged from behind the Pruitt house, a loaded shotgun in her hands. She moved swiftly as she handled her weapon with ease. Since Randall and his outlaw gang had attacked her and Alexander's home in Sacramento months ago, she'd sworn to herself: never again would she be caught off guard. She had brought with her a small arsenal of rifles, pistols, and even a spare shotgun, all strategically placed.

"Charlie, you've got another thing coming!" Martha roared, her voice cutting through the chaos. She pumped a round into the shotgun, aiming for the outlaws. The first two men barely had time to raise their rifles before Martha's buckshot tore through the air, sending them sprawling.

From the other side of the yard, Elizabeth drew her late husband's six-shooter along with hers, a blur of motion. She moved with a desperate fury, firing with surprising accuracy, dropping another outlaw who tried to flank Martha. Charlotte, not to be outdone, seemed to dance across the yard, her single six-shooter spitting fire. It was her favorite, too, its hair-trigger responding to the slightest thought of a squeeze. She targeted the men trying to get a bead on Elizabeth, her shots precise and deadly.

The air was filled with the deafening crack of gunfire. Bullets whizzed, kicked up dirt, and splintered wood. The three women moved as one, a synchronized rampage of destruction. Martha reloaded her shotgun and took down another two outlaws. Elizabeth picked off a fifth man trying to pin down Charlotte.

Charlotte, seeing her chance, used the distraction to put a final bullet into the sixth outlaw.

Within minutes, the battle was over. Charlie's men lay scattered, lifeless, around the perimeter of the yard. Only Charlie remained, staring in disbelief at his fallen men, his face contorted with rage.

Elizabeth's adrenaline surged as she said, "I'd say you're pretty stupid to foul up that bank deal. You would have been living a comfortable life for quite a while."

"If Frank had killed you, Mrs. Pruitt, when he was supposed to, then everything would have worked out fine," cried Charlie.

Elizabeth muttered, "I told him he could call me Elizabeth."

Charlotte's brows furrowed.

Charlie continued, "Frank blamed Charlotte for his bullet missing you, Elizabeth."

Elizabeth chuckled. "He called me Elizabeth."

"Are you joking at a time like this?" asked Charlotte.

"It helps to relieve the tension."

Charlotte called out to Charlie, "Come on out. This is getting tiresome."

She turned to Elizabeth and croaked, "We need to end this now. He's no match for us." Her eyes shot to Charlie's hiding place. She took a deep breath, and fire ignited in her eyes. She dropped, rolled, and fired; Charlie's leg buckled with a sickening thud. She scrambled back to the wagon. Blood had splattered the white wall of the coop, and only stillness was left.

"It's over!" yelled Charlotte. "I don't want to kill you. You're all the family I got."

Elizabeth's gaze drifted to the chicken coop where Charlie had been hiding, and then back at Charlotte. "Where did he go?"

Charlotte lowered her gun. "That stupid coward ran off to cower in a corner somewhere." She shook her head.

Her eyes lit up. Thomas was racing toward her from the road. She turned to Elizabeth. The barrel of Elizabeth's gun was looking her way. She stood frozen, her jaw slackened in disbelief.

Elizabeth gasped, her trembling hand locking Joseph's six-shooter on Charlie. He was coming at Charlotte from behind her, his gun ahead of him. He laughed maniacally.

Elizabeth pulled the trigger.

Charlotte's breath caught in her throat. Bright flashes from in front of and to the side of her blinded her. The percussion of multiple gunfire shook her. Charlotte's ears rang as bullets tore past her, hot and deafening.

Elizabeth's face was a jumble of shock. Behind Charlotte, Charlie's body jolted and crumpled as the bullets slammed into him, sending him sprawling to the ground.

Charlotte instinctively clutched her chest, a flash of fear that she'd been shot, but found no wound. Then, Thomas was there, rushing to Elizabeth.

He wasn't alone. Behind him, emerging from the brush, was Randall.

Martha gasped, her blood running cold. "Randall!" she rasped, her voice barely above a whisper.

Thomas helped Elizabeth to her feet. "I knew that scoundrel was coming here to kill you. Are you alright?"

A stunned Elizabeth said, "Thomas, it was Frank who killed Rebecca and Joseph. It was Frank!"

"I know. Frank won't ever bother you again." Thomas's jaw slackened, and he shook his head, his heart heavy with hurt. "This is all my fault."

Elizabeth said, "No! It's not."

Charlotte said, "What happened to Frank?"

Thomas's breath caught in his throat, and he rubbed his neck. "He's dead. He was about to shoot me, but Uncle Randall shot him first."

Elizabeth patted Thomas's arm. "You've made me proud. I know Joseph would have been proud of you, too."

"After what I did to Alexander, they'll hang me for sure."

"I'll talk to Sheriff August and Alexander," said Elizabeth. "We'll figure it out."

Thomas cast a sideways glance at Martha. "I don't see that helping much."

He winked at Charlotte and turned toward his horse.

Martha's eyes burned into Randall's. The hatred was a bitter taste in her mouth, but a complex, agonizing conflict warred within her. She knew a truth that could shatter Alexander's world.

Her hand tightened on the grip of her gun.

"Don't move, Randall," Martha said, her voice low and dangerous. She aimed her six-shooter squarely at his chest. "You murdered my parents. You shot me the last time we spoke."

Randall froze, his eyes meeting hers, a flicker of something unreadable passing between them.

Elizabeth said, "Martha, please."

She grimaced and brought her gun down.

Thomas started to back away.

Martha yelled, "Don't go, Thomas! You stay put. You owe this to Alexander and me. You started this mess when you tried to hang my husband, and you'll see it through by listening."

Thomas hesitated.

Martha said, "Please!"

Thomas raised his hands in surrender and nodded.

"Come over here with us," said Martha. "We're all going to work this out. You tried to kill my husband." Martha's gaze flickered from Thomas and Randall. "And you killed my parents. Both of you need to pay for what you did. Sit down!"

Randall and Thomas marched to the bench next to the chicken coop and sat.

Martha pointed to Randall. "You're going to tell Alexander the truth—about who his father is."

Randall choked; his eyes went wide with shock.

Martha said, "Oh, get over it. Everyone here knows."

Elizabeth and Charlotte nodded, their faces grim.

"We're going to wait right here until Alexander and Sheriff August arrive," Martha declared, her voice firm.

Elizabeth stepped close to Martha and whispered, "Perhaps it would be better to wait in the house. There's too much death out here."

Martha huffed. She held her gun at Thomas and Randall, "I sure hope you're not going to give us any trouble."

Randall shrugged. "No, Ma'am. I'm done running."

Thomas shook his head. He glanced at Elizabeth and then nodded. "I am, too. I'll take whatever comes."

"Elizabeth wants us all to go inside," said Martha.

Charlotte turned to Martha and said, "I got my gun at the

ready." She winked at Thomas. "Just in case."

Martha was the last to go inside. She glanced at the road. "Alexander, I hope you get here soon, my fingers are itching to mete out justice," she said as she closed the door behind her.

Alexander and Sheriff August raced to Elizabeth's place. They rode hard into the yard, pulling their horses to a sliding halt. Their eyes swept over the scene. The air was thick with silence.

The sheriff pulled his gun. "It's too quiet. Something is wrong."

Alexander drew his gun and crept to the chicken coop. The sheriff followed.

"There's blood splattered against the wall," said Alexander. He took a few steps, and the bodies came into view. "There must be half a dozen dead men here."

The sheriff rushed over. He kicked at them one after the other. "They're dead, alright. Someone took their guns."

"Elizabeth!" the sheriff called out, his heart filled with dread.

Alexander crept toward the building. He peeked around the corner.

"Alexander, you had better come over here!" said the sheriff.

Sheriff August was looking down at something by the wagon. Alexander ran over.

"It's Charlie. He's dead," said Sheriff August.

Sheriff August jumped when Elizabeth tapped his shoulder. He spun around, his gun drawn.

Elizabeth gasped and stepped back.

He holstered his gun. "Elizabeth?"

"What's all this fuss?" she asked. "Why didn't you come inside?"

She held her gun at her side. "We heard horses arrive, and then nothing."

"Are you okay?" asked the sheriff.

"We're fine. Martha is waiting for you both inside. She has something to tell you."

"I was worried about you..." Sheriff August stood confused when he saw Charlotte step out from behind Elizabeth.

Charlotte's eyes stayed sharp. "He's worried about you. How

cute."

The sheriff drew his gun.

Charlotte rolled her eyes.

Elizabeth pushed his gun down, her face stern. "Put that thing away."

Charlotte smiled at Sheriff August. "You're not going to try to arrest me again. Are you?"

Elizabeth chuckled.

Sheriff August grimaced and stowed his weapon.

Alexander asked, "Is Martha okay?"

"She's fine. She's waiting for us."

Charlotte half-smiled at Elizabeth.

Elizabeth nodded. "Let's go. We've got some business to take care of. We can have some cakes. Afterward, we've got to get rid of those dead men who tried to kill us earlier."

Alexander said, "On the way here, we found Frank Williams dead."

Charlotte's brows lifted, and she smiled. "Justice!"

Elizabeth and Charlotte walked away, their steps steady, their whispers low.

Alexander and Sheriff August stood speechless as the two women whispered to each other and continued up the trail to Elizabeth's house.

As they approached, Martha stood across from Thomas and Randall, who sat stiffly on the porch bench. Her gun was trained on them.

Alexander rushed to the porch, gun drawn, his eyes locking first on Martha, then on Randall, a man he hadn't expected to see here, alive.

Before he could speak, Martha's eyes met his, filled with a profound, almost desperate sadness. Her voice, barely a whisper, sliced through the silence like a blade, carrying a weight that felt heavier than any gunshot.

She looked over at Randall. "Tell him!"

Randall's face collapsed into shame. He shook his head.

"Alexander," Martha said, her gaze flicking to Randall, then back to her husband, tears welling in her eyes. "Randall isn't just a killer. He's your father."

CHAPTER SIXTY-TWO
Reckoning and Rebirth

Alexander stood, stunned, at Martha's revelation that his father was Randall Pruitt. Randall was slumped on the bench, his head slightly down, looking at his son.

"My father?" Alexander rasped. He stared at Randall, then at Martha. All his life, he'd never questioned the close bond he had with Randall. It suddenly made sense now.

Martha's gun remained steady, aimed at Randall, but her hand trembled almost imperceptibly. The man who killed her parents. The man she'd hated, the man she wanted dead, was also the father of her husband, the grandfather of her children. Her grip tightened on her weapon.

Elizabeth stepped forward, her voice gentle but firm. "Martha, put the gun down. We need to talk." She turned to Alexander, her eyes pleading for understanding. "We all know. Charlotte, Thomas, even Joseph knew."

The mention of Joseph stung Alexander. Joseph avoided him for years, never letting him close. Alexander never understood why until now. Joseph knew this secret all along. Alexander looked at Thomas, the man he'd so often felt at odds with —his rival, Martha's attacker —now revealed as family. Thomas... a cousin?

Thomas, still reeling from the battle and the raw wounds of revelation, finally looked at Alexander. He'd resented Alexander for capturing Martha's love, felt his judgment, and even tried to destroy him. He'd moved on from the fruitless pursuit of Martha and found love with Rebecca.

Yet, when Frank told him that Alexander was Randall's son, his feelings toward Alexander grew even colder because of their blood connection. He remembered Frank's confession, the chilling admission that he'd killed Rebecca. A twisted sense of closure, cold and unforgiving, settled over him.

Randall said, "I did everything I could to keep you safe." He looked at the mangled hand that once held a gun with deadly precision, the hand Thomas shot. "Frank... he went mad. Said I'd gone soft, lost my purpose. He was my protégé, my greatest student, and I pushed him away. It broke him, and then he killed my brother." He glanced at Thomas. "And his love."

"I ain't no better." He cast a sideways glance at Martha. "I killed her parents." He wiped his nose. "I am sorry." He looked away, his eyes filling with tears.

"Alexander," Thomas said, his voice raw. "I never meant to... Rebecca was my life. And I didn't know about Frank killing her until today. I swear." Thomas's gaze fell to Alexander's feet.

Alexander was silent. The relief he'd felt earlier, seeing a stranger's body on the road instead of Thomas's, now made a strange, painful kind of sense. His cousin. His family.

Terrible as Thomas was to both him and Martha, they hadn't died at his hands. Quite the opposite, Thomas saved Martha from a bullet from an outlaw during the stagecoach ambush. And during that same shootout, he helped Martha free his stagecoach, saving him from certain death. Perhaps, he thought, I pushed him to this.

It was Martha who faced the man who killed her parents. Alexander's eyes drifted to Randall, the man he'd called Pa once, because he felt so much more like a father to him than the man who raised him. Even now, he felt a closeness to Randall despite all the terrible things he'd done. He tapped Martha's arm, a silent thank-you for her strength. She was so much better at seeing the good in people than he was.

Alexander's gaze hardened, no longer fixed on Thomas or Randall, but looking at Martha. His father. A killer. His cousin. A betrayer, yet somehow, a victim too. The fight was over, but the real battle, the one for his understanding, had just begun.

Martha lowered her gun, slowly, her eyes never leaving Randall. The decision had to be Alexander's, but she couldn't pull the trigger. Not now.

Elizabeth moved to Sheriff August's side.

He surveyed the aftermath: the dead outlaws, the walls scarred by gunfire, and the strained faces of those gathered. The pieces of the puzzle, Thomas's accusations, and Randall's past suddenly clicked into place.

Sheriff August cleared his throat. "This changes things. A lot of things." He paused, looking at Randall. "There's a debt to pay here—for the killings, for the ambush, for the terror you caused. But with Frank and Charlie dead, we also have a massive hole in this territory. We need men who know this land, who can protect the stagecoaches." His gaze drifted to Randall, then Thomas. "How do we resolve this debt... and secure the future of this town?"

Thomas let out a breath. "I... I won't run. I'm not cut out to be a sheriff. After what I've done, my Pa would be disappointed in me. I had my chance." He glanced at Alexander. "And I messed it up badly. You need someone like Alexander. Someone who's fair and metes out justice."

Alexander shook his head and shot a brief sideways glance at Randall. "I'm happy with what I'm doing in Sacramento. We're not moving here."

Elizabeth's eyes shot to Randall. A shadow crossed Randall's face, the final hope of truly claiming his son in this new life dissolving.

CHAPTER SIXTY-THREE

Reconciliation

Elizabeth turned to August. "Sheriff, you know what this town needs."

She paused. "Auburn needs a leader who isn't afraid to get their hands dirty cleaning up this town. Someone who knows these roads, the townfolk, and how to keep them safe."

She walked up to Randall. "Randall, you know how these gangs operate. You know their weaknesses. You always said, 'Family takes care of family.' This town needs a family. It needs you."

Randall looked up, his eyes widening in disbelief. "Me? Sheriff?" The idea was so ludicrous, so far from the life he'd carved out, it almost made him chuckle, but the sound caught in his throat.

There was a long silence.

Charlotte cleared her throat. "Before we talk about new sheriffs, how about an apology, Sheriff August?" She narrowed her eyes playfully at the sheriff. "You accused me of shooting at Elizabeth, and you locked me up." She stood, arms crossed. "Just to be clear, Frank and Charlie were the ones who tried to kill Elizabeth."

Sheriff August winced, a flush rising on his neck. "Charlotte, I... you're right. I was wrong."

Charlotte stepped closer to Sheriff August. "I didn't hear an apology." She raised a brow at Elizabeth. "Did you?"

Elizabeth stifled a chuckle.

Sheriff August shook his head as his gaze swept to Charlotte.

Charlotte held a hint of a smile, her eyes on his, looking expectantly.

"I'm sorry for accusing you of..." He glanced for an instant at Elizabeth.

Elizabeth gave him an encouraging nod.

Sheriff August's breath choked in his throat until the words escaped his mouth in a rasp. "I'm sorry, Charlotte, I shouldn't have accused you of trying to harm Elizabeth. I apologize."

Charlotte grinned. She jumped up and kissed Sheriff August on his cheek. "Now that wasn't so bad. Was it?"

He blinked, stunned, as he rubbed his cheek.

She turned to Elizabeth. "This sheriff is in love with you. You better not let him get away."

Elizabeth's face grew bright red. "Charlotte!"

Charlotte's gaze drifted back to the sheriff. "Everyone here is glum and shaken."

She pointed to Alexander. "You're finding out who your father is and what Thomas did to you."

She turned to Martha. "And you're wrestling with the terrible thing Randall did to your loved ones."

She paused. "And everyone, it seems, wants to kill someone for these horrible things that were done."

Her brows lifted toward Sheriff August. "Elizabeth killed my husband, whom I loved." She turned and winked at Elizabeth. "Even so, I understand why she did it. I can look past it. And I know in my heart she and I will remain friends for a long time."

Elizabeth hugged Charlotte. "You kept me from getting shot on more than one occasion. Thank you, my dear friend."

Martha walked up to Charlotte. "Don't leave me out, friend. You remind me so much of your sister."

"I'm told I do favor her eyes."

Martha nodded. "Yes! Rebecca and I, along with my aunt, fought off half a dozen or more stagecoach robbers once. Rebecca's shooting was better than mine. But I've never seen anyone handle a gun like you. I'd love for you to teach me your techniques."

Charlotte smiled and snuck a glance at the chicken coop where Charlie was lying. "I've had lots of practice throughout the years. After my mother died, I would take my little brother out into the fields to teach him how to shoot. It took months to get him comfortable firing a gun."

She glanced away briefly as she remembered young Charlie firing a gun at their mother, killing her. Their father had given him an empty gun to toughen him up. Charlie had forgotten he'd earlier loaded a bullet he'd found on the ground. "If it weren't for that twitch in his hand, he might have been able to shoot us easily."

Martha nodded. "His bullets weren't landing well."

She turned to Elizabeth. "Charlotte is right about you and Sheriff August. I can see there's something between you two."

Elizabeth shook her head and narrowed her eyes at Charlotte and Martha. "You two are making this awkward."

Sheriff August chuckled. "Elizabeth," he stepped closer. "They're right. I… I've loved you for a long time. Longer than Joseph ever knew. Longer than I probably admitted even to myself. If there's a chance now… for us…" He trailed off.

Elizabeth's face softened. "We'll see." She looked at the house. "I'm going back to Sacramento. I'm done with this place. I'm going back to my aunt's old place in town. That's where I belong now."

She stepped closer to Randall. "I know you miss your brother." She cast a sideways glance at Sheriff August and then continued, "Would you take care of Joseph's and my house here?"

Randall's eyes grew wide, his chest heavy. His breathing seemed to stop for an instant as he finally choked out. "Here? This house?"

"I'd expect you to take care of it, be respectful of it," she said.

"I don't know what to say. I don't deserve it," said Randall.

"Just think about it. That's all I ask."

She turned to Thomas.

"I can't see myself ever coming back to live here, but I'm sure that Joseph would have wanted you to have this ranch. To build something good from all of this."

She turned back to Randall. "Joseph would have wanted you to watch out for his son, too." She paused and cast a sideways glance at Sheriff August and then leaned in toward Randall. "I don't know what the Law has planned for you, but I'm hoping you stick around and help Thomas take care of this place."

Randall nodded. "I'm grateful. I'm done running."

Thomas looked at Elizabeth. "I'll go with you to Auburn, to see Agnes. I need to explain… everything. And ask for her forgiveness. For what I did to Alexander, for everything." He looked at Alexander, a raw apology in his gaze. "Alexander, I... I can't undo what I did. The trial, the accusations. I was blind, hateful. Can you... Can we just let it go? For Joseph? For Martha?"

Alexander met Thomas's gaze. He thought of Martha, who had always seen the good in people, who had pleaded for Thomas, his cousin, his betrayer. Relief washed over him again, remembering how glad he'd been that the body he'd found earlier wasn't Thomas's. "Bygones," Alexander said at last. "Let them be bygones." He extended a hand. Thomas grasped it tight, his eyes moist with tears.

Martha turned to Randall. "Randall," she began, her voice steady. "You killed my parents. I will never forgive you for that. But you are Alexander's father. And for his sake, I will be civil with you. We will find a way to exist, if only for him. But don't mistake civility for peace."

Randall flinched, the harsh reality of her words hitting him, but then a flicker of something almost like gratitude crossed his face. It was more than he deserved.

"As for the stagecoach protection," Elizabeth continued, her gaze firm, "Thomas and Charlotte. You two are skilled with a gun. You know how those outlaws work. You'll lead the men. Protect the stages."

She saw in them not just survivors, but protectors—flawed, but fiercely loyal.

Sheriff August nodded. "It's her money, she's in charge."

Elizabeth nodded slowly. "Yes." She looked at Charlotte, waiting for a response.

Charlotte's eyes lit up, her smile unfolding across her face. "Lead a gang? I like the sound of that." She looked at Thomas, a mischievous glint in her eyes. "Looks like we're partners, brother."

Thomas looked crooked at her. "Brother?"

Charlotte rolled her eyes. "Thomas! Rebecca was my sister. That makes you my family."

Thomas's face lit up. He nodded, a small smile touching his lips. "Partners, Sister."

Sheriff August smiled with a profound sense of relief washing over him. Things were falling into place.

CHAPTER SIXTY-FOUR
Family

Sheriff August sat at the desk in the sheriff's office, the late afternoon sun casting slivers of light through the window. He looked at the carved wooden nameplate on the desk. It read, "Sheriff Thomas Pruitt." He was about to slide it into the drawer and spotted another one there. "Sheriff Joseph Pruitt." As he slid Thomas's in, it snagged on something wedged behind Joseph's nameplate. A sealed envelope, yellowed at the edges. Just a name scrawled in firm, deliberate ink: Charlotte Buchanan.

He hesitated, then opened it.

Charlotte,

I don't expect forgiveness, and I won't ask for it.

When I left Auburn all those years ago, I did so under orders I couldn't refuse and with secrets I could no longer carry. Your Sheriff Joseph knew part of it, but not the whole. I was chasing something bigger than this town—something that started with a name I wasn't supposed to speak: Silas Gentry.

He wasn't a judge back then. He was part of a network—men in high places who used law like a weapon. I tried to fight it from the inside. I failed.

I fled to New York but... To keep you safe... It's not over.

I received a frantic telegram from Joseph. He said that Gentry broke his promise.

He says you're okay. I know you've stood your ground. I'm proud of you, even if I don't deserve to say it. But Gentry will come after you.

If this reaches you, it means I'm coming back. Not to reclaim a badge, but to finish what I started.

Be careful who you trust.

—Your Pa

August slowly folded the letter, his jaw tight. He looked out the window toward the town square, where Elizabeth was walking toward the office.

He slipped the letter into his coat pocket.

"Charlotte needs to see this," he murmured.

The front door opened, and in walked Elizabeth. "Where is everyone?"

"I asked the deputies to head out to your house and pick up those dead outlaws."

"I never noticed how quiet this place is."

He nodded. "These deputies are doing a fine job of taking care of this town. But, they need a sheriff."

"Perhaps Randall should be that sheriff."

He looked at her, astonished, and then chuckled. "He's a killer!"

"Who better to become the sheriff than a reformed outlaw? Joseph told me it was once Randall's dream to work for the Law."

"Once an outlaw, always an outlaw. He'll never change. It's not possible. I could see Thomas as the sheriff, even though he tried to get Alexander hanged."

Elizabeth shook her head. "Thomas doesn't want that job. I could tell that when Joseph offered him the deputy position, he wasn't that excited about it. It's true, he loved the idea, but not the job itself. And when Joseph died, it came as a shock to him. I was so anxious to help him through his grief that I convinced the townsfolk to elect him the sheriff."

"They listen to you because they trust you."

"I think I can convince them to elect Randall, but only if you're on my side. I don't think they'd take my word alone, not after what Thomas did."

"Elizabeth, I think the town will forgive Thomas. He's the best choice for this town's Sheriff. Besides, I thought Randall's shooting hand was messed up."

"He told me he's been practicing with his left hand, and he thinks he can get his shooting hand to work again. Thomas promised to help him get his skills back."

August laughed. "How is it possible for all these people who tried to kill each other to be even talking to each other again? It doesn't make any sense."

"I wish I could say I understood why, but I know every one of them is strong-willed, an expert shooter, and determined to find happiness. At the same time, they must be tired of holding those grudges, that quest for revenge. All of them are proud and certain they are in the right."

"When Charlotte gave her speech about you killing her husband and moving on, I think that caught their attention. It certainly did mine." A smile crept onto his face. "I'm beginning to like Charlotte."

Elizabeth chuckled. "I like her too. I'm so glad she kept at me. All those times I almost got shot. I shudder to think what would have happened if she hadn't distracted Frank. That bullet might have landed straight into my chest."

"I won't disrespect her again. I'm glad she'll be working with Thomas to lead the men protecting our stagecoaches. Douglas may be surprised, but I believe he'll be pleased to see Charlotte doing a better job than Charlie."

Elizabeth shook her head. "I'm so disappointed in Charlie. I've known him for years, and I never would've expected him to turn bad."

She relaxed her shoulders. "When I showed Martha Joseph's list, she immediately noticed something was off. She has an incredible mind. She catches tiny details about people and sees straight through their masks."

A smile crossed her lips. "We talked a bit before I came here. She showed me a story in a magazine by Edgar Allan Poe, "The Murders in the Rue Morgue." She said it helped her understand what was going on."

Then her gaze locked onto August's. "There is the matter of the badge. Martha and I are of a mind that Randall is the only one fit to carry the weight of it."

August stared at her, his voice a low rasp. "Martha agrees with Randall becoming the sheriff of this town? After what he put her through? Killing her parents?"

"Yes. She said she'd be glad to kill him if he were ever to get out of line."

August choked on his breath. "That family keeps threatening to kill people."

"That family?" She chuckled. "Turns out we are all related:

Joseph, Randall, Alexander, Martha, Charlotte, and Thomas."

August smiled. "I would like to be related to you."

Elizabeth smiled. "Are you forgetting something?"

August's head jerked back, his eyes blinking.

"I'm going to have a baby. Joseph's baby."

"I know."

Elizabeth hugged August. "Now let's go. My family is waiting for us at the restaurant. Would you escort me there, Sheriff August, as a proper suitor should?"

He let out a chortle. "It would be my honor."

THE END

The Dark Sheriff series continues in
Loaded for Truth
* * *

Coming Next in the Dark Sheriff Series

Joseph Pruitt is gone. The town of Auburn stands exposed.

Judge Silas Gentry, once held at bay by Joseph's badge, now moves to claim the land, the law, and the people who remain.

Elizabeth Pruitt, grieving but resolute, turns to the one man no one expects: Randall Pruitt—outlaw, brother, and reluctant heir to the badge.

But Randall doesn't believe he deserves redemption. And Gentry doesn't plan to give him the chance. Silas Gentry is in for a rude awakening when the past reawakens with a vengeance

Loaded for Truth begins where justice ends—and where legacy, loyalty, and truth must rise from the ashes.

About the Author

Roger Mendoza lives in San Antonio, Texas, the seventh-largest city in the United States. In 2014, he moved back to his birth town of San Antonio from Parker, Colorado, where he had lived for fifteen years. Living on the outskirts of San Antonio, he still enjoys the taste of the rural life that he loves so much and the big city's conveniences.

He worked most of his life as a software engineer in the defense industry, where he cultivated his passion for computer programming, but he is now retired. Along with writing novels, Roger is also a professional photographer and can often be seen toting his camera, looking for photo opportunities in and around town. He loves to capture nature photography and beautiful scenery.

Family has always been a cornerstone of Roger's life. Born eighth in a family of ten children, he has a deep-rooted fascination with his family history. Over the years, he has painstakingly gathered his parents' family photographs and documents, cataloging and digitizing them all. He takes pride in keeping the family tree database updated with new family members, cherishing the thousands of family photographs and documents that tell the stories of his relatives.

Roger's inquisitive nature has always led him to ponder the philosophy of life, the intricacies of human behavior, and our place in the grand scheme of things. Despite life's occasional challenges, he remains a firm believer in 'happily ever after endings', a testament to his optimistic worldview that can resonate with many.

He's always been fascinated with unusual phenomena, the most common of which is the drama of life itself. It still amazes him why so much drama fills the lives of his friends and family. Perhaps it is observing that drama that sparks his imagination and gives his characters life.

Elizabeth's Queen Cakes

Makes two dozen muffin-sized cakes
Preheat oven to 350 degrees F.

½ lb. of sifted flour (1-⅔ cups)
½ lb. of sifted fine sugar (1 cup) – (*castor sugar)
½ lb. of salted butter (2 sticks)
4 large eggs
½ tsp cinnamon
2 tablespoons cream
½ tsp vanilla
1 tsp baking powder
¼ tsp salt

Optional Ingredients:
½ lb washed currants (or raisins)
1 ½ tablespoons of rosewater (instead of cinnamon)

Whisk the eggs in a bowl until they are light and fluffy, then set them aside.

In another bowl, cream the butter and sugar together until smooth. Then, add the cinnamon (or rose water), cream, vanilla, and rose water, and mix thoroughly.

Sift the flour and baking powder together.

To the butter and sugar bowl, add the egg alternately with the flour, mixing until thoroughly combined.

Add the currants and mix until they are evenly distributed.

Use a tablespoon to drop scoops into a muffin dish. Fill each half full. Bake in a 350°F oven for 20 minutes.

Press lightly with a spoon on top. If done, it will spring back up.

Sprinkle with sifted powdered sugar while the cake is still warm.

*Castor (caster) sugar – is an extra-finely ground granulated sugar. Not to be confused with 10X superfine powdered sugar.